Price
of a Kiss

LINDA KAGE

Price of a Kiss

Contact Information : linda@lindakage.com

Publishing History
Linda Kage, September 2013
Print ISBN: 978-1491296516

Credits
Cover Artist: Sarah Hansen©
Editor: Laura Josephsen
Proofreader: Claire Ashgrove

Published in the United States of America

DEDICATION

For Kurt and Lydia,
my best family.

You are both priceless.

PROLOGUE

Mason Lowe was fixing his mother's push mower so he could cut the grass when Mrs. Garrison came to collect the rent.

"Woo hoo." Her sharp, nasally call grated against his ears before she tapped on the privacy fence separating his backyard from hers. Metal hinges whined when the gate swung open. "Anyone home?"

"It's just me." He squinted into the midday glare as he glanced up. Wrench firmly gripped in his palm, he swiped the back of his forearm over his brow to wipe away dripping sweat.

"Oh! Mason." Pressing a hand to her exposed cleavage, his mother's landlady stumbled to a halt in her ridiculously high heels and blinked long, fake lashes. "I didn't see you there."

Hoping maybe if he looked busy enough that the forty-something woman would catch the hint and leave him alone, he remained crouched behind the upside-down mower, where he'd been sharpening the blade. "Need something?"

"Um..." She bit her lip and gathered her hair with one hand to hold it off her neck as she used her other to fan herself. The sparkles in her red fingernail polish flashed in the sunlight.

She boldly checked him over, her greedy gaze consuming him. Skeeved by the inspection, he squirmed on the inside, itching to reach for the T-shirt he'd stripped off half an hour ago and flung to the side.

Glancing around the yard as if she were playing lookout for a felon robbing a bank, she asked, "Where's your mother?"

Returning his attention to his task, Mason used the wrench to twist the blade into place. "She's taking my sister to another doctor's appointment," he lied, his muscles straining as he gritted his teeth.

Mom and Sarah were actually at the grocery store, but reminding Mrs. Garrison about his sister's circumstances might score their family a little sympathy and buy them some extra time to scrounge up more cash, because he was certain Mom was behind on rent again.

"Hmm. And how is the poor, sweet child?" Mrs. Garrison murmured distractedly, her attention on his hands as he worked.

Suspecting she cared nothing about Sarah's welfare, he tossed his dark bangs out of his eyes and sent her a look. "Still has cerebral palsy." He twisted a little rougher than he had before, securing the bolt tight.

"My, my." The landlady drifted closer. "You sure have grown up right. Just look at all those muscles you have now." Her shadow passed in front of him just before she set a hand on his shoulder, her long nails digging into his slick skin.

Startled by the contact, he lurched back and

snapped his gaze up.

She gave a husky, amused chuckle. "No need to be so jumpy, dear." Her nails loosened their grip, only to skim an inch down his chest in a blatant caress of appreciation. "I don't bite." Belying her words, she flashed a smile full of orthodontically perfected, white teeth. They looked as if they wanted to take a great big chunk out of his raw flesh.

Mason gulped. The gleam in her gaze had him turning cold all over, even in the hundred-degree heat. Like a panther spotting its prey, she wanted to pounce. On him.

He didn't have to be experienced at sex—and he wasn't—to know what she wanted. She'd probably seen him from her second-story window, wearing nothing but his ragged shorts, and had dolled herself up with the sole intention of coming over to play.

He felt a little ill. Not because he actually wanted to hang on to his virginity. He didn't. In fact, if the opportunity had ever arisen before, he would've lost it years ago.

It wasn't even because she was ugly. The woman might have a fake tan, fake breasts, and a little reconstructive surgery done to her face—certainly to her lips and eyebrows—but she wasn't a dog by any stretch of the imagination. She had big boobs, a tight ass, and shapely long legs, which, okay, yeah, they looked nice in those super-tight, super-short jean shorts.

And it wasn't because she was married, because she wasn't that either. He wasn't sure why everyone called her Mrs. Garrison. He was pretty sure there'd never been a Mr. Garrison in the picture.

No, it all had to do with her age. Cougars just

didn't do it for him, and her digits had to multiply his own by two. At least.

Mrs. Robinson—er, Garrison—must've been thinking about the numbers thing too because she arched an interested brow and asked, "How old are you now, Mason?"

"Eighteen." He glanced away, cursing himself even as he admitted the truth. Damn, why hadn't he lied about that too? Seventeen suddenly seemed so much...safer.

But he had a sneaking suspicion she already knew exactly how old he was.

A predatory grin spread across her painted lips with a mocking gloat as if she assumed she'd already caught him in her web. "So...you're legal, then."

Mason made a choking sound. But holy shit. He hadn't actually thought she'd have the nerve to come right out and say that aloud.

She chuckled huskily. "I see I've shocked you."

He shook his head, more in denial of the moment than actually saying no. She smiled with approval as if proud of him for his answer. "Your mother owes me over three thousand dollars. Did you know that, Mason?"

Wait, had she said three *thousand* dollars?

He stared hard at the old, run-down lawn mower and tried not to pass out. "No. I didn't."

Christ, that was a lot of money.

As if feeling his pain and offering him a measure of comfort, Mrs. Garrison crouched beside him and set her hand on his bare knee. He glanced at her, thinking maybe he'd see some compassion in her gaze. Maybe she'd give them a couple of months to hunt up three grand.

Except, with that calculating gleam glistening within her callous, hazel depths, she didn't look very sympathetic. Her palm shifted on his leg, sliding up to mid-thigh, and he nearly leapt out of his shorts.

Damn, did she plan on giving him a hand job right here in the middle of his mother's backyard or what? While a part of his brain screamed *gross*, the little guy in his pants perked to attention, deciding her slim fingers felt rather nice moving up his leg and would probably feel even nicer resting on his enflamed head.

An electric pulse jumped through his system. He wanted to shove her away and glare at her for doing this to him, for making his body react against his will. But he couldn't shove her anywhere, couldn't tell her off, couldn't even give her a scathing glare. His mother owed her over three *thousand* dollars.

How many freaking months of rent *was* that?

Panic set deep into his veins. He needed to divert this before it went straight to where he feared it was already going.

"I'm sure Mom has the money," he tried. "Sh-she and Sarah should be home in an hour or two. She can pay you then."

"Really?" Mrs. Garrison brightened. "So we have an hour or two to do whatever we want?"

Mason didn't know what to say. He didn't know what to do. He wanted to run, but he had a bad feeling those fingernails of hers would bite into his leg and rip him to shreds if he tried.

He felt trapped.

She leaned in closer, the heat from her palm scorching his thigh. A coconut smell wafted over him. "I'm not stupid, you know. Your mother doesn't have that kind of cash. And she won't pay me anything whenever she gets home from her *doctor's* appointment. But I'd be willing to cut what she owes me in, let's say, *half* if you'd perchance be willing to make a side arrangement with me."

Holy mother of God.

Mrs. Garrison had just asked him to have sex with her.

For fifteen hundred dollars.

He didn't even know her first name.

"You know what I'm asking, don't you, Mason?"

Leaning away, he closed his eyes and nodded.

"Good." She sounded pleased. And disgustingly smug. "So your answer would be...?"

Unable to actually voice his refusal, he gave a vigorous shake of his head.

When she didn't respond, a tense silence met his ears. His curiosity got the best of him, and he opened his lashes.

She studied him with a shrewd expression, as if she knew a small, microscopic part of him wanted to say yes. But seriously, what eighteen-year-old guy wanted to say no to sex, even if it meant losing it to an old chick?

"Is that your final answer?" she asked, sounding amused.

He messed up by opening his mouth. "Yes! I'm absolutely positive. I won't have sex with you. I wouldn't..." He glanced away. "I wouldn't even know what to do."

Why he went and confessed *that*, he had no idea. But he hoped to God it scared her off, because any woman who wanted a fumbling virgin to bang her had to be out of her ever-loving mind.

Instead of jerking her hand off him in revulsion, however, her fingers tightened on his leg. Hazel eyes widened, and she licked her lips.

"Oh, sweetie," she breathed. "You just made me wet."

Mason blinked. Huh?

"Don't worry if it's your first time, darling. I could teach you everything you need to know. And more. It would be an honor to train a young buck like you to learn my...preferences." Her fingers began to slide farther up his leg.

He grabbed her wrist before she reached the hem of his shorts because he knew she wouldn't stop there. She wouldn't stop until she had a handful. His dick throbbed, knowing full well this was as close as any female had ever come to touching him. Stupid dick.

Gritting his teeth, he tightened his grip on her to warn her away. But hell, she began to breathe harder as if his manhandling turned her on even more.

With her gaze glazing to a fevered pitch, she drew in a heavy pant. "Damn, you have strong hands. You're hard for me right now, aren't you?"

Disgusted with her as much as he was with his own betraying body, he threw her hand off and lurched to his feet, turning slightly away so she couldn't see anything bulging from his shorts.

"You need to leave," he bit out. It had to be the most surreal, embarrassing, awkward moment of his life, standing petrified in his mother's backyard in front of a broken lawn mower, sporting a woody and discussing sex for sale with the landlady. "I told you no."

"Fine." She huffed out an indignant sniff as she pushed to her feet. The heat from her glare burned into the back of his neck. "Tell your mother to pay up by the end of the week then, or she'll be receiving an eviction notice."

Mason spun around to gape at her.

She wouldn't.

Oh, holy hell, she would.

She pretended to admire her fingernails, preening in front of him as if proud of herself for besting him. Then, with a jaunty wave, she chirped, "Toodles," and twirled away on her heels, humming a bubbly tune under her breath. Her hips swung in a saucy manner as she strolled toward the gate.

Mason gaped after her, sick to his stomach and scared out of his mind. She'd never threatened eviction before. Then again, she'd never solicited him for sex before, either.

His mother already worked two full-time jobs, and what money she'd been saving back was to buy a motorized wheelchair for Sarah.

Mason clenched his teeth, feeling like the worst son ever, the worst older brother ever. He'd been part-timing it at the car wash after school, but that hadn't even made a dent in helping Mom pay the bills. If he could assist his family in any way, he should be jumping at the chance to do anything and everything possible.

Even the landlady.

Closing his eyes against a wave of dizziness for what he was about to do, Mason rasped out the word, "Wait," half hoping she didn't hear him.

But her hand froze on the gate latch. Slowly, she rotated on her heels. "Yes?"

He hated the way her eyes flickered with triumph. He hated her, period.

He worked his mouth a few times before he actually spoke. "Let me...let me just wash up first."

She laughed and shook her head. "Oh, honey, don't you dare. Before this afternoon is over, I plan to lick every inch of sweat off that taut, glistening young body."

He nearly lost his lunch.

She must've sensed he was a split second from backing out of the whole deal, because she crooked her index finger, beckoning him forward. "Follow me, handsome."

When she turned away and opened the gate, he followed.

Three hours later, he returned home a completely different person. And Mrs. Garrison had pardoned him all of his mother's back rent on the condition that he would return whenever she summoned him again.

CHAPTER **ONE**

Two Years, Three Months, and Twelve Days Later

Okay, so maybe I was about to start drooling just the teeny tiniest bit when my cousin bumped her elbow into mine, distracting me from feasting on the hunk of man candy across the quad I might possibly have been—i.e., was totally—undressing with my gaze.

"Girl, don't even think about it. You couldn't afford him if you emptied all the money in your piggy bank."

I blinked, cleared my throat, and murmured, "I'm sorry, what?"

"I said, uh-uh. No way. You can't afford him."

Wrinkling my nose, I kept staring because, well, really, how could I stop? He was hotness exemplified. That was my new name for him, actually: Hotness.

"What? Is he, like, *for sale* or something?" I snickered at my own joke.

Eva patted my knee in a sympathetic gesture. "Yes. Actually, he is."

My grin slipped. "Huh?"

Seated on one of the benches outside the main building of Waterford County Community College, Eva and I had been sipping on our morning dose of caffeine and sugar, arguing over who was wearing the cutest shoes, when Hotness himself had crossed my line of vision at the very corner of my eye. I'd glanced over to catch the whole picture and yeah...Shoes? What were shoes?

But seriously. He was wickedly beautiful. With the strap of his messenger bag slung diagonally across his chest, he leaned against one of the campus's many bronzed animal statues as he chatted with a handful of other guys.

Wearing jeans and a simple T-shirt, he shouldn't have stood out among the pack. But he did. Oh my, he did. His dark, wavy hair called to me—*Reese, Reese! Run your fingers through my wild, gorgeous, untamed mane*. It did. For real.

So maybe I didn't have a detailed, up-close-and-personal view of him. I mean, I couldn't even make out his facial attributes from here—and a striking face was what usually drew me first. But none of that seemed to matter, because I had this gut feeling deep inside that his smile was an absolute heartbreaker.

It was breaking *my* heart that very second.

There was just something about his aura that screamed sensual, confident, charming beast. It radiated off him in waves as he relaxed in a comfortable, total guy stance, casually draping an arm across the back of a frozen stallion. The boy was a piece of art, and hella more alluring than the chunk of metal currently supporting his weight.

I could not take my eyes off him. "Just tell me

he doesn't stalk and stab his ex-girlfriends."

"Nope," Eva assured me. "He doesn't even have ex-girlfriends. Because he's a gigolo."

Oh, yes she did. Out loud. In the middle of a busy campus. Like it was an everyday fact.

I ripped my stare away from Hotness to gape at my cousin, who, sure, sometimes said some crazy-ass shit. But really, this was up there with the best of her whoppers. "Excuse me?"

Eva smirked. "He sells his body for sex."

As if I needed the dictionary definition for a gigolo. Hello. "What the heck are you talking about?"

"I'm talking about Mason Lowe, that guy you keep sexually harassing with your eyes." She tipped her head in the direction of Hotness still leaning against the bucking horse statue. "You can't stop staring, I know. He's stunning, I have to agree. He was two classes ahead of me in high school, and we shared a fourth-hour math class my sophomore year, so yeah, I've drooled over him a time or two myself. But trust me, sweetie, he's not available. Because he's a frigging gigolo."

When I did nothing but blink at her because, um, what was I *supposed* to say to that, Eva insistently added, "I'm serious!"

"You mean figuratively, right?"

"I mean exactly what I said, literally."

I cocked an eyebrow. "And...you would know this because...?"

"I don't know. I just...know. *Everyone* knows. Except the cops, of course. Otherwise, he'd be in jail for illegal prostitution or something. It's a well-known rumor he works at the Country Club as some kind of cover to set up appointments with his clients, who just happen to be some of the richest, horniest women in the county who pay him boocoos of cash to pleasure them...any way they want. I'm certain some of my mom's cronies have had him."

My mouth fell open. I scrutinized her an entire minute before snorting out a laugh and shoving at her shoulder. "Oh, my God. You are *such* a liar. Jeez, E., you totally had me going for a second."

"What?" Eva managed to look insulted. "I swear to God, I'm not lying. Do you want to go ask him?" She hooked her arm through mine and tried to stand up, dragging me with her.

Um, yeah. Not going to happen. I'd internally combust from hormone overdose if I went anywhere near Hotness right now. Like getting too close to the sun, he'd probably burn me with one of his deadly testosterone rays. And I *so* wasn't wearing enough SPF for that kind of action.

I yanked both our asses back down. "What do you think you're doing? You can't just go up to someone and ask him if he's a gigolo?" *Gah!*

Eva responded in typical Eva fashion. She shrugged and tossed her hair. "Why not? I doubt he'd lie about it. It certainly doesn't seem to be a secret."

I threw my head back and shouted out a laugh. But, wow. Sometimes Eva was just too much. The things she could think up were, well...they were outlandish. I kind of loved that about her, and yet it also embarrassed the heck out of me. Sadly, I wasn't quite as outgoing as my vivid counterpart. I was much more prone to moments of horrified blushing than feats of extroverted greatness. I mean, I wasn't shy by any stretch of the imagination, but I was by no means an Eva Mercer.

As if he sensed I was blushing over him that very second, Hotness—or as Eva had dubbed him, Mason Lowe—glanced in our direction and made eye contact. With me.

I stopped laughing. Stopped smiling. Pretty much stopped breathing. Gawd, but the boy sure knew how to hold a heated stare.

"Lord have mercy," Eva murmured next to me.

I didn't respond—couldn't if I'd wanted to. I was too busy being electrocuted from the inside out. My fingertips sizzled and toes curled as if an invisible, kinetically charged bolt tethered me to the hunk fifty yards away, who seemed to bind us together with his stare alone.

Yes, the chemical current between us was exactly that powerful. I'm not even exaggerating. Okay, maybe a little. But not much.

He broke the connection by shifting his attention to Eva. I gasped from the release as if someone had just ripped a Band-Aid off my soul.

Not that I could really tell, but I swore his eyes narrowed when he focused on my cousin. He sent me another quick dart, which suddenly seemed full of accusation, and swiftly turned back to his group, dismissing us both entirely.

Never before had a mere glance rattled me so deeply.

Blowing out an unsteady breath, I set my hand against my wildly thumping heart. If I had just flatlined and someone had used a defibrillator to bring me back to life, I don't think I would've felt more jolted than I did now. "Whoa."

"Yeah," Eva murmured, sounding similarly affected. "I think I need a cigarette."

I turned to her and blinked. "You don't smoke."

She rolled her eyes. "I swear, sometimes, we cannot possibly be related. You weren't supposed to take that literally, ReeRee. Gah."

My rational cognition was still too fried for me to think properly, so I merely murmured, "Oh."

Then I shrugged. "Well, my sparkly ballet flats still kick your sandals' ass."

"Dream on." She snorted. "Sandals are so in this season." And with that, she chomped her gaze back on *my* piece of man candy.

"Whatever," I mumbled with a petulant sniff, battling this insane urge to pull her hair and scream that I'd seen him first, or at the very least remind her *she* had a boyfriend. "Chillax, E. I was just looking anyway. It's not like I want to get married and set up house with him. I am so not ready for another relationship right now."

"Whatever," Eva repeated right back, but in a much nastier tone than I'd used. "I told you he was unattainable."

Damn, what had crawled into her Wheaties and died? And why did she keep staring at him? Seriously, it pissed me off something crucial, because now I couldn't sneak another peek. Two girls eye-gushing over the same guy was just plain pathetic.

Oh, hell, it didn't matter if she wanted to hog all the ogling to herself. I was a little too intimidated to look at him again, anyway. I mean, what if he looked back? I wasn't sure I could take that kind of shockwave twice in one day.

I assume no one had ever actually overdosed from a lusty glance before, but with Hotness around, I had a bad feeling I'd probably be the first.

So, I focused my attention on my class schedule I'd pulled up on my cell phone two-point-five seconds before becoming intensely aware of Mason Lowe's existence. Draining the rest of my latte, I looked up the room number for my first class. The heat and steam from the drink burned all the way down, but I kind of welcomed the pain. It kept me distracted from you-know-who.

Gasping out a silent gulp to cool my inflamed esophagus, I blinked back tears. "So..." It took me a few tries before I could add, "You said you had Brit Lit with me, right?"

"Right," Eva answered. From her breathy reply, I could tell she was still busy staring.

"Well, it starts in...three minutes. Maybe we should get going." At this point, anything to get her to heel and take her eyes off my hunk would do, even attending Early British Literature.

Spotting a trashcan nearby, I took aim and sank my empty cup, nothing but net, thanks to three years on the high school basketball team. "So let's do this," I announced, gathering my backpack and getting ready to stand.

But Eva slid over, slamming her body into mine until she smashed us together, hip to hip. "Wait." Her voice went hushed and serious as her hand landed on my leg, holding me in place. "He's coming this way."

Drawing in a sharp breath, I glanced up. He'd abandoned his bronco statue and was strolling down the sidewalk by himself toward the main entrance of the school. Problem was, the bench Eva and I inhabited sat along the edge of that very path. He was going to walk right by us.

Nothing but ten feet of dead air was going to separate him from me.

Dear Lord in heaven, please deliver me. Could I survive such close proximity? I honestly didn't know. My chest heaved from the sudden unsteady rhythm of my breathing.

"Watch this," Eva whispered in my ear.

I glanced at her, hoping to find some kind of direction, for her to tell me what to do. But she didn't look a bit aware of my approaching panic attack. The girl looked damn mischievous.

I grabbed her wrist. "Oh, God. What're you going to do?"

Eva merely smiled her infamous Cheshire cat grin as she settled her gaze on the passing hottie. "Good morning, Mason," she called.

Every muscle in my body tightening, I dug my nails deep into her wrist, warning her to shut it. But her greeting had already captured his attention.

He glanced over, his gaze indifferent. Jerking his chin in that way guys had of greeting someone with their head, he nodded. "Sup?"

I melted, and a dreamy whimper oozed out. But, wow, he had a compelling voice to go with that compelling body. It was deep, yet smooth, and entirely too sinful to belong to someone so pretty. It made me want to close my eyes, and just...liquefy.

"Looking good today," Eva told him, her tone full of feminine wiles and not-so-hidden invitation. Tipping her face just enough for the sunlight to catch her flawless complexion, she let her beautiful mane of platinum blonde hair spill over her shoulder to bounce down her sizable chest. She couldn't have said come-and-get-me-big-boy any more flamboyantly than if she'd shrieked it aloud. "What say we skip class this morning and do something...fun instead?"

Mason Lowe snorted out his disinterest at the same moment I gasped, "E.!" I really was going to have to remind her she had a boyfriend, wasn't I?

At my reprimanding hiss, Hotness zipped his attention to me, and suddenly his expression was no longer unresponsive. His intense gaze burned into me, and yes, I was going to need a whole vat of Aloe Vera to soothe the delicious sting it left behind.

Again, our immediate connection held me prisoner. His heavy stare cemented me into place as if it made every organ in my body weigh a million pounds each. I could do nothing but gape back. Like a punch to the solar plexus, he left me breathless. I sucked in air, seeking oxygen.

He looked even better from ten feet away than he had fifty yards away. Separating himself from his guy-pack hadn't even diminished his appeal.

And that face. I swear, angels sprouted up around him and began to sing in harmonious worship of that glorious face. Straight nose, prominent brow, über-defined square jaw, dimpled chin. He had every alpha male feature a guy could possibly possess. Even his eyebrows were thick and rugged. There was simply a hallowed kind of masculine perfection about him.

When he tore his gaze away, I felt wrung out and abandoned. I watched him pass by us and stroll all the way to the front door. Then I watched him disappear inside. Licking my parched lips, I turned to my cousin in a daze.

"Okay," I heard my own voice say, the tone a trifle faint to my ears. "Maybe I could believe women paid him for sex."

"Hells yeah," Eva purred. "If I had the cash, I'd definitely do him."

She sounded a little too invested in her statement, so I nudged my knee into hers, aghast. "What about Alec?"

She gave me an empty stare. "Hmm? Who?"

I lifted one eyebrow. "Your boyfriend."

"Oh." Blinking, she seemed to return to herself. With an airy shrug, she pushed to her feet and swung her bag over her shoulder in a fluid, graceful way only a supermodel could accomplish. "Mason is only a pipe dream. Like I said, we could never afford him."

Something about the way she worded that

made me think she'd actually tried. It worried me, but I didn't question it. Guys were the very last thing I wanted to get tangled in right now. And true gigolo or not, Hotness had sticky mess written all over him. Eva obviously had some kind of prior claim.

For once in my life, I let my curiosity lie dormant. Silently, I trailed Eva toward the front doors of Waterford County Community College and into my new life as Reese Alison Randall

CHAPTER **TWO**

A year ago, I'd had grand plans of attending the local university in my hometown. It had a wicked, awesome medical program, and I'd dreamed of becoming a virologist, one of those surprisingly cool lab geeks you see on NCIS or some such TV show, who's always studying bacteria under a microscope and solving the crime of the day.

Anyway, nearly four months ago, my plans for that perfect future had changed. Drastically.

I blame my psycho stalker ex-boyfriend. I mean, sure, I'll take some culpability by saying I was a little too open about telling everyone where I wanted to go to college and what I wanted to become. He would know exactly where to look for me, meaning I could no longer go there. And yes, if I'd turned Jeremy down flat that fateful day my freshman year of high school when he'd first asked me out, we never would've dated, he never would've become obsessed, and I would've been able to avoid all of this. Sure.

But other than that, he was the sole reason I'd lost my big dream.

Because of him, here I was, hiding out halfway across the country, attending a no-name, small-town, lame-ass community college and living above my aunt and uncle's garage. Talk about major suck zone. My life in the past couple of months had been nothing as I'd imagined it would be for my first year of college.

But seriously, no one had tried to kill me here, so I guess I couldn't whine and complain too much.

Pity party cut short.

After Brit Lit with Eva, I had a free hour before my calculus class started. I spent that time stopping by the library. Since I'd been hired there as a work-study assistant, I still needed to talk to my new supervisor about a schedule. So we did, and I was pleased to learn I could weave all my work time in during the day between classes. I left my impromptu meeting with ten minutes left to find my math class.

I found it in five. Whoosh!

My calculus professor dove right into numbers and equations as soon as he skimmed over the syllabus. He was passionate about his numbers and equations too, which reminded me a lot of my dad, and made me a teensy bit homesick. But Dr. Kolarick kept us almost five minutes over, which my time-conscious father would never do. By the time he let us go, the next class had gathered outside in the hall and was ready to pile in.

I rushed, trying to hurry from my seat and get to Humanities next. But as soon as I stood and took two steps up the aisle between desk rows, one of the dangling straps on my book bag caught on a nearby chair and tipped the pack upside down, spilling all my belongings to the floor.

Horrified, I bent down and fumbled frantically to gather notebooks, texts, pens, and stray little pieces of papers with embarrassing doodles on them. Haphazardly shoving stuff into my bag, I was so busy watching what I was doing that I didn't pay attention to where I was going. As I surged to my feet, I totally missed the guy coming down the aisle to find a seat for the next class.

That is, I didn't notice him until I plowed into him, ramming my bag into a very taut, very sturdy stomach.

He grunted in pain, and I screeched in surprise.

I'd like to say I'm usually much more graceful. But I'm not the best liar in the world either, so yeah, I confess; I'm a total klutz.

Losing control of my book bag, I spilled everything inside onto the floor. Again.

Note to self: Zip my freaking backpack closed next time.

"Oh, my God. Sorry," I said, instantly falling back to my knees. "I didn't see you. I'm so sor—"

I glanced up and forgot what I was going to say.

From fifty yards, he'd taken my breath away. From ten feet, I'd been ready to have his babies. With a bare foot of nothing separating us in that cramped aisle between desks, there I was, on my knees in front of him.

Need I say more?

"Holy crap," I squawked.

What the hell was he doing here? He wasn't supposed to be here. Okay, maybe he was. I didn't know his class schedule. But I certainly wasn't supposed to be bumping into him...or sitting on my knees in front of him with my face mere inches from his—

Good God, how mortifying.

Hotness stared down at me, looking as startled as I felt.

"I...sorry—sorry." I rushed out the words and blindly reached for my things, inadvertently shifting closer to his crotch as I snagged a handful of stray papers.

He lurched backward, dislodging two of my textbooks that had landed on his sneaker.

"Are you okay?" I bit my lip as I looked up, hoping I appeared as apologetic as I felt. But looking at him was always such a distraction. I was so breathless, I probably sounded like a one-nine-hundred operator when I said, "I'm so sorry."

He had the look of a lifeguard with his lean build but wider upper body and defined muscles covered by some deliciously golden, sunbaked skin. His face was the most appealing feature about him. His incredible tan made the whites of his eyes and his perfect teeth stand out. It also drew more attention to his full lower lip, his dimpled chin underneath, and the gray intensity of his eyes above. Insert dreamy sigh here, because their brilliant pewter color reminded me of a cloudy sky right before a gentle rain shower.

"I'm fine." He gave me a tight smile. A get-away-from-me-because-you-smell-bad kind of smile.

Oh, God. I *repulsed* him.

He finally bent down and retrieved the books that had been lying on his feet. When he handed them to me, I mumbled, "Thanks." I was determined not to bawl in the presence of the gorgeous gigolo I *repulsed*.

Unintentionally—yes, unintentionally, jeez! — my hand brushed his as I took the books. Sparks of electricity shot up my arm. I gasped and jolted backward, shocked—both literally and figuratively—by the current that crackled between us. It nearly made me drop my books again.

Needing to know if he'd felt it too, I glanced up and shoved my hair out of my face, only to discover how strained and uncomfortable he appeared. His face had darkened to a dull red as if he were holding his breath to keep from smelling me. Every female instinct in me wanted to reach out and trace the wrinkles in his brow he was making as he frowned.

Must. Soothe. The hottie.

But really, why was he scowling? Did I honestly stink that bad? Or did he just not like making sparks with me?

Both options sucked.

Then it struck me. Maybe he hadn't felt the sparks. Maybe he thought the way I'd yanked my hand away from his magnetic touch was rude. It would certainly appear rude if he had no idea what was going on in my head, which, wow, he really didn't have a clue, did he?

Oopsie.

I opened my mouth to apologize, but he turned on his heel and slid into the nearest chair, avoiding me as well as giving me an open path to the exit—so I could leave him alone.

I blinked, deciding he was even ruder than I was. Would a forgiving pat on the arm or a simple it's-okay, no-big-whoop have killed him? I really was sorry for bumping into him.

"Jerk," I muttered to myself as soon as I lit out of the classroom and escaped.

Okay, okay, I suppose I could give him the benefit of the doubt. All hotties deserved a second chance, right? So...he might not be a jerk. I *had* been the one to plow into him and spill a load of books on his feet, and he'd actually been kind enough to bend down and pick them up for me. And just because a guy wasn't big on the whole communication and I-forgive-you thing or obviously couldn't smile did not automatically make him a jerk.

But it stung to consider the possibility that he just didn't like me. Thinking of him as a jerk settled my ego much more nicely.

So, yeah. He was such a jerk face.

I lifted the collar of my shirt and sniffed. Smelling nothing but clean laundry detergent, a hint of my Sweet Pea lotion, and Fresh Breeze deodorant, I scowled. I did not stink.

He was definitely a jerk.

As luck would have it, the rest of my day was spill-free. I didn't spot Hotness, the jerk face, again. And no one tried to stab me to death.

I'd call that progress.

The weather had warmed considerably since I'd left my above-the-garage apartment that morning. But, wow, was Florida hot and muggy in August, or what? I was so tempted to pull my hair up into ponytail to catch a little breeze that my fingers actually ached with the urge to start gathering stray strands.

Except the scar on the back of my neck was still pretty fresh—only four months old. Every time I checked a reflection of it in my hand mirror, the wound looked dark and ugly. So ponytails were completely out of the question. If too many people saw it and asked questions, I might get caught in one of my lies, and the truth would come out. That couldn't happen. Ever. So I continued to hide it every day by wearing my hair down.

It was almost four in the afternoon when I returned to my new home.

Aunt Mads and Uncle Shaw had been amazing to let me stay there. I had been worried, what with Jeremy's nasty death threat hanging over my head, that everyone would push me away as if I had the plague. I was dangerous to be around. But the Mercers had taken me in when I'd needed them the most. Plus I didn't have to pay rent, a water bill, electric bill, or heating and air. Life—in that regard—was pretty spectacular.

My book bag weighed down one shoulder as I trooped up the steps outside my aunt and uncle's four-bay garage. When I reached the top landing, I had to swing the bag's strap around so I could fish out my apartment key I had tucked away in the front pocket.

Finding it exactly where I'd zipped it this morning, I pulled my key ring free, squinting as the brass surface glinted in the bright daylight, momentarily blinding me until I fit it into the lock and twisted the door open.

As soon as I stepped inside, I jerked to a frozen halt.

The newspaper I'd bought this weekend to search for a couple more part-time jobs was no longer sitting on the breakfast table, folded nice and neat where I'd left it this morning. The pages were opened and strewn across the floor while one sheet draped half off the table.

Someone had been in my apartment.

Fear paralyzed me in surreal waves. I'd trained for this, trained all summer with Eva and Aunt Mads at a self-defense class. And in none of my courses had the instructor said to stand frozen like a stupid nincompoop when the threat of danger arose.

Finally, I shook my head, denying it. He couldn't have found me. Not yet. He was still halfway across the country with no idea of who or where I was.

Wasn't he?

I tried to back out of the apartment; I told myself to run. But my sparkly ballet flats wouldn't budge. I just stood there, too terrified to move, or scream, or even think.

Then the window-unit air conditioner kicked on. The sudden blast of frigid air caused the last bit of newspaper to soar off the table and flutter across the room until it floated down, adding to the already cluttered mess on the floor.

A relieved sob screamed from my lungs as I covered my mouth and wilted against the doorframe.

Not an intruder. It had only been the stupid, bleeping air conditioner. And, of course, the A/C hadn't been running this morning when I'd left—it hadn't been warm enough to kick on yet—so I wouldn't have known it would blow the newspaper onto the floor.

Whew.

But seriously, talk about cardiac city.

Limp from the sudden surge of blood through my veins and then the just-as-sudden liberation, I staggered into the apartment. After slamming the door, I locked and bolted it. Then I collapsed onto the couch in a drained, hot mess.

I lay there ten seconds, trying to fight off the overdose of adrenaline in my system. But I felt eyes watching me from every corner, so I leapt to my feet and decided it wouldn't hurt to run a quick check around the apartment to make sure no one was lurking about.

After what I had survived, it was smart to stay paranoid.

The newspaper scare left me rattled. Trying to

do homework was an impossibility, so I spent some time writing in my notebook and signing my new name on a sheet of paper.

Mom had instructed me to do this in an attempt to help me get used to it. *"When I was newly married, I used my maiden name more than I didn't for those first five years. It wasn't until I had to start signing it all the time that I finally adjusted."*

Well, I hadn't gotten married as she had in order to get a new name, and I didn't have five years to acclimate myself to being Reese Randall. Since I'd legally changed it to escape a psycho stalker ex-boyfriend, I needed to have my shit together a bit more immediately.

I filled two pages and tried about fifty different signature styles. I'd just decided I could have heaps more fun signing the R in Reese than the boring ol' T I'd had before, when my cell phone rang.

The number that appeared on the screen wasn't programmed into my address book. I was instantly cautious. But I'd applied for a few job openings on Saturday, so—keeping my voice low and hard to distinguish—I answered in the hopes someone was getting back to me about employment.

And what do you know, someone was!

My work-study at the college library only covered ten hours a week. That was barely latte money. With Mom and Dad paying my car payment and insurance, plus sending me a monthly gas allowance, I was okay there. It was food and everything else I had to worry about. And honestly, after my first grocery-shopping venture with E. this summer, I was scandalized by how much food actually cost. I was so never going to whine again over how my mom had never bought my favorite brand of cereal and OJ. Name brands were utterly overrated. Except when it came to clothes. Or shoes. Or bacon.

Okay, okay, I loved all my name brands. Why, oh, why did they have to be so stinking expensive?

To say the least, a ten-hour-a-week job at minimum wage didn't sound as if it would cover my lavish preferences, especially like an emergency shopping spree or trip to a hair stylist, both of which Eva and I had done just last week. Hey, I couldn't help it if my cousin was a spoiled rich girl who needed to part with her cash frequently or she might become physically ill, and she felt the need to drag me along to every boutique and shopping mall she patronized.

I had to be a good, supportive friend and go with her, didn't I?

Well, I went with her anyway.

So, yeah, I was thrilled to hear from Dawn Arnosta. A single mother with a twelve-year-old daughter, she had one full-time day job at a glass factory. But she also worked every Monday, Wednesday, and Friday evening as a waitress at an all-night café. With her last evening babysitter leaving for Gainesville to attend the University of Florida, that left a big fat opening...for me, I hoped.

I got some good vibes off Mrs. Arnosta, and I know I impressed her with my credentials.

"I know CPR and have first aid training, plus I used to babysit a special needs boy with autism when I was in high school. I also worked as a lifeguard back home at our city pool for one summer, so if you have a pool, I could totally handle that."

Oh, how I could handle that.

Please, please, have a pool.

She didn't have a pool, but that was okay,

because she said, "Well, you certainly sound more qualified than any of the other applicants we've had. Can you start Wednesday?"

My heart thumped hard and happy in my chest. Fisting my hand, I mouthed the word, *"Score!"* while aloud, I remained much more professional. "Sure. Whenever you need me."

And so I had a second job for the semester. I was super psyched about it...until I actually arrived at the Arnosta house.

CHAPTER **THREE**

I showed up thirty-five minutes early on Wednesday. Dawn, as Mrs. Arnosta insisted I call her, asked me to arrive half an hour before my usual time because she needed to give me instructions before she left for work. I wasn't sure how many instructions I needed for a twelve-year-old, but I guess I was about to find out.

She lived less than ten minutes away from the Mercers, which would help a lot during the winter in case the weather got nasty and road conditions were—

Wait. What was I saying? This was Florida. I was no longer in the Midwest. A nasty winter here was probably a bracing forty degrees with a slight breeze.

Okay, so scratch that last part.

The short drive would...help me save a lot on gas money. Yeah.

The neighborhood was nice, with professionally tended lawns and huge, beautiful houses lining wide, well-paved streets. I began to get excited, thinking I'd get to chill on extra-long leather sofas and watch late-night shows on large-screen televisions while I snacked on gourmet popcorn after my ward went to sleep. But then I parked in front of the correct address, and my hopes crashed. Kaput. Suddenly, I remembered Dawn was a single mother who had to work a second job to support her family. No extra-long leather sofas for her. Or me.

Her place was obviously owned by her neighbor to the right because the style of architecture plus the blue and white color schemes of both places matched. I deduced that her house must be an old guest cottage the owner had turned into a rental.

Hooking the strap of my knock-off Prada purse over my shoulder, I locked my car and trudged up the sidewalk to the front door. Mr. Landlord to the right was a total ass. His own house was freshly painted, while the worn siding on his guest cottage had begun to peel in places, and the lawn sported brown patches of dead grass.

I'd just leaped over a deep chasm a giant might consider a small crack in the sidewalk when the front door opened. A thirty-eight-year-old woman— if my internal age radar was reading her correctly— peered out at me. Willow slim, she'd tied her dark hair up into a perky ponytail.

I know, I know. My own hair was bawling with jealousy to do the same. Someday, I swore, I'd get to wear my hair up again.

Despite the youthful locks, her eyes looked tired and were double ringed with fatigue, while her shoulders stooped as if taking on the weight of the world. But she had a friendly smile, so I instantly liked her and felt bad for her in equal measures.

She just looked so exhausted and worn down.

"Reese?" she asked.

I nodded and made my own guess. "Mrs. Arnosta?"

"Oh, it's just Dawn." Hearing my address made her wince with a pained expression, but she stepped aside and opened the door wide to let me in.

Her last name must give her fits or maybe memories of a bad spouse. This was the second time she'd asked me to use her first name...a little too forcefully.

"Right." I cringed. "Sorry." I definitely wouldn't make that mistake again.

With a forgiving nod, she graciously ushered me into the house. For some reason, I instantly smelled sickness. I breathed it in deeply, reminded of one of my childhood friends from home who'd had a little brother with leukemia. There had always been this sterile scent of medicine in the air whenever I had visited. That same pharmaceutical bouquet hung heavy in Dawn's front room, telling me someone living here was not one hundred percent healthy.

Glancing at her, I checked her over, wondering if she was okay. Did she have cancer? That would definitely account for the weary, threadbare look about her.

"Sarah's back here," she said, sending me an almost guilty glance before motioning me to follow as she started down a long, dark, narrow hall.

As we approached the lighted room at the end, I heard a voice saying, "Hey, I know you wanted to go to that slumber party your classmates didn't invite you to tonight, but don't sweat it, okay. I bet you're not missing anything fun at all. I mean, what kind of—"

"Mason!" Dawn interrupted the speaker,

sounding surprised as she entered the kitchen just ahead of me. "There you are. I didn't realize you were still home. But since you're here, the new evening sitter just arrived, and I'd like you to meet her."

Hearing that name, I stumbled and tripped over my own feet before bumping into the wall and jostling a hanging framed portrait of a young Mason.

Yes, a young Mason, as in Hotness from Waterford County Community College, Mason *Lowe.*

I gawked at the face in that photograph—though, aww, he'd even been a cutie patootie when he'd been missing his two front teeth—and suddenly, I didn't want to enter the kitchen. Thinking quickly, I tried to concoct a plan to not exit the hallway. But honestly, there was no way to avoid it, unless I wanted to abandon this babysitting gig altogether. Which just seemed totally irresponsible and not at all like me.

"Reese?" Dawn asked, her voice full of concern as she appeared in the opening of the hallway. "Are you okay?"

No, not really. But I nodded and stepped into the room, smoothing down my shirt as I went, so I hopefully wouldn't look like a total dork. But when my gaze latched onto a pair of familiar gray eyes, I experienced a mad case of word vomit. "I'm fine. Sorry about that. I'm just the queen of clumsy." And a total dork.

"Reese," Dawn said again, this time with amusement in her eyes. "This is my son, Mason. He works most evenings at the Country Club, so you may or may not see him coming and going whenever you're here. Mason, this is Reese Randall."

Mason gaped at me with the most horrified expression I think I've ever seen. A second later, he shook his head and cleared his throat before glancing away and distractedly mumbling, "Hey."

"H-hi," I croaked.

But what the hell? Hotness was Dawn Arnosta's *son*? That couldn't be. They didn't have the same last name.

Even though I knew this was all a big, awful coincidence, I felt tricked.

With him decked out in his work uniform—a pale blue polo shirt with an oval logo for the Waterford County Country Club over his left pec and Khaki pants to match—I was suddenly reminded of what Eva had said about him being a gigolo.

Holy crap, she hadn't been lying about the Country Club thing; what if she hadn't been lying about—

My eyes grew round. And his narrowed as he stared back, his lips tightening as if he could read my mind.

"...Mason just started taking classes at the community college this semester too," Dawn was telling me. "Maybe you two will see each other there."

"Yeah," I murmured, half out of it as I smiled tightly at the mother before turning back to the son. "I...I think I might've seen you around campus already."

"You dumped a bag full of books on my feet before my calculus class on Monday," he reminded me dryly.

"Right," I agreed slowly before trilling out a guilty little laugh. "That *was* you, wasn't it? Yeah, sorry about that...again."

His stare was borderline hostile, telling me I

didn't impress him in the least. But it still held a powerful punch.

Whenever he'd glanced at Eva on that first day of classes, it was as if he'd stared straight through her. With me, it was the complete opposite.

He *saw* me. He just didn't approve of what he saw, for some unknown reason.

"Oh, so you two have already met, then." Dawn seemed pleased to learn this. "That's great."

I sent her a horrified glance to let her know she was crazy. Mason and I had certainly never "met" before. But she was too busy pointing to something he was blocking with his body like some kind of protective papa bear.

"I guess that leaves one introduction. Reese, this is Sarah." Taking Mason's elbow, Dawn manually dragged his resisting body aside to reveal the little girl sitting in a wheelchair behind him.

Yeah, I said wheelchair. Sarah, the twelve-year-old I was supposed to babysit, sat in a wheelchair.

This, I had not expected.

Trying not to show my shock, I clasped my hands together and gave the girl such a huge smile it stretched my lips to unbelievable proportions. "Hi, Sarah. I'm so happy to meet you," I said aloud when internally, I screamed, *Oh, my God. Oh, my God. Why didn't Dawn mention this in the phone interview?*

In response, Sarah flailed her head and arms, limbs and neck spasms floundering her out of control as her torso went limp and floppy. A low, garbled sound, like a sick cow on drugs, moaned its way from her throat.

I'm not too sure, but I think she said, "Hello."

I freaked.

How the hell was I supposed to watch a special needs child in a wheelchair? I wasn't trained for this. Artie, the autistic boy I'd watched once or twice two years ago, had had such a mild case that sometimes I'd forgotten he was different at all. But there would be no forgetting it with Sarah. I didn't know the first thing about...well, whatever it was she had.

"Sarah, this is Reese." Dawn crouched next to her and set her hand gently on the girl's shoulder. "She's going to stay with you in the evenings now that Ashley's gone."

I smiled encouragingly at Sarah, hoping she understood I was a good guy, hoping she understood anything.

Sarah moaned out another inarticulate sound that didn't give my hope a lot of room to breathe.

Damn it. *Why* had Dawn kept this a secret?

Mason stiffened. Don't ask me how I knew that, but I felt a blast of angry chill attack me from his direction, so I glanced over. He glared with so much pent-up anger I actually shrank back. But the meaning in his glower was clear. If I did anything to hurt his little sister, he would make me regret it.

I was tempted to hold my thumbs up in a message-received signal but restrained myself. Bad timing and all that.

"Sarah has CP," Dawn told me.

"Oh." I nodded as if I knew what that meant and unconsciously turned Mason's way with a questioning wrinkle in my brows.

"That's short for cerebral palsy," he said, his voice damn near a challenge, daring me to run screaming from the house.

Except I wasn't really the running and screaming type.

Again, I nodded as if I totally understood and had no problem with it. Really, though, what the hell was cerebral palsy? I'd heard the term plenty of times but had no idea what it actually entailed.

"It's a muscle disorder," Dawn answered my unspoken question. "Sarah was born premature, and it injured the motor part of her brain, affecting the muscles in her entire body, from her limbs to trunk to even her tongue and eye muscles. It takes an extreme effort for her just to talk, or chew, or even blink."

Ohhh. Good to know. But poor Sarah. That kind of life had to suck monkey butt. I glanced at her with a commiserating grimace, which seemed to tick her big brother off something fierce.

"I need to get going," he broke in, as if he couldn't bear to stand in the same house with me a second longer.

Bending slightly to kiss Sarah's cheek—and my, my, how nicely those pants fit his rear to perfection—he said, "Take care, kiddo," before he stood and ruffled her oak-colored locks, which were the same shade as his own. Then he glanced at his mother and waved goodbye.

When he turned toward me, because he had to since I was standing right by the hallway entrance, his eyes were stormy and filled with silent warning. He didn't even nod as he brushed past before disappearing down the hall. A second later, I heard the front door open and close. And he was gone.

I felt rattled after his departure, but his mother didn't seem to notice anything strange at all.

"So this is Sarah's picture board," she told me. I jerked to attention, not daring to miss any vital piece of information. "If she has trouble understanding something you're saying, you can always point at a picture to communicate. And likewise, she can do the same in order to speak to you."

I nodded, soaking in as much as I could.

"Her supper's already ready. I have her meal

blended and sitting in the refrigerator. Just pop a straw in. We keep them in this cupboard." Dawn paused to open a nearby cabinet door so she could point out their location. "And hold it to her mouth for her. She'll probably try to talk you into letting her hold it on her own, but trust me, it's always less messy if you do it. Make sure she eats in about half an hour. Her evening meal is at 8:30 every night."

Another nod. Was I soaking this up well enough? I was still so freaked it felt like I was forgetting more directions than retaining. Half an hour suddenly didn't seem like nearly enough time to learn how to care for Dawn's daughter.

But she seemed to think I'd do just fine as she showed me Sarah's bathing chair in the bathtub and explained the girl's nightly routine.

"Cleaning her teeth is important. But we've been having trouble using a toothbrush. It used to be she'd let Mason brush them. But lately, he can't even get her to open up. She just doesn't like the bristles. So use a cotton swab and soak it in some toothpaste if you have to. Just do the best you can, and beware of these chompers." With a grin she tapped Sarah's chin. "She can bite."

Oh, joy. I looked forward to the rest of this evening more and more. Not.

We moved through the house, Dawn talking in rapid-fire succession as she pushed the wheelchair ahead of her, making me forget more and more of what she said. As we entered the front room, Dawn stopped Sarah in front of the muted television and smiled at me.

"Oh, and if she has a seizure," she added as she slipped on her café apron and picked her purse up off the coffee table, "don't try to stop it, because you can't. Just make sure she can't do anything to harm herself and wait it out. Call 911 if she turns colors or if she has more than one."

With that, she kissed Sarah's cheek. "Take care, munchkin. I'll be home by the time you're awake in the morning."

And she was out the door.

I panicked. Seizures should never be addressed in a parting comment, I decided. Seizures were scary. And serious. I'd just been left alone with a CP kid I had no idea how to even talk to who had seizures.

I turned slowly from the doorway, praying she wouldn't fall into convulsions that very second.

"So…" My voice trembled as I clasped my hands together. I was afraid to step toward her, and I had no idea why. She didn't smell bad or anything. I knew she wasn't contagious. I was just…ignorant.

But I stretched out my arm as far as I could without moving close and tapped a picture on her board. "Do you want to watch some television?" I asked in a slow, drawling voice.

Sarah knocked the picture board off her lap with a flailing hand—I suspect she did it on purpose. Then, she moaned out the word, "no," and despite all the bobbing her head did, I could tell she rolled her eyes at me.

Yes, she did. She rolled her freaking eyes.

The child thought I was lame. And that just wasn't acceptable. I was one of the most un-lame people I knew.

But really, the rolling eyes thing bespoke of a rebellious move and calmed me down more than anything else had since arriving at the Arnosta house. It was comprehendible tweenie behavior. And comprehendible behavior, I could get.

Narrowing my eyes, I smiled. Game on, brat.

"So…I overheard you and your brother talking about how all your friends are at a slumber party tonight," I started, folding my arms over my chest in a ha-take-that manner. "And you weren't invited."

She wailed out a groan, telling me I was trudging on dangerous ground for bringing up such a sensitive subject.

I tsked out a sympathetic sound and sat on the chair beside her wheelchair so we could be eye-to-eye. "That's really too bad, you know. I bet they're having loads of fun right now, putting on makeup and doing each other's hair, maybe having a campfire in the back yard and eating s'mores while they tell spooky ghost stories." I shivered for effect, really rubbing it in.

But then the damndest thing happened. Miserable, fat teardrops glistened in Sarah's eyes. When she blinked them away, my throat went dry.

Now *I* was the total jerk face.

Here, I'd been trying to prove I wasn't some pathetic, pushover babysitter, and my ward had been suffering from honest-to-God heartbreak. Ashamed of myself for being so cruel, I shut up and cleared my throat.

I had to fix this. Like right now.

And suddenly, as if the genius god had visited me, I had an idea. I've been known to have occasional, random streaks of brilliance, sure, but this one took the cake.

"Yeah, it's too bad," I repeated in the same fake-compassionate voice I'd been using. "Because those girls aren't going to have *nearly* as much fun as we will tonight." Then I let out an enthusiastic cheer and surged to my feet. "Let's get this party started."

Sarah glanced at me with a confused wrinkle in her brows.

I sighed and rolled my own eyes. "Let's do each

other's hair and put on makeup. I swear, I have an entire cosmetic kit in my purse. We don't need a bunch of other lame girls around to have fun. We can have it all by ourselves."

Before she could nix the idea, I hurried to my purse I'd left on the floor by the front door and returned to the chair beside her, pulling out everything I had on me and lining each item on the coffee table.

"You sit here," I ordered as if she wasn't already sitting, "And I'll glam you up."

That's what happened too. I babbled and applied while she sat and listened.

"The key to putting on makeup," I murmured ten minutes later, holding my mouth just right to mimic how I wanted hers to purse while I applied glittery gloss to her lips, "is to make it look like you're not wearing any at all. I mean, to be honest, if you're not going out club-hopping, too much makeup these days is just tacky and gauche."

"Then...why...put...it...on..."

Since the long question was such an effort for her, I hopped in, interrupting. "Why put it on at all?"

When she nodded, letting me know that's exactly what she was curious about, I grinned. "Oh, Sarah, Sarah, Sarah. I have so much to teach you, my little grasshopper. You see, beauty is all in the eye of the beholder. Some people will think you're lovely no matter how much you doll yourself up. Others will think you're hideous. It doesn't matter who you are. It's just a fact of life. So, honestly, the only opinion that really matters is your own. And I say...as long as you *feel* pretty, you will be. When you take out special time each morning to beautify yourself, it's just easier to feel that way. Tilt your chin up for me, will you, precious?"

I was pretty sure my whacked out speech on life and beauty would horrify Sarah's mother. But...Dawn wasn't here, so I kept gushing on as I grasped her chin to keep it as steady as possible when she tried to move it up herself but couldn't quite manage.

When I playfully dusted blush across her nose, she giggled a hoarse, keening moan.

I think I loved her laugh.

"There," I murmured, tilting her face from the left to the right as if examining every inch for flaws. Surprisingly, I found none. "You're simply beautiful, *dawhling*."

And she really was. There was a certain glow to her perfectly formed cheeks. I could see how she was related to Mason. They both had gray eyes and dark eyebrows. On him, the eyebrows looked sexy. On her, I might've wanted to pull out my tweezers and start plucking, but they still gave her a certain charming character. She looked amazing.

"I always feel like dancing when I put on makeup just for fun," I told her. "Do you feel like dancing?"

She nodded, and I grinned. "Well then what are we waiting for, chickie? Let's boogie."

Grabbing her wheelchair, I rolled her down the hall and back to the kitchen, which had a nice big open space in the center of it.

I booted up some Flo Rida on my iPhone, set the volume to full blast, and we got a "Good Feeling" going. Holding hands, we whirled around the linoleum, dancing in our own way.

We totally connected. She loved how I sang off key to the song and made the wheels on her chair skid into a circle.

"Only...Mason...dances...with me," she confessed a few minutes later when I plopped into a kitchen chair beside her, exhausted after our workout.

Something warm and tight trickled through me at the mention of him. "Does he? That's nice." I snagged a cookie off the center of the table, trying to sound blasé about it, when really I wanted to ooh and aww and blurt out how much my crush on him was growing that very second. "He sounds like a good brother."

"He's the best." She snatched a cookie too and began to munch.

I froze, not sure if cookies were allowed. I mean, if her supper needed to be blended, solid food must be taboo. Right?

But she grinned at me as she downed the entire thing. So, I grinned back.

And life was good.

From there, our night only got better. I found a flashlight and put a red cup over it before setting it in the middle of the living room floor—my very safe interpretation of a campfire. Using Sarah's dolls as fill-in people, I arranged our little party into a circle around the pseudo campfire. Then I helped Sarah from her chair and propped her back against the sofa with enough pillows on either side of her to keep her from tipping over.

We ate supper there—she held her own cup, of course, without a single spill—and I told her the golden arm ghost story. She loved every second and actually argued with me when I insisted it was bath time. But she ended up being helpful and pointed out the location of things when I needed to know where her soap and shampoo were kept.

By the time I got her into bed, we were both drained. She fell asleep almost immediately, and I stood over her for a minute, awed by such a wonderful, sweet child. She actually wanted to hug and kiss me goodnight, and we'd only known each other a couple of hours. When she said, "Love you," into my ear just before dropping off, I almost started bawling.

I think I loved her too; she was just too precious not to.

Lightly brushing her hair out of her face, I pressed a kiss to her temple and left her sleeping peacefully.

I settled on the couch and closed my eyes to catch my breath. And like Sarah, I fell asleep almost immediately, worn out from all the energy I'd put into entertaining my new buddy. But something jerked me from a muddled dream where Jeremy was pinning me to the door of my childhood bedroom and opening his pocketknife with an evil leer. *"I told you trying to get rid of me would be a big mistake."*

A muted light shimmered from the hallway, providing me a dim, shadowed outlook of the Arnosta living room. I had no idea what time it was, but it felt late. Groggy and disoriented, I stirred and yawned. I began to sit upright when I heard a noise from the back of the house.

A thump and then scraping wood yanked me alert.

That didn't sound right.

I panicked because I'd left my purse in the kitchen when Sarah and I had danced earlier, and the kitchen was way too close to where that sound had originated. My mace, Taser, and cell phone were in there.

Hell, yes, I owned a Taser. My psycho stalker ex-boyfriend had tried to kill me four months ago.

What was worse, I suddenly couldn't remember a thing I'd learned in self-defense training.

Oh, God. How was I supposed to protect

Sarah?

Sarah! Wait, what if she'd somehow gotten out of bed, and that was her back there, *hurt*?

I had to know what that sound was. But, Lordy, I wasn't sure if I had the courage to find out.

To be on the safe side, I snatched one of the dolls we'd used for our campout that was still sitting on the floor with its back propped against the entertainment center. Then I crept to the opening of the hallway, scared out of my gourd.

Thinking of Sarah's safety first was the only thing that gave me the nerve I needed to put one foot in front of the other, because if Jeremy had found me and followed me here, there was no way I was letting him anywhere near that sweet, innocent girl.

I paused at the partially closed doorway to her room, holding my breath, half hoping she was inside—and safe—and half hoping she wasn't—because if it wasn't her making that noise, then who the hell was?

I nudged her door the rest of the way open and peered into the darkness inside. The nightlight plugged into the wall revealed a perfectly shaped Sarah-sized lump on the bed. Then she shifted, making her mattress and sheets rustle.

Okay, so she was here. Then who *else* was in the house with us? If Dawn—or even Mason—was home, wouldn't they have woken me and told me I could go?

Something moved again in the back bathroom at the end of the hall, the one Dawn had told me not to use because the toilet didn't work right. It sounded like a drawer opening and shutting. Was someone looking for drugs or a weapon to use against me?

Shaking all over, I gripped the doll in my hands

tighter and held it like a ball bat, prepared to swing a home run if necessary.

Just as the door to Sarah's room had been, the opening to the bathroom was also hanging half open. I had to creep closer than I wanted to in order to get a peek inside. When I finally eased in just enough to see the sink, I froze solid. Hermione Granger could've pointed a wand at me and shouted, "Stupefy," and she wouldn't have had a better result. I could only stand there in shocked wonder and gawk. All fear vanished to be replaced by instant fascination.

With his back to me, a sopping wet Mason Lowe wore nothing but a towel as he leaned over the vanity and held onto its sides as if the sink were the only thing keeping him upright.

I could see his slightly bowed face perfectly in the mirror above. He'd squeezed his eyes closed, and a ragged expression contorted his features while creases of haggard regret etched deep grooves into the skin around his mouth and eyes.

I gasped when I saw the scratch marks on his bare, upper back, just under his shoulder blades and right where a pair of feminine fingernails might grip him if he'd had a woman lying under him very recently.

Lashes popping open, he looked up and saw me in the mirror.

CHAPTER **FOUR**

"**S**hit!"

As Mason cursed from obvious shock and reeled around, I squeaked out my own surprise and leapt back, freaked because I'd been caught ogling him. We gaped at each other with wide eyes through the opened doorway of the bathroom.

I know, I know. He was naked under that strip of terrycloth—please, God, don't remind me. The ladylike thing to do in this situation would have been—let me repeat, *would have been*—to instantly turn away and apologize for intruding into his shower time, and then flee in mortified embarrassment as fast as my legs could carry me. I fully realized that.

But seriously. He was *naked* under that terrycloth. Hello. Fully clothed, Mason Lowe was one hell of a yumsicle. But shirtless, he was simply indescribable. Since I'm so giving, however, I will certainly attempt to describe him to the best of my ability, even though it'll be *such* a hardship.

The white towel draped around his waist was loose and had slipped just enough to hang low, showcasing his flat, toned abdomen. A light sprinkle of dark hair growing around his innie bellybutton stretched down, disappearing under the towel, making me want to lick my lips and purr—or more to the point, it made me want to lick those perfect abs and that enticing happy trail.

And brace yourself for this one, ladies: He had a tattoo. I know. I almost spontaneously combusted right then and there. Stretching across his left bulging hip muscle was an honest to God tattoo. It said one, maybe two, words in what looked to be one of those impossible-to-read fonts. And it was somewhat obscured by the beginning of that aggravating towel.

Unable to help myself—hey, you try to restrain with a half-naked, tattooed Mason Lowe in front of you—I tilted my head to the side and leaned forward, squinting in an effort to read—

He snatched up a handful of towel, pulling it snug around his hips and lifting the waistline enough to hide his tattoo completely—the fun hater. Grabbing the door with his other hand as if he was going to slam it in my face, he demanded, "What the hell are you doing here?"

I looked up at his face, and Lord have mercy, I suddenly realized I'd totally neglected to check out the upper half of him. Yeah, I can't believe I almost missed out on that eye-party, either.

With his hair wet, his thick locks looked extra dark—almost black—and curled even more around his ears and neck. Water droplets dripped off the clumped strands and splashed down the side of his face and throat. More beads streaked across his chest, some having the good sense to cling possessively to his über-defined guns and pecs. Not that I blamed them. If I was a droplet of water and had the great fortune of landing on Mason Lowe, I'd cleave to his muscles too.

He still had that rugged sharp face I adored, but his cheekbones and the cleft in his chin looked extra pronounced in the florescent glow of the bathroom light, while his eyes took on a dreamy silver hue.

A very pissed off dreamy silver hue.

Scowling at me, he lifted his thick eyebrows as if to say, *"Well?"* which reminded me I hadn't answered his question yet.

Whoops.

"I...I'm babysitting." *Duh.*

But he looked so condemning, as if he thought I'd purposely snuck into his house and had staked out this very bathroom just to catch a peek of him in a towel and try to read his tattoo. It got my dander up.

I scowled back, growing defensive. "What the hell are you doing, taking a shower with the door *wide open* while I'm babysitting?" I set my hands on my hips and arched my own eyebrows.

Yeah, answer that one, buddy.

"I didn't know you were *here*," he snapped back. "And the latch doesn't work. I shut it as best as I could, but it still floats open when the exhaust fan is on."

Oh. Hmm, maybe that's what Dawn had told me: that the door latch—not the toilet—was broken. My bad.

But that still didn't excuse his crotchety attitude.

I tried—really—to keep my stare above his neck, but that was like plopping someone onto the ledge of a hundred-story skyscraper and telling them not to look down.

I *so* looked down. And yep, he was still sexy from head to toe.

He cleared his throat in a disgusted, do-you-mind kind of way.

Busted. I jerked my gaze back up.

"Isn't my mom home yet?" he asked when he finally had my attention on his face.

When he made it sound as if it were my fault that she wasn't, I huffed out an impatient breath. "Apparently *not*."

But really, what a tragedy. A guy with his level of hotness turning out to be a rude jerk was like stumbling across a steaming hot strip of perfectly fried bacon only to turn it over and realize it had mold growing on it. Not cool.

"I fell asleep on the couch after putting Sarah to bed and no one woke me. Wouldn't she have woken me if she'd come home?"

"She must be working overtime for someone, then." He closed his eyes and silently mouthed something, but I'd never been good at reading lips, so I had no clue what he said. Finally, he sighed as if forfeiting a mental battle he was having with himself and ran a hand through his thick, wet, dark hair. "Well, I didn't know you were here, okay," he said, not for the first time, but at least he sounded defensive instead of offended this time.

It was minimal progress if you ask me. Now...if *I'd* had control over his lines, I would've had him apologizing profusely for snapping at me by now.

"And I didn't know you were here either," I smarted back. "You scared the crap out of me. When I woke up and heard something back here, I thought a burglar had broken in."

The incredulous look he sent me told me he wasn't buying it. "You thought someone broke in...to use the *shower*?"

"I didn't hear the water running. Jeez." And now *I* sounded just as defensive as he did. But really. "I only heard doors, or drawers, or something opening and shutting. I didn't know what was going on."

He glanced at the doll in my hand that I still held as a weapon. "Well, swell. I suppose I should feel so much better now, knowing Sarah is safe in your hands. If someone breaks in, you can just wield your doll there and play tea party with them to death."

Oh, no, he didn't.

Instead of bringing up Mr. Taser and Mace Man hanging out in my purse, I scowled. "Hey! I'll have you know the plastic head on this doll is *pretty* hard. Trust me. Your sister caught me in the noggin with it earlier." I sank my fingers into my hair and immediately found the tender goose egg she'd left behind. With a wince, I added, "You just wait. After they finish with all the gun bans, they'll be outlawing these suckers next."

I waved the doll for emphasis. Its limp body lobbed back and forth in a pathetic attempt at intimidation.

Mason didn't even crack a smile at my joke. Watching me rub the side of my head, he blinked, looking horrified. "She *hit* you?"

"Oh, not on purpose, no. It's nothing," I dropped my hand from my hair. "No big whoop. We were having a good time. She was excited. Arms started flailing a little too wildly." I mean, how could they not when I'd been wailing, *'Give me back my golden arm?'* "But it's all good. Don't worry about it."

He studied me a moment longer. I couldn't read one discernible thought from his guarded expression. Then he shook his head as if to clear his thoughts and turned his attention away from me. "I guess I should pay you. My mom said eight dollars an hour, right?"

He continued to hold the towel in place as he bent to pick up a pair of rumpled, discarded Khakis off the floor. But as he shifted, the terrycloth stretched down in the back, and I swear I saw a peek of crack.

Oh, how I could become addicted to crack, especially when those two taut, tanned globes hugging that blessed crevice molded so perfectly to the back of his towel. They were like twin mounds of ecstasy.

Not noticing me gobbling up his rear end, he dug a hand into the pocket of his pants until he came up with a thick wad of cash. I lurched a step back, gaping at the bills he pulled free. Dear God, I *sooo* did not want to know where he'd gotten that money.

Whether it was true or not, Eva's rumor about him being a gigolo had me rattled.

"Umm..." I panicked. "D-don't worry about it. I'll just square it up with Dawn later."

He tilted his head as he eyed me, dissecting me to bits with his penetrating gaze. "Trust me." He waved the cash in his hand. "You're going to get paid from these exact bills right here. Does it really matter whether I give them to you now or if I pass them along to my mother, who probably won't remember to give them to you until next week...if not later?"

I stalled, still not wanting to touch his allegedly dirty money. But I really had earned that cash tonight. I wouldn't be surprised if I was nominated into the babysitter hall of fame after the way I'd pampered Sarah—excluding the first few minutes of the evening, of course.

Still, it was kind of sad to realize he was taking on this kind of responsibility for his sibling. My older sister had certainly never worried about paying my babysitters before. I wondered what kind of weight had been thrust onto Mason Lowe's shoulders so early in his life.

His eyes narrowed with defiance, daring me to reject his offer as he peeled back two twenties and handed them to me.

"Well...when you put it that way...." I tried to sound all nonchalant, but I knew he could tell how not-casual I felt about taking his money.

A little sick to my stomach, I felt this irrepressible need to turn on my heels and escape. But slowly, I reached out and slipped the bills from his long fingers, making sure not to touch his heated skin in the process. "Thanks."

When a surprisingly feminine smell caught my senses after the cash passed hands, I twitched my nose. Lifting the twenties to my nostrils, I inhaled deeply.

Mason's brows burrowed as he sent me a perplexed frown.

I blushed. "Sorry. I just...They smell like...Is that...Chanel No. 5?"

As his face blanched of color, I knew immediately. Everything Eva had said about him was absolutely true. Rich women paid him for sex. My skin prickled with a chilling awareness, realizing exactly what kind of things he'd done to earn this cash.

His jaw bulged. "I wouldn't know," he bit out from between clenched teeth. "I don't ask."

I wanted to drop the tainted, illegally gained funds. But holy guacamole. I was standing in the doorway of a steamy bathroom, staring at an honest-to-God gigolo who was wet and naked and covered by nothing but a bath towel. This was *so* going in the Christmas letter I was going to write to all my girlfriends.

The whole situation must've affected me way more than I realized, because without planning what I was going to say, I blurted, "What *do* you ask, then?"

He shrugged and studied me with a mocking kind of insolence. "Not much. My clients aren't exactly the shy type. They tell me what they want and typically don't leave a lot of room for questions."

My mouth fell open.

Oh. My. God.

"Oh, wow. So you're actually admitting you're a...a..."

He straightened pulling back slightly. "What? Haven't you heard the rumors? As tight as you appeared to be with Eva Mercer on campus the other day, I would've assumed she'd told you every dirty detail about me by now."

I sputtered and flushed hard. "I...Yeah...I mean, she told me some crazy gossip, but...I'm not sure if I believed any of it."

He didn't confirm or deny. He just watched me, waiting for my next move.

I figured people had two distinct responses to him: They either got as far away from him as feasibly possible or they moved closer in an effort to find out just how good he was at his job.

I did neither.

"Does your mom know?" I asked, rooted to the spot.

Dawn seemed way too nice—and moral—to allow her son to do such a thing.

He glanced away, and I once again caught a glimpse of the regret I'd seen on his face when I'd first spotted him in the bathroom. "I have a feeling she suspects."

Whoa. This was big. This was so big. "This is just..." I shook my head, not sure what to say. "Yeah."

Poor Dawn. She seemed so nice. If I were her and knew my twenty-year-old son was selling his body for sex, I'd—well, I wasn't too certain what I'd do. It was obvious they could use more money, but this seemed kind of extreme.

I settled him with a probing stare. "Doesn't it bother you that she knows—"

"No, it makes me feel all warm and fuzzy inside," he snapped with a glare. "Jesus. How do you *think* I feel about her knowing?"

All righty, then.

I opened my mouth to apologize, but he shook his head. "No. No more. The question and answer portion of this evening is over. You have your babysitting money, and I'm home to stay with Sarah. You can go."

"I..." Realizing enough was enough, I nodded. "Okay."

Ducking my head, I turned away, barely pausing to collect my things before I hurried from the house.

CHAPTER **FIVE**

The next morning, I felt craptacular as I slunk across campus, lugging my breakfast I'd stopped along the way to buy. Wallowing in my solitude, I was glad I wouldn't see Eva in any of my classes today, because I probably would've been all bitchy and crabby to her.

The night before still bothered me. How could I have been that rude and nosey to Mason? I couldn't believe I'd come right out and asked him such intrusive questions about his secret lifestyle.

I mean, I knew I had a snoopy side and it usually went to extreme lengths to appease its curiosity, but I had been so incredibly insensitive.

I hoped I wouldn't see him every evening I had to babysit. That could get awkward real fast.

And on the flip side: How could such an amazingly hot hottie be so completely unavailable, live such a corrupt life...and act so hostile?

Nothing made sense anymore.

Trudging past the bronze statues in front of the

main campus building, I was trying to think up a way to get past this when I caught sight of Hotness himself sitting on one of the benches along the sidewalk paths. With one leg crossed over the other and his ankle resting on his opposite knee, he'd spread open a textbook on his lap. He wrote madly in a notepad, pausing every few seconds to consult the book.

I reacted instantly, jerking to an abrupt halt. God, he looked good. Up close, from a distance, it didn't matter. The boy didn't have a bad side.

He's a gigolo, Reese, my inner conscience reminded me. *That means off limits*. Way *off limits*.

But he was also a gigolo who hated me, and a gigolo whose good side I needed to get on if I wanted my babysitting duties to progress smoothly. And he was just so pretty.

Changing my course, I turned his way and approached boldly. He didn't notice me until I stood right in front of him and said, "Here." In a peace offering attempt, I thrust forward the steaming cup and small brown paper bag I'd been carrying.

He looked up, brushed the hair out of his eyes with the end of his pen, and blinked at my gifts before returning his confused gaze back to me.

"This is my apology," I explained, "for being such a rude, nosey bitch to you last night. I'm... really sorry. I mean, what you do in your personal life is totally none of my business, and I shouldn't have been meddlesome. Please believe me when I say I never meant to offend you."

When he didn't reply and didn't reach for my breakfast, I shifted nervously. Okay, so maybe things between us *could* get more awkward.

This was so not helpful.

A stubborn streak bit me and suddenly I

refused to give up on my apology. I set the covered cup and baggie beside him on the bench with a plunk. "It's a bear claw in the bag and a white chocolate mocha espresso in the cup," I explained. "I don't...I wasn't sure what you'd like. So...I hope it'll do."

There. Pleased with myself for making it sound as if I'd bought my breakfast for him all along, I blasted him with a wide smile. When he didn't return it, my own dropped.

"Okay, then." I cleared my throat. "Have a good day."

I turned away, and the jerk face didn't call after me. So I walked off before he could respond.

Oh, who was I kidding? I'd given him plenty of time to respond. There's been a good five-second pause of uncomfortable silence after each sentence I'd said. And he hadn't gifted me with one word from his beautiful voice. The bastard.

I was irrationally hurt. But, hello. He wouldn't forgive me for *anything*. Truly repentant people should be forgiven. *Gah*.

Marching faster with each lungful of rising ire, I veered right toward the nursing center, a smaller, oval-shaped building beside the main hall, where my first class of the day took place. Instead of entering it, however, I hurried around the side and paused before sneaking a peek back to where Mason was sitting.

He stared at my breakfast as if it might be hazardous. I'd just convinced myself he was going to stand up and walk away without touching either the cup or the baggie when he reached out a cautious hand and gingerly picked up the latte. He held it another second, simply studying the brand on the container before he brought it to his mouth and took a timid sip, quickly pulling back.

Scowling at the cup, he licked his lips. My breathing stalled in my chest as I waited. Then he drank again, longer this time, tipping the bottom up as his throat worked through each swallow.

A pleasant buzz of warmth stole through me, as if he were drinking in a piece of me instead of my espresso.

With his next pass, he guzzled with abandon, draining the contents dry. Looking much less intimidating and much more approachable now, he set the latte aside, smacking his lips as he opened the sack to pull out my bear claw. He took a hearty bite from the fried dough and chewed with a cheek full before returning his attention to his homework. As he set his pen back to the page, the foot he had crossed over his ankle bobbed in a merry manner.

Hmm. At least he looked pleased by my gift...even if he couldn't bother to exonerate me aloud to my face.

Strangely satisfied by his reaction, I turned away and strolled to class, unable to stop smiling.

~$~

It had taken me all of thirty seconds on Tuesday to decide my General Virology course was going to suck ass. After my second round of it this morning, I almost considered changing my major entirely.

But at least I wasn't alone in my frustrations. As soon as class let out, complaining started all around me.

"We really need to start a study group," Ethan, the guy who'd sat beside me on the first day, announced to the room at large.

I could definitely get in on a little of that action, so I raised my hand. "Ooh! Count me in."

"Me too," a couple more people spoke up.

And thus, I had a study group arranged for Tuesday evenings after my library shift. My schedule was filling by the day. If I wasn't careful, I might actually appear to have a life soon.

Tickled that things were working out for me better in Waterford than I had expected they would, I trooped to the cafeteria next, starved since I'd given my breakfast away to the ungrateful bastard jerk face, who was still more beautiful than any man should be.

After purchasing a fully loaded salad-to-go, I found a deserted table outside and parked myself. I'd just opened the plastic lid to my lunch, my mouth watering for some ripe, green lettuce, when a shadow fell over my food, jarring me alert.

"Wha—" I glanced up, almost expecting to see Jeremy's leering grin, but gasped when I found Mason Lowe instead, hovering next to my table with his messenger bag once again strapped diagonally across his chest.

"What'd you say that drink you gave me this morning was called again?"

"Umm..." I blinked, unable to stop staring at him standing only three feet away. "Uh, it was a...a white chocolate mocha espresso. Why?"

Yikes, I hope it hadn't given him the scoots. That might get nasty.

But he made a pleasant humming sound in the back of his throat. "Mmm. It wasn't bad. Thanks."

Thanks?

Dizziness swamped me. The appreciative way he spoke sounded so genuine, so...so sexy, my entire body responded.

"Well...." I cleared my throat. *Respond, Reese. Freaking say something back to him already.* "Yeah." I swung out my hand as if to sign 'you're welcome'. "And...and thank *you* for, you know, forgiving me for the way I acted last night."

Okay, he hadn't quite said, '*you're forgiven for the way you acted last night*', but I was going to interpret his presence as just that.

I blew out a relieved-sounding breath. "I thought you totally hated me."

Yeah, yeah, I said that out loud. I'm a dork. Put it on my epitaph already. Though, honestly, I hadn't meant to say it; it just kind of projectile vomited from my mouth.

Mason gazed at me with a slight squint. I felt his stare all the way to the tips of my toes. It left my chest tight and my head muzzy. I couldn't make heads or tails of what he was thinking, but no matter what thoughts flowed through his brain— good or bad—they were definitely intense.

Finally, he glanced away and licked his lips. "No. I don't...I don't hate you."

His voice was low and serious, and damn, he might as well have said '*I love you*' by the way it affected me. I found breathing was suddenly impossible.

I opened my mouth, but no words came out, which was probably a good thing, because I'm pretty sure anything I would've said in that instant would've left me eternally mortified.

He shifted on his feet as if he were going to take off. But his eyebrows wrinkled, harboring conflicted thoughts, before he ran a hand through his hair. Never in my life had I wanted to be a hand as much as I wanted to be his hand right then.

"So I talked to Sarah this morning." He rushed out the words and played with the strap of his bag in a nervous manner.

"Oh, God," I moaned, squeezing my eyes closed and clutching my head, feeling eternally mortified anyway. "She told you about the makeup, didn't she? Oh...fudge. Is Dawn pissed? Is she going to fire me? I swear, I removed every inch of it before she went to bed. We even—"

"No. Yes." He muttered something under his breath and pressed a fist to his forehead as if he was embarrassed about how my rant flustered him.

Heat flooded me. I was unreasonably flattered that I'd actually managed to fluster him at all, and that he was embarrassed about being flustered in front of me.

"Yes," he finally said, straightening and speaking precisely. "Sarah told me about the makeup. She told me about *everything* you two did last night. And no, Mom is *not* going to fire you. She's probably going to give you a bear hug the next time she sees you. Sarah was absolutely glowing this morning. I've...I've honestly never seen her so happy. So whatever you think you did to annoy me last night after my shower has been erased tenfold by everything you did for my sister."

My jaw dropped as I watched him gaze at me with a sincerity that tore open my chest and made my crush for him expand into a wicked, hot mess.

After I cleared my throat, I straightened my spine and tried to calm myself. *Resist the hunky gigolo, Reese. Resist!*

"And you couldn't have said anything like this to me earlier this morning because...?" I arched an eyebrow, actually proud of myself for standing firm against his oozing sensuality.

But that's when it happened.

His face lit up and he grinned.

He *grinned.*

It was the first real grin I'd ever seen him give. And it was all for me. It fried a couple of my nerve endings. I definitely felt overheated. Might've even smelled smoke.

With a carefree shrug, he answered, "You were giving me food...and apologizing. If I had said anything then, you might've taken that bear claw back."

He had a point. I would have. Bear claws were very important to me. Unless he had pulled out that sweet grin this morning. In which case, I probably would've sat on his lap and hand fed him the damn doughnut.

But I snorted and shook my head, because I needed to fight my attraction.

Fight it!

"You are such a guy." I said it as if it was an insult, but he smiled again as if I'd complimented him.

Seriously, we were going to have to do something about that smile. It was way too powerful.

I rolled my eyes and let out a big sigh. When I realized he was still just standing there, watching me, I lifted an eyebrow. "So, are you going to sit down or not?"

His smile fell flat. "You don't mind?"

Mind? Sitting beside the most gorgeous guy on the planet? He obviously needed to get to know me better.

The surprise in his voice made my throat go dry, however. If he could look so stunned by a girl asking him to sit by her, then it must be a rare occurrence. Did his gigolo status really make him that much of an outcast?

Needing to keep things casual before I turned misty-eyed with sympathy, I lifted my hand to the back of my neck and pretended to knead strained muscles. "I mind this crick in my neck you're giving me by making me look up at you," I said, startled when my fingers drifted over my scar.

Crap, I'd completely forgotten about my scar. I never forgot about my scar. Dropping my hand, I swished my head to make sure my hair fell back over the area, concealing any and all red, puckered flesh. "Sit down already."

Scrutinizing my face as if he expected me to retract my invitation, Mason slowly looped the strap of his messenger bag from around his head. Then even more slowly, he lowered himself onto the bench seat beside me, leaving two feet of space between us and keeping his back to the table with his feet braced firmly on the ground—probably for a quick getaway. He set his bag gingerly on the bench between us, using it like some kind of shield. His shoulders looked so stiff I swear he was holding his breath.

I grinned, feeling the itching need to tease. "Comfy?"

He shot me a short glance before his shoulders visibly dropped a fraction of an inch as if to appease me.

Turning my attention back to my lunch, I tried to start a casual conversation. "I feel like your mom totally played me, by the way."

Mason cringed. "I know. I'm sorry about that. I told her she needs to tell people about Sarah's condition whenever she interviews them. But she insists it takes her five times longer to find a willing sitter when she does."

He had a point. Dawn really *should've* told me about Sarah in the interview. But then, I guess Dawn had a point too. I bet it did take her significantly longer when she was up front and honest. I'm ashamed to admit it, but if I'd known about the CP thing before I'd gotten the job, I totally would've declined it.

"I don't see how I'm allowed to watch Sarah at all," I said. "Not that I'm complaining, because your sister is absolutely the sweetest thing ever, but...doesn't she need, like, a trained medical professional watching her or something?"

"No." He shrugged and made a face as if he'd never considered that scenario before. "I watch her all the time, and I have no medical training. It's not like you have to give her any of her prescriptions or treatments when you watch her either. That all lands on the day sitter, who, okay, *is* a retired nurse, but government programs pay *her* wages, whereas your job is off the records since you only work part time every couple of evenings. Mom and I pay *you* cash out of pocket."

"Oh." I sat back, my brow wrinkled in thought. When I glanced at Mason, he was staring at me again with that unreadable scrutiny that made me want to fluff my hair and pull up a mirror to check my face. What the hell did he see when he looked at me like that?

Needing to fill the silence between us, I drew in a quick breath and pushed my hair out of my face. "You know, I kind of freaked out when I saw her picture board. I thought she couldn't talk at all."

I wasn't going to admit that wasn't the only thing to freak me out last night, but I felt more honest by confessing one of them.

Mason barked out an incredulous sound. "The *picture board*? Mom didn't really show you that, did she? God, Sarah hasn't used that stupid thing in over a year, and she only needed it in extreme situations when she was too excited or distressed to talk properly." He rumbled out a frustrated sound. "I swear, I love my mother to death, but sometimes the woman is way too overprotective. She can treat Sarah as if she's still two."

I grinned, because I'd had the exact same thought last night. "Yeah, I figured the board was unnecessary about one-point-eight seconds after your mom left when I touched a picture of the TV and Sarah *rolled* her eyes at me."

Mason chuckled, and oh, my God, the sound was amazing. "That sounds like Sarah."

I nodded, waiting a moment to talk so I could catch my breath. "And the whole blended supper thing—"

"Also unnecessary." Mason shook his head in disgust.

I snorted. "Well, I should hope so. When she took a cookie off the table, I almost had a heart attack, trying to remember the steps to CPR in case she choked." Leaning closer, I confessed, "Actually, after seeing that, I made us some s'mores for our campfire later on."

He leaned in close too, pitching his voice low and intimate. "I know. She told me."

Right. I'd forgotten he'd already said Sarah had told him everything.

God, he smelled good.

Holding my breath so I wouldn't give in to temptation and lean any further his way to inhale copious gulps of his scent, I straightened and turned to my lunch. "She's a sweet girl."

Sarah. Sarah was our only reason for communication. *Don't forget that, Reese.*

"She is," Mason agreed affably as he watched me open my ranch dressing packet and liberally smother my salad.

I sighed. "It's a shame she wasn't invited to that slumber party."

"Oh, you don't have to convince me. I know." Then he threw me for a loop by asking, "Do you always eat rabbit food?"

"Hmm?" I glanced at my salad, then sent him a strange look. "Uh, you ate what I was going to have for breakfast. What do you think?"

His eyes gleamed with a victory that confused me until he pointed an accusing finger. "Aha. I knew that was *your* breakfast you gave me."

Crap. Busted. I hated it when I opened my big mouth and ousted myself. "Whatever," I grumbled moodily. "I bet you didn't."

"Oh, I knew." He lifted one eyebrow, and oh my *gawd*, he looked really good doing that. Not fair. "You think a drink bought for a *guy* would be a white chocolate mocha espresso? Really?"

I sniffed. "Hey, I thought you said you liked it."

"I did. It was way too sweet though. Like girly sweet." His smile grew seductive as he added, "Must be your lucky day. I just so happen to like it extra sweet."

Holy guacamole. Was that a double entendre? I swear that was a double entendre. Someone hold my panties on for me because Mason Lowe was freaking *flirting* with me, using double entendres.

Shaking my head, I muttered, "You are so..."

He grinned. "Charming? Handsome? Intriguing?"

All three, not that I'd ever admit it to him. He appeared to have a big enough ego as it was. I scowled hard. "I was going to say confusing."

"Ahh." He nodded in an astute manner. "We'll slot that under intriguing."

"Actually, I think it really deserves its own classification."

"Fine. Whatever you like." Shrugging as if it made no difference to him, he sent me a look full of smug, glittering eyes.

Oh, now he was just being overly placating to make the little woman feel better. Grr. Every breath he took irritated me. Or maybe it was just me that irritated me, because as much as I wanted my emotions to stand firm against him, I was too utterly thrilled to be sitting next to him, talking to him, breathing in his handsome, charming, intriguing essence.

Man, I was lame. But I didn't care. I was eating lunch with Mason Lowe. *Squee*!

Rolling my eyes to conceal the thrill party going on inside me, I smarted back, "I *do* like."

As I picked my tomatoes off the top of my salad and piled them onto a napkin to the side, Mason's gaze zoomed in on them like some kind of heat-seeking missile. "Aren't you going to eat those?" He sounded scandalized that I was setting them aside.

I wrinkled my nose. "What? My tomatoes? Eww."

He shook his head. "How can you not like tomatoes?"

"I don't know. It's nothing personal against them. I'm sure they're very pleasant in a social setting, and they're fine in, like, ketchup and spaghetti and stuff. I just don't want them on my salad."

He continued to gaze longingly at them like they were bacon...or chocolate...or bacon-chocolate muffins. Okay, that sounded nasty, but you get where I was going with that, right?

"Do...you want them?" I offered.

He had the tomato-laden napkin sliding across the table away from me before I could fully finish the question. After setting his bag on the table, he threw one leg over the bench until he straddled it, facing me.

"Thanks," he said, his voice muffled as he popped a tomato chunk into his mouth and spoke while he chewed. "Mmm. These are perfect. Nice and juicy."

I guess the boy liked tomatoes. And had he just said *juicy*? He should always say words like juicy, just to rile a girl's imagination towards all kinds if naughty thoughts. Not that I should be having naughty thoughts about a gigolo. Certainly not.

"Do you have any salt?" he asked, breaking into my naughty thoughts as he licked his fingers.

Salt? How was *salt* naughty? Though the finger-licking...oh, yeah, that was naughty.

"Uh..." I glanced around and picked up the condiment package my napkin and plastic fork had come in.

When I spotted a miniature container of salt and pepper left inside, I brightened. And hey, it suddenly struck me how naughty salt could be if it was sprinkled on his naked chest and then licked off his sculpted pecs, or out of his innie belly-button, or away from his mysterious tattoo.

Clearing my throat, I fished the salt package free. "You're in luck. I do." I tossed it his way, trying not to mourn the loss of all the things I could do with that salt.

Hotness totally impressed me when he caught the packet with one hand. "Thanks. Again."

I watched him sprinkle the tomatoes.

"What?" he asked when he caught me staring— and totally not thinking about salt. "Don't you put salt on your tomatoes?"

Apparently I wouldn't be putting salt on *anything*. "Seeing as I don't even eat tomatoes, no. I was just...sorry." I blushed hard, trying to forget what he had looked like in that towel last night. "I seem to have a slight staring problem today."

His eyes sparkled as he chewed. "I noticed." He didn't seem to mind, though. He looked amused by my staring problem.

I wrinkled my nose to make a face, my sneaky way of showing him I wasn't affected by his playful charm.

But he merely grinned. "Not only do you *eat* rabbit food, but I swear you must be one."

I paused chewing. "Huh?"

"That's the second time you've wrinkled your nose at me. Total bunny move."

Oh, crap. He'd noticed my one bad habit. Yes, I just have *one*. Hush.

Wait! He'd noticed my nose-wrinkling habit and was counting how many times I did it? That was...whoa. That was the sign of an interested male right there.

But no way could Mason Lowe be interested in me. He was a freaking gigolo. Gigolos didn't bother themselves with insignificant, nose-wrinkling, lame college girls.

Did they?

Feeling as if I was being sucked into something bigger than I could control, I glanced away from Mason, reminding myself there was still life around us. We were not the only two people left on the planet, sitting at that table, discussing nose-wrinkling habits. Away from this moment, he did things I could never condone. I needed to distance myself from any guy who lived such an intolerable lifestyle. Jeremy had taught me that lesson, and I would never forget it.

When I looked away, I caught sight of one of my professors strolling by, carrying her briefcase as if she was on her way to teach a class. Needing a diversion away from the captivating guy eating with me, I lifted my hand and waved.

Big mistake.

CHAPTER SIX

"Hey, Dr. Janison," I called as I flagged her down with my hand. "Good morning. Those are some kick-ass shoes."

Dr. Janison was my favorite professor at Waterford, and not just because she knew a damn fine Jimmy Choo when she saw one. I loved her teaching style too. She knew how to make Early British Literature interesting when I was not a fan of that particular period in the least.

She gave me a vague nod. "Good morning," she said in that polite, distant way that told me she didn't know I was one of her students. Then she glanced at her pumps. "And thank you."

I was opening my mouth to explain which class of hers I attended when she glanced toward Mason and instantly paled.

Face blanched of all color, she skipped a step back as if she was about to take flight in her four-inch Jimmys. "Mr. Lowe," she nearly whispered, sounding terrified as she gaped at him with wide eyes.

He didn't make eye contact, merely mumbled, "Dr. Janison."

Realizing the professor had probably heard rumor of his reputation—and didn't approve—I felt suddenly protective.

Gah, just because he was a gigolo didn't mean he had the plague.

I set my hand on the arm he had resting on the tabletop. I only wanted to banish some of her worries, assure her he wasn't diseased. But when Dr. Janison's gaze darted to where my fingers sizzled against his skin, she didn't appear reassured. She looked even more disturbed as she glanced between us.

Not sure how to kill all the awkward floating around us, I forced a bigger smile. "I found a pair of knock-off Jimmy Choos similar to that style online one time, in a silver pump, and I wanted them so bad. But even the replicas were more than I could afford."

If the pair she was wearing was original, then the woman was easily standing on eight hundred dollars.

But instead of revealing the secret to me about whether they were knock-offs or not, she sent me a knowing kind of smile. "I do have expensive taste."

When her gaze flittered back to Mason, all the muscles in his arm under my hand tensed.

"Is our meeting to discuss your class schedule still on for this Thursday, Mr. Lowe?" She looked pointedly at me as if she expected any negative answer from him would be my fault.

Understanding, I suddenly forgot how to breathe. Oh, my God. *Dr. Janison*? And Mason? No way.

His voice wasn't tight or strained as he

answered, "Of course," but I could've sworn he was talking through clenched teeth, and he still refused to look at her.

She gave a single nod. "Good." I swear she looked relieved by his answer. With one last glance at me, she murmured, "I look forward to seeing you then." Turning away, she strolled off in her kick-ass shoes, which I suddenly had the urge to boot out from under her.

I whirled to Mason. "You don't have any classes with her, do you?"

He popped his jaw as he clenched his teeth. "No."

I shut my gaping mouth. "Oh."

Hissing something under his breath I couldn't quite catch, he snapped his messenger bag off the table with vicious force. "This was a mistake. I never should've sat beside you."

My heart thudded against my chest. "Well, thanks a lot." I forced my voice to sound offended instead of hurt, when honestly, I was a whole lot of both. "I had a sucktactular time talking to you too."

Jerk face.

"I didn't..." He closed his eyes and fisted his hands before sitting back down. "Reese, I didn't mean it that way. I swear."

"Then how exactly did you mean it? Because it sounded pretty rude from every angle I heard it."

His lashes fluttered open before he pierced me with one of his intense, paralyzing stares. "Don't you get it?" He glanced around the courtyard. "I just doomed you. By talking to you in public, by sitting with you at this table..." He whooshed out his arm to motion to our surroundings. "Everyone here thinks we've had sex."

I snorted out a laugh. "Oh, whatever. I seriously doubt that. I barely even touched your arm. People do not..." But my words faded off as I glanced around. Everyone really was stealing speculative glances in our direction and talking behind their hands. I sank lower in my seat, feeling instantly ostracized. "Or maybe they do."

Holy salted tomatoes, Batman. He must have a mighty heavy reputation if simply sitting beside him automatically made me a slut. "So...uh, Dr. Janison is really one of your, umm, clients then?"

He snorted but didn't answer.

I groaned and closed my eyes. "Wow. This is going to make my next Early British Literature class way awkward."

"Wait." He grasped my forearm, and I swear I felt his touch explode out the tips of my toes. Maybe it wasn't so farfetched to think he had such a heavy reputation. "Are you saying you have a class with her? With Dr. Janison?" When I nodded, he closed his eyes briefly. "Shit."

Well, that didn't sound good. "What? What does that mean?"

"Look." He sighed, sounding incredibly tired. "If she starts giving you a tough time, or failing you or...*anything*, let me know. I'll talk to her."

"Whoa, whoa, whoa. Why...why would she *fail* me just for sitting next to you on a public bench?" And setting my hand on his arm as if we were dating, and...oh, crap.

But wait. "That makes no sense. Even if we had...you know, had sex or whatever, she has no reason to get jealous. Doesn't she know she can't possibly be your only...customer?"

"Of course she knows. But you're obviously *not* a customer. She might feel slighted if she thinks I gave you a..." He glanced away and waved his hand. "You know, a freebie."

"Wow. Okay. But wow. Not only is this the

strangest conversation ever but, wow. A *freebie*?"

Mason sent me a dark glance as if he didn't think I was taking the situation seriously enough. "You know what I mean."

I barked out a laugh, because okay, yeah, the whole conversation did feel incredibly ridiculous. "Just convince her I paid for it then, that I'm, you know, a client too, just like her."

He blinked. "What? You don't want me to tell her we're not fooling around at all?"

Flushing hard, I cleared my throat and glanced away. "Or that. That...I mean, sure, the truth would probably be best. Yeah. Let's stick with the truth."

Mason shook his head, looking entertained and frustrated in equal parts. "Except she won't buy it. And she knows you can't be a client."

"Hey. Why couldn't I be a client?"

Was I too young? Not classy enough? Not his type?

His lips tightened as if he was trying not to smile. But his eyes lit with amusement. "Reese, you just admitted you couldn't afford the same kind of shoes as her. There's no way you could afford me."

Oh, now he sounded like Eva.

I didn't want him to know it, but that kind of offended me.

"Really?" I arched an eyebrow and set my hands on my hips. "Just how much do you cost, Mr. Ego?"

Leaning in close, he whispered an amount in my ear. My mouth dropped open. "Okay, yeah. I couldn't afford that. But...wow, I don't know." I flailed my hand. "Don't you have a payment plan or something? Reduced prices for the lower income?"

He sputtered through a startled laugh. "No, I do *not* offer payment plans. Are you for real? I play the expensive way, or I don't play at all. I don't do this for my health, you know."

"Then why—"

"Because being a decent, moral *upstanding* citizen didn't keep the eviction notices away," he snapped. "It didn't get my sister a new wheelchair, and it didn't put food on my mother's table, or keep the electric company from turning off our power in the middle of the hottest day of the year. And it sure as hell didn't get me enrolled in college this semester. This is all about the money. *Only* about the money. Got it?"

"Got it," I said in a small voice. Then I offered him a smile. "Actually, that explanation makes you sound kind of noble, you know, with you falling on the sword of absolute depravity to save your family. You'd probably make a good Saturday afternoon movie."

There. I hoped that sounded frivolous enough, like I really didn't care what he did with his life.

But Mason blinked at me. "You're...insane."

"Only on Thursdays." I wrinkled my nose since he was counting my nose-wrinkles and all.

He grinned—unwillingly, I think, but hey, at least I'd managed to ease some tension from the moment.

Popping a salted tomato between his perfect lips, he chewed with vigor...until I went and asked, "So, you don't give out freebies? Like ever?" That just sounded so bizarre to me. I would've thought a gigolo would be a complete man-whore, even off the clock.

But when his jaw went dead still as he stopped chewing and he said, "Are you...*asking* for one?" I wanted to smack myself on the forehead.

Crap, I hadn't meant to make my question sound so hopeful. "What? No!" Then for good measure, I made an incredulous sound. "*God*, no."

He gaped at me, telling me he didn't believe me.

I flushed and looked away. "I'm not—" It was on the tip of my tongue to tell him sleeping with him would break my heart. But admitting that couldn't end well, so I repeated, "No!" just to be clear. "I'm not like that. I need to be in, you know, a committed, monogamous relationship, and...in love, and stuff, before I...sleep with someone."

Shifting closer and setting an elbow on the table to study me until I squirmed on the inside, he softly asked, "Have you ever been in love?"

My mouth fell open. "Are you asking if I'm a virgin? Because I'm not—"

Lifting his hand, he waved it softly to stop my flow of embarrassing words. "That's not what I'm asking."

"Oh." I cleared my throat and glanced away. More self-conscious than I'd ever been, I bit my lip and winced. "Well...I don't..." I shook my head. His question was too complicated to answer with a simply yes or no. "I'm not sure what I was, if it was stupid, too-young-to-know-better infatuation or what, but it definitely wasn't love. And I'm not about to make the mistake of not knowing the difference ever again."

His lips tilted up in a smile, almost as if he were proud of me. "Good."

Huh? I wasn't sure which part of that he approved of so much, but the admiring gleam in his eyes made me a touch too warm. I promptly turned the subject back to him and back to why I needed to stay away. "So, if it's common knowledge around here that you're really, you know, what you are, then how have you never been arrested before?"

"It's not common knowledge. It's a common rumor." He squinted as if he wanted to say more on the topic but sighed instead. "You're not going to leave this alone, are you?"

"Hey, it's not every day I meet a gigolo."

He choked on a tomato when I said gigolo aloud, because my vocal chords might've risen a touch too vociferously, but I kept going. More quietly, of course.

"Can you blame me for being curious? I have, like, a million questions." I held up a hand, remembering how uptight it had made him last night when I'd gotten nosey. "But only if you're cool with answering them."

He eyed me a moment longer before shaking his head. "You read a lot of Nancy Drew mysteries when you were a kid, didn't you?"

I wrinkled my nose. "No. I've never even read one. Harry Potter is more my style, and yeah, his curiosity got him into trouble a lot too. As you well know."

"No," he murmured, looking almost regretful. "I've never read *Harry Potter*."

Gasping, I set my hand over my heart and stared at him as if he were an alien. "Are you kidding me? But...*everyone's* read *Harry Potter*."

He shrugged and didn't even have the grace to look ashamed or guilty. "Not me."

"But...but...they're so...amazing. Don't worry," I instantly reassured, reaching out to pat his arm. "I have all the books in the series sitting in my apartment. Next time I babysit Sarah, I'll bring the first one over for you to see what you think."

The muscles under my fingertips twitched as if my touch burned him. I noticed his expression then as he stared at my hand still resting on his forearm. I wanted to jerk my fingers away because he seemed so transfixed by our connection, but I couldn't move. He just looked so...tempted.

I liked it.

Slowly, he slid his arm out from under my gentle grip, severing our contact. "I don't do freebies," he said in a throaty voice. "Ever."

Wow. Okay, then. That had kind of come out of left field.

Had he really thought I'd been coming onto him to score a freebie?

Jeez, *had* I been coming onto him?

"But I wasn't..." Scowling, I turned back to my lunch. "Whatever." Then just as quickly, my snoopy Harry Potter syndrome struck again. Crunching on a crouton, I asked, "What about your personal life, though? What about dating and—" I broke off when he laughed. "What's so funny?" I totally hated missing out on a joke.

He arched his eyebrows. "Dating? Personal life? Are you serious? The only girls who sniff around me are willing to pay or they're looking for free services rendered, which only pisses me off."

"But—"

"And all you monogamous, *relationship-conscious* ladies stay as far away from me as possible for obvious reasons."

I made a face. "That can't be true. I'm sure plenty of—"

"Reese." He stopped me mid-word by lifting his hand. "Honestly, would *you* date a...person of my occupation?"

I gulped. Hells to the no, I would not. "Good point."

"Yeah." He let out a long, lonely sigh. "Exactly."

"Well, that's just sad," I finally decided. "You can't date or have recreational...fun, or even fall in love just because you went to drastic measures to save your family?"

Yes, I was feeling bad for a gigolo. Sue me.

He shook his head as if stumped by my sympathy. "I was eighteen when I fell into this. At the time, I was too young and stupid to think about how it would impact my future...so." He shrugged. "There you have it. Now I'm stuck."

"No. You can't be stuck. Surely, there's *something* else you could do to make money. Something *legal* and...and..."

"Moral?" he guessed.

"Yes, and moral. And..."

He chuckled and touched my cheek briefly. "You're cute, Reese. Cheerful. Optimistic. Funny. But completely deluded." Grasping his bag, he stood up abruptly, letting me know he was done talking. "Thanks for making my sister smile. And thanks for the tomatoes. I'll see you around."

As I watched him take off, I wanted to call after him and make him come back. He'd looked so lonely when he'd said he was stuck. The pain in his eyes had cried for help. It had cried for a friend.

And I could always use a new friend. But I'd have to be extra careful. Because that's all he could be.

CHAPTER **SEVEN**

"**Y**ou'll never guess what rumor I heard yesterday."

Eva's voice startled me Friday morning before Brit Lit as she slid into the seat beside mine. I'd been downloading a few songs Sarah and I could boogie to onto my phone.

"What's that?" I asked, returning my attention to the four-inch screen to purchase a little Black Eyed Peas.

"I heard my favorite cousin on earth was spotted eating lunch with Waterford's very own hunky, mysterious gigolo yesterday."

"Hmm? Oh, yeah, he—Oh, I forgot to tell you." I lowered the phone. "That babysitting gig I got— the one I started Wednesday—it's his sister, Sarah. She has cerebral palsy. Did you know that?"

"About his sister? Yes, I've heard." Eva made a grumbly sound in the back of her throat as she waved her hand. "How does that have anything to do with you sitting all alone in the middle of campus with her brother...*yesterday*?"

"Well, I guess I'm a kick-ass babysitter." I tossed my hair over my shoulder as I flashed her a smug grin, preening over my awesomeness. "Miss Sarah raved about her evening with me to him, and he wanted to...I don't know, thank me, I guess, for being so nice to her."

Eva's mouth dropped open as if she didn't buy such a lame excuse. "Really? That's *all* he said to you during your forty-five-minute conversation?"

Wow, our gossiping eavesdroppers had actually been timing us? Weird. And had we really talked for forty-five minutes? No way. It hadn't felt that long. But then, it hadn't felt nearly long enough, either.

"Well..." I frowned. "Mostly, yeah. After talking about Sarah, we moved on to a couple other topics, but—"

"What other topics? Like his *work*?"

I rolled my eyes. My God, she could be even more curious than I was sometimes. "Well...sort of. That was on the list. But we talked about all kinds of—"

"Oh, my God, so he *admitted* what he is."

"You said he would."

"But...but everything I've ever heard about him was just...hearsay. This is actually...fact." Her mouth fell open as she whispered, "Holy shit, he's really a gigolo."

At that moment, our professor walked into the classroom. A sharp-dressed woman, Dr. Janison wore fitted skirt suits as you could imagine some executive in high fashion might wear. It was too bad I had to hate her now; she really did teach well and knew how to put together an awesome ensemble.

But thinking of her anywhere near Mason made me feel all heartbroken and depressed. And kind of vengeful.

Unable to help myself, I motioned to her with my eyes and leaned across the aisle to whisper, "And guess who one of his clients is."

Mouth falling open, Eva turned to watch our teacher set her briefcase on top of her desk and click it open. "No freaking way."

A niggle of guilt gnawed at my conscience. Mason hadn't acted like it was a big secret, but I suddenly felt ashamed about spreading gossip about him—even though it was true and I was only telling my favorite relative and personal confidant.

Still.

"But you didn't hear that," I was quick to add. Both the professor and Mason would find themselves in a world of trouble if someone leaked their association.

"Oh, hell, yes, I did," Eva whispered, unable to take her eyes off Dr. Janison. "I wonder what position she likes it in."

Seriously? "You did not just say that."

"Whatever. Tell me to my face you're not a little jealous of her right now. I mean, the man *ate lunch* with you yesterday. Mason Lowe just doesn't...interact with females in public. I think you have more claim over him now than any girl, like, ever." She turned back to me. "You should be the most jealous of us all."

"I...*no*," I insisted a little too emphatically. But did I really have more claim over him than any other girl ever? "I mean, no. I don't hate Jessica for having Justin, do I?"

How could anyone hate another woman for having a man who was totally out of her league?

Eva wrinkled her face in confusion. "Jessica and Justin?"

I gasped. How could she not know who Jessica and Justin were? "Justin *Timberlake*," I clarified with that are-you-kidding-me kind of expression all over my face. "Jessica Biel. Only one of Hollywood's hottest couples."

Now she really looked mystified. "You like Justin Timberlake?"

"Hello." The look I sent her said, *Yes! Duh.* "He brought sexy back."

Ooh, and now that I was thinking of it, that would be a good song to add to my phone for Sarah to groove to.

"Well, whatever," E. murmured beside me as I searched for "SexyBack" since "Let's Get It Started" had finished downloading. "*You* can deny jealousy all you want. I don't think Dr. Janison is going to be so forgiving, though."

I whipped my head up. "What do you mean?"

"Honey, she's going to flunk you hard for playing with her boy toy...without paying for him."

I swear, she and Mason sounded too much alike sometimes. I opened my mouth to tell her our professor was a professional; she would *not* flunk me just because I had one lunch with her gigolo.

But Dr. Janison interrupted me by beginning class. "Good morning. Today, we're going to start studying a new author. I think everyone will get a kick out of Chaucer—"

She broke off mid-word when her gaze caught mine where I sat near the right side of the room midway down the aisle. Recognition lit her gaze, and her face drained of all color. Then her eyes narrowed ominously. When everyone turned to glance at me, I shrank lower in my seat.

"You are so flunked," E. hissed under her breath.

Oh, God. I was.

~$~

"We're getting our noses pierced this weekend."

I paused eating my lunch to gape at E. "Say what?"

I'd been so deep in thought, wondering if I should transfer out of my literature class, I hadn't been paying a whole lot of attention to her prattling. But I swore I'd just heard something along the lines of—

"You, me, nose rings. This weekend."

She sat next to me on the bench to the table I had decided was going to be my lunch spot for the rest of the semester. My memory of sitting here with Mason the day before had pretty much cemented that decision—even if sitting with him was going to get me flunked from my English class. It was as if we'd christened it as ours.

It actually kind of felt like a betrayal to sit here with Eva instead of him.

But I suspected she was hanging around me so much today in the hopes I'd be granted another "gigolo-sighting," as she was calling it.

"I'm not piercing my nose. Are you insane?"

"But they'd look so cute." She stole one of my fries and decidedly stated, "I saw Alec checking out a girl wearing one yesterday. So, yeah, we're getting them."

I snorted. "If you want to go poking holes in strange places on your body just to impress your wandering-eye boyfriend, be my guest. But I will not be getting one with you."

She merely sent me a cool smile and shrugged. "We'll see. Oh, by the way, Mom and Dad are taking off early next Friday to spend Labor Day weekend at our beach house. They won't be back until late Monday night. I'm thinking...party at my place,

Friday."

"Beach house? I had no idea you guys had a beach house. Oh, my God, why aren't you going with them?"

Eva yawned as she flipped open her pink and black tiger-striped planner with a matching fuzzy pen. "Um...because I'm not *ten*. How lame would it be to spend Labor Day weekend with the rents? Seriously, ReeRee. I have so much to teach you."

If my parents had a beach house, I'd be there every weekend. I don't care how lame spending time with them might look. But this was Eva we were talking about. So I just shrugged. "Well, I can't make it on any Friday. I have to babysit."

Eva scowled. "Who? The gigolo's retarded sister?"

I sent her a glare to kill. "Her name is *Sarah*. And yes, I'm talking about Mason's *special needs* sister. Don't ever call her retarded in that derogatory way again."

With a roll of her eyes, she relented. "Okay, fine. How about Saturday night? Are you baby-sitting any freaks then?"

I ignored the bash against my little buddy by gritting my teeth and dipping one of my fries into a vat of nacho cheese. "Just how big of a party are we talking here?"

Ever since Jeremy, I had soured to huge gatherings full of too many strangers.

But Eva brightened. "Epic." Then she spotted a group of guys passing our table. "Hey, boys. Party at my place. The Saturday of Labor Day weekend. You in?"

They grinned and gave her the thumbs up. "An Eva Mercer party? Oh, we are *in*."

"Great. See you then." She turned back to me, looking smug.

I blew out a lungful of irritation. "I guess we'll be throwing a party, then. And now I know why my mom was so worried you might become a bad influence."

"Oh, let's not call it a bad influence." She slung an arm over my shoulder and grinned. "Let's call it bringing a little color into your life."

Behind us, someone snorted. "Only you would call it that, Mercer."

The breath whooshed from my lungs as the owner of that voice rounded the table to sit across from us.

Mason.

Damn, he looked good today, all fresh and friendly with a charcoal gray v-neck that made his eyes look lighter than usual. He grinned at me and promptly scoped out what I was eating.

"Ooh, chili cheese fries. Good choice. Better than the rabbit food you had yesterday." He stole one off my plate and popped it into his mouth.

"Well, look who's come to visit Miss Deluded," I snarked back, hiding my intense reaction of all things excitable to his presence. "Do you ever eat your *own* food? Or do you just get a perverse pleasure out of eating mine?"

"That's for me to know and you to find out." He sent me a grin full of promise and hidden meaning. I fell into a mini trance, watching his lips purse and move as he chewed. Then my attention fell to his tanned throat as he swallowed.

Seriously. Eating a chili cheese fry should not look that sinful.

"Umm. Can we help you? *Mason*?" Eva asked pointedly, glaring daggers at him.

He sent her a strained smile. "Nope. Just eating my lunch."

"*My* lunch," I cut in right before he pulled a

plastic-wrapped sub sandwich from his bag. He waved it tauntingly, letting me know he *had* brought his own food.

I scowled back because, really, I hated being bested.

Watching him unwrap his meal and take a bite, Eva muttered, "Do you seriously have to eat here? With us?"

"Eva!" I gasped. What was her deal? Earlier in Brit Lit, she'd acted as if being in his presence was the bomb. Now, she was just...a bitch.

"Jesus, Mercer." Mason scowled as he lowered the hoagie. "I'm not contagious."

"Are you sure about that? I mean, who knows what kind of nasty STD—"

"Okay, okay, okay," I broke in, lifting my hands and waving them in the universal white-flag gesture. "I'm sensing a disturbance in the Force between you two. Is there some kind of history here I'm not aware of?" Then I gasped. "Oh, my God. You two have slept together. Haven't you?"

Eva huffed out an aggravated sound and wrote something in her planner vigorously enough to make the fuzzy tassel on the end of her pen bob sporadically.

Mason merely stared at me in awe as he shook his head. "Wow, your curiosity has no filter whatsoever, does it?"

I scowled back because he was purposely avoiding my question. Glancing at my cousin, I said, "E.?"

"It's nothing," she muttered, suddenly very interested in turning the page and checking future dates.

With a roll of my eyes, I whirled to face Mason with a pointed look.

"What?" he asked, pulling back with an overly

innocent expression. He cast a questioning glance at Eva before focusing on me. "She said it was nothing."

I opened my mouth, but Eva must've had a change of heart.

"*Nothing*?" she repeated in an offended voice. Slamming her planner shut, she narrowed her eyes. "Okay, fine." She finally gave me her attention. "One night at a party about, oh, a year ago, I'd had a little too much to drink and I ended up throwing myself at him." Her gaze pierced Mason with hateful shards. "And he turned me down. Flat."

I frowned, confused. Umm...wasn't that kind of what a guy was supposed to do when a drunk girl came onto him?

"And *she* proceeded to call me a pretentious bastard for it," Mason added, glaring right back at Eva.

"Well, you are," she hissed.

"...who had no right to act so self-righteous because I'm nothing but a high-priced whore with a pretty face, who'll end up an overweight, broke, balding no one by the time I'm forty." His jaw tightened. "Isn't that how you worded it?"

I gasped and pinned my cousin with an incredulous glance. "You called him a *whore*?"

She shrugged. "He *is* a whore."

"So that's what I get for trying to be a gentleman and not take advantage of the stumbling, slurring drunk girl." Looking pissed and a trifle hurt, Mason reached across the table and picked up my cup as if he needed it to console himself. But after taking a deep drink through the straw, he winced and pulled back. "What *is* this?"

I wrinkled my nose at him and pushed my hair out of my face. My drink didn't taste that bad. "It's a diet cola."

Okay, maybe it did taste that bad.

He set it back in front of me, looking deceived. "So...you eat chili cheese fries loaded with grease, calories, and carbs. Then get a *diet* cola?" He gave an amused laugh. "You're such a girl."

I tossed my hair again and leveled him with a fake scowl. "Maybe I just ordered a nasty-tasting drink because I knew you'd try to steal it. This could've been the only way to protect what's mine."

"A," he said with a smile. "That won't work on me. I'll always steal whatever food or beverage you have. And B." He fluttered his lashes. The feminine move should've looked ridiculous on him. Which, okay, it kind of did. But it also looked drop-dead sexy and somehow masculine. "I'm flattered you took the time to think of me at all."

"Oh, gag me," Eva howled. "If you two are done eye-humping each other, I'd like to go throw up now."

I sent her a glower, promising a good strangulation later. I even opened my mouth to tell her in no uncertain terms that Mason and I were *not* flirting.

But he ignored her and said to me, "Are you watching Sarah tonight?"

I gave him some major brownie points for being able to totally blow off Eva's rude comment. But the tightening around his mouth told me her words hadn't left him unaffected.

Following his example, I decided to ignore her too. "Yep. I think I'm going to give her a mani-pedi and paint her fingernails and toenails some wicked awesome color."

He nodded approvingly as he rewrapped his sandwich and slid his lunch back into his messenger bag. "She'll get a kick out of that. I'll see you at the house, then." He knocked on the table in front of me as he stood. "And don't forget that book you promised to lend me."

"Right." I sucked in a sharp breath, tickled he'd remembered. "Yeah, okay. I won't."

"Good." With a warm, congenial smile for me, he stole one more of my fries. "And for the record, I like deluded." Then he strolled away without once glancing at Eva.

My cheeks flamed. I loved knowing he liked me just the way I was, naïve tendencies or not.

I didn't notice how Eva had spun to me with an expectant arch in her eyebrows until she demanded, "What book?"

I played with my fries without eating any. "*Harry Potter*. He said he's never read the series before. Can you believe that? So I offered to loan him mine."

"Really? *Harry Potter*?"

She sounded so skeptical, I sighed. "No, we were talking about a *Kama Sutra* book. *Yes*! *Harry Potter*. Why is that so hard to believe?"

Eva shrugged. "I just can't see Mason Lowe reading *Harry Potter*. I can't see him reading anything." Then she made a face, letting me know she'd thought up an allowance. "Except maybe *Kama Sutra*."

I shoved my fries away and turned to pin her with a frown. "You know, he's not that bad of a person. Once you actually talk to him, he's just another guy."

Just another guy who made my body heat, my pulse pound, and my throat go dry. Another guy who was fun to talk to, got my jokes, and liked my taste in food. Another guy who made me forget I was leery of the opposite gender these days. Yeah, just another guy.

"I don't understand why you'll talk about him

behind his back like he's some kind of god, but you just treated him like crap to his face."

"Oh, sweetie." Eva's features filled with sympathy as she grasped my hands. "You poor, deluded thing. I'm going to have to explain the social pyramid to you, aren't I? Mason Lowe is an honest-to-God gigolo. Guys like him are fun to gossip about. They're fun to flirt with when nobody else is around, and I'm sure they're fun, period, when you employ their services. But you do not *sit* with them in public and talk to them like they're *just* another guy. Because they're not." She sighed and patted my hand. "I knew I needed to keep an extra-close watch on you today. Because look what happened. He came sniffing around, trying to ruin your reputation, and—"

I yanked my hands away from hers and lurched to my feet, not about to listen to another word. "If he's such bad news, then why did *you* try to get a freebie from him?"

Eva flushed even as her eyes narrowed with outrage. "Okay, *one*, I was drunk and I am still absolutely humiliated I did that. And *two*, I could actually handle him without getting in too deep. *You'd* probably go and fall in love with a piece of underworld scum like him if he ever had sex with you. And that's completely unacceptable, ReeRee. A prostitute doesn't belong anywhere near you. You're too sweet and innocent."

My mouth fell open as I openly gaped with outright disgust. "Oh, my God, E. I'm going to ignore the way you just totally insulted me because I think you were coming at it from a good place. But I will not sit here and listen to you bash Mason like that." I stood and gathered my things. "He may have made a...bad career decision, but he is by no means—"

"Dear God, you're already falling for him, aren't you?" Eva scooted across the bench toward me, her eyes pleading. "Don't do it, sweetie. You're just going to get hurt. It'll be Jeremy all over again."

"Whatever," I muttered as I swept my book bag over my shoulder and whirled away. "I'm out of here."

I stewed all the way to my next class. Eva was wrong; Mason would never be another Jeremy. First of all, I would never date Mason. I *knew* he was off limits. *Not* that he was unworthy, just that he was incapable of being faithful, due to his job and all. I knew I could crush on him from afar but never hope for more. I *knew* that. And secondly: Mason didn't give off one control-freak vibe, not the way Jeremy had exhaled them like carbon dioxide. He was most certainly not the girlfriend-beating type.

But I remained moody for the rest of the day because Eva had said one thing that had completely freaked me out. Despite knowing I would never date Mason, I thought he could still hurt me, because I was pretty sure I *was* falling for him on a level I couldn't stop.

He would be able to hurt me in a way Jeremy never had. I might have told my first boyfriend I'd loved him when he'd expected me to say it, but I'd never really given my heart to him. There was something about Mason though that told me I could give it to *him*.

A little too easily.

CHAPTER **EIGHT**

When I went to babysit on Friday evening, and the Monday after that, I didn't get to see Mason either day. He'd already left for his "country club" job by the time I arrived. And Dawn got home from work before he did on both nights, meaning he'd stayed late...with a client, no doubt.

The thought made me burn with...I don't know. Lots of emotions. Anger, jealousy, sadness, depression. I was pretty much a tangled, hot mess inside.

And his mother forgot to pay me—yes, on both nights. But then, Mason had warned me she was a tad on the forgetful side when it came to settling her debts.

The only bright spot on both of those evenings had been getting to spend time with the sweetest little girl with cerebral palsy on the face of the planet. I was quickly falling in love with Sarah, and her smile.

After I painted her fingers and toes with Purple

Passion on Monday, then topped them off with some plastic jeweled bling, the biggest, brightest smile lit her face. I was tempted to pull her into a big ol' bear hug and kiss her all over her adorable face.

I put her to sleep by reading her the first chapter of *Harry Potter*, which I'd brought for Mason. Then I dragged myself into the Arnosta kitchen and tried to catch up on a little homework. I gagged my way through a Humanities assignment before Dawn showed up about twenty minutes after midnight.

Bummed that I hadn't even caught a glimpse of Mason, and even more bummed because I knew why, I drove home and did a walkthrough of my apartment to make sure nothing looked disturbed. When I collapsed on my bed, I forgot to set my alarm clock.

So of course, I slept in on Tuesday.

With no time to do my hair or put on makeup after a quickie shower, I dashed out the door, figuring I'd buy breakfast on campus. But, *au contraire*. Remembering I was low on funds for a couple more days, I dashed back into my apartment and snagged a banana from my rarely picked-from fruit basket sitting on my kitchen counter.

I reached campus ten minutes before my class started, which made me gnash my teeth and wonder if I'd had time to primp after all. Oh, well. It was just going to have to be a grunge day.

My usual table where I'd first eaten lunch with Mason was taken. Taken! I know, I was going to have to carve my name into it. I slumped to a nearby tree and collapsed on a sunny patch of grass. Digging my banana from my bag, I wrinkled my nose at the brown, aged spots on the peeling and decided I was too tired to eat anyway. So I closed my eyes and waited until it was an acceptable time to drag my bootie to class.

I was trying to boost myself to stand when a shadow blocked out the sunlight. I sensed someone standing over me a split second before that voice I loved and loathed at the same time—because it made me want things I couldn't have—said, "Question."

I opened one eye to see Mason. He looked perfect. As usual. Wearing loose, scruffy pants and a form-fitting, dark-plaid top, he grinned down at me, holding his hands behind his back.

"What?" I mumbled drowsily.

"Why are we sitting on the grass this morning?"

We? When had we become a *we*?

God, I loved how he said *we*.

Damn it, we could never be a *we*.

Life was so freaking unfair.

I flung a lazy hand in the direction of my table. "If you haven't noticed, *our* table is already occupied."

He glanced over, and then looked back to me. "Really? Hmm. Actually, I hadn't noticed."

I lifted my face from my book bag I was using as a pillow—a really sucky, lumpy, hard pillow—and craned my neck as far as my body would allow without exerting any more energy than absolutely necessary. When I saw our table was indeed empty again, I groaned and dropped my head back with a thump.

"Well, it *was* occupied when I got here, so I opted for this lovely spot of fresh grass. And don't even think about making me get up to move now. I'm too"—I paused to yawn—"tired."

"Ah," he said with an understanding nod. "I see." He didn't sit next to me but remained standing with his hands behind his back. When he rocked back onto his heels, I squinted at him, wondering what the heck his deal was.

"So I saw you here, lounging on the grass," he finally told me, "and I said to myself, what is wrong with this picture...besides the fact that you were practically passed out on the ground."

"Oh, God." My hand immediately went to my hair. It had dried into a clumpy mess. "My hair looks like crap, I know. And I'm not wearing any makeup. I slept in, okay. I didn't have time to doll myself up, and—"

"Not that," he said, shaking his head and grinning. His gaze went to my hair before it skimmed my face. "Actually, I hadn't even noticed. You do seem more natural today, though. Looks nice."

Lordy, I needed to ignore how warm that compliment made me feel.

Forcing my mind past it, I kicked up a leg, showing him my footwear. "Is it because I'm wearing sandals instead of flats?"

Yeah, yeah, Eva had converted me to the dark side. But my feet could breathe so much easier in sandals. I could show off my own sparkly painted toenails—plus a new toe ring I'd just gotten—and besides, they were adorable, sexy and practical all rolled into one with a bunch of straps to make my ankles look incredible. I hadn't been able to resist buying them.

Mason glanced at my new sandals. "Uh...no. Sorry."

I let my foot plop back to earth. "Okay, I give up." When he just grinned at me, I rolled my eyes and feigned some seriously pathetic interest. "Why, whatever did you notice missing about me this morning, Mason?"

"I'm so glad you asked, Reese, because I noticed you don't have your usual latte today."

I moaned and muttered, "Thanks a lot. Remind me I'm lacking my caffeine intake on top of everything else." I sniffed, pettily. But hey, I was tired; I couldn't help it. "My piggy bank is running a little dry at the moment"—damn you, cute strappy sandals that had been on clearance, fifty percent off—"so I'm going to have to postpone my espresso treats for a while until—"

"Mom didn't pay you again, did she?"

I cringed. Crap. I hadn't meant for that to come up. This wasn't his problem, but I knew he'd make it his.

When I refused to answer, he gave a big sigh. "I don't have all the cash on me to cover what she owes, but I'll make sure you get paid. Okay?"

"It's fine," I started, but he shook his head to hush me.

"It's still a shame you can't have your daily latte, though."

I slumped my face back onto my bag. "Yeah."

"But look on the bright side."

Bright side? There was a bright side to this? I lifted one eyebrow, waiting for him to enlighten me about this unforeseen bright side.

Mason winked and pulled his hands from behind his back, holding two Styrofoam cups, one in each hand. "You've befriended Mr. Money Bags who *can* afford them."

My mouth fell open. "You bought me a latte?"

He'd bought me a latte?

I melted, my emotions softening into this huge, gooey ball of adoration. I wanted to laugh and cry and hug him until I decided having a boyfriend who slept with scores of other women for money wasn't really that big of a deal.

Okay, it was still too huge of a big deal for me to ever get past. But wow. Mason had bought me a latte when I was at my lowest of lows.

How sweet could one guy get?

"Don't get too excited," he warned as if he could read my mind. "I have an ulterior motive."

I sat up immediately, no longer tired at all. It was as if the caffeine in the drinks he held had somehow already shot straight into my bloodstream.

"Fine." I lifted my hands and wiggled them impatiently. "You can have my firstborn. Now *gimme.*"

Mason laughed and handed one of the cups over. "I hadn't realized you requested the chocolate shavings on top special." He sighed as if refreshed when he settled himself in the grass beside me Indian style. "I was halfway across campus before I noticed them missing and had to go back again."

He'd gone back to get me chocolate shavings?

Oh. My. God.

It was official. Mason Lowe was perfect. Well, beside the whole gigolo part. But yeah, other than that, no one else could even compare.

I took my first sip. When I moaned, he arched an amused brow. "Would you two like to be alone?"

I tucked my latte protectively close. "Yes. Could you give us fifteen, twenty minutes tops? I have a feeling things are about to get real obscene up in this house."

He laughed again as I took another drink, my toes curling as I swallowed.

His warm, affectionate gaze on me, plus the shot of instant caffeine to my system, brought me to life in a way I couldn't even describe. But I was suddenly very alive.

I grinned back without an ounce of my inner

whiney, childish crabby-pants anywhere to be seen. "Thank you, Mason. I was afraid I'd have to eat this banana I brought from home." Making a sour face, I held it up to show him how ripe it had gotten. "But the idea turned my stomach. For some reason, healthy food first thing in the morning bothers me."

He pointed, looking scandalized. "So...you're not going to eat that?"

I saw where this was headed and rolled my eyes. "You want?" I offered it to him, and he snatched it immediately.

"Thanks."

I drank as he peeled the banana and tore off a third of it, popping the entire section into his mouth. He still looked entirely too gorgeous while chewing, even with fruit bulging from the side of his cheek.

I glanced away and picked at a piece of plastic on the lid of my cup. "Did you get your book? I'm sorry I forgot about it Friday and didn't bring it over until last night." I didn't want to think about why he hadn't been there to accept it himself, but I did anyway.

He nodded as he took a small sip to wash down the banana. "Yes. Sarah made absolutely certain it was in my hands first thing this morning. At five o'clock."

I winced. Ouch. He'd gotten home later than I had last night and had been up way before I'd opened my eyes. If anyone had a reason to be a tired be-otch today, it was him. But he looked too content for any of that as he added, "And she showed me all twenty of her newly painted nails. Nice job, babysitter."

"Why, thank you," I said with a not-so humble bow—well, as much of a bow as I could manage while sitting on the ground.

"Sarah's the reason I need to talk to you, actually."

"Right." I emptied my cup and frowned. Had I finished my latte already? Bummer. I focused on him. "The ulterior motive. I remember."

"Right," he repeated with a nod. "So I've heard a rumor from a little birdie that you have a...charm bracelet."

I frowned, completely confused by this line of questioning. "Umm...yeah."

"Can I see it sometime? Sarah has been gushing about it. So I was thinking of getting her one for her birthday next month."

I perked to attention. "Her birthday's next month?"

"Yep. She's going to be the big one-three." Without waiting for me to lift my arm and show him my wrist, Mason spotted my bracelet and took matters into his own hand, gently wrapping warm fingers around my forearm and lifting it to examine the piece of jewelry draped over the base of my hand. "Mom and I were going to give her a birthday party on the twenty-third if you want to come."

"Hell, yes, I want to come. And I'll buy a charm to go on the bracelet as my present to her. Are you going to invite any of her school friends?"

Mason's good mood immediately soured. He let go of me with me a hard look. "Sarah doesn't *have* any friends from school."

"Jeez, sorry." I lifted a hand to calm his scowl. "I guess I should've worded that differently. What I meant to say was: Are you going to invite any of her *classmates*?"

The dark fury on his face said *hell, no*. "Why should we? They never invite her to any of their stupid parties."

"I know, I know." I gave a relenting sigh.

"But...this is middle school. It's a really eye-opening time for her. She's beginning to see how the world works and is realizing how much having no friends sucks. I just think if there was any way to get someone her age to be nice to her, even for an hour-long birthday party, we should at least *try* to help her adapt to her social peers. I mean, she's going to be *thirteen*. That age is the toughest time, I swear."

Mason blew out a breath, looking reluctant, but he admitted, "No doubt. I hated middle school. Nothing good comes from adolescence."

"Oh, I don't know about that." I playfully bumped my shoulder against his. "You learn where the most painful pimples grow."

With a grimace, he made a mustache with his index finger. "Right here, under your nose."

"I know, right." I laughed. "Most painful place ever."

"My eyes would always water when I tried to pop them."

"*Uhhmm.*" I mimicked a you're-in-trouble-now sound. "You're not supposed to pop pimples. Bad Mason."

His mouth dropped open as he sent me an incredulous gawk. "How you can you *not* pop them?"

Caving, I nodded and confessed. "Okay, fine. I always had to pop them too." When we shared another smile, I grew a little too fascinated with staring at his perfect features. I frowned. "I can't imagine you with acne."

Mason rolled his eyes. "Trust me. I had my fair share of craters."

"Well, your skin is flawless now." I sent him a suddenly suspicious, arch-of-the-eyebrows look. "You exfoliate, don't you?"

He choked on the sip he was taking. After

coughing and wiping a dribble of latte out of the dimple in his chin, he dryly reported, "Yes, you caught me. I put that green crap on my face and cucumbers over my eyes every night."

"Hey, don't bash the cucumbers. Those actually work."

"Wait. You *do* that?" I'd shocked him yet again.

"What? I'm a girl, aren't I? It's like required to try the green mask of beautification at least once in a woman's life. It's part of Girly Girl Law or something." And hey, there was something else I could do with Sarah.

After studying me as if he'd just met a new person, he asked, "Do you eat the cucumbers when you're done?"

Only Mason, the food vacuum, would ask that.

I made a face. "Eww. No way. What if an eye booger got on them?"

Mason threw his head back and shouted out a laugh. He'd been laughing a lot this morning. I kind of, sort of, totally loved it.

Shaking his head, he gave me a look full of amusement. "I think this is the first time I've ever discussed zits and eye boogers with a girl before."

It was a first time for me to discuss such things with a boy too. Feeling suddenly awkward around him because his words somehow reminded me my hair was a disaster and my face was bare, I hugged my empty latte cup with both hands and glanced around the campus...only to frown.

"Wow. Does it seem unusually quiet all of the sudden?"

Mason checked his wrist. "Shit!" He lurched upright. "I'm late to class."

"Oh, my God. What time is it?"

"Almost fifteen after." He jumped to his feet, his messenger bag already slung over his shoulder.

Fifteen after? "No way!" How had I gotten so distracted?

I scrambled for my own bag, and Mason caught my elbow, helping me up even as he snagged it for me. "Here you go."

"Thanks."

He kept pace with me as we rushed toward the entrance of the school.

When he reached out ahead of me to open the door, his fingers lightly cradled the small of my back. The sensation of his hand there sent sparks up my spine and exploded in the base of my skull with blissful fireworks until I experienced a full body throb.

Ignoring the reaction, I started to turn right toward my Brit Lit class when it struck me—I actually had virology today...in the other building.

Crap. I began to rotate back around and noticed Mason was going left. We realized at the same moment we had to part ways.

He halted and opened his mouth. Gray eyes scanned my face.

More than curious to know what he wanted to say, I froze in my sandals and held my breath.

"Well...bye." He winced, making me suspect he'd wanted to say more than that.

I gave him a small smile. "Yeah. Bye."

He nodded and went left. I stared after him a moment before rushing from the main building and dashing toward the nursing department.

But I wondered all day what he'd really wanted to say to me.

CHAPTER **NINE**

The rest of my week was a dream come true. Mason showed up at my lunch table every day. And he was the only one. No Eva, no jealous professor clients. Just him and me.

By Friday, we'd fallen into a rhythm. I know this sounds totally nerdy, but we worked on homework together, usually calculus since we were both in a calculus class—same professor, different times. We could bounce ideas and helpful tips off each other.

The best part was I was smarter and worked faster. Not that I'm bragging. Okay, I'm totally bragging. But it was just so awesome to be better at something than he was.

"Have you finished question three yet?" he asked about five minutes into our lunch...after he'd polished off half the chicken strips I'd gotten from the cafeteria.

I snorted. Of course I'd finished question three. He held up a hand before I could spit back something sarcastic. "Wait, scratch that question. Of *course* you're past question three already."

Aww, he was learning me so well.

"Ergo, I revise my query to, '*what* did you get for an answer on question three?' I keep coming up with sixty-four over zero. But that looks—"

"And you would be wrong." I spoke over him, making a game show's buzzing sound. "Now you have to admit you're not smarter than a fifth grader."

He sent me a scowl. "I'd like to see a fifth grader try college calculus."

"Hmm. I bet a fifth grader would've answered number three as eleven over four."

Mason threw his pen on top of his notebook full of equations. "How in the hell did you get eleven over four?"

With a grin, I leaned over and pointed out each x and limitation.

He picked his pen back up and scribbled numbers madly, working the equation the way I suggested. "Damn," he murmured when he came up with eleven over four. "Why didn't the professor explain it this way? This way is easy."

I gave a long sigh. "They rarely do explain anything the easy way. Their brains just don't function the same as a normal person's, so it's harder for them to translate equations in layman's terms. My dad's a high school math teacher, so I know."

Mason looked surprised as he glanced at me. "Really? That's cool. I guess I shouldn't be surprised you know your way so well around numbers. Must run in the genes."

I shrugged, modest about my geeky side. "Hmm." Tucking a piece of hair behind my ear when a breeze caught it and sent it fluttering in my face, I asked, "What did you inherit from your dad?"

As soon as I asked, I remembered Dawn was a single mother. Wincing, I held up a hand, "Sorry. I didn't mean to impose. I totally forgot your mom's—"

Mason waved a hand. "No. It's fine. My dad died when I was four, so I don't remember much about him. I just know he was in the army."

I set my hand over my chest. "I'm so sorry. Was he killed in the Middle East?"

Sending me a telling look that seemed to snarl, *you just had to ask that, didn't you*, Mason sighed. "No. He never went to combat. He got tanked one night and killed a family of four, plus himself, in a drunk driving accident."

My mouth fell open. *Whoops*. "Oh, my God, Mason. That...sucks."

"Yeah, pretty much. And in this small town of a community, everyone knows how he died, so I can't even fabricate some hero's death for him."

I chewed on the end of my pen as I stared at the calculus book in front of me. "So...can I ask about Sarah's dad?"

His narrowed eyes told me I shouldn't have asked about that guy either, but he answered me. "Butch Arnosta. That loser ran off after we learned about Sarah's condition. Mom met him when I was seven. They had a quickie romance, she got knocked up, they got married, and then he was gone again as quickly as the doctor said the words cerebral palsy. After that, I think Mom gave up on men completely. She never really dated again."

I made a sympathetic sound in the back of my throat. "Well, I don't blame her any. Sounds like she has as bad a track record with men as I do."

Mason shot me an incredulous glance. "How

can you have a bad track record? You're only, what, eighteen?"

I sniffed. "Eighteen and a *half.*"

He grinned at my joke. I loved how he always knew when I was trying to make a funny, even if it was a corny, really bad funny.

"I beg your pardon, old woman." He held out his hand as if asking me to pass something to him. "Let me see your palm, Miss Eighteen and a Half. I'll take a look at your love line and tell you just how bad your track record really is."

I crinkled my brow, untrusting. "You read palms?"

"No, I just want to hold your hand." His voice was so serious, I couldn't actually tell if he was teasing or not. Then he rolled his eyes and shook his fingers impatiently. "Gimme."

I had nothing to lose, so I held out my arm.

He took my wrist and gently turned my fingers over. "Let's see here," he murmured, deep in thought. He brought my hand closer to his face for inspection just before he blew on the skin.

His warm, stirring breath made every hair on my body stand on end. Holy freaking cow. The boy sure knew how to arouse.

"What are you doing?" I gasped. *Besides totally turning me on in the middle of a college campus.*

"Hmm?" He glanced up, looking innocent. "Oh, I was just blowing the dust off my crystal ball here. It's obviously been a while since you've had a good palm reading." Felt more like palm foreplay to me. But... whatever. I certainly wasn't going to tell him to stop blowing on me.

"You are such a dork," I said with a snort to hide the emotions I was feeling.

"Hey, don't insult the fortune teller while he's working. He might predict something...unpleasant."

I couldn't imagine anything worse than my past relationship, so...bring it.

But I told him, "Oh, I'm so sorry, wise one." Leaning in toward him just enough to smell his clean, male scent, I pretended to study my palm too. "So, what's my love life look like?"

He turned his attention to my hand and studied it a moment before running his index finger along one creased groove. It sent a delicious shiver down my spine.

"It looks good. Says here you'll have a long and happy love life. You'll meet your soul mate early on and marry straight out of college. The two of you will move to"—he squinted and leaned closer, making waves of lush, oak hair spill across his forehead—"Rhode Island, where you'll each make at least eighty grand a year, have two point five children, and buy a dog named...Hundley."

I lifted my eyebrows. "Is that so? Hundley? As in the dachshund off *Curious George*?"

"Yep. Says so right here." He tapped my palm as if that should convince me completely.

I shook my head slowly, tickled by this playful side of him. "So what's the name of my soul mate then?"

Mason frowned. "How the hell am I supposed to read some guy's name off a couple of lines on your hand?"

I scowled right back. "But you know what my *dog's* name is going to be?"

"No." A mischievous grin lit his face. "I told you I don't read palms."

"Oh, my God." I shoved at his shoulder. "You're ridiculous."

He didn't seem to mind that I nearly shoved him off the bench; he was too busy shouting out a laugh. "Ridiculous, huh?" Curling my fingers in to make my hand ball into a fist, he brushed his thumb across my knuckles. "We'll slot that under charming."

"Ridiculous most definitely does not go under charming."

He didn't answer; he was too busy studying my middle finger that bent at a funny angle. "What happened here?" He wiggled it a little, making it lay straight.

"Hmm? Oh, I jammed it out of place while playing basketball in high school."

He looked up. "You played ball?"

I nodded, trying to ignore the way his thumb kept moving over my suddenly sensitive flesh. "For three years."

"Why not all four?"

Shrugging to cover the tremble of distress that passed through me as I remembered a particularly horrible moment, I distractedly murmured, "I, um...I broke my arm just before the season my senior year. Couldn't play."

His gaze went up my arm and straight to my elbow as if he knew exactly where the bone had shattered. "How'd you break your arm?"

Glancing away, I watched a group of guys fooling around over by the garden of bronze statues, climbing onto the back of the bucking stallion and pretending to ride it. "I took a tumble down some stairs." *Right after Jeremy shoved me into them.*

Mason studied me as if he could read the horrifying memory from of my brain. Then he grinned. "Well, I guess you *are* fairly accident prone. My toes are still smarting from those books you dropped on them."

"Hey." Only half offended, I tried to pull my

hand out of his grasp, but he tightened his grip so he could kiss my mangled middle finger.

Yes, yes, I know. He put his mouth on a part of my body. I'm surprised I'm still conscious enough to talk about it.

Examining my finger, he pulled his lips away. "I wouldn't have taken you for the athletic type. You don't move like a jock."

I lifted one eyebrow. "Just how do I move?"

He shrugged before shooting me a wink. "Well, when you're not tripping all over the place, you move like a girl." He bunched up the features in his face as if deep in thought before adding, "Maybe like a cheerleader."

I grimaced. "I don't think so, scooter. All the cheerleaders at my school were dirty, vengeful sluts. I only dated one person all through high school, thank you very much."

Jeremy had threatened away every other guy who came within twenty feet of me after I'd broken up with him.

"Oh, ho! So the truth comes out." Mason cocked me an I-got-you-now smirk. "Pray tell, Miss Randall, how do you have such an awful track record when you've only had *one* boyfriend?"

I straightened my spine. "Sometimes it's more about the quality than the quantity that counts."

His eyes darkened with feeling. "That bad, huh?" His features softened as if he might want to comfort me, which, okay, I wouldn't mind. Really. "What did he do? Cheat on you?"

I tried to pull my hand away again. No luck. But I didn't try too hard. I didn't really want him to let go, and it warmed me that he initially refused.

"Among other things." I kept my voice light, trying to play it down.

Mason's face darkened. "*What* other things?"

Thank God I was saved from answering, because my mind went blank, trying to concoct a good lie.

"See, they *are* dating," a voice said as a trio of girls passed by our table about twenty feet away. "He's holding her hand. I told you he couldn't be a gigolo."

Mason jerked his hand from mine and scooted backward to put some space between us. The way he shuttered away his expression, like a house yanking down its blinds, sent a bolt of fury straight through me. I wanted to maim everyone who'd ever hurt him with their barbed gossip.

I glared at the passing girls. "We can *hear* you, you know."

All three of them snapped their gazes to us and just as quickly looked away again. Hustling into a light jog, they hurried off until their giggling echoed back.

"Don't listen to them," I told Mason. "They're...ignorant"

"Doesn't matter." He shook his head as he slammed his calculus book shut and shoved it into his bag. Sending me a tight smile, he stood up. "Have a good Labor Day weekend, okay?"

Before I could respond, he turned and strode off, his shoulders rigid and hands fisted at his sides.

I sighed. Depression hit hard as I remembered it really was going to be Labor Day weekend. Dawn had taken off work at her night job for Friday, and the café where she worked would be closed on Monday, so I wouldn't be going to the Arnosta house until the next Wednesday. And since school was closed for the holiday, I wouldn't even have a good reason to see Mason around campus until Tuesday.

Strangely, I missed him already.

CHAPTER **TEN**

I'd give my cousin this: The girl sure knew how to throw a party.

As I watched the music-thumping activities around me, my nostril smarted from the diamond stud embedded in the side of my nose. Yes, Eva had finally peer pressured me into it.

Hey, I'm not perfect.

My weakness had started as soon as I'd seen how cute the silver hoop she'd gotten for herself looked. Then she'd glanced at me, said, "Jeremy would hate seeing you with a nose ring," and my resistance had sunk like the Titanic. God forbid I do anything *he* would approve of.

Worried how much goo would catch on it whenever I sneezed, however, I had opted for a stud instead of a hoop. The redness and swelling had gone down, and it had never bled the way Eva's piercing had, so no one could tell it was only a couple of hours old.

I glanced across Aunt Mads and Uncle Shaw's

living room to watch Alec lift a shot of tequila from Eva's cleavage with his teeth and tip the jigger up without touching it. E. cheered him on as a trickle of alcohol dribbled down his chin. But she licked it off him as soon as he dropped his shot glass into his hands.

I shook my head even as my lips quirked with amusement. Crazy kids.

I'd been worried about her and Alec dating when I'd first met him. He seemed as rich, spoiled, and pretentious as Eva was. Two likes, in that regard, usually didn't attract. I figured they wouldn't last a week, each of them expecting the other to pamper them as much as their parents did.

But they'd been together almost three months now and still seemed content.

Standing with my back against a wall so I could take it all in without missing anything, I felt like I was supervising instead of joining the fun. Ever since May, though, I'd been a little too leery of diving into a group of complete strangers.

I'd just taken a sip from my plastic red cup when someone approached me from the side. "Hey. You were looking lonely standing over here all by yourself. Thought I'd keep you company."

"Oh!" I almost spilled frothy beer down my shirt, I jumped so hard. Wiping my chin and feeling like a moron, I turned to the stranger. "I didn't see you there."

He grinned, his teeth perfect enough to tell me he must've worn braces at some point. "Sorry. I guess all my secret ninja training is paying off after all."

I smiled but couldn't manage a laugh.

He held out his hand. "I'm Ty."

"Reese." I shook with him, pulling back immediately.

I swear I didn't throw off any flirty signals. But he still leaned against the wall beside me as if I'd invited him and took a drink from the longneck bottle he held. Surveying the crowd with me, he asked, "So, do you know Eva or did you just hear about the party?"

"I know Eva." I turned to watch him instead of everyone else, since he seemed like the bigger threat. "She's my cousin."

"Hmm." He stopped people watching to twist to me as well. "She's never mentioned you before."

I shrugged. Eva and I may have grown up halfway across the country from each other, but every holiday our families had gotten together; we'd always been inseparable. Facebook had helped keep us tight too. But I had no idea why this stranger thought she ever should've mentioned me to him.

His dark brown eyes were direct and told me they appreciated what they saw. I wasn't sure what to think of that. I mean, he wasn't ugly. He wasn't gigolo status hot, but he wasn't repulsive by any means. I had simply been totally honest with E. when I'd told her I wasn't looking for any kind of relationship.

If my history with Jeremy had taught me anything, it was to be very cautious of anyone putting out the kind of signals Ty currently was. He was looking to get laid tonight, which made me nervous. Actually, every guy lately, except Mason, made me nervous. Okay, I definitely had a fit of nerves around Mason too, but a totally different kind. With Ty, I kept wondering how mad he got if a girl didn't kiss him the right way. How soon after he became serious did he nix girls' night out? How many weapons did he own?

Maybe thoughts like that never crossed my mind when I was around Mason because there was an element of security between us. He was forbidden. Ergo, I was safe from experiencing any relationship horrors with him. We could both be ourselves without reservation.

"Are you always so quiet?" Ty asked, looking amused by how intensely I was staring at him.

I blushed and waved my hand. "You caught me. I just stand here and look pretty."

He laughed and his eyes glittered hungrily. "Yes, you do."

Yikes. I cleared my throat and winced, wishing he hadn't thought I'd been fishing for a compliment. Needing a change of subject, I was opening my mouth to ask if he attended Waterford too when Eva appeared in front of us. Thank God.

"Ty! You made it." She hugged him and then bumped her cheeks against his in a pretend kiss.

As she pulled back, Ty inspected her from head to foot, still holding both her hands in his. "Eva. You're as lovely as ever. New nose ring, I see. It looks sexy."

"Why, thank you." Gracefully severing her contact with him, Eva continued to smile her hostess smile as she linked her arm through mine. "ReeRee and I got both of ours done just today. Now, if you'll excuse me, I need to borrow this lady right here."

He nodded, his eyes simmering with barely repressed heat as he glanced at me. "Only if you bring her back when you're done with her."

Eva laughed and turned us away from him to march me through a crowd of people toward the kitchen. I was about to thank her for saving me when she muttered, "Not on your life, pal."

"E!" I hissed, glancing back to make sure he hadn't overheard. "What was that about?"

"Oh, Reese, honey. You must have a serious

bad boy fetish. I swear, you are the queen of impossible relationships."

"Am not," I muttered peevishly and jerked my elbow free. She always found a way to make me feel naïve in the relationship department.

"Just...stay away from Ty, okay? Trust me on this one."

I hadn't been planning on staying near him, but I grew alert at Eva's serious tone and pulled her to a halt in the middle of the empty hallway. "Why? Did he take a knife to his last girlfriend?"

She rolled her eyes. "No."

"Is he a gigolo?" I couldn't help but ask.

"No, but—"

"Then he already has two brownie points in his favor."

Why I was defending him, I had no idea. I think I just wanted to argue with Eva because she was pissing me off. Did she think I had no head on my shoulders at all when it came to guys, just because I'd been so awfully wrong about Jeremy?

Hell, did everyone who knew me think I was a complete ninny now?

I spun toward the kitchen to refill my cup and get rip-roaring drunk over this new insight, but Eva pulled me around to face her. "I dated him for three months last year," she explained on a sigh.

Oh.

I wrinkled my nose. "Eww." Dating one of Eva's exes had to be just as bad as dating one of my sister's ex-boyfriends. "Why didn't he mention that? I even told him we were related."

"Welcome to Ty Lasher," Eva said. "He doesn't have a moral bone in his body. The bastard cheated on me, *twice*, in the three months we were together."

"Yeesh. Thanks for the warning." I would not

be returning to a conversation with that douche. "So, wait. If you two have such a bad past, why is he at one of your parties?" And why had she been so cordial about greeting him?

"Because anyone who's anyone comes to my parties. They are the bomb, baby."

"Unfortunately, she's right," a voice said, tingling my spine, as someone stepped into the hallway behind me. "Mercer does know how to throw a hell of a party."

"Mason," Eva hissed, her eyes narrowing. "What a surprise. I rarely see you at these. And I don't recall *inviting* you to this one, either."

I thought that was a strange observation. Eva probably hadn't invited most the people here.

"No," Mason agreed. When I dared to turn around, I saw his sneer was just as hard as my cousin's. "But your boyfriend did."

Eva's lips tightened. "And I will be having a few words with Alec about that. Trust me."

"Okay, hold on." I adjusted my stance so I could see both Eva and Mason. I lifted my hands and shook them. "I don't get this. Mason *didn't* take advantage of you when you were drunk, and you don't want him here. Yet that Ty guy cheated on you twice and you just *hugged* him in welcome. That makes no sense."

Eva blinked as if she didn't understand my confusion. "ReeRee, Ty is the son of a judge. This...person is nothing but a holier-than-thou male *prostitute*."

"A prostitute who turned *you* down," Mason taunted. "Pride stung much?"

She glared at him. "You are such a smug—"

"—bastard," he finished for her, his voice pleasant. "Yeah, I remember."

"You don't belong here." She balled her hands

into fists, damn near vibrating with fury. "How dare you crash *my* party? You're a nobody from nowhere who—"

"Hey!" I jumped in front of him, facing off with my cousin. "Back off. You invited everyone and their dog to this party tonight. Stop being such a stuck-up snob. I want Mason to stay. He's fun to talk to."

E. stared at me hard, as if searching for something before glancing over my shoulder. Eyes narrowing, she clutched my arm. Keeping a censorious gaze on him, she spoke quietly in my ear. "Remember what I told you, ReeRee. Don't do it." Then she plowed past us, shoulder checking Mason as she left.

I stared after her, confused as ever with the burning need to apologize for her.

"Don't do what?" Mason asked from behind me.

I whirled to face him and my breath caught. God, it was too late; I had totally disregarded Eva's warning already and fallen big time. Into what, I wasn't exactly sure. But Mason Lowe definitely had a hold on my emotions.

"I think she's worried I'll follow in her footsteps and try to throw myself at you like she did."

"You think?" His eyes scanned my face. "Well, you do tend to act like her little lemming."

I gasped, appalled and hurt he saw that in me. "I do not."

His eyes gleamed with amusement before he tapped the end of my nose. "New nose ring," he noticed, sealing his point.

I covered my diamond stud with my hand, hiding the evidence. "Okay, but I don't follow her over the cliff *every* time."

"No," he agreed amicably. "But I'm glad you did this time. That ring makes you look incredibly... hot."

He sounded surprised by that fact.

I was surprised he thought so. Clearing my throat, I glanced away, knowing I should respond somehow, but I just couldn't.

Mason blew out a breath. "I knew you'd be here tonight."

Whirling back, I gawked badly. "You...you're here because of *me*?"

He shifted, glancing away briefly, looking uncomfortable before he turned back and suddenly thrust something at me that I hadn't even realized he'd been holding. "Here. I wanted to return this."

I stared down at my *Harry Potter* book in shock. Frowning, I took it slowly. After slipping it from his hand, I looked up. "What? You mean, you *finished* it? Already?"

He nodded and actually blushed. "Sarah...she kept pestering me to read it to her. I think I missed a couple of homework assignments because we had to read it every free chance I had." He breathed in a deep breath, lifting his shoulders. "So...what's the name of the second one? *The Secret Chamber,* or something like that?"

I sputtered and gaped down at the book in my hands, still stunned he'd actually read it. He was definitely turning out to be full of surprises. "It's *The Chamber of Secrets,*" I corrected as I ran my thumb up the spine of *The Sorcerer's Stone.* When I looked at him, I squinted suspiciously. "Did you really, *really* finish this already?"

"Yes!" He sounded flustered and kind of embarrassed. "Do you want to quiz me about it, or do you want to give me the next book already?"

My mouth popped open. "You want to read the

next one?" A smirk knotted my lips. "You *liked* it, didn't you?"

He shook his head. "Sarah wants to know what happens next."

"But you do too," I taunted and leaned closer. "Admit it. You liked it."

He sent me a warning scowl. "Don't even think about saying I told you so."

"Ha!" I crowed, shooting my hands into the air, one full of alcohol, the other full of *Harry Potter*. "I knew it! I knew it! I knew it! I *so* told you so."

"I see you're one of those gracious, humble types of winners," he said dryly, though his lips twitched with amusement.

"This is so awesome," I went on, totally ignoring him. "I created a *Harry Potter* fan. You know, if this keeps up, J.K. is going to have to give me a cut of her royalties. Don't you think?"

"I think you're pushing it, Randall."

For a second, I blinked, wondering why the heck he'd called me Randall before it clicked into place. Oh, right. My new last name.

Reese Randall, Reese Randall. Don't forget it.

"Whatever," I rolled my eyes as I grinned. "This is still awesome. I can go get you book two right now if you really want it."

He frowned. "You carry *Harry Potter* books around with you to college keggers?"

I lifted the volume he'd just given me and shook it in his face. "What? You do too."

He laughed. "Wow, you really are aiming to be the top recruiter of the year."

"You know it." I grinned and tapped the dimple in his chin playfully with the edge of my book. "But seriously, my apartment is right above the garage, which is, like, twenty feet away from that back door, so...I can get it for you in two minutes tops."

Mason glanced at the back door. Then he turned to me, his eyes squinting with suspicion. "You're staying above the Mercers' *garage*?"

"Yep, and I know what you're thinking, but trust me. The place is super cool. It's honestly like a mini apartment up there with a kitchenette, bedroom, bathroom, and living room. And the privacy is...awesome." I had to sing the word *awesome*. "Eva is so jealous. She had no idea what kind of gem was on her property until I moved in. I swear, she'd probably kick me out and move in herself if her closet wasn't twice the size of my entire bedroom."

"Hmm." He looked utterly confounded. "Wow. I could tell you and Eva were close, but I had no idea her parents would let you move in."

"Oh! I'm sorry; I guess you didn't realize Eva's my cousin. Her mom, Aunt Mads, is my mom's little sister."

Mason paled. "Yeah," he drew out the word. "I didn't know that."

"Okay, seriously," I growled, suddenly dead sober. "Is there more to this thing between you and E. than you two are letting on?"

"No." He shook his head. "No, I just...no. Not at all. I was only worried the contention between her and me would bother you. I mean, you're not going to stop talking to me now in loyalty to your *cousin*, are you?"

I arched a suspicious eyebrow. "If I haven't stopped by now because of her, then I'm probably not going to stop later either because of her."

His shoulders relaxed. "Okay, good. It's just...I know she doesn't consider me to be from her...ilk. It'd be a shame if you jumped over that cliff with her."

Eva might've coaxed me into going all sandal.

She might've talked me into getting a diamond jammed into my nose. But no one could talk me out of being friends with Mason Lowe, except maybe Mason Lowe.

I sighed. "I may love my cousin to pieces and go all fashion crazy with her on occasion, but trust me, I *do* know how to be my own person. If I ever become as condescending as Eva Mercer, please shoot me, okay?"

Mason's expression was a little stiff, as if he didn't believe me. But he nodded. "Okay."

I grinned. "Great. Now that we have *that* settled, wait right here. I'll be back in a jiffy with your next book."

CHAPTER **ELEVEN**

I had intended to dash up to my apartment by myself and return to Mason with the book, but when I glanced back and saw him following me out the back door and into the warm night, I gulped.

"Or...you could just, you know, come *with* me," I revised, pretty sure I didn't want him to come with me at all.

Mason. Alone with me in my apartment. The two together threw my breathing all out of whack and made Eva's warning—*don't do it, don't do it*—whirl through my brain.

He snorted. "Hey, you're not leaving me in there by myself with fifty other Eva Mercers lurking about. I might be molested before you returned."

I rolled my eyes. "Oh, my God. Drama much?" But really, I wasn't all that certain he was joking.

Did *every* drunk girl throw herself at him?

Okay, that was a stupid question. If I were drunk right now and all my inhibitions went bye-bye into alcohol land, *I'd* be throwing myself at him.

"Well, just don't expect me to jump in front of you like some kind of human shield if any frisky females come flying out the shadows to ambush you for a freebie."

He chuckled as we started up the steps to my apartment. "I'll be sure to toss you in front of me against your will, then."

"Ha, real funny, smart ass." I paused to fiddle with my keys in the dark.

To be perfectly honest, I was kind of glad to have him with me. There wasn't a nightlight outside the doorway to my loft, and standing in the dark alone during one of Eva's keggers didn't sound appealing. What if some drunk Jeremy-wannabe stumbled across me and tried to get frisky?

Mason was quiet as I fumbled, and I relished the sturdy, protective feel of his presence.

"Here we go." Finding the right key, I unlocked the door and pushed my way inside.

I hadn't thought to clean before leaving for the party. My place wasn't a disaster by any means, but it looked well lived in. My Brit Lit book hung open on the coffee table. Yes, I was still in Dr. Janison's class, and passing—whew. A throw blanket lay wadded on the couch. A handful of dishes were piled in the sink, and I'd yet to toss the empty latte cup I'd run out to get this morning for breakfast.

Mason seemed to take everything in as he slowly wandered around the living room and kitchen space.

Nodding, he murmured, "Yeah, I have to say, you were right. This is pretty awesome. I could live here with no problem." He strolled toward the table in front of the window unit and snagged an apple from my fruit basket.

I shook my head. "You just couldn't resist, could you?"

His eyes glittered with amusement as he sank his teeth in the apple's pulp. "What? Resist your forbidden fruit? Hell no." Then he winked as he chewed. "What do you think of them apples?"

I snorted and rolled my eyes. "I think your pun is corny and pathetic." And completely *adorable*.

He laughed and took another massive bite. "So, where's this book?"

"In my room." Hugging book one of the series to my chest, I left him eating and dashed into my small sleeping nook. Flipping on the light, I tossed *The Sorcerer's Stone* onto my unmade bed and knelt in front of the mini bookshelf set up under my window.

Finding book number two almost immediately, I slid it free and stood. Whirling away to hurry back to Mason, I found him the doorway, still chewing slowly as he watched me.

"Oh!" I yelped and skidded to a halt. "There you are."

Heat covered my body like a rash. I suddenly felt the presence of my full-size bed only three feet away as if it were a living thing, breathing hot air down the back of my neck to remind me of its existence. I pulled my hair into my hand only to let it go again. But the sensation remained. I think as long as Mason stood in my room, I'd be hyperaware of any available flat surface.

"Do you...I mean..." I swallowed and took a breath. "You can take the entire series now if you'd like. That way you won't have to wait between each book until I can get the next one to you."

"I don't mind waiting." His gaze was direct and meaningful. "In fact, I like building up the anticipation."

Whoa. Were we still talking about books?

I couldn't breathe, couldn't think.

As if completely oblivious to my growing arousal, Mason turned toward my dresser and examined all my personal effects on top. I felt exposed, probably more exposed than if I'd been standing in front of him naked. He smiled softly as he set his half-eaten apple down and picked up my favorite lotion.

Knees turning to jelly as he flipped open the top and took a deep sniff, I could only watch as he glanced at me. "You wore this Friday."

No way in the world could my vocal chords work. I simply nodded.

He turned the label and read it aloud. "Sweet Pea." When his grin broadened, I thought I was going to pass out from hormone overdose. "So fitting."

Slowly, I reached out and slid it from his hand because watching him hold my lotion was doing wicked, evil, wonderful things to me. "I was thinking of getting a bottle for Sarah. Do you think she'd like this fragrance?"

Mason frowned and shook his head. "Don't you dare. This is *your* scent. It would be too weird to smell on my little sister."

After setting the Sweet Pea back on the dresser, I pushed my hair out of my face. "I guess I could get her some cucumber melon then. Or warm vanil—"

He caught my hand when I lifted it to my hair again. "If your hair getting in your face bothers you that much, why don't you ever tie it back?"

Startled and pleased, I gaped up at him. "You know I never tie my hair back?"

His nostrils flared as he leaned in to smell the Sweet Pea...off my skin. "I know you're always pushing it out of your eyes."

My body went into a dazed kind of shock. In sensory overload, I scrambled to think properly. "I don't know," I said with a loose shrug. "Don't... don't you guys prefer long, flowing hair?"

Mason caught a strand of my hair and ran it through his fingers. "I can't speak for other guys, but, yeah, I guess I do like it long and flowing." He glanced at me with a disappointed expression. "So...this is to attract a guy then? Anyone specific?"

I flushed and ducked my face. "No. Not necessarily. I just...I personally think I look best this way."

He picked up another piece of hair that had been lying on my opposite shoulder. With both hands full on either side of my face, he almost appeared as if he were holding a pair of reins, about to bridle me in close to him.

"Does this mean you'll have caught your guy whenever you show up on campus someday with your hair in a ponytail?"

I shot him a strange look. "Well, then I'll have to *keep* his attention, so...probably not."

Mason gathered my locks at the back of my head as if preparing to put it into a ponytail. Once he had a hold of it all in one hand, he stroked a couple of knuckles down the side of my exposed jawline. "I don't think you ever have to worry about what your hair looks like in order to attract a guy. You have too many other intriguing attributes to keep them interested."

My lips parted and my entire body throbbed. "Mason?" I said slowly, my voice timid. "What're you doing?"

"Something I probably shouldn't." His voice sounded hoarse and tender as he dipped his face and pressed his forehead against mine.

I began to tremble. I don't know if it was because of anticipation, utter excitement, dread, or outright fear. "If...if you shouldn't, then...don't."

A throaty whimper like a wounded cougar tore from his voice box. "Easier said than done." With his fingers slipping through my hair, he curled his hand around to the back of my neck, urging my face up, probably to align me into position for a kiss. Then he whispered my name.

God, the achy, husky way he said it was like a silken caress to every erogenous nerve in my body.

"I think...I think it'd be best if you stopped." My voice shook as badly as my limbs. But even as I spoke, my hormones cried out for him to continue.

"Okay," he said, but his breath continued to beat against my lips and his forehead remained tattooed to mine.

I think an inch separated our mouths. I could sneeze and accidentally crush my lips against his. Damn it, why wasn't my new nose ring making me sneeze?

But no way was I going to purposely be the one to cross the line that seemed to be drawn in that inch of space. Crossing it would change everything. He tilted his head, keeping our brows attached, and shifted to the side, but he kept that inch secure between us.

I knew he wanted to breech it as badly as I did. But the invisible barrier must've been stronger than both of our cravings. We feared what the change would bring.

His palm flattened on my neck, and when his touch slid over my scar, he frowned and paused. His eyes questioned me before he turned me around and gathered my hair out of the way to examine the nasty gash.

Feeling bare as a light breeze washed across my nape, I closed my eyes and tightened my fingers around the book I was holding. "So you see, that's why I don't pull my hair up anymore."

His fingers were gentle as he touched the numb, deadened area. "This looks deep. What happened?"

I licked my lips. "I was cut."

"I see that. What cut you?"

"A knife."

Jeez. I'd already told him too much. If he asked anything else, I wasn't sure what I'd say. My original lie was to tell people I'd gotten it in a small car crash. What was I supposed to come up with now?

An urge bubbled inside me. I actually wanted to tell Mason the whole story. Everything. But the fewer who knew the truth, the better. And no matter how much he affected me, rationally I knew I hadn't known him nearly long enough to trust him with a secret of this magnitude.

"A knife," he repeated. "Did it cut you on purpose?"

"Maybe." *Definitely*. And if I hadn't whirled away to run from Jeremy any faster than I had, this scar wouldn't have been on the back of my neck either. It would have been in the front, and I probably wouldn't be standing here today.

I shuddered, trying not to remember that night, trying not to relive the fear.

As if sensing the panic that was clawing its way up my throat, Mason leaned forward and pressed his lips to the scar.

I whimpered and closed my eyes, biting my lip to stop my chin from quivering. If I started crying now, that would be it. I'd forfeit everything.

"If you don't give away freebies," I said, bracing myself to say what I needed to say to stop this from progressing further, "then are you going to charge me for that?"

"No." He kissed the spot again, his lips

lingering over the area. I listened to him breathe in as he smelled my hair. It sent a shockwave of awareness down my spine and cramped the muscles low in my belly. I wanted this to last. I wanted him to spin me around and give me a real kiss.

"It wasn't mouth to mouth, so...no charge."

I turned to face him, hating myself even before I continued. "So if you kissed me, say, on the breasts, that would be free since it's not mouth to mouth?"

His gaze turned hard. "No. That's part of foreplay; it's off limits."

"And what you just did *isn't* foreplay?" I knew I was being cruel, but I also knew the fastest way to get him to retreat was to remind him of his profession. And he needed to retreat, because I was pretty sure I couldn't.

"*That* was a friend comforting another friend." His eyes sparked with anger as he clenched his teeth.

"I see." With a nod, I asked, "So, you weren't about to kiss me—mouth to mouth—just before you discovered my scar?"

"Jesus," he railed, swiping his hands through his hair and taking a big step back. "Yes, okay. I almost kissed you. But I didn't. Mistake averted. No harm done. We're good."

"Are we?" I charged.

He stared at me, his mouth slightly fallen open. His expression looked wounded. "What're you saying, Reese?"

I closed my eyes and groaned. "I don't know. It doesn't matter. We can't ever kiss or anything else because you sleep with women for money. End of story."

He rumbled out a sound of utter frustration.

"Why do you always have to remind me of that? Trust me, I haven't forgotten."

"I'm not reminding *you*," I snapped, flashing my eyes open to glare. "I'm reminding *me*."

God, I was such an idiot. I cannot believe I just stood there and pretty much confessed I cared about him as more than a friend, and the only thing holding me back was his...job.

Understanding dawned in his eyes. They sparked with interest and joy. He took a step toward me.

I darted a leery leap back. "We're just friends, Mason."

He stopped in his tracks, turmoil swirling in his gaze. Then he closed his eyes. "Right." When he opened them, the desire was gone. He reached out, tugged the book I'd forgotten I was still holding out of my arms, and waved it once. "Thanks for loaning this to me...*friend*."

Brushing my hair to one side, he tipped his head so he could lean around and kiss my scar one last time with a brief but warm peck. Once he straightened, he said nothing and barely held my gaze before he turned away and walked from my apartment.

I waited until I heard the door close before I strayed back into my living room to lock and bolt it behind him. Then I collapsed onto my couch and buried my face into my hands.

What the hell had I gotten myself into?

CHAPTER **TWELVE**

I had been fourteen, barely a freshman in high school, when Jeremy Walden approached me for a date. He was a junior and so much more experienced and sophisticated than I was. He was also popular, good-looking, and came from money. Being with him had been exciting, and sure, the vain part of me can admit I liked what being his girlfriend did for my image.

For a year or so, things coasted along, not perfectly, but okay. Since he was a little older and had been the one to draw me into *his* crowd of people, we naturally started our relationship with him being the more dominant, controlling figure. And that didn't bother me.

For a while.

Okay, it bothered me. But I didn't do a whole lot about it at first.

When his senior year started, and his dad began to pressure him more about picking out the perfect college, the not-so wonderful side of him grew more defined. He'd always had a cruel streak. He could bully with the best of them. But when he turned his bullying on me, I wasn't impressed.

The occasional slaps he'd given me before and bruises he'd left from grabbing me too hard grew to be not so occasional. It was embarrassing to think I could be one of those abused women who put up with that kind of crap. I convinced myself his small acts of totally minor violence here and there were no big deal. He'd never actually *hurt* me, hurt me.

But it still got to me.

As I matured and my personality developed, we began to argue more. He didn't like me standing up for myself, and I didn't like him manhandling me and dictating to me every little thing he wanted me to do. The sad part was, it wasn't even his violence that broke us apart the first time. One of his friends told me he'd seen Jeremy making out with one of the skanky cheerleaders.

I confronted him about it, of course, and after I said something snide and sarcastic—yeah, imagine that—he whirled around with his hand out. He caught me in the cheek and ended up cracking my jaw.

I broke up with him while he drove me to the hospital.

After our split, my friends he'd isolated me away from during our time together were wonderful and returned to me, nursing my wounded ego back to health.

But Jeremy came sobbing back to me—literally. He fell on his knees before me, hugged my legs, and begged me to take him back. Somehow, he managed to convince me the whole broken-jaw thing had been a complete accident. He hadn't purposely hit me that hard; I'd just been standing too close when he'd swung around. And he insisted his friend had lied about the other girl.

Stupid me, I'd believed him.

After two months of being apart, we got back together.

For a while, he was careful not to be too controlling, and I tried to not branch out away from him more than he could stand. But...a person can't help who they are. I needed my me-space; he needed to oversee every little thing I did. I broke up with him again during my senior year.

I was very amicable about it. Really. I sat him down and kept my voice calm when I told him we were two totally different kinds of people, and we just didn't mesh well together. I think the part he didn't like so much was when I told him—as gently as possible—that he needed to seek counseling to help him deal with his anger management problems.

Yeah, he beat me black and blue for that one. The worst damage came to my arm, which shattered with a nice, painful crunch after he pushed me down a flight of stairs.

He was well on his way to becoming a woman beater.

Finally, I learned my lesson. I knew better than to let him anywhere near me. My parents threatened to take out a restraining order against him, but his lawyer father jumped in, saying we didn't need to take any legal measures yet. He assured us Jeremy would keep his distance. To him, his son was flawless and perfect, and it had been all my fault his perfect child had felt the need to act out.

Since it was all so very disconcerting for me— and my family and his family as well—both our parents tried to keep the situation low-key. As long as it severed my contact with Jeremy, I didn't care.

I just wanted him out of my life.

But *Jeremy* wasn't entirely on board. After being with me for two and a half years, he'd grown attached. He actually thought he loved me. So, in his mind, he fought for me.

To me, he turned into a psycho stalker crazy ex-boyfriend who'd break into my room when I wasn't home and leave me letters and poems and gifts, frantic to get me back.

He was very careful to stay away from me physically. But he harassed me on every other level possible, constantly hanging around outside school whenever classes let out, finding ways to post things on my Facebook page, texting me, emailing me, leaving gross videos on my phone of how he had to pleasure himself since he no longer had me.

I ignored him for the most part, sometimes yelling at him to leave me alone already, but nothing worked. He wouldn't stop.

Eventually, his control broke. One evening, when my parents were out to dinner and I was home by myself, he snuck into my house to pay me a visit. He had his pocketknife with him—which had seemed more like a collapsible machete at the time.

After he pinned me to the door of my bedroom, he told me in no uncertain terms that if he couldn't have me, he was going to make sure no one else could either. Then he pressed the blade to my throat.

I'd never been as afraid as I was then, knowing he was fully capable of killing me and realizing he totally planned to do just that. I blocked some of that moment to the darkest, coldest recesses of my mind. I didn't think I'd ever fully remember everything that happened. But I remember how cold, and pale, and sweaty his face was as he leaned in close until our foreheads touched.

"No one will ever love you the way I do, Reese's Pieces. And if you won't let me have you now, I'll just make sure we're together for all eternity."

I had no idea if he'd planned a murder/suicide or what. But I didn't want to find out. I was also not too clear how I did it, but somehow one of my hands grappled behind me until I found the doorknob. Just as he began to press the knife into my flesh, I opened the door and spun away.

He sliced me the deepest on the back left side. And if I hadn't been wearing my hair up in a ponytail, he probably would've whacked off my beautiful brunette locks too.

My mother contracting food poisoning from the restaurant saved my life. Dad had rushed her home early. They came through the back door to find me screaming and hurtling myself toward them with my psycho stalking ex-boyfriend charging after me, his bloody knife raised and ready to plunge again.

And here was where I had to pause and take a breath, remind myself I was fine. I was okay. All that was over.

Whew.

Well, mostly over. Jeremy's rich daddy bailed him out of jail the very night he committed his crime, so he didn't spend any time behind bars, hence me changing my name and fleeing halfway across the country. But my parents felt confident he would be charged guilty during his trial—if his father finally stopped finding ways to delay it—and then he'd go to prison for a long, long time. It wouldn't even matter that he'd find out my new name when I testified against him, because afterward, he'd be locked away for good.

Then, everything really would be okay. I could

go back to my birth name. And it'd all be over.

If I didn't have such a unique—sure, we'll call it unique—personality, my time with Jeremy might've left me an unbalanced, frightened mess. I still have moments of fear. I still experience some of that submissive compliance he tried to brainwash into me—though rarely, thank God. And I've grown a little more judgmental around new people.

My parents tried to talk me into seeing a therapist, but I think I handled everything okay. I dealt with it. I survived and I actually kind of felt as if I was flourishing here in Waterford. I still missed Ellamore. It would always be home.

But I was doing okay. And the lunches I had shared with Mason on campus everyday were a big part of that. He had a way of making me feel normal and yet exhilarated all in the same breath. He accepted me for what I was, and he actually seemed to like my unique personality.

He got me.

That was why, despite the three years of hell I'd lived through under Jeremy Walden's thumb, the two weeks following Eva's party were the most miserable days of my life.

After our near kiss, Mason suddenly dropped off the grid, avoiding me altogether. He no longer sought me out at lunch, even though I made sure to always sit at our table. On the nights I watched Sarah, he was gone before I showed up at his house, and he stayed away long after I left.

I tried not to wonder what he was doing every night he worked late, or which woman he was servicing, or how much she made him touch her, or why he kept living that stupid, freaking lifestyle. But it drove me crazy, thinking about it.

Things had changed between us. Our friend-ship had shattered. And he knew it too; otherwise he wouldn't have stayed away.

I was so tempted to slip into his bedroom and leave a letter on his bed, just to tell him how much I missed him and how I could still be his friend; we could get past that stupid, almost kiss. I wanted to study with him at lunch again, watch him steal a portion of whatever I was eating, tease him about whatever topic we were discussing, and just...be in his company.

But leaving him a note felt too Jeremy-ish. So I never once even opened the door to his bedroom, not even to peek inside.

And in return, a part of my soul ached on a daily basis. A chunk of me felt missing.

I needed Mason back in my life.

CHAPTER THIRTEEN

I guess it was bound to happen eventually, but I still wasn't prepared when it did.

Thirteen days after Eva's Labor Day party—a.k.a. the night Mason Lowe almost kissed me mouth to mouth and thereafter totally abandoned me—Sarah had her first seizure. Well, her first one around me, anyway.

Yeah, I totally freaked.

One second, I was assisting my little buddy in the bathtub, making her giggle over the corniest knock-knock jokes on the planet. The next she was lurching from her bathing chair, her entire body convulsing. It was a miracle I caught her slippery, wet torso before she took a serious nosedive.

"Sarah?" I screamed. "Oh, God. What's wrong? What's wrong, baby?"

She couldn't answer me. I had to clutch her tight so she didn't shake right out of my arms. It took me a bit to work through the panic and realize what was happening. But it didn't reassure me in the least once I did.

A seizure.

But, oh, holy shit. A freaking *seizure*.

My mind went blank; I couldn't remember one thing Dawn had told me about seizures except there was nothing to do to stop them. Oh, and I had to make sure she didn't hurt herself in the middle of one.

Since the bathroom seemed too confined and suddenly hella dangerous, I half carried, half dragged her into the hallway.

Laying her contorted body on the carpet, I knelt beside her and stroked her shoulder once before dashing into the bathroom to grab all the towels I could see.

After covering her, I stepped back and burst into tears. Biting my knuckles to hold in my sobs, I tore down the hall and into the kitchen to scramble for my phone in my purse. I snatched the emergency contact list off the fridge in the next breath.

I was only gone from her for about three seconds, but it felt way too long by the time I returned, falling to my knees at her side.

Almost expecting to see foam spewing from her mouth as if she'd turned rabid, I wiped wet clumps of hair out of her face and clutched my phone with my free hand.

Dawn didn't answer her cell within four rings— and I swear these were the four longest freaking rings of my life. I think I had about three mini heart attacks between each one.

I couldn't handle waiting for a fifth, so I disconnected and found the next number in line on the contact list. Mason's cell phone. My fingers shook so badly and my brain was so overloaded with fear, I knew I had to be punching in the wrong digits, but I continued jabbing until a ring echoed into my ear.

I wiped a buttload of tears off my cheeks and listened to the echoing silence after the first ring. I could count each heartbeat as it pounded in my chest. God, if he was with a client right now, I was going to kill him.

Just as the second ring started, he answered, and I swear, his voice had never sounded so wonderful.

"Mason, I need you; I don't know what to do." I rushed out the words, making one long, breathless, run-on sentence. "Sarah's having a seizure, and I don't know what to do. She won't stop shaking, and Dawn's not answering her phone. I'm so freaked out right now. I don't know what to do."

Had I mentioned that I didn't know what to do?

Mason didn't answer immediately. After a painfully long pause, he said, "Reese?"

Oh, my God! There was no time for *introductions*. "Yes!" I screamed in a frustrated, get-with-the-program-already kind of way. "Who the hell do you think it is? Did you hear me? I said your sister's having a seizure."

"Yeah, okay. I heard. I think. Just...first of all, calm down."

Calm down? *Calm down*? Was he mental? This was not a time to calm down.

"You can't help her if you're flipping out."

Shit. His steady, grounding tone trickled past the panic and somehow found the only rational section of my brain. I blew out as calming a breath as I could manage.

"Did you get her out of her wheelchair?" he asked. "Is she lying down?"

I nodded. "Yes. We're on the floor in the hall. I

was giving her a bath when—"

"Good," he butted in, obviously not needing details. "Keep her there and just stay with her. Talk to her. Let her know she's not alone. I'll be home in a minute."

"Do I call for an ambulance?"

"Is she turning blue or changing any color?"

"No."

"Not yet, then. This is fairly typical, but I'll know more when I get there."

"Okay. Okay." I clutched the phone gratefully. "Hurry."

"I will."

He hung up before I could thank him. And I really, really wanted to thank him for being there and answering my call.

But...later.

Tossing my phone aside, I crawled to Sarah and held her hand, stroking the back of her knuckles where her curled, contorted wrist seemed to wrap around my fingers, begging for help.

"It's okay, honey," I cooed. "It's okay. Reese is here. And Mason's coming." Sniffing, I didn't even wince when I bumped the still tender area around my nose ring when I wiped the back of my hand across my face.

For some reason, I remembered something I'd heard once about epileptic people and how you had to make sure they didn't swallow their tongue during a seizure. I tried to look into Sarah's mouth, but her jaw was clamped tight. She didn't appear to be choking, so I prayed she hadn't swallowed anything that wasn't supposed to be swallowed. A trail of drool seeped from the corner of her pressed lips. I wiped it away, figuring no girl would want to be caught drooling, especially if the paramedics who might need to come save her were as sexy as hell.

Then a breath later, she fell still and went catatonic.

"Sarah?"

She didn't respond. Her eyes were open but they stared sightlessly. My level of scared rose to a whole new level. I checked for a pulse and when I found one, I began to cry even harder. The relief was more than I could handle.

"Oh, God. Oh, God. Oh, God. Please be okay, little buddy."

I didn't know if unconsciousness was common after a seizure, but I didn't want to call Mason again; I wanted him to concentrate on the road so he could drive as fast as possible to get here.

Since Sarah was no longer juddering about, I hurried into the bathroom and collected her nightclothes. If I were her, I wouldn't want everyone to see me in my birthday suit while I was out cold.

With her being wet and unconscious, it took me three times as long as it usually did to dress her. My fumbling fingers, which wouldn't stop shaking, didn't help matters. And it was impossible to see clearly through all the tears that kept falling and blurring my vision.

I'd just pulled her shirt on over her head when the front door flew open.

"Reese?"

I wiped my nose with a trembling hand and sniffed. "We're here."

Mason appeared in the hallway.

"I was just getting her nightclothes on," I explained needlessly as I smoothed Sarah's shirt down her torso. "She passed out. I didn't know if that was normal."

He knelt beside us and pressed two fingers to

her throat. "Sometimes. How long has she been like this?"

"Umm." I shook my head. "A few minutes. Three. Four." I looked at him. He was wearing his Country Club valet uniform. "You got here fast."

His glanced up. "You sounded pretty shaken."

I was *still* shaken. "How...how long will she be like this?"

"Not much longer. So you need to keep it together, okay. If she sees you upset, she's going to get upset too. We don't need anything triggering another episode." His gaze was steady but determined. "Think you can do that?"

No, absolutely not. I wanted to keep bawling my eyes out, curl into a fetal ball, and call my mommy while drinking hot cocoa and stroking my childhood blankie.

But, I nodded and stopped wringing my hands to wipe all the wetness off my cheeks. If it helped my little buddy, I'd do whatever I had to.

Mason's eyes softened. Voice low and soothing, he said, "Good. She'll probably need a drink when she wakes up."

"Okay." I began to stand. "I'll get her some water."

But he grasped my wrist, his grip gentle. When I paused to look at him, I was shocked by the concern in his gaze—as if he was concerned about *me*. "I'll get it." After urging me back down to return to Sarah's side, he stood and loped down the hall.

Sarah's lashes fluttered just as he returned.

"Hey," Mason murmured as he rejoined us on the floor. "Welcome back, kiddo. You had a little spell there, but you're okay now."

He helped her sit up and propped her back against his chest as he held the cup to her mouth and tipped it just enough to give her a drink.

Smacking her hydrated lips, Sarah gazed around in a daze. When she saw me, she reached out her hand.

It took everything I had not to burst into tears all over again. Taking her fingers, I moved close until my knee bumped Mason's. "I guess my knock-knock jokes were just too funny, huh?"

She grinned and said, "Knock-knock," in her precious, throaty voice.

"Who's there?" I returned, squeezing her fingers tight.

"Boo," she answered.

Together Mason and I said, "Boo who?"

Sarah thought this was hilarious and began to cackle. She was so busy laughing she couldn't even finish the joke to ask us why we were crying.

Every muscle in my body clenched, afraid she'd laugh herself into another seizure.

But Mason chuckled right along with her as he hefted her into his arms. "Let's get you into bed, kiddo. We're missing out on some valuable *Harry Potter* story time."

"Well, we can't have that." I followed them into Sarah's room and pulled back the blankets for Mason to place her on the mattress. After the first night I'd delivered the book to her, I hadn't read any of the series with Sarah, because it seemed like an infringement on her and Mason's special time. But tonight, I sat on the opposite side of her as him while he cracked open *The Chamber of Secrets* and started chapter seven.

Her attack must've worn her out, though, because she fell asleep before learning Draco was the new seeker for Slytherin. She didn't even wish us a good night or demand hugs and kisses as she usually did. Her lashes merely fluttered closed and she was breathing heavily.

Mason's deep, lulling voice fell quiet when he glanced at her. Then he looked at me across the bed. My chin trembled. More tears filled my eyes. The urge to fling myself into his arms and weep actually made my limbs feel stiff and sore.

Slowly, he closed the book. After setting it on the nightstand, he kissed Sarah's forehead and slid off the mattress. I fussed over her a moment longer, making sure the blankets were secure and tucked in tight before I pressed my lips to her sweet, soft cheek.

"'Night, little buddy. I love you. So much."

Mason was waiting for me in the hall. "Are you okay?" he asked as soon as I closed Sarah's door behind me and turned to face him.

I snorted and wiped at my eyes before hugging myself. "I'm not the one who just had a seizure."

He shook his head. "Don't worry about her. She's going to be fine." Taking my hand, he started to lead me down the hallway toward the kitchen. "Come on. Let's get you a drink."

But I resisted. "I need to clean up the bathroom. I think there's still water in the tub and the towels are everywhere and..." Thank God, we'd already rinsed the soap out of Sarah's hair before her attack had started.

"Don't worry about that either. I'll clean the bathroom later. Just...come and sit down for a second. You look like you need to get off your feet."

A break did sound tempting, preferably one in the Bahamas while I was stretched out on a beach towel, watching an amazing sunset off an ocean view while a shirtless Mason served me a piña colada with a tiny umbrella in it, shish-kebobbing a stack of rum-soaked fruit.

I blinked at him to realize he'd ushered me into

the dimly lit kitchen. Instead of a colorful sunset, I saw a stack of dirty dishes sitting by the sink. Mason was most definitely not shirtless—grr—and the cup he thrust at me was full of drab, boring ice water.

Feeling ancient all of the sudden, I eyed the glass without taking it. I couldn't drink right now if a masked gunman held a pistol to my temple and told me to swallow or die.

My gaze sought Mason's desperately. I was still terrified for Sarah's sake. "Are you sure she's going to be okay?"

He stared at me before shaking his head. Then his lips tilted into a soft smile, and the skin around his eyes crinkled with amusement. "You know, your eyes look really big and blue when you've been crying."

My mouth fell open. "How can you possibly think about *eyes* at a time like this? Your sister just—"

"Shh." After setting the cup of water on the table, Mason took my hand and pulled me to my feet. "Come here."

He tugged me to him, and I sank against his chest, clutching his shirt hard as I balled my hands into fists. Burying my face in his shoulder and seeking comfort, I held on to him for dear life. My eyes watered some more when my sore nose bumped against his collar bone, but I didn't care. This was heaven. He rubbed my back and pressed his cheek to my temple, giving me exactly what I needed.

"She's going to be fine," he reassured me for a second time. "She *is* fine."

"How do you know?" I looked up and saw blue and yellow flecks in his silver irises. They were exquisite, like reflections of the beauty within were sparkling through a magnificent stained-glass window.

His lips twitched. "Well. I have this theory. If you love someone enough, you can make them invincible. Like your feelings for them are so strong they work as a magical shield, protecting them from all harm and pain."

I sniffed. "Like the protective spell Harry's mom used to save his life from Voldemort? Her love protected him."

Mason chuckled and kissed my nose. "Yeah. Kind of exactly like that."

"I like that theory." I lowered my head to rest my cheek back against his shoulder. "I wish it were really true."

Lips brushed my temple as Mason blew out a shuddered breath. "Yeah. So do I." His voice was hoarse with emotion as his arms tightened around me, forming a protective shell as if he wanted to protect *me* from all harm and pain.

I closed my eyes, soaking up the comforting warmth emanating off him. We stood there in his mother's kitchen, embracing forever. I grew drowsy and languid. I was so drained I might have even dozed off.

"Thank you so much for coming home," I slurred against his chest, even more sedated by his drugging smell. He gave off some kind of clean musk that made me breathe in deeper, falling further into a tranquilized state.

"Why wouldn't I?" He stroked my hair, just like my mom used to do to put me to sleep after I'd had a nightmare when I was young.

God, he was trying to knock me unconscious, wasn't he?

Oh, well. That was okay. I'd totally let him.

"I don't know," I murmured. "I was...I was

worried you were busy. With a woman."

As if throwing a bucket of arctic ice water all over both of us, my question broke the spell.

Mason tensed and dropped his hand from my hair. "No." His voice went hard. Abrupt. "I don't get off work at the club until after eleven. I was still there."

"Oh." I lifted my face, but his eyes were averted. "Well, thank you anyway. I don't know what I would've done if you hadn't calmed me down."

He stepped back. And every place he'd been pressing against me—warming me—turned cold and bereft from his sudden absence. "You handled it just fine," he said, though he even sounded cold. "You found a safe place for her and got help. There's not much else to do when she's having an episode."

I studied the side of his face. He couldn't even look at me since I'd brought up his job.

Sick and tired of being evaded like this for the past thirteen most miserable days of my life, I said, "I've missed you."

I know how pathetic I sounded. Any woman who admits that to a guy who's been avoiding her might as well just tear her heart from her chest and hand it over to him, begging, *"Here, please stomp all over this and rip it into little bitty pieces for me, will you? Thanks."*

But I couldn't help it. The words just spilled out. I *had* missed him. Too damn much. It wasn't healthy to miss anyone the way I'd missed him.

He darted a quick glance at me, furrowing his brows as if my comment confused him. "I haven't gone anywhere." But he wasn't fooling me. I saw the guilt and the misery in his stormy eyes before he turned away.

"You know what I mean," I muttered, crossing my arms over my chest because I felt too exposed. "I thought we were *friends*."

He whirled back. "We are." This time, his confusion was genuine.

"Oh, really?" I cocked my hip and lifted an eyebrow. "Well, friends don't avoid friends. You've been *avoiding* me. On purpose. I still sit at the exact same table every day for lunch. And we still keep getting calculus assignments to work on."

"I know," he broke in with a tortured wince as he blew out a breath. "I know. I just..." Closing his eyes, he bowed his head and squeezed the bridge of his nose before looking up again. "We got a little too close that night. I still want to be your friend, Reese. I *will* be your friend. I just...I need some time and space to control my...my horny guy urges."

He thought we'd gotten too close?

My curiosity was killing me to find out exactly in what way he thought we'd gotten close. The horny-guy-urges comment—which, I loved by the way; I might have to steal that phrase soon—made me think maybe he was only talking about sex. But the depth of feeling in his gaze said it was more than that. It said something so much deeper than a little physical interaction.

I wondered if the boy had just confessed he'd fallen for me.

My heart gave a happy lurch, almost pounding its way through my ribcage.

Needing to taunt him, just a little, I stepped forward, coming so close to him I'm sure he could feel my breath on his face.

He stumbled back until his spine hit the wall. And when I kept closing in, he exhaled, his entire body tensing. I finally stopped with a bare inch of space between us. That familiar inch was always keeping us apart.

"Jesus," he breathed.

"So you thought we got too close, huh?"

His gaze fell to my mouth, and he appeared completely unable to look away. With a vacant nod, he murmured, "Yes."

"I see." I made myself stare at his chin, since it seemed like the least likely thing to turn me on, even though the dimple there was a total turn on. "And you haven't had enough time or space to control those pesky urges yet?"

He gulped. I was so close I could actually hear the swallow shift down his throat. "Not... quite...yet." Damn, he sounded sexy when he was breathless.

I made a sympathetic sound. "Gee, I'm sorry to hear that." Even though, I totally wasn't. I loved knowing I turned him on. I tapped on his dimple playfully. "Make sure to let me know when they're gone. Okay? I'm ready to have my friend back."

He reached out and took hold of the edge of the kitchen counter as if he needed to grab on to something to keep from reaching for me. Shaking his head, he let out a breath. "You are so evil. If I didn't like you so much, I'd take you right now."

Sweet Baby Jesus. Talk about turning my panties to mush.

The euphoria that surged through my veins was unreal. The first time I'd seen Mason Lowe, he'd been like this mythical, totally inaccessible erotic beast I probably wasn't even fit to stare at. To be standing so close to him, actually turning him on, was so unreal and amazing I wanted to dance, and scream, and burst with joy.

"Really?" I said. "How?"

Heat flared in his expression. "Probably hard

and fast against this wall."

"Hmm." I bit my lip, trying not to react. But I stared at the wall behind him, picturing it...vividly. "That sounds...fun." And wow, it really kind of did.

But he *was* my friend, and I'd probably tortured him enough for one night. I managed a friendly grin. "I guess since we're friends and you're not going to take me, I'll give you that time and space you need then."

I took a step back, and then a few more, retreating until the air in his lungs hissed out as he wilted his shoulders.

Shaking his head, he murmured, "Evil, evil, evil."

As he rested his butt against the side of the counter, looking drained, I shrugged. "Would you *really* have given me a freebie just now?"

He glanced up, his eyes swirling. "Just say the word."

Hot damn.

My grin stretched wide, loving the power I wielded. I could actually make the unbendable Mason Lowe break one of his sacred rules and give a girl a freebie. "Cool," I admitted. Scooping up my purse from the table, I remembered I'd left my phone on the floor in the hallway.

"My phone," I told him before I disappeared for a second. When I returned with it, he'd slunk to the table and was sitting in a chair with his elbows resting on the tabletop and his face cradled in his trembling hands.

Tucking my phone away, I said, "I guess I'll see you around then."

When I slung my purse strap over my shoulder, he lifted his weary gaze. "Are you seriously going to walk out of here right now after I just confessed my soul to you, cool as a cucumber, without reciprocating *at all*?"

"What?" I sent him a blank look. Then I rolled my eyes and reached out to ruffle his amazing hair. "Mason Lowe, if you don't know by now that I'm attracted as hell to you, you're freaking blind."

He stared at me a moment before muttering, "There. Was that so hard to admit?"

I stuck out my tongue and started for the door. "Good night, Hotness."

"'Night, Reese." I heard his much softer response as I slipped into the warm night.

I stood with my back to the closed door and my hand pressed over my heart for a solid minute. Crap, but that had taken all the willpower I possessed to act blasé and leave with my head up. I still wanted to rush back inside and get myself that hard-and-fast-against-the-wall freebie. I would love to take anything I could get from Mason, just so I could spend more time with him.

Shaken to the core, I finally staggered to my car. Usually, I was more alert when I was alone outside at night. But I was so worried about Sarah and still utterly bowled over by Mason's admission, I didn't see the woman until she spoke.

"Nice night, isn't it?"

I screamed and dropped my purse.

A middle-age female stepped from the shadows in the neighbor's yard and strolled toward me, the heels of her shoes clicking against the drive. "Sorry about that, darling. Didn't mean to startle you."

"It's okay." I bent and scrambled for my purse, hoping I hadn't spilled any of the contents, because there was no way to find them in the dark. "You just"—I gave a nervous laugh—"totally scared the living shit out of me. No biggie."

She laughed too, but it was husky and amused, not the least bit on edge like mine. She lifted a cigarette to her lips, the red glow from the butt brightening as she inhaled. "You seem a little pre-occupied."

"Oh." I cursed myself. Not paying attention to my surroundings could land me in a heap of trouble. I needed to be more careful. If Jeremy ever found me—

Well, I didn't want to think about that scenario.

"Yeah," I told the woman. "You could say that." Or she could say *preoccupied* was a huge under-statement. Whatever. "It's been a...wild night."

"Hmm." She took another drag. I couldn't make out much of her appearance through the dark, but I sensed her watching me as if she had night vision and could dissect every detail.

That's exactly what it felt like, anyway: a dissection.

"Are you a friend of Mason's?" she finally asked.

"What?" Rattled by the question, I shook my head. "No. I mean..." I flushed and flailed my hand, not sure how to answer. "I guess so." I didn't know what we were anymore. "I'm Sarah's babysitter," I explained.

"Ah." Her knowing voice said that answered everything. "The replacement for Ashley."

Since I remembered Dawn calling Sarah's former evening sitter Ashley, I nodded. "Right. Are you Mrs. Arnosta's neighbor?"

Shifting my weight from one foot to the other, I managed a tight smile, though I sure she couldn't see it in the dark. I didn't really want to stand out here all night, talking to her. But she was in no hurry to let me go.

"I'm Patricia Garrison," she said. "Dawn and Mason's landlady."

"Oh." The way she totally left Sarah out of that

equation irritated me. I mean, seriously. Why mention Mason and forget his sister?

Rude much?

"Are you a student?" Mrs. Garrison asked, fishing a little too deeply for my taste.

Not wanting to upset the woman who owned Dawn, Sarah, and Mason's home, I nodded. "Yeah. I attend Waterford."

"With Mason," she added.

Wow, she certainly liked to bring him up. That was kind of...really creepy.

"Umm...I guess," I hedged. "We don't have any classes together, though."

"I see."

I had no idea what she really saw. The entire conversation was growing way beyond my scope of understanding, so I shifted closer to my driver's side door and found my car keys. "Well, it was nice to meet you." I waved and smiled again.

"You too, Reese. Have a nice night."

I didn't realize until I was halfway home that she'd called me Reese, and I'd never told her my name.

CHAPTER **FOURTEEN**

Another week passed. Things between Mason and I stayed distant, and yet not. He still refused to sit with me at lunch, but we remained friends of a sort. After our talk on the night of Sarah's seizure, our relationship morphed into friends-that-flirted status.

On Tuesday, I saw him across the courtyard while I was snacking on cheeseburger sliders and curly fries—both of which I'm sure he would've stolen if he'd been close enough—and everything inside me brightened. I straightened and waved. When he returned the wave, I patted the seat next to me and gave him an encouraging thumbs-up. He smiled but shook his head and kept walking.

I slumped back into doldrums land.

A second later, my phone buzzed with a text.

Still need some space to cool off.

Groaning, I typed back: *These pesky horny guy urges are beginning to annoy me.* See, told you I was going to steal that phrase.

Well they might go away faster if you stopped being so...you.

That did it. I was crazy about this guy. He could've told me to stop licking my lips, or tossing my hair, or wearing revealing clothes, or simply to stop being so hot. But he went after my personality. How was a girl supposed to resist that?

Too pleased not to turn playful, I set my phone on video mode and clicked record when I saw my own face reflected on the screen.

"Would you rather I be Eva instead?" I asked the phone aloud. Giving the best impersonation of my cousin as I could manage, I mimicked, "Good morning, Mason. Looking good today. What say we skip classes and have some...fun." Then I toyed with the collar of my blouse and let the camera see me undo one button before I focused it on my face again and winked.

A minute after sending that bad boy off, he returned with: *Need more cleavage please.*

The 'please' part made me throw my head back and shout out a laugh. I typed, *Perv*, and almost as soon as I hit send, a text came back to me.

See, your laugh is exactly what's keeping me away, woman. I just want to kiss those lips and hoard that sound all to myself.

My breath caught in my throat. Suddenly the amount he'd told me he charged his customers seemed like a mere pittance. If he talked like that when he was on the clock, no wonder why he had such a lucrative business going. Damn it.

My throat was a little constricted and it was hard for me to draw in air because I felt so full of emotion. It took me a moment to realize he'd just admitted he'd *seen* me laugh.

Face zipping up, I glanced around, shocked to learn he was nearby.

Are you stalking me?

I'm sitting on the bench by the eagle statue. I thought you saw me.

When I looked, he lifted his hand. Rolling my eyes, I typed him a new message. *Mason, you goober, just come sit by me already.*

From where I sat, I saw him shake his head. *Not yet. I need to get to class anyway.*

As he gathered his bag and stood, I sniffed. I'd eaten lunch with him enough to know he didn't have class for another half hour. But if he wanted to keep dodging me...

Before you go, just one thing. I know I tease you A LOT about your "urges," but I am glad you told me about them so I understand. Thank you for that.

He was almost to the entrance of the main building when he paused and dug his phone out of his pocket. I watched his back and the way his dark head bent as he read what I'd written. When he was finished, he looked back at me.

I returned the stare, waiting. But he rotated away and entered the college. A disappointed hiss of air leaked from my lungs. God, I was so pathetic, crushing on a freaking gigolo and then flirting with him mercilessly.

I mean, how much more forbidden could a guy get? I could tell myself a million times over that I just wanted to be his friend, but that would be a lie...a million times over.

Thirty seconds later, my phone dinged, and it was scary how happy that made me.

Are we getting serious now?

I sighed and idly fiddled with my nose ring, because I still hadn't gotten used to it being there, and typed back: *Apparently,*

I really needed to get over this guy and move

on. But then he wrote: *In that case, thanks for staying my friend even though I want to jump your bones.*

Amusement and tenderness fizzled inside me. I think a part of my personality was beginning to rub off on him. He could be sweet, charming, flirty, and kind of crude all in the same breath.

A man after my own heart.

The feeling is mutual, you know, I felt compelled to tell him. *Girls get urges too.*

He'd be out of a job of they didn't.

A second later, my phone buzzed. *You probably shouldn't have told me that. Now I'm going to have to stay away longer.*

With a frown, I responded: *Hey I can control MY urges, thank you very much.*

With you, I'm not so sure I can control mine. You're getting hard to resist.

I couldn't help it; I had to tease: *Don't say hard. You just sent my mind straight to dirty girl land.*

Now who's the perv?

I'll accept that award. Want to hear my thank-you speech?

No time. I really do need to go. Flirt with you later.

Buzzkill.

He honestly must've had somewhere to be, because he never did reply. Our conversation left me in a strange mix of moods for the rest of the day. Whenever I'd remember something he had typed, I'd grin and feel lighthearted. A few times, I even pulled out my phone to reread some of his messages. *I just want to kiss those lips and hoard that sound all to myself* was my all-time favorite.

I wanted to hoard him all to myself too. It wasn't fair that a bunch of strangers who knew nothing about him got to be with him in ways I never would. And...then I was reminded all over again why we could only flirt through texts, and my emotions would plummet. I wanted him to plop down on the bench across from me at our lunch table and steal some of my food.

I wanted Mason back.

~$~

On Thursday afternoon, I was doing some homework outside in the courtyard while I waited for my time to clock in at the library. Dr. Janison, who'd yet to flunk me, had assigned my class Chaucer's *Canterbury Tales*...in Middle English.

Yeah, I know. *Middle* English.

I was trying to decipher the *Wife of Bath's Tale* as I sat in the midday sunlight, soaking up some warm Florida rays, when I came to the line "*By verray force, he rafte hire maydenhed.*"

Huh? Okay, pretty much every line of the epic poem left me with a great big *huh*? And this one was no different. Pulling up my handy dandy translation book I'd bought last week, I found the corresponding line.

When I realized it said something along the lines of "he took her maidenhead by force," I jerked back in surprise. What the heck was Dr. Janison making us read? A heroic knight raping a virgin was not my idea of classic literature.

But it did grasp my attention a little more firmly. I was busy deciphering and reading about how Queen Guinevere convinced her sweet hubby, Arthur, to leave the rapist's punishment up to her— yeah, you go, girl; hang that bastard by the balls— when a commotion across the lawn caught my attention.

A group of guys had been playing around the entire time I'd been sitting at my table, attempting to jump from one bronzed statue to the next. But no one had yet succeeded in making it from the charging bull with a ring in its nose to the oversized eagle spreading its wings.

By the cheers that rose, I gathered they had a new champion.

When I looked over, Mason, of all people, stood on top of the eagle's back, his arms spread almost as wide as the wings fanning underneath him as he shouted out his triumph.

I rolled my eyes but had to smile. As if feeling my gaze on him, he turned in the direction of our table and gave me the thumbs-up sign. I returned it, congratulating him, and he blew me a kiss before a group of guys caught him by the legs and began to carry him around in some kind of whacked-out victory parade.

Apparently, the male portion of the world thought he could do no wrong.

Laughing softly, I checked the screen of my cell phone for the time. Realizing I needed to get to work, I closed Chaucer and packed away my homework.

After clocking in, I chatted a minute with the head librarian and his two assistants, who were the only full-time staff in the library. Then I got started reading call numbers.

I know, it was *sooo* exciting, but I wanted a little peace and quiet today, so I didn't mind the boring task. I headed upstairs to a small section above the offices, where only reference books were kept. No one ever, *ever* came up here, so I knew I wouldn't be bothered.

Strangely enough, though, I was halfway through the first shelf when I heard footsteps.

Someone settled onto one of the three pieces of furniture clumped by the stairs, and my curiosity got the best of me. I squinted through the bookshelves, only to catch sight of Mason.

Mason?

Pressure built behind my ribcage. Anticipation and hope. Did he know I was up here? Had he come to see me? Did this mean we were still friends— friends who actually spoke face to face?

Appearing as if he had no idea I was near, he stretched out on an avocado green couch. After propping his head on the armrest of one end, he crossed his ankles and set them on the other end. Then he opened my copy of *The Chamber of Secrets* I'd loaned to him and began to read. He turned a page every minute or so and seemed to be three quarters of the way through, making me think he was really reading it.

I'd been scanning the shelves that were facing away from him, but I gave in to temptation and turned around to read the other shelves behind me, so all I'd have to do to see him was squat half an inch to peek over the tops of a row of books.

Between all my reading and peeking, I found a total screw up in the call numbers. An entire shelf was out of order. I pulled every book off the ledge and piled them on the floor. I was just beginning to put them back in the correct order when I heard, "Hello, Mason," in a low, private voice.

Crouched on the floor, I peeked through an open gap and saw Dr. Janison standing above him.

My heart sank into my stomach. Oh, holy shit. Had he come up here to meet a *client*?

Mason jerked upright and set the open book in his lap. He looked startled to see her. Thank God. That gave me some hope that he hadn't planned this little encounter.

"You shouldn't be talking to me," he murmured, glancing meaningfully toward the stairs.

"Don't worry," Dr. Janison answered just as quietly. "No one ever comes up here. We won't be caught together." Shifting closer, she eyed his lap. "What're you reading there?"

Without waiting for an answer, she reached out, caught the edge of the book, and tilted it forward just enough to see the cover.

An amused smile lit her face. "I approve," she murmured in a husky purr. "I have a preference for British Literature myself."

Mason peered up at her with a wary squint. "I'm not...I can't schedule a meeting with you to...to talk about classes again." He said it so quietly I had to strain to hear him. "I've dropped out of *those* courses and changed my major completely."

For a second, I wasn't sure if Dr. Janison had heard him either, or if she had deciphered his code correctly. Heck, maybe I hadn't deciphered his code correctly.

But after studying him for an overly long five seconds, the professor smiled a slow, knowing smirk. "So you're raising your prices again?"

My mouth fell open. What?

Mason seemed similarly struck. "What?"

Dr. Janison chuckled. "I remember you doing something like this last year. Stopped making appointments for a few months, told everyone you were finished. But it turns out you just needed more...incentive." She leaned closer. "Don't worry. I'll pay whatever you charge."

I could only see the side of his face, but the side I saw was filled with red-hot rage. Or was it humiliation? "This isn't about money. I'm *done*."

She looked confused for a second before her face cleared. Nodding sagely, she murmured, "Ah, so it's the girl, then?"

I covered my mouth with both hands. Girl? What girl? Did he have a girl?

Oh, my God. Was *I* the girl?

I had to be. Who else could *the girl* be? I was the only girl who'd publically associated herself with him and the one girl Dr. Janison had seen him sitting beside.

"That's fine. You're young and curious. I don't mind if you play at a relationship for a while. As long as you return to where you belong when you're done." Dr. Janison reached out to touch his hair, but he shifted his head away from her seeking fingers. She dropped her hand but didn't look deterred in the least. "Just let me know when you're finished with her. And then...I'll pay whatever fee you ask." She winked. "I know you're good for it."

She took a business card from her pocket and slowly bent to set it in the spine of the open pages as if slotting in a bookmark.

Eww. Now I was going to have to spray every page with disinfectant to erase her slut cooties after Mason returned the story to me.

How dare she put her business card in *my* book? It made me hot and angry and sad and heartbroken and kind of sick with jealousy and repulsion. I even grew pissed at Mason for leading the kind of life he led, where situations like this happened.

Dr. Janison blew him a kiss, then turned and strolled off.

As soon as she was gone, Mason sliced a guilty glance in my direction.

The breath caught in my throat. Oh, God. I couldn't breathe. He *did* know I was here, which meant I just *might* be the girl.

He'd come up here to be close to me. He'd told

one of his clients he was done taking appointments. There was a girl involved. In my head, one and one and one made *holy shit, he's no longer a gigolo.*

Giddy warmth stole through me, but then I mentally slapped myself across the face.

What the hell was wrong with me? I'd just watched another woman solicit him for sex—which she planned to pay *any price* for—and I was woozy about thinking he might want to start a relationship with me?

I must've lost my damn mind.

I don't think he saw me watching him. I was still kneeling on the floor by the bottom shelf, but I moved my face out of my peephole just to be sure.

When I had to—yes, I *had* to—look again, he was picking Dr. Janison's business card out of my book with the very tips of his thumb and index finger. Handling it carefully as if it were contaminated, he flicked it into a nearby trashcan.

A huge grin spread my lips wide.

Who cared what sick plague had infected me for wanting to be with a gigolo—or possibly an ex-gigolo. He'd just turned down a client.

For me!

Well, maybe for me. But the maybe part made all the difference. I was thrilled. Euphoric.

Getting back to work in a much better mood, I sorted through the misshelved books and organized them with much more buoyancy. I couldn't stop smiling. I might've even begun to hum a cheerful tune under my breath.

I felt jovial until I heard another female voice saying Mason's name. Jesus Herbert Christ, they were like cockroaches coming out of the woodwork to swarm him.

But this voice was way too familiar.

"Well, look who's hanging out in a library,

actually reading. Or is that just a front to meet some horny skank?"

I jerked my face up and peeked through a gap in the books in time to see Eva knock my book out of Mason's hands—gasp, I know; the sacrilege of knocking *Harry Potter* to the floor was simply obscene. Then, my dear sweet cousin went and took its place, plopping onto his lap. Looping her arms around his neck, she added, "I just saw Dr. Janison up here. Isn't she one of your regulars?"

My mouth dropped open wide. What the hell was she doing?

"Eva, get off me." Grabbing her wrists that she'd seemingly super-glued around him, he struggled to untangle her arms.

Still perched on his lap, she merely smirked. "So, did you two actually do it up here, or were you only setting up your next...appointment? Personally, I think it'd be hot to do it in some place public. Like a library. Except we'd have to be too quiet."

Giving up on trying to unlace her arms from around his throat—because he was having no luck whatsoever—Mason lifted his hands in surrender. "Seriously, you need to get off me. Now."

"Seriously," she repeated, her smile teasing as she unfastened one arm from around him only to run her newly freed finger down the center of his chest. "You need to loosen up."

I went cold all over, and for the first time in my life, I wanted to do my cousin intense, bodily harm, like break that finger she kept using to touch him.

"So, I'm not drunk now," she said with a smile. "You don't have to be a gentleman any longer. Still want to turn me down?"

"Yes." He snorted. "I'm not going to sleep with you, Mercer. Ever."

Her playful expression turned dark. Eyes flashing with outrage, she hissed, "Why? Because I'm not one of your *professors*? I can't give you an automatic A for every orgasm well received?"

Oh, yeah, she totally said that.

"Actually, there are several reasons. And none of them have to do with that. First of which, you have a boyfriend, and he's one of my good friends. Not to mention, I don't *want* to have sex with you, plus your cousin is—"

Eva broke him off before I could hear what he was going to say about me. "Don't you dare mention Reese. She's been through enough and doesn't need another loser asshole hurting her. So just stay away. Got it?"

Mason blinked, looking startled. Then his face clouded with fury. "Who hurt her? Hurt her how?"

Eva didn't answer. Instead, she smiled. "She's not to be played with. If you want to play, you'll have to settle for me."

He rolled his eyes. "I'll pass."

"Oh, I'm sure I could change your mind."

She reached between his legs, and he reacted instantly, surging to his feet and dumping her off his lap to the floor in an angry heave. "Don't ever touch me again."

I wasn't sure if I wanted to defend Mason or save my cousin—since he looked pissed enough to hurt her. But I flew from my hiding spot.

"Eva!" I shout-whispered. "What the hell are you doing? That's sexual assault."

Instead of apologizing with utter embar-rassment, Eva turned indignant. Picking herself up off the floor in a huff, she scowled at me. "Whatever. He's a prostitute, ReeRee. He's nothing."

Mason's chest swelled as he sucked in a sharp

breath. His eyes glazed with emotion, but I think there was more hurt than anger in their depths.

"He's a human *being*!" I snapped. "He has just as many rights *not* to be harassed every time he turns around as you or I do. And how dare you do this to Alec. Were you seriously just going to cheat on him?"

My cousin wiped floor dust off her butt with a *humph*. "You're blind if you can't see I just did this for *you*."

"Me?" My mouth fell open. "I guess I'm totally blind then. How did you do this for *me*?"

"He's not good for you. I was trying to keep him away from you."

I sighed. "Believe it or not, E., you don't have to bother. Mason and I are just friends."

She snorted. "Yeah, right. Keep telling yourself that, sweetie. Maybe someday our dead Grandma Dixon will actually believe it." Searing Mason with a glare, she hissed, "You know better than to pant after her." Then she stalked off.

Neither he nor I moved until she disappeared. Finally, he turned to face me, worry lining his eyes. "I'm sorry."

I shook my head, making a face. "For what?" I was the one who seriously needed to apologize for my asshole relative.

He lifted his hands, his expression incredulous. "I just knocked your cousin to the floor."

If I'd been him, I would've kicked her while she was down there. "You don't have to apologize for that. I'm surprised you didn't dump her off your lap sooner."

He still looked like he wanted to keep begging for my forgiveness.

I couldn't help it; I felt bad for him. Stepping close, I hugged him hard. "I never meant to bring the wrath of Eva down on you."

He gave a startled jerk in my arms. "You didn't. I brought it on myself."

I pulled back, aghast. "Just because you had some misguided notion when you were eighteen, thinking you had to do something drastic and unnecessary to save your family, doesn't mean you deserve to be treated with such constant degradation by every woman who crosses your path."

It struck me how much even I had objectified him the first few times I'd seen him, waxing poetic about his amazing looks. I had cared nothing about his personality. About him.

I wanted to beg his forgiveness for being no better than my cousin or my professor. But the intense way he stared at me gave me a moment's pause.

He lifted his right hand and gathered a handful of hair out of my face. "You're not like anyone I've ever met before. Where did you come from, Reese Randall?"

I didn't deserve that expression of awe he was giving me. I wanted to tell him I wasn't really Reese Randall. I wanted to tell him everything. But this moment was about him, so I just stuck with the truth I *could* give. "Ellamore, Illinois."

His smile was amused and full of adoration. My chest filled tight with an echo of that same emotion a split second before he heaved me back into his arms and hugged me again.

Burrowing his nose through my hair, he found the scar on the back of my neck. After pressing his lips to the puckered skin, he whispered, "Thank you for being my friend. But Mercer was right. I do know better than to pant after you. You should never have to deal with any of my shit."

A second later, he sniffed and pulled away before bending down to pick up the *Harry Potter* book. With his things gathered, he glanced at me. "I'll see you around," which was Mason-speak for he was back to avoiding me.

I stood in that same spot for way too long after he disappeared down the stairs. Too many things had left me rattled. Eva's behavior, what she'd called him, Mason's admission to Dr. Janison that he wasn't taking any clients, and all that talk about *the* girl.

I was getting in over my head here. But I just didn't care.

I had it bad.

CHAPTER **FIFTEEN**

That weekend started out pleasantly boring. I declined an invite from Eva to go club-hopping with her and her crew, and not just because her little scene in the library still had me ticked, but I just didn't feel like leaving my nest. I wanted some peaceful solitude.

After E. called me a total buzzkill and hung up on me, I shrugged, curled up on my couch with some homework and popcorn, and started a marathon of my favorite movies.

When my cell phone rang a little before eleven, I was beginning to feel sleepy. I figured it was Eva again, drunk calling me, demanding I dress my ass up and come join her already. So I dawdled with reaching for the receiver.

Upon seeing *Home* on the caller ID, however, I suddenly wanted to bawl. I nearly attacked the phone, starved to hear my mommy's voice. I know. I actually *missed* my parents. And my annoying older sister. Our cat, Doodles. Oh, and my bedroom.

I missed them all so very, very much.

I was far and gone past homesick.

"Hey, Mom," I answered coolly, trying not to sound hella anxious to hear her voice. "Don't worry. I'm fine. School is fine. And no, Eva hasn't totally converted me to the dark side yet." I poked at my nose ring, deciding not to mention that quite yet. I'd have to gauge her mood first.

"Honey." My mother's voice touched my ear, and it was as if I were sitting at our kitchen table again, sipping on hot chocolate with a bunch of marshmallows as we played cards and talked about our day. "I don't want to alarm you, but..."

The hair on the back of my neck immediately stood on end.

But, no, no, no. I wasn't alarmed.

I was totally freaked.

"What?" I demanded.

She sighed. There must not have been any way for her to cushion the blow, because she came right out and said, "Jeremy's father found a way to get the case dropped. It's not going to trial."

"Oh, my God." My vision wavered. If I hadn't already been camped on the couch, I might have collapsed to the floor. "Oh, my God." Did this mean I was going to be stuck as Reese Randall for the rest of my life, always checking over my shoulder, never feeling safe or settled, forever pursued by a crazed, blood-hungry maniac? "When?"

"Thursday, but listen...This isn't a reason to worry. I don't want you to—"

"Thursday?" I very nearly screamed. "Thursday? But..." Oh, my God. Why hadn't she called to tell me this on Thursday? "But he was being accused of attempted *murder*. How could they just *drop* that kind of case?"

"Sweetie, his father is a very good lawyer—"

"Oh, God," I moaned, feeling queasy. I'd just *had* to find myself a rich, spoiled lawyer's son to have as a psycho stalker ex-boyfriend, hadn't I?

Super. I definitely knew how to pick 'em.

"...was broken into this evening, but—"

"Wait, what? I'm sorry, Mom. I was spacing. *What* was broken into this evening?"

"Our house, but—"

I exploded to my feet. "*WHAT!*"

"Now, this doesn't necessarily mean it was him."

"Of course it was him. Mother!" *Wake up, woman.* "Who else would it be?"

"Okay, all right." Mom's voice was a little too calm and placating for my taste. "You're right. It's a good chance it was him. Nothing was taken, though. Just a couple of papers in the office were... rifled through."

"He's looking for me," I whispered, glancing around the room as if I would spot him lurking in one of the corners. He was free and clear from all legal accusations, so now he was looking for me. For revenge.

"He's not going to find you," Mom assured me. "We have nothing in the house to connect Reese Randall to you. The only way he could possibly find you now is through your social security number, and I swear we have every document with that information on it locked away in a security deposit box in the bank. Just to be on the safe side, however, Dad's going to go in and change your cell phone number tomorrow. We'll call and let Shaw and Mads know what the new number is. All right?"

When I didn't answer soon enough—my brain was too busy whirling with thoughts—Mom repeated my name. "Reese?"

"All right," I said, shaking my head, not quite sure what I was agreeing to.

But it seemed to reassure her. "See." There was a smile in her voice. "Everything's fine. We're not going to let him get anywhere near you. You're safe."

A long sigh eased from my lungs. I had left home to stay as safe as possible. But now that danger was breaking into houses to find me, it felt as if I'd left the only place that could truly keep me protected.

I was nine hundred miles from home. Alone.

"I love you, Teresa," Mom murmured into my ear.

As I closed my eyes tight, a single tear slid down my cheek.

Everyone had always called me Reese, ever since I'd been a baby and my older sister had found it impossible to pronounce Teresa. But it felt nice to hear my birth name spoken aloud. It had been too long; I'd begun to forget who I really was.

"I love you too, Mom."

After I hung up, I did a thorough walkthrough of the entire apartment, flipping on every light and checking every window and closet. Under the bed. Behind the shower curtain. Then I returned to the front room, no longer sleepy in the least.

Staring sightlessly at the television screen, I jumped at every creak and groan I heard echo through my tiny apartment. I was tempted to call Eva and demand she come home to be with me. But she was probably so drunk by now, she'd bring her partying gang along with her. I certainly didn't want a horde of strangers prowling through my loft.

When someone knocked on my door, I screamed. The pillow I'd been clutching to my chest went flying.

I scrambled off the couch and ran away from the knock, instead of toward it. Grabbing my purse, I dumped the contents on the table and fumbled through my compact and wallet before I found my mace and Taser.

"Who is it?" I called as I crept toward the door, both my hands full of girl-power weapons.

"It's Mason."

What?

Not believing the muffled male voice in the least—because why in the world would *Mason* come see me at eleven on a Saturday night?—I peeked out the closed window blinds and gaped at Hotness standing outside my apartment door.

What in the world?

Happy to see anyone who wasn't Jeremy, and even more thrilled that 'anyone' ended up being Mason, I dropped the mace and Taser at my feet and went to work, opening the three locks keeping my door sealed against intruders.

By the time I threw it open, I was ready to fling myself into his arms and hug him for being here. I was so relieved I didn't have to suffer through the rest of the night alone.

"Mason," I gasped.

When he lifted his face, I saw instantly something was wrong. His gaze swirled with torment. "Can we talk?" he grated out. "I just...I need to talk...to someone."

Brushing my hair out of my face, I found a piece of popcorn stuck in the tresses and batted it free. "Um...okay. Sure. Come on in."

I began to open the door wider, but that seemed to intimidate him. He scuttled a step back and lifted his hand. "If this is a bad time, I can leave."

I rolled my eyes. "Mason, seriously. Get inside

now." I didn't really fancy the idea of letting my front door just hang open.

But Mr. Gigolo turned shy. He stayed rooted on the landing outside, sending me a skittish glance.

With a mutter of frustration, I grabbed his arm and tugged him into my apartment. As I bolted us inside, he paced my front room. I turned and watched him run his hands over his hair and sigh. Repeatedly. He was so distracted he didn't even notice when I scooped up my Taser and mace off the floor and discretely tucked them away.

After he prowled around for a solid minute without even acknowledging me, I perched on the arm of my couch and folded my hands in my lap. "So...what's up?"

He slumped down onto the couch and sprawled out, letting his head drop back against the backrest. After letting out a low groan, he admitted, "I almost got caught tonight."

Oh, crap.

I slid off the armrest and sat next to him. Our knees almost touched, so I leaned forward and snagged my soda off the coffee table, using it as a bad imitation of a barricade.

My hands began to shake. To disguise the tremors, I took a quick drink, but immediately realized how big of a mistake that was. The carbonation in my pop made me want to heave up all the contents in my stomach.

But damn it, damn it, damn it. I'd been so sure he'd told Dr. Janison he wasn't taking clients anymore. I thought he was stopping that lifestyle because of *the girl*, because of me. I thought all our flirt texting and near kisses meant we were getting close.

So how could he have almost gotten caught? Had Eva's warning to him scared him back to the dark side?

God, I was such an idiot.

And I was *not* going to cry about this. No. I refused.

"You...you mean by the police?" I finally found enough oomph in my voice box to ask.

"No." He swung his head back and forth, still staring up at a ceiling. "By a husband."

"Holy..." I dropped the drink I was holding, and it was a miracle my lap caught it upright. I gathered it back into my hands. "Oh, my God, you sleep with *married* women too?"

I had to cover my mouth as if to manually shove the bile back into the depths of my stomach.

He sent me a distraught glance and began to jiggle his knee. "*Most* of the women who hire me are married."

I gulped and almost gagged on the misery and pain and disappointment crowding up my esophagus. "Oh." I was a little too busy concentrating on not bawling my head off to say much else.

My lack of response seemed to irritate him though. "Jesus, why do you think they come to me? A majority of them are bored, affluent housewives who blow all the spending money their husbands give them on younger men."

He surged to his feet and began to pace again, yanking at handfuls of his hair until the strands stood up at odd angles. The sad thing was, even as upset and scattered as he was, he still looked as sexy as hell. And I still wanted to go to him and hug his pain away.

He kicked the door as he passed it. Then he froze and gawked a moment as if making sure he hadn't damaged it before wincing in my direction. "Sorry."

I shrugged and motioned for him to carry on. He could kick whatever he wanted as long as he didn't leave a dent or hole. "Hey, at least you didn't kick me."

That comment seemed to shock him. "Why would I kick *you*?"

"I don't know." Suddenly uneasy, I took a big sip. This time, the caffeine settled my stomach instead of upsetting it. He was still watching me, so I fluttered out my hand in a useless gesture. "Sometimes people feel the need to hurt other people in a way to show their power. And you're obviously feeling powerless with no control of your own life right now, so—"

He was by my side and sitting next to me before I could complete my explanation. "I would never kick you, Reese. Why would you even think..." He shook his head, and then bowed his face and squeezed his eyes shut. "I shouldn't have come here."

"No." I reached out and caught his knee. "It's fine. Really. I mean, if you need to get something off your chest, then...let it out. It's not like you can talk to just anyone about this. And we're friends, so..."

He looked up and studied me, his gaze pleading for some kind of deliverance.

But as he stared, his features collapsed. "Do you know I've never had sex just for the hell of it, just to have a little recreational fun with a partner of my choice? I have always, *always* been propositioned and paid. I've never gotten to decide when or where, or how, or with whom. I've never—"

"Then have recreational sex," I said, frowning because I couldn't see why this was so upsetting. Not for him anyway. The idea of him having recreational sex—without me involved—was incredibly upsetting for *me*. Sure. But we weren't talking about me. This was about him. "Nothing is stopping you from giving out your...freebies."

Mason pulled back as if I'd slapped him. "That wouldn't be fair to the girl. It wouldn't be fair to me. It wouldn't be fair to *anyone*."

Oh.

Hmm.

So he was a gigolo with starch standards. Damn, another thing I had to admire about him. More than admire, actually.

With a burst of clarity, I realized he wasn't a man-whore at all. In fact, if he'd never fallen into this lifestyle, I bet he'd be the commitment type, the one-woman man who never strayed or stayed in a relationship for less than two years.

He'd be perfect boyfriend material.

It was a wonder some girl hadn't snagged him up before—

"Wait." I shook my head when another thought struck. "Even your *first* time was—"

He made a sour face. "My landlady. She offered to knock off the back rent we owed if I...relented. Threatened eviction if I didn't. She's actually the one who set me up with meeting other women and got me hired at the Country Club."

My eyes could've popped out of their sockets. "You mean Mrs. Garrison? So she's like, what, your pimp?"

He huffed out a scoff. "Pimp? Yeah, I guess, in a manner of speaking. She...hey, how do you know her name?"

I shrugged. "She told me. I ran across her smoking outside when I left your house one night after babysitting."

"Damn it." And he was back on his feet with the pacing again. Seriously, the boy was going to run me dizzy. "I told her to leave you alone."

"You did?" Well, that was alarming. "When did you do that? And why were you discussing *me* with your landlady?"

"Because she's seen you coming and going and you're..." He threw out a hand to motion toward me as if I should be able to finish that sentence.

I couldn't. Straightening, I pressed my palm to my chest, already offended. "I'm what?"

"You're...beautiful," he muttered, turning away. "So, naturally, she thinks you and I..."

"Yeah." I nodded and rolled my hand. "I got that part."

Mason scrubbed his face, moaning. "God, I really hate this sometimes. Sometimes, I just want to quit it all."

My heart skipped a beat. Hope sprung eternal. "Then quit. Quit it right now."

He clenched his teeth and sent me a scowl. "I can't!"

I shook my head. "Why not?"

"I just..." He winced. "I'm not going to do this forever. I *do* have a plan. As soon as I graduate, I'm getting a kick-ass job. Then I'm setting Mom and Sarah up in a house, one they *own*, not another rental. And I'm going to find my own place. I'm going to be free."

I nodded as I listened. It was sad to hear how trapped he felt in his current life and how responsible he felt for his mom and sister. "Why can't Dawn buy her own house now? And why can't you move out now, if that's what you want?"

He sent me a scandalized blink. "Are you crazy? Mom cannot be trusted with finances. Before I stepped in, she forgot to pay...pretty much everything. She's a great mother, don't get me wrong. I would give my life for her, but the woman can't budget worth shit. Sometimes, she would forget to pay the electric bill, and the lights would just go out while we were eating dinner or I was taking a shower. Sometimes—"

"So, wait." I waved my hands to stop him. "I'm sorry, but I guess I just don't understand how you finishing college is going to teach *your mother* to learn to finance and take care of herself without you."

He stared at me as if he couldn't comprehend my concern.

"Even if you build up a big enough nest egg for her and Sarah to be set for life, she could still forget to pay for utilities after you leave."

Mason's glower was irritated. "Are you saying I'm never going to be able to move out on my own?"

"No, I'm saying you need to come at this from a different angle. It sounds like *Dawn* needs to learn a little organization." And to quit stacking so much responsibility on her son's shoulders.

"She's starting to come around," he argued. "I've worked with her for the past two years. And every couple of months, she'll pay the bills without my help."

"Well, then there you go. Maybe she *could* do it all on her own now. Ergo, you can stop doing something so drastic to save your family. They'll be okay. You don't have to keep breaking the law or your own moral code and continue doing something you obviously hate just to make more money."

"I have a plan," he repeated, his jaw going obstinately hard, telling me nothing was going to make him deviate.

I rolled my eyes and muttered, "Yeah. A *stupid* plan." My voice might've been a tad petulant, but I didn't care. His stupid plan was keeping me from jumping his bones this very second. It was keeping me from being with the one person who saw *me* and liked what he saw.

As if he understood his pigheadedness was leaving me shafted, he sat beside me. "I'm sorry, Reese. I didn't mean to dump all my problems on you. I..." He swallowed. The look he sent me said volumes in the apology department, but the words he said sounded more like, "Do you have anything to drink?"

I blurted out a hard laugh. Yeah, a stiff drink sounded perfect right about now.

"Sure. Hold on." I pushed to my feet and left him on the sofa. I needed a little space from him anyway before I slapped him silly.

In the kitchenette, I opened the top cupboard and stretched up onto my toes to reach the only bottle of alcohol I had in the place. After filling a crystal cup with ice, I poured a healthy shot and carried both the glass and bottle to the couch.

"Here."

Relief crossed his face. "Thanks." He downed the drink whole, only to sit upright, nearly spitting it out as he coughed and sputtered. "God." He grimaced and scraped the surface of his tongue against the bottom of his top teeth, wiping off the remaining flavor. "What *was* that? Tequila?"

Shocked he didn't know his liquors, I gaped. "No. It was gin." How could anyone not recognize the taste or smell of gin?

"Blech. Tasted like Pine-Sol."

Umm...Yeah. Duh.

He gave a sudden laugh. "I just meant water when I asked for a drink, you know."

"Oops." I shrugged.

He shrugged too.

"Oh, well. This'll do too." He reached out and

snagged the bottle from my hand to pour himself another shot. He merely shivered in revulsion with his next swallow. "Damn, that's nasty." He cast me an arched-eyebrow glance. "I wouldn't have taken you for a gin drinker."

"I'm not. It was in the cabinet when I moved in. Must be my aunt and uncle's."

He snorted, pouring himself more. "Nice way to tempt their underage, college-student niece into staying sober." Hissing through his teeth after shot number three, he looked at me from slightly watered eyes.

I grinned because his reaction was so darn cute. "Let me guess. You're not a big drinker."

Mason shook his head before taking a deep, bracing breath and downing number four. A green tinge touched his cheeks, but he swallowed again and kept everything down only to flash clenched teeth.

"Well, newbie. If you keep shooting them that fast, you're going to be sicker than a dog."

He eyed me, considering it. "But I'll be drunk?"

"Oh, yeah."

"Good." He slammed number five without a wince.

I had to admit; I was a little impressed. The boy was a fast learner. That or the Pine-Sol had already numbed his taste buds.

Two gulps later, I intercepted shot number eight, tugging the bottle out of his hand before he could pour. "Trust me, honey. That did the trick."

He blinked at me, swaying a little. "Are you sure? I don't feel—"

"Oh, you will, just as soon as the alcohol hits your bloodstream."

"Good."

When he nodded, trusting my word implicitly,

I had to ask. "Now, why are we getting rip-roaring drunk again? Because of the almost-getting-caught thing or because I called your plan stupid?"

"It's not stupid." He scowled before adding, "And *I'm* getting drunk," he jabbed a finger into his sternum, "because of earlier tonight. *You're* staying sober to take care of me."

"I am?" This was news to me. When I lifted my eyebrows, letting him know he should probably revise that last statement to sound a little more pleading and a lot less demanding, he merely sent me a sweet, goofy grin.

"Come on, Reese. Please. I just want to forget this evening ever happened. Forget what I am, forget *who* I am...who I..."

His words trailed off as his attention strayed to the frozen image on my television screen. "Hey, what movie is this?" Spotting my popcorn bowl, he snagged it off the coffee table, settled it into his lap and began to eat. Then he plopped his feet up on my coffee table.

Yeah, I think the alcohol was beginning to kick in.

Sighing, I slumped, defeated, onto the sofa beside him. Apparently, *we* would be watching movies together tonight while I babysat his cute, drunk ass.

Man, I was whipped.

A part of me realized I had to be the stupidest idiot *ever* to allow him to stick around. I was pretty much welcoming heartbreak. But another part of me said I was doing it for the security. Knowing Jeremy was actively pursuing me had me spooked. Even a drunkard in the house made me feel better.

But secretly, I was mostly just tickled he'd come to me—and no one else—to get drunk on and tell his personal, most private feelings to. I actually felt honored to babysit him.

"You might get a kick out of this movie," I said, relieved for a conversation changer. "I was just starting a *Harry Potter* marathon when you knocked on my door."

He perked up. "Really? *Harry Potter*?"

"Yep. I'm halfway through the first one, but I can start over if you want."

"Yeah. That sounds great. I haven't seen the movies either."

Scrounging up the remote, I shook my head. "That's so insane. I can't believe you haven't seen the movies *or* read the books. You're like...un-American, or something."

He cocked me a confused look. "How can it be un-American? I thought they were written by a British author."

I sighed. He would remember that, wouldn't he? "Well, then, you're un...*earthling*."

He laughed and tossed a kernel into the air in an attempt to catch it with his mouth. But he totally missed and the piece of popcorn bounced off his nose. So I had to laugh too.

"Feeling the buzz yet?"

CHAPTER **SIXTEEN**

I didn't get to bed until nearly two in the morning. After stealing a few more shots of gin, Mason passed out midway through the second movie, and since I was dead on my feet, I turned everything off. I removed his shoes, pulled his feet onto the sofa, and found an extra blanket to drape over him. Then I turned off the lights and stumbled to my bedroom.

I won't lie. I watched him sleep for a good ten minutes before getting off the couch. But he looked so peaceful and loveable all cozied up with his head tucked down by his shoulder. Tempted to brush away the dark piece of hair that had fallen over his eye, I finally forced myself to retreat.

I cleaned up and changed into my sleepwear before crawling under my sheets, completely exhausted, and yet hyper aware of his presence still in my apartment.

Glad another person was close so soon after learning about Jeremy, I was able to drop off pretty easily. Sleep had just overtaken me when I was jerked awake by someone lifting my blankets and crawling into bed with me.

I bolted upright. "What do you think you're doing?"

My indignant squawk only made Mason grumble. "The couch is too short. I can't sleep in there."

I chewed on my bottom lip as he plopped down beside me and didn't move. There was barely enough light in the room to see his outline. And what a striking outline he made. But really, he couldn't sleep in my bed with me.

Could he?

No! No, Reese, no. Boot his hot, gigolo ass out. Now!

"Want me to drive you home?" I asked, biting my lip and unable to do such a blasphemous thing as boot Mason Lowe anywhere away from my bed.

But he was already half passed out again. "Mmph?"

"Well, fine." I huffed and lifted the sheet. "I guess *I'll* sleep on the couch then."

Being that I had such a small room, I'd pushed my bed against the wall, and my side faced the wall. So I had to crawl over him to escape. Or maybe I should say I *tried* to crawl over him. His arm caught me around the waist and anchored me back to the bed so that I landed on my side facing away from him.

"Don't leave," he slurred.

His voice was so full of wounded plea, I fell motionless, undecided.

This was dangerous territory.

Behind me, Mason scooted close, spooning.

Oh, my God, spooning was so romantic and cuddly.

"You feel good." He rumbled out the words from a husky, sexy, sleep-clogged voice.

When he sighed, that was it. Kaput. Towel officially thrown in. I wasn't going anywhere.

I let out a relinquishing breath and relaxed against him. In return, he hummed his gratitude.

"Just don't say I didn't warn you." I tried to keep it platonic. "But sometimes I get night terrors and scream or moan while I thrash around. I might wake you or accidentally give you a black eye."

The muscles in the arm wrapped around me twitched. "You get night terrors? Like nightmares?"

I closed my eyes. "Yep."

He tucked me protectively closer to him. "Why?"

"Oh...that's another story for another day."

Patting my hip in reassurance, he whispered, "Don't worry, Reese. I'll be here to keep you safe, no matter what monster invades your dreams."

His words were so sweet, my eyes misted.

Warm fingers dusted my shoulder as if to console me, only to pause. "Shit. Are you naked?"

"What? No." His touch suddenly felt like a hot brand on my bare skin. "I'm wearing a camisole and shorts."

I *was*!

But he'd already discovered this for himself when his thumb found the spaghetti strap and the palm of his other hand caught the hem of my cami and skimmed just under it to brush across my navel.

"Can I turn the light on?"

I stiffened. "Why?"

"So I can see you." His thumb traced the camisole's strap gently, running down the back of my shoulder blade. "I want to see you so bad."

"Let's not," I said, my throat tight with the urge

to mutter, '*Screw it; take me now!*'

It had been over a year since I'd had sex. Up until this very second, I would've sworn I didn't miss it in the least. Jeremy, my one and only source of experience on the subject, hadn't exactly been famous for his giving nature. I did not have fond memories.

But Mason barely grazing my tummy had me totally reconsidering.

He leaned his face in close to the back of my head, inhaling deeply. "Damn it, Reese. I have a *plan.*"

His touch turned desperate and scorching hot. Catching my hip, he pulled me snug against him. When my bottom cradled his erection through all our clothes, I grasped a handful of pillows by my head and sucked in a lungful.

Don't grind back, Reese. Whatever you do, don't *grind back.*

I couldn't help it; I arched my tush out and rubbed against him. Hard. He groaned and slid his hand into the waistband of my shorts, cradling me low—oh, so very low—on my abdomen as if to guide my movements.

Oh, God. Oh, God. Was he going to...?

Holy hell. His palm slid between my legs, pressing against me through my panties. My breathing went short and shallow. I panted, trying to control myself, but the tingling in my breasts and the ache he was stroking with his fingers was throwing off my concentration.

"Mason," I choked out.

"We can't do this," he said, his voice full of naked need while he used the cloth of my underwear to sweep over a sensitive spot and make me cry out. "I have a plan. *Don't you understand?*"

When he leaned in to take a flesh full of my

shoulder between his teeth and grind his hips to my ass, I squeezed my eyes closed. "Yes, I...I understand. I understand I'm not part of your plan."

A strangled sob tore from him. For a micro-second, he clutched me tight like he was going to throw his stupid plan by the wayside and shag me silly. The way he clung to me made me feel like a lifeline for his tortured soul. And the press of his fingers about had rockets blasting off behind my eyes. I was so freaking close.

Then he let out a pent-up breath.

"I respect you," he grated out the words. "I admire, and adore, and respect you, Reese Randall. I will not do this."

And just like that, his body went lax and his hand eased from the waistband of my shorts.

I held my breath as his nose burrowed through my hair before his lips found my scar. He kissed it gently. "Good night, friend," he whispered before he turned away with his back abutted to mine.

Wrung out from how taut he'd wound my hormones, I let out a hard pant.

Fudge.

Mason Lowe might be a pure gentleman when it came to not taking advantage when there was alcohol involved, but he was also a damned dirty tease. I throbbed, *physically throbbed* for release.

He breathed deeply behind me, telling me he'd passed out. I was tempted to elbow him in the spine and wake his drunk butt up, demand some kind of compensation for the torture he'd just put me through.

But I admired, adored, and respected him too. And I totally dug that he felt the same. Besides, I would've regretted it in the morning because, come on, he'd almost gotten caught by a husband tonight.

He was not the kind of guy a girl could start anything with.

Eyes watering with confusion, regret, depression, and a whole lot of sexual frustration, I buried my damp cheek into my pillow and cursed when my nose ring caught on the cloth. Clamping my thighs together to ease some of the ache between my legs, I waited for the morning to come. I didn't try to climb over him again to escape, because sadly, despite all the heartache he was putting me through, there was nowhere else I wanted to be but with him.

CHAPTER **SEVENTEEN**

I woke the next morning, wrapped in a snuggly human ball of warmth and not much else. Since it had become a habit to make sure my nose ring hadn't come loose overnight, I patted my nostril to find everything in order and then let my hand settle on Mason's forearm resting on my hip. His skin felt so nice I gave a little sigh of delight, trailing my fingers up and down his arm. Then I opened my eyes and blinked at the wall only about two inches away from my face.

Snuggly Mr. Lowe had hogged so much of the bed he had me nearly pinned against the sheetrock, and all the blankets were wrapped around *him*. I probably would've been cold if it wasn't for the fact he was providing himself as my personal blanket. A toasty warm personal blanket.

Soaking in the experience of waking up in bed with him, I lay there for longer than I should have.

Despite everything, lying tangled up with him felt amazing. I could have stayed right where I was all day, but my bladder wasn't so impressed by his cuddly warmth or drugging smell. The selfish thing demanded attention. Pronto. Whimpering as I unwound his arm from around my waist, I crawled over my blanket-wrapped bed partner and scampered for the bathroom.

Since I was already there, I went ahead and took a shower, then realized too late I'd forgotten to bring fresh clothes in with me to change into. When I snuck the door open, I expected him to be up and alert. But he was still dead to the world and mummified in my sheets. I skipped across the floor to my closet and picked out an outfit in hyper speed.

Mason hadn't so much as stirred.

When a naughty touch of inspiration hit me, I couldn't stop myself. I watched the prone lump on the bed, the back of his head turned my way, as I dropped my towel to the floor. And the bastard still had no clue what kind of show I was putting on for him.

Oh, well. It was probably for the best he didn't wake up and—oopsie—catch me changing. We were just friends.

He looked as if he might snooze for another millennium or so, so I jotted a quick note—in case something shocking happened and he actually opened his eyes while I was gone—and told him I was going out to get some breakfast.

When I returned, his Jeep still sat in the drive but my apartment was quiet. I crept to my room, almost worried he'd risen and left anyway. The day had brightened considerably, and the sun had snuck in through the closed blinds to spray down on my bed, spotlighting a masterpiece.

Mason had rolled onto his back in my absence. The sheets had shifted down to the bottom of his ribcage. And holy cappuccino and white chocolate mocha espresso, he was shirtless!

Yeah, he'd been shirtless all night long while I'd been lying next to him...and I'd had no clue.

Wow.

Just...wow.

I gazed at him in all his shirtless glory—on *my* bed, squee!—and was beyond tempted to pull out my cell phone to snap off a few (dozen) pictures to keep forever and ever.

But...he might not appreciate that.

Damn, sometimes being friends with a total hottie could suck. You couldn't take nearly naked pictures of them while they were passed out on your bed against their permission without getting a serious case of the guilties.

It didn't keep me from looking though. So, I looked and looked.

And looked.

Then, like a Harry Potter lightning bolt, an idea struck me. What if he wasn't just shirtless under that sheet? What if he was completely naked?

Oh, this I had to know.

Since he was dead to the world and seemed like a really deep sleeper, I went on a fact-gathering mission. Purely academic curiosity, of course.

After setting the two lattes I was holding on my dresser, I grasped the edge of the sheets covering him and inched them very, very slowly down his sleek, tapered and tanned torso. My attention darted between his face and his chest, taking in every inch of the sexy, sculpted pecs I exposed.

When I came to the beginnings of his tattoo, I brightened, forgetting about the pants mystery for a second.

Maybe I could read what it said today. I tugged a little more insistently on the sheet and discovered at the same moment that he was still wearing his underwear but no pants and his tattoo said *Make Me.*

I gasped.

After last night, those two words made so much sense. I could see him feeling trapped and rebellious, living a life where women told him exactly what to do to pleasure them and thinking this was his only form of giving them the finger.

He wanted to break free and live his own life. He wanted control over himself.

I suddenly understood why I'd always felt connected to him. We were similar souls who'd been made to feel repressed. After years of Jeremy telling me how to wear my hair, what kind of clothes to buy, what kind of food to eat, I had grown the same rebellious, "make me" attitude.

The sad thing was, Mason was still living under his suppression, and he had the means to break free; he just wouldn't. He wouldn't stop doing what he was doing until he knew without a doubt that his mother and sister were going to be okay. *But oh, Mason, you poor deluded thing. They've already made you.*

His tat also reminded me I was acting like every other woman out there, treating him like a sex object by sneaking a stolen peek at him. Tears stung my eyes. I was about to cover him back up, give him back his dignity, but at the last second, I reached out and touched the dried ink embedded into his skin, silently apologizing for my part in making him this way.

He sucked in a breath at my touch and rolled toward me, onto his stomach, where he winced and buried his face in my pillow.

No, I didn't plan on washing that pillowcase ever again, now that you mention it. Sex object or not, he was still Mason, and I would relish every little scent he left behind on my bed.

Retreating to the doorway, I wiped my cheeks dry and snagged up both cups as if I'd just then come into the room. "Rise and shine, sleeping beauty." By my perky tone of voice, you'd never guess I'd just been on the brink of weeping my eyes out.

A second later, Mason whipped his head off my pillow. "What the hell?" His voice was hoarse and confused as he jerked his face around until he spotted me. Eyes widening, he gasped. "Reese?"

"Morning," I chirped and took a nonchalant sip from my cup. "So, I went out and bought us some breakfast. There are doughnuts in the front room." When he just stared at me, I rolled my eyes. "I know, I know. 'Reese, you're so amazing and wonderful. Thanks for thinking of me. You shouldn't have.' But, really, it's no problem. Anything for my buddy. So...*de nada.*"

He blinked and licked his lips, smacking them together a few times, probably to moisten a dry mouth. Glancing slowly around the room, he winced when he got to the window and morning sunlight blinded him, doing wonders to his hangover, I bet.

"This is your room."

I opened my mouth to spout out something sarcastic and snide, but he looked like he was in pain, so I found pity and took another sip. "Yep."

He nodded slowly and directed his bloodshot eyes my way. "What am I doing in your bed?"

I shrugged. "You said the couch was too short."

He squinted as if he was trying to remember saying any such thing. Focusing on me again, his face paled as he asked, "So, did we...?"

This time, I couldn't help myself. I had to

torture him just a little.

Hey, don't judge.

"Seriously, Mason." I gasped in mock outrage. "How could you forget the magical night we shared together?" I pressed my cup to my heart as if in heartfelt pain. "It was...beautiful."

He choked out a sound of denial. "Oh, God. We didn't."

"Hey!" I flipped up my middle finger, which was quite a feat since both my hands were full. "You could at least *pretend* as if the idea of sleeping with me doesn't completely repulse you. Gah. I thought you were into me at least a little. I mean, what about your stupid horny guy urges and that freebie you said I could have if I just *said the word*?"

"I...God, Reese. I'm sorry. I didn't mean it that way. I just...shit. This was not something I'd want to forget." He gulped and ran a hand through his sexy rumpled hair, looking a little green. "Umm... was it at least good for you?"

I burst out laughing, choking on the last sip I'd taken and barely avoiding spitting it across the room. "Wow. You don't remember anything at all, do you?"

He winced, utter devastation flushing his cheeks. "No. Nothing."

"Well, relax, Casanova. Nothing happened."

If anything, he looked even more disappointed. "It didn't?"

"Nope."

He totally didn't seem convinced. "You're saying I came in here, crawled into bed with you, and I didn't come onto you *at all*? Why do I find that impossible to believe?"

Probably because it was. So, for this one, I had to lie. I shrugged. "You were tanked. You just stumbled into my room, burrowed in beside me, and passed out cold. Oh! And then you hogged three fourths of the mattress and *all* the sheets. Which is something you really need to work on, buster, because if you ever plan on getting married one day, no wife is going to appreciate that."

His lips quirked in amusement. "I'll keep that in mind." He studied me a second longer, looking as if he needed to say something else. But instead, he swallowed and scrambled upright. "Bathroom?"

I pointed. "Right there."

"Thanks." He was out of bed and streaking across the room in a flash, gifting me with a blurred peek of him in nothing but dark boxer briefs.

Oh, the hardships of having a sexy, tanned beefcake for a close friend.

Though I wouldn't have minded another glimpse of him in that snug, form-fitting cotton, I left my bedroom to give him some privacy, because it was kind of strange listening to him pee through the bathroom door.

Leaving his latte on my dresser, I retreated to the living room and was going to hang around in front of the television until he emerged when I spotted his shirt and jeans crumpled in a pile on top of the blanket I'd covered him with last night. After picking them up off the floor and taking a nice, deep whiff of the Mason smell lingering on them, I carried them back to my room. I'd just tossed them onto my bed when I heard the toilet flush. So I hurried back out again.

This time, I shut my bedroom door before I returned to the couch. I'd just folded the blanket and draped it over the back of the couch when a knock came on my front door.

For some reason, it reminded me of my mom's phone call from the night before.

What if it was Jeremy? What if he'd already

found me?

Shit, had I remembered to lock the door after I'd gotten back from my latte run? I'd been so preoccupied and eager to see if Mason was still here, I'd totally forgotten about the added threat of danger.

The door handle turned, telling me I most definitely had not locked it.

I freaked and glanced around frantically for a weapon. Oh, God, if Jeremy found Mason here, he'd kill him.

Spotting my espresso I'd set on the coffee table, I snatched it up, ready to throw the hot, scalding brew in my psycho stalker ex-boyfriend's face. But Eva began to jabber as soon as she barged her way inside.

"*Reese*! We need to talk. Like right now."

I gaped at my cousin, alarmed by how close I'd come to burning her.

How could I have forgotten to lock my door?

She took in my frozen expression and sent me a funny look. "What?"

"I thought you were...I forgot to..."

Before I could spit out a comprehendible sentence, my bedroom door opened, and Mason emerged, still in the process of pulling his shirt on over his head. "I stole some of your ibuprofen," he said as poked his head through the collar.

When he spotted both Eva and me ogling him, he stopped short. His gaze froze on my cousin before he turned to me with a slight, apologetic wince.

I cleared my throat. "Umm...that's fine. I'm sure your hangover is"—I darted a quick glance toward Eva, who was narrowing her eyes threateningly—"killing you."

He opened his mouth and looked like he

wanted to say something important, but what came out was, "Do you know where my shoes are?"

I shook my head and sputtered my way into action. "Y-your shoes? Umm...yeah. I took them off of you after you passed out and left them by the foot of the couch."

Setting my latte back down, I knelt onto my hands and knees to search underneath the furniture.

"Here they are."

When I straightened, Mason had a particularly strained expression on his face. His smile was tight as he snagged them from my hand and rushed to shove his feet into them. "Thanks." He pointedly ignored Eva as he focused on me. "I'll see you at two, right?"

I wrinkled my brow. "Two?"

His eyes flared wide. "Sarah's birthday party is today. You're coming, aren't you?"

"Oh, yeah!" I smacked my forehead. "I totally forgot. But, yes, I'll be there. Definitely."

He cringed. "You got her a present, didn't you? She's been wondering all week what kind of gift you got her. And you said you'd get—"

"Of course I got her something." With a devilish grin, I set my hand on my hip. "And I hate to break it to you, pal, but my present is so going to spank your little present's ass."

For the first time since waking this morning, he gave me a genuine smile. "We'll see about that." His gaze cut to my cup sitting on the coffee table. "You said you got one of those for me, didn't you? And mentioned food."

I rolled my eyes. Didn't matter how awkward or uncomfortable a situation was, I could always count on Mason to take my food. "Your latte's sitting on my dresser in my bedroom. And doughnuts are on the table."

Grin growing, his eyes warmed. "You're the best."

Disappearing too briefly for Eva to say anything to me except, "Oh, no you didn't," he returned, drinking heartily from his to-go container. After snagging a doughnut out of the baggie on the table, he stamped a brief kiss to my cheek. "Thanks. For everything."

As my cheek tingled from where he'd pressed his lips, Mason turned toward the door but paused when Eva crossed her arms over her chest and glared at him, refusing to move out of the exit.

Lifting one eyebrow, he rumbled out a gruff, "Excuse me."

"Oh, that's not going to happen. After what you did to *my* cousin—"

"Eva, leave him alone. You don't know what you're talking about." When she sliced me with an incredulous glance, I muttered, "Nothing happened. He fell asleep on the couch."

There was no reason to mention he hadn't stayed there.

"You know what," E. snapped. "It doesn't matter if you two stayed up all night sitting on opposite ends of the room, reading the Bible together. Alec *saw* his Jeep parked outside your apartment when he brought me home last night. You know he's going to tell everyone."

I sighed. "I really didn't care who Alec tells. I'm not going to un-friend Mason just because some stupid, ignorant people think I'm some skanky whore now."

"Whoa," Mason broke in and spun toward Eva, looking freaked. "Are people actually saying that about her?"

"He is my *friend*," I railed, "and he really

needed a friend last night. It's not easy for him, you know."

"Oh. No, you're right, ReeRee. I can't *imagine* how awful his life must be. I mean, rich, swanky women flock to him, tucking hundred dollar bills down his pants on a daily basis. Yeah, that sounds....awful."

"You don't know anything, okay. With medical bills and his mother's crappy jobs—"

"Look, I've heard about his home life already. I know the whole story of his sad, depressing childhood. But I also know a lot of people have it hard. A lot of people go through just as much shit— if not more—and they aren't selling their bodies for money."

"You're just jealous," I muttered, turning away.

"Jealous?" She cracked out a surprised laugh. "Of *what*?"

Swinging back, I pointed at Mason and yelled, "Of that fact that he wanted nothing to do with you, only to turn around and become *my* friend."

"Friend?" Eva gave a harsh laugh. "He doesn't want to be your *friend*."

"Actually," Mason started, but E. rolled right over him.

"And the only reason I came onto him that day in the library was because I *knew* you were watching. I wanted to show you how much he couldn't be trusted."

I let out an unladylike snort. "Too bad that *thoughtful* gesture blew up in your face."

As if giving up hope on winning any argument against me, Eva swung toward Mason. "You," she sneered. "You stay away from Reese. She's so far out of your league you aren't fit to lick her shoes. In fact, if you go anywhere near her again, I'm heading straight to the police station and telling them what you are."

Mason's face drained of color. His eyes were already bloodshot, but they seemed to go extra moist as he glanced helplessly at me.

"That's enough!" Charging forward, I shoved Eva's shoulder, nudging her with a little too much force away from the doorway. Then I grasped Mason's forearm. "Don't listen to her. She will not be telling the police *anything*."

"I wasn't—" he started, but he still wasn't having any luck about getting in a word edgewise this morning.

I talked right over him as I opened my apartment door. "You and I are friends, and we're going to *stay* friends." Silently excusing him, I stepped back to let him leave even as I looked him in the eye and murmured, "I'll see you at two o'clock."

When he stared back, I had to hold in the urge to hug him. He looked devastated. Unable to help myself, I popped forward, lifted up onto my tiptoes and pressed a quick kiss to his cheek, since we seemed to be cheek-kissing friends now. He turned his face in just enough to make our skin brush for a second longer than necessary, causing heat and affection to roar through me.

Neither of us spoke as I drew back. We stared at each other a moment, and then he nodded and left the apartment.

After closing the door behind him, I turned to Eva slowly, ready to do whatever was needed to protect Mason. "I swear to God, E., if you do anything to hurt him—"

Eva burst into tears. "Oh, shut up. I'm not going to hurt your precious gigolo. Jesus." Burying her face into her hands, she sank onto my couch and began to rock herself back and forth. "I mean, I *am* worried about you, and I wanted to warn you away from him. But I was bullshitting. I just don't want anything to happen to you, ReeRee. There's still hope for *you.*"

A little thrown by the tears because Eva was by no means a crier, like ever, I neared her slowly, not sure what to think of her overly dramatic, out-of-character outburst.

With hesitant fingers, I reached out and touched her hair. "Eva?"

She looked up. I don't think she'd washed off her club-hopping makeup yet because huge black trails of eyeliner leaked down her face. "I messed up," she sobbed. "I messed up big. And I don't want the same thing to happen to you too. Be careful around him. Promise me."

Sitting beside her, I pulled her into my arms, "How did you mess up? What are you talking about?"

Shit, if she confessed that she'd had sex with Mason, I was going to lose it.

"I was..." She paused to sniff and wipe at her tears. "After seeing his Jeep here last night, I was going to come talk to you and warn you away from him anyway this morning. But I was going to wait until after he left. Then...then I woke up and was looking in my medicine cabinet for some aspirin when I spotted my tampons and realized...oh, God."

She buried her face into my shoulder and sobbed anew. I smoothed her hair out of her face and gently asked, "You realized what?"

"I'm late."

My fingers froze in her golden locks. "What?" Just as quickly, I asked, "Who?" Please, God, not Mason. "Alec?"

She sat up in order to glare at me. "*Yes*, Alec! I'm not that big of a slut. God."

Thank the Lord.

I covered my mouth. "Oh, my God, Eva. Are you sure? Does Aunt Mads know? Are you—"

"Of course I'm not sure! I just told you, I saw my tampon box, realized I was late, and I freaked. I came running straight to you and forgot about the gigolo until he strutted out of your bedroom. I'm sorry I attacked him again, okay? I know you're still pissed after the last time, and I swore I was going to ignore him altogether from here on out, so you'd forgive me. But then I saw him, and it just seemed...easier to strike out than confess."

"Okay, okay." I lifted my hands to stop her rambling. "Just...keep calm and think of Chris and Liam."

"Okay," Eva repeated. "Okay." She panted a few times as if she was already prepared to go into labor. When an expression of shock lit her face, she straightened and gaped at me. "Hey. That actually worked."

With a grin, I tossed my hair. "I know, right."

No hetero female on the planet could panic with a mental image of the Hemsworth brother combo running through her head.

We laughed together, and suddenly I knew everything would be okay.

"I guess the first thing we need to do," I said when it was time to get serious again, "is find out one way or another. So, let's get to the pharmacy and buy you a test, little mama."

Eva's face blanched and she covered her stomach with both hands. "Oh, God. Don't call me that. I'm so not ready for that."

CHAPTER **EIGHTEEN**

Well, I was going to be an aunt. Or was it a second cousin?

Oh, who cared how the relationship worked; Eva was pregnant any way you looked at it. The world was coming to an end.

I spent the rest of the morning and most of the afternoon with her, soothing her frazzled nerves. I managed to make her laugh a few times, but mostly I handed her tissue after tissue. We talked about her future, about what she wanted to do with her situation, and how she was going to tell her parents and Alec.

I think she was more worried about telling Alec than Aunt Mads and Uncle Shaw.

"He's not the one, ReeRee. I can tell you that right now. He and I aren't going to last. He's never once looked at me the way Mason looks at you, and you two are apparently *just friends*."

I straightened my shoulders. "How does Mason look at me?"

Eva shook her head and sighed wearily. "If you don't know, I'm certainly not going to tell you. I still think you should stay away from him. You have less future with him than I do with Alec. Jeez-us. But Alec is going to flip when he hears this."

I was too busy thinking about Mason to answer. But really, how the heck did he look at me?

"Shit!" I sprang off my couch, remembering the last time he'd looked at me, before I'd shut the door in his face. "Sarah's party. I totally forgot. It started five minutes ago. I'm sorry, E. I have to go."

I rushed to my room and grabbed my gift. Eva was struggling to her feet, looking panicked as I reentered the living room. "But—"

I held up a hand. "Chris and Liam. Chris and Liam," I reminded her. "It'll be fine. I'll return in a few hours and we can continue where we left off. Okay?"

Eva bit her lip but nodded. "Don't forget about me."

"Never." Glad our relationship was somewhat restored since the afternoon I'd caught her macking on Mason in the library, I gave her a quick, impulsive hug. "I love you, E. Everything will be fine. Trust me." Then I was out the door.

Dang it, how could I forget about Sarah? I had to be the worst babysitter ever.

Five minutes later, I skidded my car to a sloppy halt in front of the Arnosta house. Jittery adrenaline roared through my veins.

I jumped into the birthday festivities with both feet.

"I'm so sorry I'm late." Breathless, I blew through the front door without knocking. "I lost track of time while I was writing a paper for school. I know..." I paused to grin and pose in a jaunty kind of position, because the tension in the air almost choked me as soon as I entered. "I'm a total geek that way."

Then I turned toward the three young girls I didn't recognize. They hovered in a pack together on the opposite side of the room from Sarah. "Hi, I'm Reese," I told them, striding forward to shake their hands. "I'm Sarah's evening sitter."

Brittany, Leann, and Sorcha introduced themselves, giving me stiff smiles and casting uncomfortable glances at Mason and Sarah, who were crowded together by the loveseat.

"Well, it's nice to meet you guys. I'm sure we're going to have a blast today. Sarah is always the life of the party. Which reminds me, I need to give the birthday girl a huge hug, like right now."

I hopped over to Sarah and leaned down to enfold her into my arms before I waved her gift in front of her, letting her hear the items inside rattle. "I think you're going to love it." I set it among the pile of other gifts on the coffee table.

Sarah looked absolutely miserable. I swear tears were gathering in her eyes, and the anger oozing off Mason kind of shocked me. He wouldn't stop glaring at Sarah's classmates.

I rubbed my hands together. "So...where's Dawn?"

Mason sliced his scowl to me. Through gritted teeth, he hissed, "She's in the kitchen, setting out the food."

"Great." Ignoring his nasty mood, I forced a huge smile. "I'm starving. Let's help her." Hooking my arm through his, I dragged him to his feet and patted Sarah's shoulder as I passed. "We'll be right back, little buddy." As soon as I had Mason in the hallway, I hissed, "What the hell did I miss?"

"Brilliant idea to invite the classmates," he muttered. "They've been ignoring her the whole time and won't even stand on the same side of the room as her."

I rolled my eyes. "Well, what did you expect, with you hovering over her like a pissed off guard dog? I swear, you were foaming at the mouth as you stared at those poor little girls. I'm surprised they haven't run screaming from the house yet."

"Poor little girls, my ass. We invited every brat in her class, and only *three* of them showed up, the three who openly confessed they were only here because their parents forced them to come. Sarah is *crushed*."

Our conversation abruptly halted when we entered the kitchen to find Dawn rushing around frantically, taking ice cream out of the freezer and setting it by a bowl with no punch in it.

"Hey, Dawn," I greeted. "You look a little harried. Why don't you go visit with the guests? Mason and I can take care of this."

"Oh, Reese, you're a saint. Thank you." Dawn sent me an exhausted, yet relieved, smile—something her son had yet to do. "I've been scrambling all morning to get this party ready. It'll be nice to get off my feet for a bit."

As she left the kitchen, Mason muttered, "Thanks for volunteering me."

"What?" I asked, shocked by his bitterness... towards me. I mean, hello, I'd just walked in the freaking door. "What did *I* do?"

"Where *were* you?"

"I told you; I was at home, writing a paper." Yeah, yeah, that was a total lie. I'd finished that paper last night before my mother had called. But I couldn't tell him about Eva. She hadn't even told Alec or her parents yet.

Finding the punch mix sitting in a pitcher in the fridge, I grabbed it to pour it into the bowl as I rattled on. "It's actually a pretty interesting subject for my Brit Lit class. We had to read Chaucer in Middle English, which totally sucked monkey butt, and then translate it into today's English. But let me tell you, *The Canterbury Tales* is not just some sweet, innocent fairytale. I mean, I'm still pissed the rapist ended up in a happily ever after romance, but—"

"I don't care about your *paper*, okay." Mason threw his hands into the air. "My sister is about to cry in there. I wanted this to be the best birthday ever...but she *hates* it."

My mouth dropped open. "Oh, my God. Is it your time of the month, or what? I *said* I was sorry. I honestly lost track of time. And it *will* be the best birthday party ever. I swear. We just need to get past that first stage of awkwardness and everything will be fine. Trust me."

Running his hands through his hair, Mason watched me begin to cut the cake. Since it didn't have any cool design on it, or even an awesome slogan like *Happy Birthday, Sarah*, I assumed it was safe to cut.

"I'm sorry," he immediately relented, clutching the back of the kitchen chair and bending forward to blow out a breath. "It's just...After that thing with Eva this morning, I wasn't sure if you were going to come. Then you were late, and I thought—"

"Hey." I paused after sinking my knife into a thick layer of frosting. Keeping my voice gentle, I set the knife aside and reached for his hand, forcing him to look at me. "Don't worry about Eva, okay? We talked. She isn't going to go to the police. I swear to you, you don't have to worry about her."

His eyes were still slightly bloodshot from his night of gin. They penetrated me with meaning as he squeezed my fingers. "That wasn't the part I was worried about."

I frowned, trying to remember what other part there had been, and I realized he must mean the part where Eva had told him he wasn't good enough for me.

I let go of his hand to slap his shoulder. "Oh, whatever. You know you can't get rid of me that easily. I'm going to be that annoying friend who never leaves you alone."

His shoulders relaxed as he watched me return to cutting the cake. But his eyes remained tormented. "Promise?"

I grinned and winked. "Cross my heart and hope to die."

He snorted at my joke, but the tension in his shoulders settled. For a microsecond, anyway. Then he winced. "That's not all. Mom went and invited our *landlady* to the party. And she said yes."

"Oh, that's nice," I started, scooping up the first sliced piece to wiggle it onto a plate. Then it struck me. I glanced at him. "Wait. Is this the same landlady who was your first—"

I broke off as he seared me with a threatening glare. "Right," I finished slowly. "Well...this should be fun."

I couldn't wait to meet his cherry-popping, cougar pimp landlady again. Said no one *ever*.

Mason spun away to pace the kitchen, much the same way he'd paced my living room the night before. He even ran his hands through his hair, making it all sexy and tousled, which wouldn't do. I so did not want the cougar to see him looking sexy and tousled.

"I hate it when she comes over," he ranted quietly. "She always manages to find a way to corner me somewhere and *talk*. It makes my skin crawl."

Grabbing his arm when he passed, I paused in my slicing duties to pat his hair back into place. He was still too sexy for my comfort, but his locks no longer held that just-rolled-out-of-bed look. Standing passively before me, he let me groom him as his eyes ran over my face.

"Do you want me to protect you from the mean old cougar?" I asked sympathetically.

He dropped his head and leaned in toward me as if he wanted to rest his face on my shoulder. "Yes."

"Done." I grinned and licked frosting off the butter knife.

He glanced up and his lips quirked with amusement. "You got a little something." Stepping closer, he reached out and gently rubbed his thumb slowly—oh, my God, so agonizingly, deliciously slowly—over the corner of my lip. When he withdrew his hand, there was a dab of pink frosting on his finger.

Feeling a little breathless and dazed, I flicked out my tongue to the spot where I could still feel an echo of his touch. I was tempted to dip up a finger full of more frosting straight off the top of the cake and intentionally smear it all over my mouth just so he'd touch me like that again. But I was a good girl. Drawing in a shuddered breath, I watched him stick his thumb into his mouth and suck the icing away.

Dear God. My bra suddenly felt itchy around my way-too-sensitive girly parts, and my panties were no longer all that comfortable either. I'd never grown so turned on, like full-out aroused, by simply looking at a guy before, as in, one more lick of frosting would have me screaming out a healthy release.

But Mason Lowe let off some powerful phero-mones. My body soaked them in and begged for more.

As if he knew he was causing all my hormones to whimper and squirm, his eyes heated and he swayed toward me. A foot of space between us became six inches. Then three.

Danger. Danger, Will Robinson, my heart screamed, thudding against my ribcage as if it were pounding on the door to my head to get my attention and pull me back to reason.

Holding my breath, I turned away and snagged up the can of mixed nuts to open the lid. "You know, I might've been saving that frosting for later."

His chuckle was strained. "But you know me. If you have food on you, I'm bound to steal it."

"True." I ripped off the freshness seal to the nuts before offering him some.

"See, you *do* know me." With a sensual grin, he took out a handful.

His fingers lingered in the jar, so I frowned. "Don't take them all. The guests might want some."

His grin fell flat. "Those *guests* better start treating my sister right, or they can kiss my ass."

Not fair. If anyone was getting the honor of touching his perfect, tight tush, it really should be me, not a bunch of snobby little teens who were upsetting his sister. Really.

"Don't worry," I told him with a wink. "I have a plan for the little children. They'll be eating out of Sarah's hand before the end of the day."

Mason shook his head. "You're smiling a bit too evilly right now. I don't know whether to be awed or scared."

"Awed," I answered as I fluttered my fingers over the rough stubble on his cheek with flair. "Always be awed of me."

He smiled and swayed close, looking drugged

by my touch. "I usually am."

His reaction did naughty things to me. Things I loved but couldn't think about right now. What was important was that I had successfully calmed all his frazzled nerves. Damn, was I good or what?

But with Mason pacified, it was time to save my little buddy.

CHAPTER **NINETEEN**

"**W**e've got food," I cheered as I entered the living room in front of Mason with my arms loaded with plates full of cake and ice cream and mixed nuts. Serving Sarah first, I set her treat on the TV tray beside her chair and manually placed the plastic fork in her hand. "Here you go, my lovely. I made sure you got the most frosting on your—" I gasped. "Oh, my God, we didn't sing happy birthday and let you blow out the candles."

"Sarah has too much trouble with candles," Mason answered as he gave his mother a plate of food and then handed another to Leann. "We usually skip that part."

"Oh. Well, we could still sing to her, couldn't we?" Since Dawn looked too relaxed in her La-Z-Boy with the feet kicked up to organize a song, I began singing as I passed out snacks to Sorcha and Brittany.

Thankfully, Mason and his mom and the three guests sang along with me. Afterward, I clapped, and everyone followed suit.

"We'll be right back with drinks," I said.

Mason stumbled after me as I grabbed his arm and dragged him along.

"See," I said once we hit the hallway. "That wasn't so bad."

He snickered. "Probably because you didn't give anyone else a chance to talk."

Not appreciative of his teasing, I jabbed him in the ribs with my poky pointer finger. "Just keep watching, buddy. You're about to behold the miracle that is Reese."

"Okay," he relented on another laugh. "I'll trust you. But Mom didn't have to sit over by the brats and totally ostracize Sarah like that."

"She's *probably* trying to make them feel more comfortable." Entering the kitchen, I handed him four cups of already poured punch.

Scowling as he juggled them in his arms, he muttered, "Well, it's not helping *Sarah* feel more comfortable."

"Hey." I would've told Mason to calm down and picture Chris and Liam too. But sadly, I don't think that would've worked on him. Guys could be no fun sometimes. "I have a plan."

Instantly, I remembered when he'd said that very phrase last night, right before his fingers had—

I shuddered and shook my head, refusing to go there. So not the time.

After making sure everyone had what they needed, Mason and I served ourselves and joined the group, sitting together on the only piece of furniture left in the living room—the loveseat. Talk about a giant tease, being cozied up next to him like we were a couple.

Though the three guests were almost finished with their cake, I said to Sarah, "Why don't you open your gifts while we all eat."

"That's a good idea." Dawn kicked down her footrest so she could pick up one present off the coffee table and hand it to her daughter.

"Good thinking," Mason leaned close to murmur acerbically in my ear, tickling the sensitive skin on my neck with his warm breath. "Hurry the torture along so we can get this over with as soon as possible."

I liked him being this close to me a little too much. I even liked the smell of roasted nuts on his breath. Needing space before I lost it and threw myself at him, I elbowed him away, whispering, "Behave."

He snorted but moved respectfully back to his side of the loveseat, moodily shoveling cake into his mouth.

Sarah dove into the unwrapping ceremony with relish. Her classmates even wandered closer as she ripped open the first gift. She was so excited, she almost fell out of her wheelchair when she saw her shiny new charm bracelet from Mason.

"Thank you. Thank you, Mason, thank you," she kept saying, her smile wide and ecstatic.

It took a few minutes for Dawn to get it latched around her wrist, but Brittany, Leann and Sorcha oohed and ahhed when they slunk in toward Sarah enough to examine the swanky piece of jewelry.

"That's really pretty," Sorcha murmured, envy glittering in her gaze. "I've always wanted a charm bracelet."

I grinned at Mason and patted his knee, letting him know what a good job he'd done picking out the bracelet. He glanced at me and flushed almost bashfully.

I felt honored that Sarah wanted to open my gift last. I had actually gotten her two things and wrapped them in separate boxes, only to rewrap those together in one. Sarah seemed thrilled to get to unwrap more once she opened the outer package.

"You got her *two* things?" Mason hissed accusingly in my ear.

With a triumphant grin, I tossed my hair. "Of course."

He narrowed his eyes. "Suck up."

"You know it." I nudged my knee against his and winked.

Dawn probably thought I was the devil when she helped Sarah open the first. "It's...oh, my." She shot me a quick glance and in a small voice mumbled, "A makeup kit."

I could see on her face, no way in hell was she letting Sarah wear any of it out of the house, but maybe we could still put it on when I was baby-sitting, or if I had my way, in about thirty seconds.

The music notes charm for her bracelet—to remind Sarah of the first night we'd danced together—had a much better reception from Dawn. But in Sarah's eyes, I think it tied with the makeup. Her entire face gleamed with pleasure and thanks when she looked at me.

As her mom helped her put the new charm on, I turned my attention to the guy lounging beside me. "Do we make a good present-giving team or what?"

I lifted my hand to fist bump with him.

Giving in to a reluctant smile, he obliged me. We were in the middle of clashing our knuckles together when the front door blew open.

"Woo hoo. I heard there was a birthday party here today."

A huge box, wrapped in Mickey Mouse paper, crowded the entrance before it lumbered inside and turned to the side to the reveal Mrs. Garrison.

My cheerful smile died a tragic death.

This was the first time I'd seen her in daylight. I was expecting something totally different, maybe leathery, wrinkled skin from tanning too much, gaudily applied makeup, and tight leopard print spandex. But this woman was classy. Elegant. Her capris and blouse were stylish, conservative and age-appropriate. And, oh, my God, she had a Burberry purse hanging from her shoulder, the very design I'd been drooling over on eBay for, like, ever.

Now I really hated her.

Mason's thigh, which was pressed against mine, tensed. I wanted to reach for his hand and give it a supportive squeeze, but I was a little too shocked by the stranger who entered behind Mrs. Garrison.

Leaning in close, I breathed, "Who's he?"

"No clue." Mason shook his head slightly, his confused gaze settling on the man.

But Mrs. Garrison quickly doused all our curiosities. After setting the oversized box on the floor in front of Sarah, she introduced him. "Everyone, I would like you to meet my fiancé, Ted. Ted, this is Dawn..."

As she dragged him over to Mason's mom, I snuck a quick glance at Mason.

I swore to myself I wouldn't hurt him if he appeared to be jealous in any way of the landlady's new man. But by God, if he looked jealous in *any way*—

He didn't. Honestly, he looked shocked as he gawked at Mrs. Garrison's fiancé. Then he turned to me, and I saw relief and excitement in his eyes. "Thank God," he mouthed the words even as a smile lit up his face.

I squeezed his leg and grinned back. "Guess

you won't be needing my protective services after all."

"And Reese," Mrs. Garrison called, breaking into our moment. "I had no idea you'd be here today. Hello, again."

"Hey, Mrs. Garrison," I said, smiling sunnily at her.

Damn, I was such a good actress, though really, it wasn't all that hard to act happy to see her when I was so ecstatic to learn she wouldn't be messing with Mason ever again.

She had a fiancé now. *Woot, woot*!

After Sarah's reaction to both Mason's and my gifts, the opening of her last present was anti-climactic. But she graciously told Mrs. Garrison thank you when Dawn pulled an enormous stuffed bear from the box for her to see.

Mrs. Garrison looked at Dawn and puckered her face. "What did she say?"

Narrowing my eyes, I leaned forward. "She said thank you."

The landlady sent me a quick, glacial glance, and I swear in that brief look, she wanted to scratch my eyes out. But then her lips pursed into a tight, gracious smile. "Oh."

She didn't bother to look at Sarah again. Turning away from me, she looped her arm through Ted's and struck up a conversation with Dawn.

Sarah had tossed her bear aside and was staring longingly at her makeup, so I took this as my cue. Popping off the loveseat, I abandoned Mason and approached the wheelchair.

"So, Brittany, Leann and Sorcha," I called. "Do you guys want to help me put this makeup on Sarah? I think I have the perfect color combination that would look so boss on her."

Makeup and thirteen-year-olds always got

along, so the three classmates readily agreed and crowded around me. With their help, and Sarah's input, we dolled her up just right. Even her new friends looked awed by the outcome.

"Wow. You're so pretty," Leann cooed, sounding startled by Sarah's beauty.

Tickled by their praise, Sarah wanted to put makeup on all three of them next. When no one objected to that, we beautified the other three teens. I mostly oversaw the event as the girls jabbered and discussed what would look best on each other.

Just as I finished putting eyeliner on Sorcha, I lifted the mirror for her to examine herself. She smiled, pleased, and thanked me. Then she spotted something on the floor next to me and yelped. "Eww! A spider!"

Not to be outdone in the presence of an eight-legged creature, I had to scream louder.

"Where? Where?" When I spotted it, I jumped onto the couch to escape, my shriek gaining volume. "Oh, my God, it's huge. *Mason!*"

I put on such a show I had all three of Sarah's classmates scrambling and squealing, hopping onto the sofa cushions with me to get away from the arachnid.

"Someone save Sarah!" I cried, too petrified to wheel her to safety myself.

Thank God, Sorcha latched a hand around her chair and yanked her away from the huge, hairy spider that leered up at us as if he wanted us all for dinner.

"What the hell?" Mason detached himself from the landlady, who at some point had stolen my empty spot on the loveseat and was sitting by him—oops, I guess I sucked in my protective duties. He leapt across the room to the rescue. "What's wrong?"

The four of us on the couch pointed, and Sarah tried to point with her overactive arms.

"Oh." Mason straightened, looking relieved as he spotted the beast. "It's just a wolf spider."

Just a wolf spider? My mouth fell open. Was he *seriously* serious?

"I wasn't asking what kind it was," I roared. "Just *kill* it!"

He laughed. Yes, the bastard laughed as if spider murder was some kind of joke. He had no idea just how much peril his life was in for laughing at me. Honestly, have you ever been so freaked-out scared that you could bawl and commit murder in the same breath because someone thought your fear was *funny*? Well, I had jumped off the high dive and was swimming in a whole vat of that kind of crazy.

One more laugh, and Mr. Lowe might as well pick out the flowers I'd be leaving at his grave.

"It's harmless," he reassured. "Jeez, Reese. I thought you would be more of a humanitarian than this."

"Not when it comes to gross, hairy, eight-legged freaks. That thing is bigger than me."

He rolled his eyes. "It is not."

Now he was shaking his head as he chortled over my phobia. My claws extended and I was about to pounce on him for finding amusement in my terror when the spider saved his life by distracting me.

I screamed and nearly tackled Brittany in my frantic lurch to leap away from the edge of the couch. "Oh, my God! It moved. Kill it, kill it, kill it."

I certainly knew how to lead an upheaval because the girls started shrieking—even Sarah—begging Mason to exterminate the spider.

He sent me a vexed frown that seemed to say, *look what you started.*

I didn't care. The spider was still alive and that was not cool.

"What am I supposed to kill it with?" he demanded, looking harassed.

My hysteria rising to titanic proportions, I shrieked, "With your big freaking foot, you idiot. You have what, like, a size twenty shoe. Smash that thing."

"I wear a size *twelve*." He scowled, clearly insulted.

"I don't give a flying flip if you wear a size two, just step on it before it gets away."

And so the chant started, quickly gaining followers...and volume. "Smash it. Smash it. Smash it."

Mason started laughing. He shook his head with resigned humor and stomped his foot down over the wolf spider.

"Did you get it? Did you get it?" I clutched Leann's arm, probably cutting off her circulation as I held my breath in tense anxiety.

Mason lifted his foot and showed me the big black smudge on the carpet. "Handled," he reported proudly.

I screamed out my joy. "Oh, my God, *thank you*." I really hadn't planned on launching myself at him, but one second I was standing on the sofa, too relieved to think properly, the next, I was flying through the air, arm opens as I tackled my best good gigolo friend.

He barely caught me, a grunt of surprise gasping from him as I knocked the wind out of his lungs. We stumbled backward a few steps before he found his footing and latched an arm around my waist to brace me against him. Grateful, I hugged him hard and buried my face in that comfortable little nook at the base of his neck.

He was solid, and real, and warm, and smelled amazing. As soon as I hugged him, I realized how much trouble I'd just gotten myself into. I liked pressing against him. Too much. I didn't want to let go. But we were standing in a room full of people, one of which was his mother, another of which paid him money to have sex with her.

Awkward.

I cleared my throat and pulled back just enough to grin up at him, thinking quick to keep the situation funny instead of utterly uncomfortable. "Mason Lowe," I sighed out in a dreamy voice, purposely overdramatizing my words as I fluttered my lashes like a B-rated actress. "You're my hero."

He rolled his eyes and cracked out a laugh. Putting a hand to my forehead, he nudged me off him. "You're such a dork."

I shrugged and thankfully didn't have to respond because all the girls who'd been shrieking on the couch with me leapt off behind me so they could hug his waist too and praise him for saving them from the mean, scary spider.

After he accepted the praise from them, he turned to Sarah and bent down to hug her. "You're...my...hero...too," she told him in her halting voice.

He looked like he might start bawling. Cupping her cheek, he grinned at her and murmured, "For you. Always."

Damn. Now I wanted to bawl.

But really, did he have to be so utterly sweet when it came to his sister?

Without wanting to, I fell a little bit further than a mere crush. I was already halfway in love with this man.

~$~

After all the spider drama, Sarah wanted to dance. It was all her idea, I swear.

With Dawn's permission, I pulled up LMFAO on my phone and blasted "Sexy and I Know It," from the tiny speakers. The other girls loved how I flipped Sarah's wheelchair to manual and twirled her around the kitchen floor. They all wanted to take their own turns giving her a spin.

Mason had followed us back to the kitchen and stood just inside the opening of the hall to watch. Though he folded his arms over his chest much the same way they'd been folded when I'd first arrived to the birthday party, he at least looked relaxed, as if he might actually be having fun.

When I caught his gaze, I wrinkled my nose at him. He grinned back and rolled his eyes.

Spinning away, I bumped my hip into Sorcha's, and we boogied together while Leann spun Sarah.

"Mason," Sarah called. "Your turn." She waved him to her.

He wasn't the type to deny his little sister anything, so he pushed from the wall and strolled forward. As the two of them began to "dance," I backed away from the scene so it wouldn't get too crowded. I'd just rested my back against the very doorjamb Mason had been using when I felt a presence at my side. I looked over to find Mrs. Garrison, sans her fiancé.

Wow, were he and Dawn *still* talking about plants in the front room together? Once she and Ted had begun, they'd fallen deep into a heated discussion over perennials.

"Hi again," I said, trying to be cheerful when I

just wanted to escape the woman who'd turned Mason into a prostitute. Well, okay, I wouldn't mind chopping off her hair and stealing her purse first and *then* escaping, but...you get the drift, right?

"Hello, Reese," she murmured with a regal nod to me before turning her attention to Mason.

I shivered from revulsion as I saw a predatory gleam enter her expression, as if she truly believed she owned him.

A fissure of fear worked up my spine. When she'd introduced Ted to us, I'd been so sure that meant she was done with Mason. But the way she watched him now, I knew she wasn't.

"Nice...nose ring," she said, her eyes still on him.

I cleared my throat and played along. "Thanks. My cousin talked me into getting it." Totally pissed that she wouldn't release him from her gaze, I added, "You know, you have the perfect shape of nose to get one too."

Finally, she glanced askance at me and laughed. "Oh, sweetie. I'm way too old to be getting something like that."

I think she was trying to cut me down and make me feel immature, but...I didn't fall for her intimidation tactics so easily. Besides, I loved and embraced my immaturity.

I cocked my head to the side and gave her an innocent smile. "Really?" Sounding intrigued, I played with a piece of my hair that was so much younger and healthier than her frizzy, old mess full of split ends. Okay, fine. I didn't see any frizz or split ends on her, but she totally deserved both. "I didn't take you for the type to let a little thing like *age* bother you."

Directing my gaze to Mason, I made my

meaning obvious. When I turned back to her, she went still and her face drained of color. A muscle in her jaw twitched and her eyes narrowed and hardened.

Ooh, the bitch didn't like me knowing her little secret.

Score one for Reese-meister, the contender. Boo-yah.

"Hmm." Turning on her heel, she strolled back down the hall to the front room, where the rest of the *older* adults still were.

Ending his dance with a kiss to Sarah's cheek, Mason stepped backward to stand beside me.

"I don't know what you said to scare her off," he said from the side of his mouth, "but I think I love you for it." His eyes glinted a warm pewter as he grinned at me. Then he flashed forward to dance with Leann.

I stared after him, too affected to respond. I knew he'd been teasing. But the l-word coming from him sounded so darn amazing. It made me tingle from head to toe.

I was still glowing like a love-struck idiot when his pants rang.

He let go of Leann to dig his hand into his pocket and pulled out his cell phone. When he read the ID on his screen, he sliced me an awkward look. Swiftly turning away, he murmured, "Excuse me," and hurried into the back bathroom before he answered.

Acid swirled through my veins. There could be only one reason he wouldn't want anyone to hear his conversation.

He was speaking to a client.

I tried to shrug it off—honest—but I couldn't.

What he'd said to Dr. Janison in the library on Thursday must've been a complete lie, because he hadn't stopped scheduling clients at all. He was setting up a meeting with one right now. And he'd almost gotten caught by a husband last night.

Heartache cramped my chest. My throat went dry and my eyes moist.

Why I kept doing this to myself, letting the hope grow up like weeds around me and choke out all my common sense, I didn't know. I could never be anything more than just a friend to Mason Lowe.

Since it was beginning to get dark outside, and I'd been freaked out since my mom's phone call the night before, I took this as my cue to leave. I wanted to be home before the sun set with all my doors and windows locked and my Taser and mace strapped to both of my hands.

Besides, Eva might still be waiting for me. She needed me. Mason obviously did not.

I didn't wait for him to get off the phone. I hugged and kissed Sarah goodbye, waved a friendly farewell to her friends, and slipped out the back door, hurrying to my car before anyone could stop me.

CHAPTER **TWENTY**

I hated homework. Always had.

Before I had started kindergarten, my older sister, Becca, had told me my teacher would give me a homework assignment if she thought I was dumb. And sure enough, at the end of my very first day of school, my teacher, Miss Zeigler, had clasped her hands together cheerfully.

"For homework, I want all of you to go home and practice writing the letter A."

I'd promptly stuck out my bottom lip and burst into tears, thinking I was the ultimate epitome of stupid.

Through the years, I'd slowly overcome homework apprehension and had yet to bawl over another class assignment. However, the urge to sob like my old kindergarten self bubbled to the surface the next Tuesday morning when my General Virology professor gleefully doled out eight pages of research questions and then announced we'd go over the answers the next time class met.

That gave me forty-eight hours to look up and find fifty responses that were in no way easy or simple to uncover.

That evening, I had two textbooks flipped open and three handouts spread across the table in front of me. Around me, the college library stayed fairly quiet, yet every scrape of a chair, shuffle of paper, or cough from a passing patron distracted me.

The guy sitting next to me, leisurely rubbing the toe of his shoe up and down my shin, didn't help matters either. I wanted to tell Bradley to scram, but he was a part of my Tuesday evening study group, though I wasn't too sure *why* he was a member. He didn't seem too interested in the whole concept of actually doing homework. I figured he must've joined hoping to get the answers solved for him.

Thus far, I had gone with the whole "I'm trying to ignore you" plan. But unfortunately, he wasn't catching the hint.

Across from us, Ethan Riker hovered over his own textbook as he squinted through thick-rimmed glasses and worked out what appeared to be a particularly difficult problem. I frowned as I glanced over and noticed he was three questions ahead of me.

Gasp! Not acceptable.

Clenching my teeth in competitive irritation, I once again focused on my worksheet and suddenly wished Mason were a Virology major. *He* had never tried to play footsie with me when we'd studied together—though with him, it would have been welcomed—and I had always worked faster than him.

But no, Mason was working toward an electrical engineering major. The buzzkill.

Besides, I was still avoiding him. Kind of. Okay,

not at all. But I hadn't seen him since Sunday evening at Sarah's party because he was back to keeping his distance from me.

I nearly jumped out of my chair when I felt a very bare toe creep over my calf. Eww! If Bradley was rubbing some nasty foot fungus onto me, he was so dead.

As I scooted my chair a couple of inches away from him, he didn't get the hint.

"Hey, Reese?" he whispered.

Not daring to give him any more incentive to harass me, I didn't even glance up as I murmured, "Hmm?" in the utmost distracted tone I could fake.

"Can you help me find which animal the prion disease, scrapie, affects?"

I almost groaned. That was part of the first question on the worksheet. Good God Almighty. Bradley needed to get a move on it if he was going to finish the handout tonight. And he really needed to get his grubby feet off me before I kicked him.

Seriously.

Seeming to have mercy on me, Ethan looked up. "It's sheep. Says right here in the textbook on page thirteen."

"Oh," Bradley mumbled unenthusiastically. "Thanks," He sent a not-so-grateful look Ethan's way. As he jotted down the answer, I glanced across the table. I wanted to send Ethan a discreet *Thank you for getting him off my leg* smile, but he already had his nose buried back in the worksheet.

And, damn it, now he was four questions ahead of me. Bradley lifted his face, turned toward me and opened his mouth as if he was going to ask for help on the second question. My teeth grated. On the edge of losing my cool completely, I seared him with an evil, don't-you-dare glare.

Before Bradley could speak—or even attempt

to—and I could blow up and tell him to keep his toes off me, a voice broke over the intercom. "The library will be closing in twenty minutes."

Ah...saved by the closing library.

Next to Ethan, Debby slapped her book shut. "Thank God. I'm so out of here. I can't answer another question on this stupid assignment tonight."

Chase, who was sitting between Debby and Bradley, followed suit. "Who the hell cares about virus classifications anyway?"

Bradley watched with wide eyes as both Debby and Chase began to pack their things. It was a little too obvious he didn't want to stick around the last twenty minutes either. And since I hadn't fallen under the spell of his icky leg-massaging efforts, he no doubt wanted to flee with the others.

"Well, I should get ready for work," he said.

As the three deserters stood simultaneously, I lifted my gaze toward Ethan, who was glancing expectantly back at me.

"You going to leave now too?" I asked.

He shook his head. "Nope. I can't. This is the only night I have time to study. And I need to get this stuff done."

I let out a relieved breath. "Good." Great, actually. Ethan was the only group member I liked to study with...even if he did work faster than me. "It's the only free night I have, too."

He studied me with a slight smile before shaking his head and looking at his homework. "Uh...did you find the answer to number eight? I had to skip it because I couldn't find anything."

Tickled he actually needed *my* help, I checked my work. "Oh, that one was in the worksheet Professor Chin passed out in class last Thursday."

Ethan muttered something irritable under his breath. Propping his arm on the table, he buried his face in the crook of his elbow with a defeated groan. "I *knew* I should've gone to class that morning, but I was so tired after working late I couldn't even drudge up the energy to turn off the alarm clock."

I grabbed my copy of the worksheet and passed it across the table to him. "You can use mine."

There was a pause before he lifted his face, sent me a mystified stare, and then slowly slid the sheet from my hand. "Thanks." A second later, he asked, "Mind if I make a copy of this?"

"Hmm?" I glanced up and wow, he looked so studious and... yummy, sitting there, looking at me.

Ethan had sandy brown hair with natural blond highlights. He must not have been a big supporter of his barber, because his locks usually looked pretty shaggy. And his glasses gave him that sexy, young professor look.

I blinked, taken aback. Wow. Ethan wasn't bad looking. How strange. I used to know whenever a guy was attractive the second I met him. But ever since Mason Lowe had entered my sphere, my hot-guy meter had bleeped out. It was as if no other male existed.

"Umm..." *Brain, Reese. Use it.* "Uh...yeah," I mumbled, furrowing my brow as if to let on that he'd broken my *homework* concentration. I ducked my face and pretended to read a passage from one of the two huge volumes in front of me.

"Yeah, you mind?" he asked. "Or yeah, I can make a copy?"

"Huh?" I looked up and gave a slight shake of my head. "Why would I mind if you made a copy?"

Belatedly, I noticed the amused glimmer in his gaze a split second before he full-out grinned. The magnetism of his smile didn't quite reach off-the-chart Mason levels, but it was pretty darn cute.

"You have personal notes in the margins," he

said. "Some people would mind."

I stared at him a moment longer before saying, "I don't mind."

His smile warmed, rising his looks a couple of notches on the Richter scale. "Well...thank you."

I watched him stroll away, considering the possibilities there, and surprisingly enough, they didn't totally suck.

"Hmm." That was nice to know. There might still be life for me after I'd totally ruined myself over a certain psycho stalker ex-boyfriend and then become completely hung up on a non-retired gigolo.

When Ethan returned, he set my worksheet down to the side of my books. "Here's your original."

"Thanks. Have you looked at number nineteen yet?"

"Just a sec." Ethan dropped into his chair and consulted his worksheet. "Yeah, I remember reading about this." Morphing out of sexy co-ed mode and back into bland study partner, Ethan flipped through one of his own numerous textbooks. "Here." Quoting a passage aloud, he read, "'Human diseases that are believed to be caused by prions are...'"

As he spoke, I scooted my chair around in order to sit next to him. He faltered in his reading to glance at me. Then he grinned, his cheeks flushed, and he kept on until he'd quoted the entire paragraph.

"There it is," I murmured. "Thanks."

"No problem." He cleared his throat and focused on his assignment.

"Oh, hey. And what Baltimore classification type did you put down for Parvoviridae?"

"I put down group two."

I soaked in his answer and continued to stare at the question before wrinkling my nose. "But isn't Parvoviridae double-stranded?"

Glancing up at the question, Ethan read it through again. "Oh, hell," he muttered. He started to erase what he'd originally put. "Good catch."

I grinned, feeling a little smug that I'd corrected the brilliant Ethan Riker.

"It's fine." I tossed my hair in my yes-I'm-awesome manner. "Would you put it into group one then?"

"Yeah," he muttered. "It'd have go there, don't you think? It's a DNA virus and it's not reverse transcribing, so..."

"Group one it is," I announced.

"May I have your attention, please?" a voice spoke from the library's speakers. "The library will be closing in five minutes."

Groaning in disappointment, Ethan looked at his homework. "I'm not going to finish this assignment before they close."

I gulped. "Neither am I." Oh, the gloom.

I had to finish the assignment tonight or I wouldn't—"Hey, how late is the student center open?"

Ethan checked his watch. "It closed an hour ago."

I rolled my eyes. "Wonderful."

Ethan's stomach growled as if it agreed, which reminded me I hadn't eaten either.

Not wanting to think about food because my kitchen shelves looked pretty bleak, I yawned and stretched, hoping to keep the sudden hunger pangs at bay.

"Have you eaten?" Ethan asked, bringing up the issue anyway.

I could've strangled him. Thanks, bud. Go and

remind me I was down to my last box of brown rice and mac and cheese. It would have to stretch until my next money installment from my parents or one of my jobs.

I shook my head no.

"Well, I'm starving." He shut his book. "If you don't mind two roommates who'll probably be playing Zombie Invasion as loud as the speakers will permit, I say we go to my dorm, where we can spread this crap out more and not get kicked out at closing. That way, we can order a pizza or something. My treat. I need to eat before I drop."

I watched him warily, wondering if he had some kind of ulterior motive behind his invitation. But when he glanced at me, he didn't look like some sex-crazed maniac who wanted to lure the first unsuspecting girl back to his lair. He looked like a tired and starving college kid who just wanted to finish his homework and go to sleep.

Realizing this was *Ethan*—not Jeremy—I was talking to, I shook my head free of concern. "I could eat. But let's go to my apartment instead. I don't have any zombie-addicted roomies who'll bother us."

Ethan looked stunned by my invite but quickly stumbled his way into accepting. When his face flushed, it finally struck me, wow, I think the guy might have a mini crush on me.

He turned suddenly awkward. "Do, uh, do you want me to follow you home then?"

"That'd be great."

I have to admit, I had an ulterior motive. I didn't want to go to Ethan's now, while there was still some daylight left, only to leave his place later on when it was dark and scary out. Plus I liked the idea of having someone else around when I got home. Eva had been at my place so much lately, I felt a little spoiled. She might have been dealing with her own issues—she still hadn't told her parents about the baby because Alec had totally flipped out when she'd told him—but her mere presence had helped keep my Jeremy terror at bay.

When Ethan followed me home and up to my apartment, he was unusually quiet. "Neat place," was pretty much all he said after he followed me inside.

"It's growing on me." I tossed my book bag onto the coffee table and scrounged up my cell phone. "Is there any specific pizza place you want to order from?"

He shook his head as he wandered curiously around the front room. "Anywhere's fine. I'll take pepperoni."

I dialed my favorite delivery and placed our order. By the time I hung up, Ethan had made his way to the refrigerator and was staring at the only picture I had pinned up with a magnet.

"Who's this?"

I grinned fondly at the snapshot of Sarah sitting in her wheelchair and perfecting a thumbs-up for the camera.

"That's the little girl I babysit. Her name's Sarah, and she is *sooo* precious."

Ethan nodded. "What's wrong with her?"

I scowled and wanted to snap, "*Nothing's wrong with her. She's perfect in every way*," but I knew what he meant.

"She has cerebral palsy. It kind of freaked me out a little when I first met her," I confessed. "But once you spend five minutes in her company, you don't see the wheelchair at all. She's just...she's a bundle of sunshine."

"She sounds special."

"She is. Oh! You might know who her brother

is. He goes to Waterford too. Mason Lowe?" I don't know why I had to say his name aloud. It just tumbled out of me.

Ethan snapped alert. "Mason Lowe? Yeah, I know who Mason is. *He's* her brother?"

I nodded. "Yep. He could tell you how awesome Sarah is too."

"I...I've actually seen you and Mason around campus together a few times."

I shrugged, trying not to react to his curious gaze. "Sure. We became friends because of her."

"Friends," he repeated. Flushing, he glanced away. "I thought...I'm sorry. I'd just always assumed you two were...dating."

I shook my head, though my neck felt sluggish and my cheeks suddenly hot. "No. No, we're just... friends."

Sadly.

"Well, that's kind of a relief. I'd heard...I mean." He bit his bottom lip. "I've heard some pretty crazy rumors about him."

Hadn't everyone? I wanted to scream and cry and throw stuff on Mason's behalf. And on my own behalf too.

But I forced utter nonchalance. With a grin and roll of my eyes, I said, "Let me guess. You heard he's a gigolo who works at the Country Club as a front to set up all the meetings with his rich, older, female clients."

Ethan turned beet red. "Uh, yeah. Something like that. So..." He lifted his eyebrows above his glasses. "It's not true, then?"

"Umm..." I made a strange face. "Wouldn't he be, like, *in jail* by now if he was practicing prostitution so openly?"

With a shrug, Ethan said, "I guess. But it doesn't matter. I'm just relieved he's not dating you."

"Why?" I asked, immediately alarmed. "What else have you heard about him?"

"Nothing. I just..." He drew in a long breath. "I've always wanted to ask you out."

My mouth fell open. "Really?" Wow, shy Ethan Riker might not be so shy after all.

He nodded bashfully and glanced away. "So what do you say?" he pushed. "This Friday? Do you want to, I don't know, do something with me?"

I began to shake my head and turn him down. But then I paused and remembered how crushed I'd felt on Sunday when Mason had gotten that phone call and ducked into the bathroom for a private word with his client. I remembered how it had hurt to listen to him talk about how he'd almost been caught by a husband. I remembered all the reasons we could never be together.

Mason certainly wasn't acting like a monk just because he wanted to be with me. Why should I act like a nun just because he was the only person I wanted to be with?

I had no reason to be faithful. We certainly weren't dating. We could never date.

We were just friends.

And I needed to move on with my life. If I could get over what had happened with Jeremy only to get stuck on Mason, I was going to end up back on square one. Nowhere.

But I was still uncertain. "I'm supposed to babysit Sarah every Friday," I said with a wince.

When Ethan's shoulders fell and a crushed look crossed his face, I felt evil. I didn't mean to, but I quickly added, "How about Saturday?"

He instantly brightened. "Saturday would be great. Pick you up at seven?"

CHAPTER **TWENTY-ONE**

My stomach churned through the rest of the week. I think it was filled with a nice, acidic regret. And maybe some guilt too, though that one made less sense. I wasn't attached to anyone; I shouldn't have felt any qualms about telling Ethan I'd go out with him. But I did.

I never should've said yes. I wasn't really in the dating mood; well, not in the mood to date anyone but one person. And that one person wasn't Ethan Riker.

But that one person *was* utterly forbidden and I should move on. I mean, if his visit Saturday night to tell me about his escapades with married woman and detail his stupid plan—that totally didn't involve me—hadn't convinced me he was forbidden, then Wednesday night certainly did.

I arrived for my babysitting duties to find he had already left for work—typical—but an envelope full of money had been stuck to the refrigerator with a magnet. My name and the words *babysitting*

$ had been scribbled on the front in his heavy scrawl. Somehow he'd known exactly how much Dawn owed me.

It hit me then. Like *really, Reese, wake up and smell the lattes* hit me.

His sense of responsibility toward his family was everything to him. Everything. He didn't care if his obligations made him do things that caused him to feel trapped or had him feeling dirty until he hated a part of himself. He wasn't going to stop taking care of Dawn and Sarah in the only way he knew how. He had sold his soul to ensure every bill his mother forgot to pay was taken care of, even the fricking babysitter's bill.

A part of me hated him for that, since I was the one who got shafted because of his unwavering, altruistic commitment. But another part of me admired and respected him for his love and sacrifice for his mother and sister. He did it because he cared so much for them, and I adored the way he loved those closest to him. It made me ache to become a member of that exclusive circle.

I almost ignored the money. Its origins made me sick. Plus he needed it for important things, certainly not some of the trivial things I'd used it for, like those cute earrings I'd ordered online that totally matched my nose ring. And I didn't care if no one ever paid me another cent for spending time with Sarah. But I took it anyway, because I knew it would make Mason feel even cheaper and dirtier if I didn't.

I'd donate it to some charity, or maybe to the baby fund I had a bad feeling Eva was going to need.

And I told myself that I would only be friends with Mason from here on out. No more flirty texts, no more forbidden thoughts—okay, that one was impossible to do, but I would at least try—and sadly, no more lunches together. He didn't need me attempting to tempt him away from his goals of supporting his family.

I was set on this plan until Mason actually appeared by my table during my lunch break on Friday and plopped his bag onto the bench across from me.

"Hey." He paused to draw in a deep breath before adding, "Sweet Pea," with a large, knowing smile.

Damn. My plans to stay away and respect his decisions fizzled completely.

But I couldn't help it. I was beginning to have withdrawals. After getting to see so much of him this past weekend—literally and figuratively, wink, wink—no Mason in five days just felt...wrong. Besides, he had come to me. So even as I told myself to shoo him along, my pulse raced with joy as he seated himself.

Feigning a heart attack, I slapped my hand over my chest and gasped. "What is this? You're sitting with me...*in public*? Have the horny guy urges subsided then? Have I lost my seductive appeal completely? Say it ain't so."

He chuckled and rolled his eyes. "No. They have not subsided. I've simply come to the conclusion we're going to have to accept that the urges will probably be a permanent facet of our relationship from here on out. And if you say you can control yours, then I'll try to control mine."

I wrinkled my nose. "Big of you."

A full, throaty laugh rumbled from his chest. "That and I can't see your nose wrinkling from all the way across the courtyard. You have no idea how much I've missed that."

His cute and playful side got to me like nothing

else. Needing to control my own urges, I sighed and went back to my homework I'd been trying to work on before he'd appeared. "Yeah, yeah. I bet you're just falling behind in calculus and need my help."

Without denying it, he gave a shrug. "Since you mentioned it..." He pulled his calculus book from his messenger bag and flipped it open to the page where his homework sat, half finished. As he searched for a pencil, he asked, "What're you feeding me today?"

His smile was so fresh and alive, it sparked a piece of life back into me, something that had wilted in the past few days without a good dose of him around.

I still couldn't believe Mason was here, across the table from me, being my friend again. Without saying one sarcastic comment, I slid what was left of my mini bag of potato chips across the table to him, since I had finished all I was going to eat, and I probably would've offered him one of my most cherished lattes at this point because I was so thrilled he was here.

He nodded in approval and snagged my chip bag. "Nacho cheese. Nice." As he pulled out a handful, he glanced at me. "Turn in your English paper yet?"

I lifted my eyebrows. "Oh, so you care about my English paper *today*, huh?"

His shoulders slumped. "Reese. Come on. I'm sorry I said that to you at the party. I was in a mood." He set his hand over his heart and sent me a pout of sincere apology. "I care about *everything* you do."

I groaned to cover the whimper of melting emotions. "Okay, enough already. The bullshit around here is getting too deep to wade through."

"What?" He had the gall to look offended. "I'm

serious."

I rolled my eyes. "Whatever. So let me guess. Your landlady still thinks you and I are riding the baby-making train together, doesn't she?"

With a sigh, he dusted the nacho cheese dust off his fingers. "Pretty much."

"Wow." I sighed as if ashamed of Mrs. Garrison for her prejudiced opinion. "Why is it so hard for people to think we're just friends?"

Mason studied me a moment, his expression probing and indistinguishable, before he gave a non-answer shrug. I could tell he didn't want to discuss the topic.

"She insulted me when she had you cornered at Sarah's birthday party, didn't she?"

"Yep." This time, his distraction tactic was to open his bag and pull out my copy of *The Prisoner of Azkaban*, which I'd left with Sarah a week ago.

Snapping my fingers, I crowed. "I knew it! Typical, petty, jealous move. What'd she say? She said I have a big butt, didn't she?"

Rolling his eyes, Mason muffled out his answer from a full mouth. "She did not say you have a big butt. Trust me, your butt is...perfect."

I swallowed. Then swallowed again. I don't know why his compliments totally came at me from left field. He gave me plenty of them. Still, I was never prepared for the impact his flattering words wrought.

Not quite sure how to respond, I waved my hand and kept talking about Mrs. Garrison, because I felt petty and jealous myself. "Then what did she say about me?"

"Nothing worth repeating." He wouldn't look me in the eye as he tipped the bottom of the chip bag up to make sure he had freed every last crumb. "Don't worry about it."

My mouth fell open. "Oh, now you *have* to tell me."

What the heck had that evil cougar *said*? I knew I wasn't perfect by any stretch of the imagination. But I couldn't think of any of my body parts that were so abnormal that Mason couldn't divulge her insult.

He sent me a warning frown, asking me to drop it. So not going to happen.

"Come on," I pressed. "Just tell me. I'll be your best friend." I fluttered my lashes.

He rolled his eyes. "You already *are* my best friend."

I was? I straightened, alarmed, flattered, and extremely touched. Aww...another unprepared compliment. I blossomed with delight. "Well...thank you. But as my new bestie, you're now obligated to tell me what she said."

"Reese," he groaned.

My alarm grew. "Oh, my God. How bad *was* it?"

"It wasn't even true. So...just drop it. Please."

Oh, hell, no. "If it wasn't true, then why can't you tell—"

"Fine. She said you were an attention seeker. Okay? She said you were stealing the limelight away from Sarah on her own birthday, which wasn't—"

"Oh, my God. Did I?" I set my hand over my chest, where an acute ache had started.

I couldn't believe that witch. She'd just totally broken jealous girl code number one. When insulting the *other* woman, you went after her looks...not her personality. God. What a nasty blow below the belt.

Her dirty tactics had definitely done the job though. I felt awful.

Well played, skanky pimp landlady, well

played.

But I'd only acted so *out there* at the party to help ease the awkwardness. I'd wanted to show the other girls how sweet, and loveable, and fun Sarah was. I'd been trying to place the attention *on* her, not steal it *from* her.

"No!" Mason broke in emphatically. "I *told* you, what she said wasn't true."

"But—"

"Listen to me." He leaned partially over the table to look me straight in the eye. "Before you showed up on Sunday, my sister was absolutely miserable. The next morning, she said it was the best birthday she'd ever had. And that was because of you, got it? *You* made those other girls interact with her. And now, that tall one, Sorcha, she's even coming back on Saturday afternoon to spend the day with Sarah."

"Really?" I brightened, excited to learn this. "That's great. *Oh!* I liked Sorcha." And now, I totally loved her.

Mason shook his head and gave me a slight grin. "You are the least selfish person I know."

I wrinkled my nose. "Well...I can be a little selfish."

Okay, a lot selfish. *Jeez.* Picky much?

He didn't look convinced. "I don't see it. That day in the library...with Dr. Janison and Eva."

Wincing, I remembered.

"Every woman treats me that way, Reese. I'm not a person to them. I'm just...a good time or something vile to be avoided at all costs. And then you came along and you...you *hugged* me. You are the first person who sees me, Mason, not *sex* for sale. And that kind of compassion is not a sign of a selfish person. At all."

"I..." My lashes beat like a hummingbird's

wings, batting away any possible tears. "Well, thank you. But you *are* a person, and—"

He lifted a finger to hush me. "We're not talking about me. We're talking about you. And you are...you're..." He paused to shake his head.

"I'm...?" I prompted, not sure if I wanted to know where this was going, but my curiosity was too intrigued not to push for more.

"You're quirky...and yet conventional. Innocent but worldly. Reserved yet outgoing. Candid yet guarded. Trendy but also practical. And childlike while still managing to be mature. It's like...you're the perfect contradiction."

I gulped, gaping at him and unable to say a single word. For him to come up with that kind of explanation, he'd really had to think it through. Knowing Mason had thought of me so thoroughly took my breath away.

He stared at me a moment longer as if he wanted to say more, something probably mean-ingful enough to knock me on my butt, but he cleared this throat and glanced down. Seeing the book in his hand, he handed it across the table to me. "Anyway...here. I think I can officially say I'm addicted to *Harry Potter*. Sarah and I couldn't wait to borrow *The Goblet of Fire*. We bought our own copy and started it yesterday."

I cleared my throat, trying to catch up with the one-eighty he'd just taken in our conversation. "Wow." I swiped at my cheeks to make sure they were dry—which they were, thank you, God—before I took *The Prisoner of Azkaban* back. "You and Sarah are just cruising through the series. I'm impressed."

"That going-back-in-time scene was really cool. I couldn't put it down."

Grinning, I hugged the hardback to my chest.

"It was always one of my favorites too. Especially when they saved Buckbeak."

"I ended up reading it twice. Once when I read ahead, and then again when Sarah wanted it read to her." His eyes warmed as he smiled. "Which reminds me..."

He half stood so he could slide his hand into the front pocket of his jeans and dig something out. Curling his fingers around whatever he'd retrieved, he grinned mischievously enough to make me suspicious as he sat back down.

I leaned in slightly. "What do you have there?"

His lips spread wider. "Something for you. I had it made. This guy I know takes an advanced metal crafting class and put it together."

Totally not expecting that, I straightened. "You did what?"

He extended his hand and uncurled his fingers. "I know it's pretty crude, but I thought it might fit on your bracelet."

A tiny silver charm blinked up at me in the sunlight. My mouth fell open. His friend had somehow crafted the Harry Potter logo, making the initials H.P. with the lightning bolt in the P and everything. To me, it didn't look crude at all. It looked perfect.

"Oh, my God." I took it from his fingers with gentle reverence. "This is amazing, Mason."

"He almost ruined the surprise on Sunday when he called during Sarah's birthday party to tell me he was done. I'd been hoping he'd finish before then."

I glanced up, shocked to learn that call had been about a surprise for me...not a client setting up an appointment. And here, that had been one of the biggest deciding factors I'd had for telling Ethan I would—

I shook my head, not wanting to think about that right now. Mason had ordered a present to be made especially for me.

"I had one made for Sarah too. Yours was actually the prototype. So I think it might contain a few more mistakes."

"What mistakes?" I shook my head as I used the tiny hook that had been made to attach it to my bracelet. "It's flawless." I held my wrist up so I could see all the charms dangle. The HP was by far my favorite. I looked up with a big goofy grin, my heart full of affection. "Thank you."

He opened his mouth to answer when someone sat on the bench seat beside me. I wasn't expecting Eva today, but when I turned, I thought it would be her.

Ethan's face totally caught me off guard. He grinned. "Hey."

I fumbled. "Umm. Hi...Ethan." A blush hit me so hard I could feel it spread from the roots of my hair all the way down my neck. "I...I'm not used to seeing you on a Friday."

He chuckled. "I know. But I saw you over here and thought I'd say hi." Then he glanced across the table. "Hey, Mason." Giving a friendly wave, he seemed nothing but congenial and courteous.

And yet Mason reacted as if he'd been flipped the bird. "Riker," he bit out in a tense voice, pulling back slightly in his seat to send a suspicious, narrow-eyed stare back and forth between us.

"Oh! You two know already each other?" I blurted out, wanting to keep things as kosher as Mason obviously didn't want them to be. "Great. That saves me from making introductions because obviously...I forgot to make introductions." I snorted at my own lame joke, revealing just how nervous I was.

Ethan grinned like a gentleman, but Mason looked at me as if I'd lost my mind. My grin died a quick, painful death.

"So, I'm really excited about tomorrow night," Ethan went on. "And I forgot to ask: Was there anywhere special you wanted to go?"

"Umm..." I bit my lip, desperately trying to ignore the way Mason swung his head to gape at me. Color leeched from my face, and I grasped for reasonable thought. But why did I suddenly feel... awful?

"No," I croaked. "I can't think of anything. Just...wherever is fine. I'm not too familiar with Waterford yet."

"Great." Ethan's smile was slow and pleased. "I have a couple places in mind." He glanced at his wristwatch and let out an impatient breath. "I have to get to class. See you tomorrow."

He stood up just as quickly as he'd sat down. Then he bent toward me and stamped a quick kiss to my cheek before I even realized what he had planned.

"Whoa!" I blurted out and leaned away, even though he'd already pulled back.

He paused to squint his eyes at me questioningly. I flushed and opened my mouth to apologize. But the waves of anger coming across the table from Mason made me stop. With a tense smile, I said, "See you tomorrow."

He nodded, darted a glance to Mason, and took off.

I stared after him, biting my lip, too afraid to breathe. Maybe if I didn't mention anything, Mason wouldn't question it. But when I risked a glance his way, I knew immediately, he would question it. Big time.

"You're going out with him? *Tomorrow?*"

CHAPTER **TWENTY-TWO**

Oh, God. Oh, God. What should I tell him?

My mind went blank, so I had to stick with the truth. "Umm...yes?" The answer came out as a question and I wanted to slug myself. Why was I being so meek all of the sudden?

Probably because Mason's body looked strangely still. I mean, not that he usually fidgeted, but nothing on him even twitched, not even his hard gray eyes that bored right into me as if I'd betrayed him.

Strangely, I felt as if I *had* betrayed him.

His jaw went rigid as he looked down, staring blindly at his opened calculus book. "Why didn't you tell me?"

"I..." I floundered. "Well, for one, I haven't seen you since *Sunday*. Then I...I completely forgot about it until he showed up just now, and..." I shrugged. "By then, you already knew."

"When?" Mason demanded.

I frowned. "When what?"

"When did he ask you out?"

"Oh. Um...Tuesday night. Why?"

Mason's eyes narrowed. "I thought you had study group on Tuesday nights."

I was startled he actually remembered my schedule. "I do. I mean, I did. He's *in* my study group." When Mason flinched at that as if it physically hurt him to learn I had something in common with Ethan that I didn't with him, I rushed on, hoping my explanation somehow soothed him. "When the library closed, we weren't finished with our assignment, so he came back to my apartment and we worked on it—"

"He did *what*?" Mason boomed, looking like he wanted to jump off his bench and chase Ethan down to remove a couple of the guy's teeth...with his knuckles.

"Hey, what is *wrong* with you?" I demanded.

"Oh, I don't know," he sneered. "Maybe it's this irresistible urge I have to *break Ethan Riker's face*."

My mouth fell open. "Excuse me?"

"You heard me," he damn near bellowed again.

"Mason," I hissed, glancing around to see if anyone was staring at us. "What the hell? It's not like I have to babysit Sarah that night."

"This isn't about Sarah. And you *know* it."

Of course I knew it. But I thought we were still in denial, only flirting around the issue and holding tight to the whole just-friends lie. I had no idea he suddenly wanted to come out.

I swallowed and tried to rein in my racing nerves, having a bad feeling the rest of this conversation was going to leave me shredded inside.

"You said we were just friends." My voice went hoarse as I studied his taut features. "I thought—"

"We *are*." He glanced away and closed his eyes.

254

"Damn it. We are, but the only reason we're *just friends* is because there's no way we could possibly *ever* be anything more."

"You want..." My lungs spasmed. It freaked me out, and I understood how Sarah must feel all the time with no control over her muscles, even her breathing muscles. I couldn't catch my breath, and it scared me.

"Do you really...want more?" I whispered in a trembling voice.

The emotions leaking into his face gave him that haggard, regretful look I'd seen the first night I'd caught him in a bath towel. "Don't you?" he whispered back. Then he gave a harsh laugh and glanced away. "Or is this only sexual attraction for you?"

My chest ached. I still couldn't catch a good lungful. "You know it's not."

"Then why the hell are you so confused about why I'm flying off the handle?"

"I don't know." I winced. "Because it's easier to play dumb?" And because he'd made it abundantly clear he'd chosen his job over me. I had every right to date whomever I wanted...whether I technically felt that way or not.

"Well, you're not dumb. Don't play dumb." When he shoved his calculus book into his bag and began to gather his things, I panicked.

"Mason? What're you doing? Where are you going?"

"I'm *leaving*. What does it look like I'm doing?"

And just as quickly as the panic came, it dissolved into pissed off outrage. Slamming my hand over his half-finished calculus paper that had fluttered across the table, I jerked it out of his grasp as soon as he reached for it. When he glared at me, I scowled. "So if you can't have me, then I'm not allowed to date *anyone*? Is that what you're saying? My God, Mason. Do you realize how much of a douche bag you sound like right now?"

"*Yes*, damn it!"

The admission came so freely from his lips, I blinked, startled to actually hear him confirm it.

Chest heaving, he sent me that tortured, haggard look of his again. "I realize exactly what I sound like. And I'm trying to stop, Reese." His voice broke. "I'm *trying* here. Jesus, why do you think I'm taking off right now? If I stay, I'm only going to say something worse."

I think his agony got to me more than my own. Tears filled my eyes. When I blinked them away, he choked out a sound of misery.

"Christ, don't cry."

I probably should've warned him that once I started with the waterworks, they didn't just dry up on command.

"What do you want me to do?" I sobbed. "Do you want me to call it off? Tell him no?"

I have no idea what happened to all my girl power. A guy I couldn't have was acting like a butt because I was going to spend a little time with another man. I should be cussing him up one wall and down the next for his asshole attitude. But there I sat, in tears and begging to know what I could do to make him happy.

Man, I was whipped.

His face contorted and turned an angry red as if he was going to start bawling right along with me. But then his features cleared and he shook his head savagely. "No. Don't call it off. I want you to be happy. I'm sorry for being a drama queen. Okay? I want you to have fun with…whomever. Just have fun and be happy. Keep being you."

More tears filled my eyes. Cursing under his

breath, he practically leaped across the table to snag his homework out of my hand. Crumpling it in his fist, he shoved it into his bag.

"I have to go," he muttered, swiping the palm of his hands across his eyes before he rushed off as if the hounds of hell were after him.

As I watched him stride away, it struck me how much I'd hurt him by agreeing to go on a date with Ethan. That hadn't been my intention at all. I'd only wanted to save myself from getting hurt. I'd wanted to force Reese Randall to move on with her life. But watching him in pain ripped me up inside.

I was in love with him.

Dear God.

I was in love with a gigolo.

It was crazy insane; I was fully aware of that. But this was *Mason*. My spider killer. My leftover food vacuum. My fellow Harry Potter fan. He was my soul mate. It was easy to look past the gigolo detail when I was with him.

And so it was easy for me to scramble off my bench and fight for him.

Though he hadn't actually *run* away, he'd been moving fast when he'd left. Chasing him, I entered the main building, only to spot him nowhere in the glass-ceilinged main atrium. I glanced left down one hall with no luck. When I looked the other way, I saw his retreating back and took off in hot pursuit.

"Mason!"

He heard me and slowed to a stop but didn't turn around.

"I can't believe you just walked away from me like that," I began to rail as soon as I was ten feet away. "We are *so* not done talking about this."

He whirled around, catching me by surprise. I gasped when he grasped my arm, his grip hot and firm but not painful. Spinning me toward an opened nearby doorway, he corralled me into an empty classroom and slammed the door shut to pin me against it.

The breath rushed from my lungs as his body pressed into mine. He felt...oh, my God...really nice. Warm, protective, muscled, male. My insides wept from the beauty of it.

With a tortured groan, he lightly pounded his forehead to the door and our cheeks brushed by each other. Then he bowed his face and rested his chin on top of my shoulder.

"Was he in your apartment all night? Did he sleep on your couch? Did he touch you? Did he *kiss* you?" Another sound escaped him. A kind of sob, kind of curse. Grazing the side of my neck, he shifted his fingers around lightly until he found my scar. "Did you tell *him* the secret behind this?"

"No. Mason, stop." It was killing me to listen to his misery. When I cupped his cheek, he lifted his forehead from the door to look down at me.

His whole body shuddered, and I knew it was from regret. "God. Reese, I'm trying to be cool about this. I'm trying not to blow off the handle. And I know I'm failing. But damn..."

His thumb traced the curve of my cheekbone until he swiped away some moisture from my recent sob fest.

A look of utter wonder and sadness crossed his face.

Then he shook his head and gritted his teeth. "This sucks. He can ask you out and take you to dinner and try to steal a goodnight kiss. He can go as far into it as you'll let him take you. And I can't even compete." He grinned, though his eyes were still full of agony. "I think I fell for you the moment I heard you laugh across the campus courtyard. When I looked over and saw you, I knew. You were something different. Something incredible. I knew from that first glance that nothing was ever going to be the same again. You were...a complete game changer. Even when I realized you were sitting with Eva and might be like her, I didn't care. I wanted to know everything about you."

I shook my head, too amazed to think clearly. "And here I thought you hated me from that first glance."

He shook his head. "I never hated you. You just scared the shit out of me, so I tried to stay away. I was afraid to get to know you because I wanted to so badly. I thought surely you couldn't be as good as I'd already built you up to be in my head. Except every time I turned around, there you were, and you ended up being better than I ever imagined." His grin fell. "The more I got to know you, the more I knew I should stay away. I could only hurt you. But I could never quite stay far enough away."

As if he couldn't stay away now either, he sank closer, his breath caressing my lips. When his eyes slid closed, I knew he was going to kiss me. I wanted it more than my next meal, but I needed to be certain of one thing first.

"Are you still a gigolo?"

He froze, then drew in a breath and pulled back to send me a ragged look, begging me not to go there. "I'll always be a gigolo, Reese."

My chest collapsed in on my lungs. "No." I shook my head. "No, I don't believe that. You can stop. You can—"

"Don't you get it yet?" He stepped away some more until we no longer touched. "It doesn't matter if I stop or not. This stigma, this *curse*, will never go away. Eighty years from now, people will read my obituary and say, 'Mason Lowe? Wasn't he that gigolo?' God!" He squeezed his eyes closed and whipped his hand through his hair, grabbing fistfuls. "That even rhymes. They'll probably make a damn limerick out of me and I'll become an immortal *prostitute*."

He began to turn away but I caught his arm. "Mason, I don't care about your reputation. I don't like your past, but I don't care about that either. All I want to know about is right now. So right now... are you still having sex with other women?"

He dropped his hand from his head and studied me. I had the strangest notion he was debating with himself over whether he should lie or not. Then he winced and glanced away. "Well, I think you *do* care about my reputation. Ethan Riker is pristine white and you agreed to go on a date with *him*, didn't you?"

That wasn't fair. I clenched my teeth. "Mason."

When I reached for his arm, he lifted it to ward me back. "Don't. It's fine, okay. I'm not the type to bring home to your parents. I get it."

"No, you *don't* get it!" Growling out my frustrations, I flashed my teeth at him. "Just shut up for a second."

Blowing out a harassed breath, I massaged my aching temples. We were arguing two totally different points, and it was confusing me. I wanted to tell him I'd be proud to show him off to my mom and dad, but I had to know if he was honestly free from a certain lifestyle first.

After arching my eyebrows at him in warning to silently tell him not to stray off the topic again, I took a breath and started fresh.

"In the library that day," I said, trying a different tact, "you told Dr. Janison you weren't scheduling any more clients."

His face paled, making his eyes sparkle like polished silver. "Jesus, do you have elephant ears?

You weren't supposed to hear that."

"Well, I did. And it made me think...I thought you were... *retiring*. But then...then you came to my apartment and started in about almost getting caught by a husband, and I wasn't sure anymore."

Mason closed his eyes and bowed his head. "I lied about the husband. I haven't...I haven't taken a client since..."

"Since when?"

He shook his head. "It doesn't matter."

"Yes! It does." When he sent me a sharp glance, I snarled at the obstinate ass. "So why did you lie about the husband thing then? What really happened there?"

He winced. "Nothing. I turned down a persistent woman wanting services, and she got nasty, that's all. She called me..." He wrinkled his face into a grimace. "She called me some names. Nothing I hadn't heard before, but it left me stewing afterward, and I wanted to...I had to...I just needed to see you. I needed to be around someone who *didn't* think of me that way."

When he glanced at me, tears filled my eyes. "Oh, Mason," I whispered. "Why didn't you just tell me the truth?"

He took another step back, putting more space between us. "Because if I'd told you the truth and you knew I'd stopping whoring myself out for money, I was scared you'd let me do things to you that I was dying to do."

I pressed my hand to my aching temples. "Okay, let me get this straight. You stopped your...practice because you wanted me, and then you turned around and lied about it, making me think you were still doing it in order to keep me away."

He gulped. "Maybe."

Damn it! Would he just give me a straight answer?

I sent him an irritated glower. "That makes no sense. If you stopped so you could have me, then why did you lie to keep me away?"

"I didn't stop so I could have you. I *know* I can never have you."

I frowned. "What? Why can't you ever have me?"

"Because," he sputtered, sending me an incredulous look as if he thought I shouldn't even have to ask such a ridiculous question. "We just went over this. I could never deserve you. You're too good for me. You're out of my reach. You're...you're Reese Randall."

"You're wrong. I'm not." I wasn't really Reese Randall, and I certainly wasn't out of his reach. "All you have to do is stretch out your hand, Mason." Pressing my palm against my chest, I whispered, "I'm right here."

He shook his head. "I can't. I'm tainted."

"No." To my own doom, I stepped away from the door, going to him, my arms outstretched to hold him and soothe his wounded soul.

But he dodged around me and darted toward the escape. Yanking the door open, he paused and turned just enough to address me but not look at me. "I thought we could just be friends. But we can't. I won't be sitting with you at lunch anymore. I won't be doing anything with you anymore. I hope you enjoy your date."

When he slipped from the empty classroom, he left the door hanging open.

His departure annihilated me. And let me tell you, the gloomy, miserable, angst-ridden look *so* did not look good on me.

CHAPTER **TWENTY-THREE**

The rest of the day passed in a blur. After my fight—or whatever it was—with Mason, I drove home and skipped my afternoon classes. Eva did too. She and Alec had broken up, and when she saw my car pull into the drive, she arrived at my apartment to cry on my shoulder.

I think consoling her was the only thing that kept me from sobbing for myself. It felt as if I'd lost Mason forever.

God, maybe I had.

When E. curled up on my couch and took a nap, I called Ethan and broke off my plans with him, since I knew that was going to be a flop before it even started.

He didn't seem too surprised, though he did have the grace to sound disappointed. "Lowe didn't take the news well, did he?"

I couldn't think up a reason to lie, so I shook my head. "No, he didn't."

After a moment of silence, Ethan said, "You

know, you don't have to turn me down just because he..." He must've realized he was about to say something that would totally offend me because he stopped abruptly, his words fading into a sad chuckle. "Right. Good luck with him, then."

Good luck. Yeah, I needed more than luck to get Mason back. I needed a freaking miracle. Or maybe a crowbar to beat some sense into him. Or maybe I needed to beat some sense into myself, because hell, I couldn't tell which one of us was being the stupidest right now.

The only good thing about all this was that I was too heartbroken over Mason to worry about my paranoia over Jeremy. I still locked all my doors and checked my purse for my mace and Taser, but at least my fear had settled back down to the level it had been before my mom's fateful phone call.

Damn, had that only been last Saturday that she had called? So much had happened in the past six days. So many people had been hurt.

To avoid the pain, I decided to keep going and follow my typical routine, hoping the regularity of my actions could settle me into a blank state of blissful oblivion.

At my regular babysitting time, I arrived at Dawn's house, opening the front door without knocking and stepping inside. The television ran the evening news with the volume turned low.

I thought about calling a greeting but decided to go the sneaky route and surprise Sarah. She did like the attention of people jumping out at her and screeching, "Boo."

I had a feeling my little buddy was the type who would adore bloody, slasher, horror movies, but I wasn't ready to go there quite yet, mostly because I was definitely *not* that type. Give me romantic comedy any day of the week. Or *Harry*

Potter; that was about as dark as I got.

As I moved down the narrow passage toward the kitchen, I approached Sarah's bedroom and noticed immediately that across the hallway, Mason's bedroom door hung open.

He never left his door open. What was more, there was someone talking inside his room.

I paused. He wasn't home, was he? Crap. I hadn't paid enough attention when I'd pulled to the curb to remember if his Jeep had been sitting in the driveway or not. I wasn't sure if I could face him right now without breaking down and weeping.

But I was curious to know what his room looked like. I crept forward, stepping easily so the creak midway down the hall didn't give away my presence.

The lights were off inside, but I knew he—or someone—was in there when I heard bedsprings squeak.

The talking paused, only to start again. The voice sounded vaguely familiar, even as muffled as it was. I scanned the dark blue walls before I had a full glimpse inside, surprised he wasn't the messy type. He didn't hang many pictures and he didn't have a cluttered floor. I wouldn't have called the space stark, but he definitely wasn't a junk collector.

Then I saw his bed with a plaid comforter thrown neatly over the mattress. Mason sat on the edge, his feet on the floor as he focused all his attention on his cell phone he held in his lap. He was watching a video where a fuzzy image shifted across the small screen.

"*...be Eva instead,*" the pitchy phone speakers blared out my voice. "*Good morning, Mason. Looking good today. What say we skip classes and have some...fun.*"

My mouth dropped open as I watched a grin spread across his face. He wiped his thumb over the phone screen, touching the video version of me.

Oh, my God. He hadn't deleted that stupid, impulsively made video yet?

Oh, my God, times two. Was he watching it *again*?

I clapped my hand over my mouth because my grin kept spreading wider and wider as a smile consumed me. My eyes grew watery.

He loved me.

If this didn't prove he loved me, nothing did.

Mason Lowe loved me.

Sensing my presence, he lifted his face. When he saw me, his eyes grew big. He dropped his phone screen-down on his bed and surged to his feet. "Reese! What're you doing here?"

He was dressed to go to work, his brown loafers adorning his size-twelve feet and his pale blue Country Club shirt tucked into his pleated slacks. I had to look away because staring at him made me feel achy and full of depressing angst.

"It's Friday," I said blankly and shook my head, confused. "I always babysit on Friday."

"But..." He glanced down at his watch. "Shit. I'm running late."

I watched him scurry around to grab his cell phone and wallet. When he turned toward the doorway to find me blocking his path, and not budging, he faltered, looking a little panicked and trapped.

"I thought you might like to know I cancelled my date."

Eyes flaring with liquid heat, he grasped my elbow. "What? I told you, you didn't have to do that. Why did you cancel? Did he do something to you? Are you okay?"

"I'm fine. I just...I can't go out with him."

"You..." Mason stepped even closer, right into my personal space, his clean, musky scent invading my senses. "Why?"

I turned my face aside and wiggled my elbow out if his grip. "Now who's playing dumb?"

"Jesus." He spun away, ripping his hands through his hair. "I *knew* I shouldn't have said anything to you. I swear to God, I'm sorry. I was a jealous tool, and you deserve to date and be happy and...and live your life however you want."

His love for me showed through every pore of his being. I could tell it killed him to say this, but he honestly thought it was for the best to let me go.

At that moment, I knew. I would do whatever I had to do to make him mine. "Well, thank you, Mason," I said, gifting him with a bright smile. "I'm so glad I have your approval to live my life however I want, because I plan to do just that."

I tried to walk away, but he caught my arm, looking way too suspicious.

"Why do I have a bad feeling there's an ulterior motive behind that statement?"

"I don't know," I said. "Maybe you're para-noid." When he opened his mouth, I cleared my throat and smoothed my hand over my stomach because I think watching Eva doing that fifty times an hour was beginning to rub off on me. "Where's Sarah?"

"Right...here."

My little buddy saved me from getting more questions by rolling her chair to the doorway of Mason's room.

Without glancing at her brother, I hurried to her and spent the rest of my time with her before he left for work. He didn't get to interrogate me further.

He looked pissed as he walked out the door, though. His gaze burned into me with promise for retribution. I wasn't too certain what had gotten his panties in a wad. I hadn't threatened, warned, or intimidated him in any way. I had backed off as he seemed to *want* me to. I'd even cancelled my date for him. Yet he looked more tormented than ever.

Gah, Mason Lowe was going to be one hard shell to crack.

After he left, my evening with Sarah lagged on. She went to bed half an hour after her usual time, which was fine with me because tonight I liked her staying up with me; I *needed* her companionship. With her asleep, I trudged from her room, my shoulders dragging with depression.

Lonely, all I could think about was Mason. What if he never thought he was good enough for me? Hell, *why* didn't he think he was good enough? I wasn't anything special. Was he completely blind to all my strange habits, whiny traits, and impulsive comments? A man who could look past all that and still like what he saw in me was worth...well, he was worth everything.

I slumped to the kitchen to get myself a glass of ice water, not expecting to see anyone sitting at the table. So when I did, I yelped and stumbled into the arched entryway. At first, I thought it was Jeremy. I'd been so stupid and careless these past few days; he'd finally found me.

But then I focused on his face, and wow, he looked nothing like my psycho stalker ex-boyfriend.

I set my hand over my heart and slumped against the wall, beyond relieved. "Oh, my God. Mason. What're you doing home so early?"

He glanced up from the chair where he sat slouched and sent me a look of utter defeat. "Fate hates me."

"Huh?"

A bitter laugh rumbled from his chest. "I was sent home early and suspended for a week."

Oh, shit. Had the country club learned about his past? I pushed away from the wall. "What happened?"

He snorted and rolled his eyes. "I was freaking distracted and backed into a valet car when I was parking another one. Dinged both of them." Plopping his face forward until he thumped his forehead against the tabletop, he let out a drained sigh. "I think the only reason my boss didn't fire me on the spot was because I'm usually a good employee."

Knowing I had to be the reason for his suspension, I gulped in a lungful of guilt and reached for his back but pulled away at the last second. Folding my arms over my waist, I whispered, "I'm so sorry."

"For what?" When he looked up, he squinted at me in confusion.

I fluttered out my hand. "You know, for causing your distraction."

"You didn't. I..." He pushed his chair back and stood, his eyes full of concern. "My suspension had nothing to do with you." He took a step toward me, and my heart beat through my entire body. "It was all me. You...you're not to blame for *anything*. You're the good part in all of this." Two steps later, he was all up in my grill in a very pleasing, overwhelming, I-couldn't-breathe-I-was-so-excited way. But it was so, yeah, *overwhelming*, I moved back, only to find myself trapped between him and that wall, the very wall he'd wanted to take me hard and fast against.

"You're the warm sun that shines when everything else is dark," he went on, lifting his hands to rest them against the wall on either side of my face.

"A smile and a hug in a roomful of disapproval. You're..." Wincing, he pressed his forehead against mine. "You're everything."

A single tear trickled down my cheek. My smile trembled with effort. "I love you too."

Mason choked out a sound and then shook his head. "You...No. You shouldn't."

I touched the side of his face. "But I do."

Closing his eyes, he muttered something under his breath right before he sealed our mouths together. We both made a sound as our lips locked. He pulled back just enough to gaze at me. And then he went back for more.

It was everything I'd ever dreamed about and so much more. As his lips plundered persistently, I wrapped my arms around him and tipped my face up for more.

Tethering me around the waist, he pulled us flush as his tongue stroked the roof of my mouth before tangling with mine. My legs went around his waist, and he hoisted me higher, cupping my butt.

We tipped to the side, disturbing a row of keys hanging by the back door until a couple jingled to the floor. Stumbling into the cabinets, he propped me on the counter and deepened our kisses with long, drugging pulls that left me gasping for more. His body pushed more firmly into mine as he cradled my face. Then he ran his hands down my neck and over my back.

Even through my clothes, he knew how to make me react when he cupped my breasts. I choked out a surprised sound of need and threw my head back, cracking it on the cabinets behind me.

"Shit," Mason gasped, his lips tearing themselves from mine. Rubbing my noggin for me, he muttered, "We can't do this."

But he still burrowed his face against my

shoulder as he panted. I clung to him shamelessly, tucking my own cheek into his neck. Stroking his back, I whispered, "If this is going to be the only time I get to touch you, then can you wait at least a minute longer before coming to your senses?"

He released a breath. "Okay."

Damn, my powers of persuasion amazed even me.

I lifted my face to him, he lifted his to mine, and the kiss was on again. I loved the feel of his jaw under my fingers. I loved his hands that slipped up the back of my shirt and caressed my spine. I loved the entire experience.

"Okay, we should stop now." He gave it another halfhearted attempt, though his lips clung to mine and his thumbs became fascinated with each bump on my vertebrae. "Reese, we should stop. I need to stop before it's too late."

"Why?" I kissed my way down his neck.

He groaned and cupped my waist, sending thrilling tingles along my nerve endings. Then his mouth was on my throat and he was tugging me to the edge of the counter to snuggle our bodies closer.

When the heat of his erection nudged me through his jeans and my shorts, we both sucked in a harsh breath.

"Damn it." He broke away from me, severing all contact before he backed away, putting a good five feet of space between us.

I had no starch left in my body, so I wilted against the wall as I slid off the counter. I could still feel him everywhere. Mason wiped a hand over his face before leaning his forearms against another wall and bowing his head.

"Do you realize what you're doing to me, Reese?" His voice sounded broken as he thunked his forehead forward. "Making me choose like this..."

Excuse me? I lifted my hands, beyond insulted. "I haven't made you choose *anything*. Have you ever once heard me ask you to make any kind of decision? I understand completely why you do this. You don't have to *choose*."

Mason closed his eyes and snuffled out a bitter sound. "Except I already have. I have declined every offer I've gotten lately because the only person I want is you."

Hearing him openly admit it lit up my hope like the Griswold house at Christmas. "S-since when?"

Emotion swam in his eyes as he shook his head and glanced at me. "Since the night before we almost kissed in your apartment during Eva's party."

I gulped, overwhelmed with joy.

It was official then. He was no longer a gigolo. He'd quit. For me.

I stepped away from the wall, but he croaked, "It might not last," as if saying that threw up some kind of force field to keep me away.

Strangely enough, it worked. I stopped in my tracks. "What do you mean?"

Grief filled his face. "I tried getting out a year ago. I refused everyone for four months straight. But it didn't change how people treated me. Then the bills started piling up. Not as bad as they had been before. But it worried me, made me fear that our lives would plummet again. Then one day, this client got so desperate, she offered me double my price to keep me from refusing. So...I agreed. And everyone else began to pay that price. Before I knew it, I was all the way back in again." He looked at me and shook his head. "I want to say I'll never go back to it, but I did before."

I shook my head, maybe denying the whole situation, or maybe I was just that sure he wouldn't go back.

Mason glanced at me, looking restless and edgy as he jiggled his knee. "I never should've told you how I felt. When I learned he was going to take you out, I should've just gritted my teeth and kept my mouth shut. At least we'd still be friends."

I gave a small, helpless shrug. "But then we never would've kissed."

His gaze lifted, and he actually smiled. "Yeah." Except now he sounded more depressed than ever.

I pushed away from the wall and went to him, opening my arms and hugging him. He exhaled and wound me tight in his embrace, burying his face in my hair. "You are the most amazing person I've ever known. I love your spunk, your crazy thoughts on life, your caring soul."

"And I love you, period," I said.

He must've known I wasn't going to take any kind of rejection from him, because he didn't even attempt to pull away when I slid my mouth to his.

CHAPTER **TWENTY-FOUR**

Everything transgressed from hug into kiss so seamlessly, I couldn't tell where one ended and the other began. Mason sank his hands into my hair and held my head steady as his lips worshiped mine. After I shifted my face just enough to align our lips better, he moaned out a needy sound. His mouth wasn't demanding but begging, and I couldn't handle letting him beg. So I opened up, and we deepened the moment.

I couldn't stop kissing him. Our mouths took on the intimate dance of getting to know each other, learning each hidden crevice and sensitive nook. One wet embrace bled into another, until we both had to come up for air. And even then, we held each other, our cheeks pressed firmly together as our hands skated over clothes until they found their way under them.

His chest was sleek and warm, so taut under my fingers. I needed to know every muscle and freckle he had. Catching the bottom of his shirt, I pulled it up. He lifted his arms to help me, and a second later, he was shirtless.

I sucked in a breath, just staring. "You are so...beautiful."

He reached out and pulled me back to him. "Not nearly as beautiful as you."

My fingers became addicted to touching him. He felt so good.

Mason pressed his mouth to my closed eyelids, my cheeks, my forehead, my chin. As he began down my neck, I slid my hands around to the base of his spine. Pressing my palms flat against heated flesh, I lowered them, dipping into the back waistband of his jeans.

He sucked in a breath and clutched my face with one palm. His other hand shifted up the inside of my shirt to my bra, and under the cup. Arching against him, I—

A ringing from his front pocket startled me into yelping. I tugged my fingers from his pants and jerked back.

Mason's jaw went tense. He closed his eyes and cursed under his breath. Slowly, he slid his hand out from under my shirt. His gaze flickered up to watch my face as he made sure the backs of his fingers trailed along my abdomen before they left me. Only then did he yank his phone from his pocket. When he looked at the screen, his face drained of color.

I knew it was over then. Whatever farce of a relationship we'd just started had shattered. Because he had a client on the line.

Turning his back to me, Mason pressed the phone to his ear. He didn't answer, but his caller must've known he was on the line because I heard a muted female voice saying something to him. A second later, he spun toward the nearest window and jerked the blinds down, nearly yanking them from the wall in his rush.

"Whatever," he hissed and disconnected before he flung his phone onto the counter as if it was contaminated. "Damn it." He kicked the wall and ran his hand through his hair.

I didn't say anything. I didn't want to hear the truth aloud, even though I already knew.

"We had an eavesdropper," he said, his voice low and barely controlled with a wrath that surprised me.

When he glanced toward the closed window blinds, it struck me.

Oh, God.

I set my hand over my mouth. "Mrs. Garrison?"

He nodded. "Apparently, she didn't like seeing us kiss."

Ripping my fingers from my lips, I balled them into a fist. "Then maybe she shouldn't have *watched.*"

Mason bent down and snagged up his shirt. "I have to go. I got the royal summons from the wicked bitch herself." As he yanked the cloth back over his head, making his sexy tousled hair look even sexier, I wilted.

It was hard to believe I'd just had my hands in that hair. And now he was going to let another woman put her hands in it.

Shaking my head, I denied that this moment was happening. "You're not really going over there, are you?"

"I *have* to, Reese. She owns this house. She owns my mother, and Sarah, and me. I have to see what she wants."

Well, that wasn't hard to guess. The cougar pimp wanted *him*.

"She may own this house, but she doesn't own

you, or your family. You do *not* have to go over there."

"I'm just going to see what she wants. That's all." When he glanced at me, his expression turned vulnerable and uncertain. "Will you be here when I get back?"

My mouth fell open. "Are you on crack? Hell, no, I won't be here! You *know* what she wants, Mason. She wants you naked in her bed. If she'd wanted anything else, she would've told you over the phone, or better yet, she wouldn't have interrupted our kiss at all."

From the stubborn look on his face, I knew I hadn't convinced him to stay. "I'll only be gone a few minutes. I won't even go inside her house."

I turned away. "Fine. Whatever. Go over there. Fuck her. I don't care. I'm out of here."

I swiped my purse off the table and marched toward the back door.

"Reese." He lunged after me and wrapped his arms around me from behind. His chest was so warm, and so Mason, I almost melted on the spot. "Don't leave like this. Please don't leave like this. I promise you, I will not sleep with her. I don't care what she tries to hang over my head. I just want to tell her to leave me alone."

Shaking my head, I snorted out a sound of disbelief. "And you could have told her to leave you alone over the phone too."

His arms tightened around me. "Reese. Please."

I closed my eyes and pulled up every ounce of willpower I had inside me. "You might not have charged me a fee, but kissing you is too big of a price for me. I didn't sign up for this. Now let me go."

He sobbed out a choked sound against my back

but loosened his arms. I squirmed free of the rest of his hold and stumbled toward the door, shoving my way outside.

I didn't look back once. I know, my willpower even startled me. When I got behind the steering wheel of my car and started the engine, I didn't look up at his house. I simply put the gear into drive and pulled away from the curb.

I got a block and a half down the street before my hands started to shake. Gritting my teeth, I pulled to the curb and called myself every vile name in the book. Then I killed the engine and yanked the door open to stumble out into the warm evening. I sprinted all the way back to his house, my chest heaving, unable to stay away.

Hey, I never claimed to be a wise, rational person.

Yeah, okay, this probably topped my impulsive list. Going back there was the cherry on the double fudge icing of my stupid cake.

I was stupid, stupid, stupid. I *know*!

But I had to see if he was really going to go to her. I just had to.

Keeping close to the shadows, I stole into his back yard. I almost threw up when I saw his back door open.

A Mason-shaped figure darted to the gate separating his yard from hers.

I couldn't believe it. He *was* going to her. After everything he'd just confessed to me—

"Can you make this little talk quick?" Mason snapped. "My sister is home alone."

I tiptoed closer to the gate and kept just out of sight.

"Well, it looks like you're already worked up and ready to go," the evil voice of Patricia Garrison cooed back. "So, don't worry. I doubt it'll take us long at all."

"*It's* not going to happen." Mason's voice was hard and unforgiving. "And do you mind never spying on me again? Your rude-creepy vibe just went through the roof."

"I thought you said the little babysitter was just your friend."

"And I thought I said it was none of your *damn* business. That part's still true."

"Tsk, tsk. There's no reason to be insolent, Mason."

"Jesus, why do you care if I get a girlfriend or not? What do you care if I have sex with every female in Florida? You're the one who sent me to other women in the first place."

"But, darling, sex is not the problem. Everything would've been perfectly fine if you'd only screwed her and moved on. It's you falling in love with her that's the problem. Because once you fall in love, you'll want to be all monogamous or some such horseshit. I know you, you will. And judging by the way you look at her, you already have. But I can't allow it. I can't allow some silly little twit cheerleader of a girl to play havoc on *my* extra-curricular activities. I'm not finished with you yet."

"Well, I assumed you were. You brought your fiancé over to Sarah's party and paraded him around in front of my mother like you were taunting her for not having her own man. You don't *need* me anymore."

"Mason, Mason, Mason, you poor deluded boy. You couldn't be further from the truth. Ted is a dear, sweet man. Rich, charming, handsome. In fact, I will love being married to him."

"Then you probably shouldn't cheat on him."

"But, sweetie. I won't be able to help it. He just doesn't do it for me in the bedroom. Not the way

I've trained you to. I need you more than you realize."

"Well, that's too bad, because I'm never touching you again. We haven't been behind on our rent in over a year."

"Well...with inflation and the economy the way it is, I'm afraid I might have to raise your rent."

"I don't care. We'll pay it. Whatever it is. And if it gets too ridiculous, we'll just *move*. You have no hold over me whatsoever."

From the shadows, I fisted my hand and pumped it into the air, silently cheering him on. *You go, Lowe! Keep it up.*

"Is that so?" Mrs. Garrison gave a small, amused laugh. "And what if I called a certain police officer I know to tell him about an illegal prostitution scandal going on over at the country club?"

Mason's return chuckle was low and hard. "Go ahead, Patricia. I don't give a damn. I've already stopped taking clients anyway. No one is going to arrest me for speculation and since I'm finished, no one can catch me in the act."

"Wow, you think you have it all figured out, don't you?"

"Yeah, for once, I do. Now when are *you* going to get it through your thick head that it's over? I will *never* have sex with you again. There's nothing you can say or do to get me to walk back into your house."

"I'm sorry to hear that. Really. Because I was just about to tell you I know your girlfriend's little secret."

Say what?

My skin went ice cold as I crept closer to the gate, peeking through the cracks to see Mason's stiff back as he faced the half-opened back door, unintentionally blocking his landlady from my view.

He sounded suspicious and leery when he demanded, "What the hell are you talking about?"

"Nothing, really. I mean, I'm sure she's told you all about Teresa Margaret Nolan. Hasn't she?"

"Oh, my God." I slapped my hands over my mouth to muffle my shock.

She knew.

How in God's name did she *know*?

"Who?" Mason asked, sounding clueless.

I closed my eyes and shook my head. This wasn't happening. He wasn't finding out the truth from *her*.

"Oh, Mason." Mrs. Garrison tsked, sounding wickedly delighted. "Didn't she ever tell you her *real* name? That concerns me. It doesn't sound as if there's enough trust and honesty in your sweet little monogamous relationship if the girl hasn't even told you she legally changed her name to Reese Alison Randall just a few short months ago. I mean, not that I blame her. If my ex-boyfriend tried to kill me and promised he'd finish the job the next time he saw me, well, I'd probably run halfway across the country and change my name too."

"No," Mason said, his voice trembling with uncertainty.

Tears filled my lashes. I wiped at them desperately, my heart breaking because he was learning the truth like this. *I* was supposed to be the one to tell him.

"You think I'm making this up?" His pimp laughed. "He cut her. With a knife. It was actually life threatening; she was in the hospital for over a week. I'm sure you've seen the scar. It's somewhere on her neck, I believe."

Mason's thick silence killed me. A second later, he croaked, "Oh, God. What happened?"

Mrs. Garrison made a sympathetic sound.

"Your girl has quite the taste in boys, let me tell you. It was nasty. Nasty business indeed. I guess they were high school sweethearts, and all was well with that until he started to get a little too controlling for her taste. The first time she tried to break up with him, her sophomore year, he dislocated her jaw. The second time, during her senior year, he broke her arm...after pushing her down a flight of stairs."

More tears trickled down my cheeks. But how in God's name did this woman know so much about me? Where had she gotten her information?

"That's when she finally decided enough was enough. But he still refused to take no for an answer. He stalked her and harassed her for months after she dumped him until he broke into her parents' house to kill her. And he nearly succeeded."

"Jesus," Mason rasped.

"Miss Teresa missed her high school graduation because she was in the hospital. And her naughty boyfriend got out on bail almost immediately. So she skipped town with a new name. And since the case against him was dropped, Mr. Jeremy Walden has been completely pardoned. Ergo, he started looking for her. Her parents' home was broken into last week. I'll give you three guesses who I think did it."

Mason's voice wavered as he asked, "Did he find anything?"

The landlady hummed. "It's hard to say, though I will tell you, that boy will do anything, *anything*, to get his Reese's Pieces back."

The name Jeremy had always called me made me gag. I clutched my stomach and closed my eyes, forcing myself to breathe through my mouth until the nausea subsided.

"Just think, Mason. If he almost killed her when he was in love with her and wanted to *rekindle* their relationship, just think what he'll do this time, now that he wants revenge. Wouldn't it be awful—simply horrible—if someone accidently *leaked* her whereabouts?"

I swayed and would've gone down if I hadn't clutched the gate latch for support.

"You wouldn't," Mason warned.

"Of course I wouldn't, sweetheart." Mrs. Garrison's insulted voice sounded fake.

I dug my nails into the metal handle, wanting to reach out and physically hurt her.

"I would never do anything to upset you. Not when you're going to give me what I want." Her tone changed from cajoling to severe in an instant. "Right?"

"No!" I cried out, shoving my way into her backyard.

"Reese?" Mason spun around and caught my elbow. Pulling me close, he wrapped his arms around me tight. "Christ. What're you doing here?"

I clung to him, my tears soaking his shirt. "You said yourself. My curiosity has no filter. I had to know if you were really going to go to her."

"Damn it," he muttered even as his hands turned gentle and he held me against him, petting my hair. "How much did you hear?"

"All of it. And you can't sleep with her. You told her no. That should be enough. She's blackmailing you. What she's doing is...it's demented. It's a violation of you in the most personal, private, vile way imaginable. I refuse to just stand here and let you fall for this, especially because of me."

He didn't answer, simply held me close as I trembled and sobbed against him. When he cupped my face and drew far enough away to look into my eyes, a bad feeling crept up my spine.

He looked...resigned. "Is it true?"

Another tear slipped down my cheek. I should've told him she'd made everything up. But I couldn't lie to him. Not ever again.

"Yes." I sniffed as more tears fell. "I'm sorry. I'm so sorry. I should've told you sooner, but—"

"Shh. It's okay. It's all right." He kissed my forehead. Then his fingers chased a teardrop down my jaw before skimming around to the back of my neck so he could touch my scar. A choked sob left his throat. "I swear, Reese. I'll never let him find you. He won't ever hurt you again."

Then he dropped his hand from me and took a step back. The sorrow and pain in his eyes told me goodbye. Forever.

"Mason." I reached for him.

He whirled away and marched toward Mrs. Garrison's back door. She rested her half-dressed body against the doorjamb, and when he strode past her, his shoulder cracked against hers, knocking her off balance, before he disappeared inside.

"Perfect timing, Teresa," Mrs. Garrison purred as she straightened herself. "I love it when he's riled up...all wild and untamed, and extra aggressive. There's just something so *sensual* about that boy when his passion has been unleashed." She shivered and let out a dreamy sigh. "Thank you." Then she too turned away and shut the door.

I stood there, staring at her house, trembling from head to toe.

Vibrating with outrage, I wanted to explode. I wanted to scream. I wanted to race inside and drag him back out, away from that evil, evil woman.

But he'd made his decision.

He'd chosen her.

And he'd done it for me.

CHAPTER TWENTY-FIVE

I should've left. I should've gone home, curled into a ball in bed, and sobbed the rest of the night away.

But I couldn't.

I slunk back to Mason's house, and, feeling numb to the core, I let myself in through the unlocked back door. Collapsing into a chair at the kitchen table, I started my sob fest, shaking uncontrollably as I held on to my arms for dear life.

I swear, a piece of my soul tore away from my chest because I cried so hard it physically hurt right in the center of my breastbone, making proper breathing impossible.

My eyes were swollen, my nose was running like a sieve, and I was hyperventilating to the point of dizziness when the back door opened and Mason stepped wearily inside.

I had no idea how much time had passed. It didn't feel like that long. Then again, it felt like forever.

I lifted my face. When he caught sight of me, he jerked to a halt in the doorway. The expression in his gaze was flighty; he wanted to run.

I pushed out of my chair, still hugging myself. "Are you...is it done?"

Guilt and devastation oozed off him. "Reese? What...what're you *doing* here?"

"S-Sarah." My voice was empty, my limbs were heavy and, my mind was muzzy. "Sarah was home alone."

But we both knew that wasn't why I was here.

He shook his head as if he wanted to deny my presence. "But your car's not outside."

"I parked a few blocks down and walked back. Did you really do it?"

"Christ." He covered his face with both hands, and a hoarse moan of agony escaped him.

I stumbled forward, needing to hold him, needing him to hold me.

He shied away, refusing to look at me. "Don't. I'm not clean."

Oh, God. He'd really done it. I kept walking to him anyway.

He held up both hands and hissed. "Stop! Jesus, Reese. This is why we're supposed to be just friends. This is why...God damn it!" He touched my face and looked me over, from my swollen, tear-stained eyes to my red nose. Then he set his palm flush against my heaving chest as if he could calm my stuttered breathing with his touch alone. "Look what I did to you. This is exactly what I wanted to avoid. I never wanted to hurt you. I would give anything to keep this from you."

I clutched two handfuls of his shirt and balled them into my fists. "Then let me help you."

He shook his head. "How?" He sounded broken and disheartened.

We shared a mutual ache between us. And the only way I could think to help myself was to help him and give him what he needed most. Drawing in a deep breath, I wiped at my wet cheeks. "Do you want to be clean?"

He glanced at me, his eyes crushed yet full of hope. "Yes."

"Then I'll clean you."

When I reached for his hand, he let me interlace our fingers. I led him to the bathroom, and he followed without resistance.

He stopped a few steps inside and just stood there, staring at nothing, appearing almost comatose. I shut the door behind us and snagged the wire toilet paper bin that Dawn had sitting by the commode to tuck under the doorknob, keeping it closed.

"What a good idea," Mason said behind me, his voice dazed. "Why hadn't I ever thought to do that?"

I turned to send him a soft smile. "Because you need me around to show you the right way."

He flinched. "I should've listened to you. I shouldn't have gone over there. I shouldn't have—"

"Shh." I grasped the hem of his shirt and began to pull it up. "No more regrets. What's done is done and we're not going to think about it again."

He lifted his arms to help me take his shirt off, but he still asked, "What're you doing?"

"I'm giving you a shower. I told you I was going to clean you and—"

The words strangled in my throat as I took in the bright red hickey on the upper right side of his chest.

Catching my reaction, he frowned. "What?" When he looked down and saw the mark, he slapped his hand over it, covering the spot.

His faced jerked up, and he opened his mouth. I saw apology thick in his expression. On its tail came fear and revulsion.

I think the revulsion won out. He spun away from me, fell to his knees and slammed up the toilet seat. As he vomited, I turned away and covered my mouth. More tears fell. With trembling hands, I reached for the cup by the sink and filled it with water.

By the time he finished, I was sitting on the floor beside him, ready and waiting with a cup of water and toothbrush full of paste.

"Thank you." He took the water first, swished it around in his mouth and spit. After a few more rounds of that, he began to scrub his teeth vigorously. And all the while, he kept his arm held over his chest, hiding the stain she'd left on him.

"I'll get your shower water warm," I offered, pushing to my feet and feeling robotic as I worked.

"Are you really going to stay in here while I shower?" He didn't sound as if he wanted me to leave; he just sounded perplexed by the notion.

"I said I was going to clean you." The truth was, I didn't think I could be away from him right then.

Opening the door to the shower stall, I started the water, not caring how stray droplets coated my arms and began to soak my shirt. I held my knuckles under the stream until I had the temperature just right for Mason.

Behind me, he stood and put his cup and tooth-brush away. When his pants hit the floor, I jumped.

Last month, I would've peeked. Heck, earlier that day, I would have looked. But I didn't even want to now, and not because I was repulsed over the fact that he'd had his penis inside another woman only minutes ago.

I just couldn't violate his privacy. He'd been

violated enough for one night.

When I glanced back, my gaze landed on his face. "I suppose I can let you do this part by yourself."

His eyes looked extra silver in the room's fluorescent light. They focused on me, searching my face. With a silent nod, he stepped past me and shut himself inside the shower. The glass was opaque, so I could only see a blurry, peach outline of him through the door.

Leaving briefly to ransack his room and find some fresh clothes for him to wear, I tossed his Country Club uniform into his dirty clothes hamper and returned to the steamy bathroom, where the door hung partially open. I returned the TP bin in front of it and closed the toilet lid to sit and wait.

I swear, he soaped everything down three times. But that was okay with me. Whatever he had to do to make himself feel clean again was fine.

When the water shut off, I was there with a towel.

He looked surprised when he opened the door and saw me. With another muted, humble thank you, he took the terrycloth and dried himself before wrapping it around his waist.

I sat back down on the toilet seat and brought my knees up to my chest to loop my arms around my legs. "I feel like *I'm* the one who had to do that with her, like she tore down the most basic part of me and left the rest abused and cast off. I feel worthless and cheap, and...and used."

He nodded once and slid his boxer briefs on under the towel. "Yeah, that pretty much covers what it does to you."

I couldn't help it; I began to cry again. Tears sprouted from my eyes and poured down my cheeks before I even realized they'd started. "And you're okay with that?"

Covering his face with his hand, he whispered, "Reese," on a choked rasp. "I'm sor—"

"Don't you dare apologize," I sobbed. "I'm the one who did this to you. It's my fault you went through this tonight."

His lashes flashed open. "No. God, no. You didn't. Nothing was your fault."

Dropping his towel, he knelt down in front of me. Against my will, I looked at his chest only to see he'd replaced his hickey with a huge red welt where he'd tried to scrub it off.

"I'm sorry." He lunged sideways for his shirt.

Once he pulled it on, I reached out, grabbed two handfuls of cloth, and leaned toward him.

He tugged me off the commode and into his arms, where he held me in his lap on the floor of the bathroom.

"It's okay," he kept murmuring. "I swear to you, Reese. It wasn't that bad. I didn't even finish. As soon as she was done, I—"

"*I don't want details*," I screeched, horrified.

But, really. I hated Mrs. Garrison. Not only had she manipulated him into doing what she wanted; she'd messed with his head, toyed with his body, and prevented him from the only gratification he might've actually gotten from tonight.

I know, that was really messed up thinking. But I *felt* messed up.

"I'm sorry." His face drained of color. When he tried to shift backward, I only sobbed harder and curled my fingers around handfuls of his soft cotton shirt to hug him tighter. Breathing in heavy drudges of the dryer-sheet-scented cloth, I clung to him, unable to stop bawling.

"It's going to be okay." He kissed my hair and stroked matted tangles free from the damp tresses.

I barked out an incredulous laugh. "Okay? I am so far from okay right now, I don't even remember what okay feels like."

He pressed his face against my neck. "I can't tell you how sorry I am. I can't...I can't...Why the hell did you stay? You shouldn't have stayed to see this."

"I don't know. I couldn't leave." I clutched him a little tighter. "Don't make me leave."

"Never." He drew his knuckles down my cheek. "Tell me what to do. I'll do it. I swear. Just tell me how to make this better."

"It's already done." I rested against him, limp and defeated. The only thing left to do now was for me to adjust and accept. Since not doing so didn't seem to be an option without losing him completely, I closed my eyes and burrowed close.

I had stuck around to help keep *him* together, but there we were, and he was the one preventing me from falling apart. The irony wasn't lost on me.

He tucked his face into my hair and sniffled. "I thought I loved you enough that my feelings could protect you," he confessed, his voice ragged and hoarse. "I thought I could keep you from being hurt. Damn it, I was so sure I could spit in her face and end it for good. I was so stupid and cocky. And you got hurt because of it."

"No." I smoothed my hand down his arm. "You did protect me. You kept her from contacting Jeremy. You saved me."

He sniffed again and kissed my hair. "Come on." Holding me tight in his arms, he stood and carried me from the bathroom to his bedroom. He laid me in the center of the mattress and pulled out the sheet and blanket from under me before drawing them up to my chest.

After a quick peck on my forehead, he crawled

in beside me.

We faced each other on the mattress without touching. He hadn't turned the lamp on, but I could see his face clearly from the light glowing in from the hallway.

"It wasn't always so bad," he murmured. "When I first started, it was kind of cool. I mean, beautiful, rich, fancy women were paying attention to me, stuffing hundred-dollar bills in my clothes. I was getting laid three or four times a week. It gave me a confidence I never had before. But it got old real fast and by the time I realized those woman didn't respect me—I wasn't even a person to them—it was too late. I had this *reputation*, I was their puppet, and I felt stuck."

Reaching out with a soft smile, he tucked a piece of my hair behind my ear. "I can't regret it, though. If I'd never accepted her offer that afternoon, I wouldn't have started my clientele at the country club. I never would've made enough money to feel like I could go to college. And I never would've met you."

I sniffed and wiped my face. "I don't think I'm worth it."

He laughed softly, his expression indulgent with tenderness. "Trust me. You're *more* than worth it." With a kiss on my nose, he sighed. "Okay, so I spilled my soul to you. Your turn."

I didn't know what to say. My soul felt empty of stories.

Mason's fingers lightly traced the scar on the back of my neck. "Will you tell me about this?"

With a shudder, I closed my eyes. "She pretty much covered it all. There's not much left to tell."

"I want to hear it anyway. I want to hear it from you."

So I told him, and afterward, he pulled me

close. "I'll do whatever I can to keep him from hurting you again."

"I know." It's what I feared most.

I rested my cheek on his chest, glad to be with him, and doubly glad he hadn't called me stupid for allowing Jeremy to manhandle me for so long. I fell asleep wrapped in his arms.

Dawn woke us when she came home, gasping loudly the moment she saw the babysitter in bed with her son.

Both Mason and I jerked upright as we sprang awake.

"Mom," he said, slapping a hand over his heart, only to fall backward into his pillows and close his eyes. "Jesus, you gave me a heart attack."

"I'm *so* sorry," she bit out, throwing laser beams my way. "I wasn't expecting to check on you and find you in bed...with Reese."

Mason's brow burrowed with disbelief. "You still check on me at night?"

"Yes! I'm your mother, aren't I? Now, are you going to explain what you're doing in bed with the babysitter or not?"

"Oh." He sat up again and glanced at me. "Jeez, Mom, nothing happened. Look. We still have our clothes on."

Dawn lifted one eyebrow, obviously not impressed. I edged a little closer to Mason. He found my hand under the blanket and clutched it hard.

"Sarah...she had a seizure," he explained, "and Reese flipped out. She tried calling you first, but I don't know, maybe she dialed the wrong number. Anyway, she couldn't reach you, so she called me next. After we put the munchkin to sleep, Reese sort of lost it and started crying. I wasn't sure what to do to help her. So I made her lie down and talk things through. Then we both fell asleep, and you came home, and that's where we are now."

His mother stared at him for a moment before she glanced at me. "Sarah had a seizure? Is she okay?"

"She's fine," Mason assured. "She seemed lucid and alert after it was over. We read some *Harry Potter* together before she went to bed."

Dawn nodded and rubbed her forehead. "Good. Thanks for being here, Reese." She glanced at me and frowned in concern. "Poor dear, you still look shaken. Your eyes are red and swollen."

I glanced down, not sure how to lie as well as Mason had. He wrapped an arm around my shoulder and tugged me against his side. "I'm going to drive her home. Her friend called and needed to borrow her car, so she needs a ride."

Startled by his quick thinking, I lifted my face. My brain still felt fried and overcooked. But he was so convincing, I almost found myself believing him. He even talked his mom into leaving his room before he crawled out of bed so she wouldn't know he'd only been wearing boxer briefs under the covers.

"I can't believe you just totally lied to her," I hissed as soon as she was gone.

He sent me a scowl, telling me to keep my voice down. "I didn't *lie*. Sarah really did have an attack and I calmed you down afterward. Just not to-night."

I snorted and rolled my eyes but ended up grinning. He grinned back and took my hand, kissing my knuckles.

For that brief moment, everything felt almost normal.

Dawn was removing a pitcher of iced tea from the refrigerator when we passed through the kitchen to the back door. Struck by her everyday behavior as if nothing out of the ordinary had happened tonight, I wanted to hate her for making Mason feel as if he had to sacrifice himself for the past two years. But I stopped myself. If I looked for flaws in everyone I encountered, I'd find them one hundred percent of the time, and I'd always be disappointed. I didn't want to be disappointed in this woman. She had raised two of my favorite people on earth. She was their mother.

Instead of glaring, I stepped toward her and pulled her into an impulsive hug. "I just want you to know you have some amazing children."

She seemed startled at first, but then she relaxed and hugged me back. "I do, don't I? And I know they're both very fond of you too."

When we pulled away from each other, Mason was there to take my hand. "I'll be back in the morning," he told Dawn before dragging my tripping, surprised self out the back door.

"Mason! Oh, my God. I can't believe you just told her that."

"What?" When he looked at me, he appeared confused. "I thought you didn't want me to lie to her."

So, I guess he planned on staying all night with me then. My heart jerked with relief because I didn't want to be apart from him either.

"But now she's going to think we'll be having sex all night."

He merely shrugged. "Well...a guy can dream, can't he?"

CHAPTER **TWENTY-SIX**

Once we reached my apartment, Mason held my hand as he walked me up to my door.

After stroking my hair in the most loving caress, he had me stand just inside the entrance as he checked the entire loft, making sure no psycho stalker ex-boyfriends were lingering about. I treasured the sweetness of his actions.

When he returned to me and took my hand again to lead me to my room, I followed in giddy exultation.

We undressed ourselves, facing each other as we stripped down to our underwear. His eyes heated as I pulled my dried tee over my head and my breasts pushed taut against the cups of my bra. I knew he was aroused; he revealed an impressive bulge in his boxer briefs when he pushed his jeans down his legs. But instead of reaching for me, he rotated away and turned down the sheets of my bed.

"After you." His gaze was filled with care and

devotion. "I swear I will refrain from hogging the mattress and blankets tonight."

I paused before climbing in, as relieved as I was disappointed that he didn't put the moves on me. We deserved a little physical connection. I needed to get close to him and share my body with him in the most intimate, bonding way possible.

But later. Not tonight.

Sex wasn't the main thing he needed from me just now. It wasn't the main thing I needed from him either. For the time being, we both could do with a little emotional comfort.

So instead of the horizontal tango, what followed were some of the sweetest, yet most platonic, hours of my life. Mason managed to turn the utter depression I'd begun in his neighbor's backyard into unreserved bliss.

He wrapped me in his arms and snuggled with me, talking about trivial things like Harry Potter, and lattes, and college, and spiders, and our futures. We drew on each other's hands with our fingers and guessed what pictures we'd made. We tried to have a thumb war under the covers...with our toes. Then we lay in tranquil silence, holding hands and listening to our breaths slow until we both fell into a dreamless oblivion.

I had a lovely, solid rest. When I woke, I didn't feel as if I'd spent any of last night bawling my eyes out until they'd nearly swollen shut. I felt refreshed and warm as I snuggled into my soul mate, who had kept his promise and hadn't hogged the mattress or the sheets.

Rolling around to face him, I watched him slumber next to me. It was like witnessing a miracle. He was beautiful. Inside and out.

As if sensing my stare, he stirred, his breath catching before he turned his head my way and fluttered his thick, stubby lashes open. A tired smile lit his face, and I seriously can't even describe how amazing it felt to be the recipient of it.

"Hey, Sweet Pea," he rasped.

If I wasn't turned on before, I certainly was now. His morning voice put his regular voice to shame, all sleep-clogged and sexy with the perfect amount of huskiness to it.

"Hey, Hotness," I returned, my fingers itching to reach out and just...pet him. Giving in to temptation, I asked, "Can I touch you?"

His lashes closed, resting against the tops of his tanned, sculpted cheeks as his smile grew broad. "You don't have to ask."

I reached out immediately but paused within inches of contact. He must've sensed my hesitation because he reopened his eyes. "What's wrong?"

I swallowed, utterly overwhelmed. "I don't know where to start."

Mason's gaze warmed. He wrapped strong warm fingers around my wrist and drew my palm forward, leading me where he wanted my hand to follow. When he set it on the center of his chest, right over his heart and pressed my flesh flush to his as if fingerprinting my soul to his, I blinked back gratified tears.

"Start here. No one's ever touched me here before."

I rubbed a circle on his chest over his heart. It thumped strong and steady under my fingers, so I leaned in and set my lips to the precious spot, sealing the moment with a kiss.

Remembering a certain hickey from the night before, I glanced over without thinking, only to find all traces of Mrs. Garrison completely gone. His unmarked chest gleamed, sculpted and magnificent like a clean slate. And all mine to touch as I wished.

Unable to stop grinning, I glanced up and bit my lip before I took the plunge. "Word," I said.

His sexy brows lowered with confusion. "What?"

I chuckled. "I thought you told me to just say the word when I was ready. So...word. Or should I say '*the word*'?"

Mason sucked in a sharp breath, looking suddenly uncertain. "Reese—"

He began to sit up, but I nudged him back down. Since my hand was still covering his heart, it didn't take much effort to apply a little pressure and topple him back onto the mattress.

"It's okay, Mason," I assured him. "I love you, and I want to show you how much. I want you to have that recreational fun you've never had. I want to pamper and spoil you as no one ever has before." Or ever will. "And I want to wash away all their rules and restrictions until you feel free to do whatever you like with me."

His eyes darkened with feeling. Lifting his hand, he cupped my face gently. "God, I don't deserve you."

"And yet you have me anyway." I grinned and moved my touch over him, exploring to my heart's content, starting at his face with his rough, unshaven jaw and working my way down.

"So, you're about to give your first freebie, Mr. Lowe, the amazing gigolo." Teasing, I slid the tip of my nose along the side of his neck. "Would you like to pause and say a little something to mark the occasion?"

His expression crackled with heat as he lay passively under me, watching my every move. "Oh, but this isn't going to be my first freebie."

"What?" My stomach dropped into my toes. "But you said—"

"Shh." He cut me off by setting his finger over my lips before I could sit upright. With a light, reassuring kiss on my forehead, he kissed my cheek next. Then my jaw...Mmm. My neck. "It's not going to be a freebie at all. I plan to make you pay. Big time."

"Oh, I'm going to pay, am I?" I pulled back as much as he would allow to arch my eyebrows. But the press of his lips against my collarbone made my entire body shudder with hunger. Sensing I might actually like where this was headed, I licked my lips. "I'm getting the girlfriend discount, right?"

Mason merely shook his head, amusement lacing his chuckle. "Nope. You're going to owe me more than anyone ever has before."

"Really? Hmm. What do you plan to charge?"

Stealing my bad habit, he wrinkled his nose. "Just your body. Your heart. And all of your soul."

I let out a happy sigh and threaded my fingers through his hair. "But I've already given you those."

His grin was slow and devastating. "Well, there's my first then. A woman who pre-pays."

I giggled. "In that case, sonny, lie back. I'm not done investigating my purchase."

He gave me a toothy grin. "Need to check my teeth?"

I lifted one eyebrow. "Not quite the spot I had in mind."

"My armpit?" When he lifted his arm, I threw my head back and laughed.

"Put your arm down, you dork." I manually put it down for him, hiding his hairy pits. "Maybe I was talking about your tattoo, huh."

I traced my fingers over the words *Make Me*, stunned I was actually touching it, that he was letting me anywhere near it. Goose bumps sprouted on his abdomen as I ran my fingertip along each letter.

His smile faded as he glanced at his ink. "I was pissed and feeling defiant after the first time I stopped accepting clients."

"I thought as much." Leaning forward, I kissed the words. His stomach muscles tensed under my lips and his hand petting my hair told me how much he liked the attention.

After obsessing over his navel, I skipped down his body, moving directly to his feet.

He sat up, resting his weight on his elbows so he could watch me. An amused crinkle lit up his eyes. "Hey, you missed a spot."

I waved him silent. "Don't worry. I'll get to your ears, I swear."

He shook his head. "That's not what I was talking about."

Glancing at the bulge in his underwear and seeing a wet mark spreading on the cloth, I blanked out for a second, overcome by this urge to climb into his lap and ride him that very second. I could almost feel the thick glide of him entering me already.

But I didn't want to do something that would remind him of anything...nasty. Unsure, I met his gaze. "I just... I thought maybe your...I was worried a couple of overeager clients might've touched it more than you wanted, so I didn't want to...intrude." I mean, if *I* had been paying him boocoos of money for it, I'd demand a little playtime with that specific body part too. "I didn't want to—"

He tossed his head back and laughed. "Reese. Jesus, you are too cute. I don't care about them. I just know I want *you* to touch it. I want *your* hands on me. Right here."

When he skimmed his fingers over the exact

spot we were discussing, I caught my breath, forgetting all about who had come before me. But holy tattooed gigolos, seeing Mason touch himself there was freaking *hawt*.

"My goodness, Mr. Lowe," I breathed, trying to control my racing pulse by keeping very, very still. "I think that was just about the sexiest thing I've ever seen."

"Then you haven't seen nothing yet." With a wink, he wrapped his fingers around himself through the cloth of his underwear. As he pumped slowly, my jaws throbbed from the way my mouth watered. "I ache so bad for you right now, Reese, just thinking about sliding into you has me..." He closed his eyes and gave a full-body shiver as he groaned.

I think I might've had a mini orgasm. Seriously. A shockwave of awareness lit through me so hard and fast, I caught my breath in surprise.

"Well, we can't have that." Before he realized what I was about to do, I grasped his underwear and slid them down his legs, dislodging his hand from his junk, which was a damn shame. But what sprang free, all naked and exposed, left me with a whole new eye-party of astonishment. "Holy Mary, mother of God. That's definitely the biggest I've ever seen."

Mason's eyes narrowed even as his cheeks flushed from the compliment. "Just how many have you seen?"

"Including you? Two." Ignoring the suspicious question in his gaze, I returned my attention to his penis. Crouching hesitantly close, I cooed, "Hey there, big fellow. You don't bite, do you?"

Mason laughed and groaned at the same time. "Damn it, Reese. Your sense of humor is going to drive me crazy before this day is over."

"What?" I asked innocently, honestly confused.

"Just touch it already," he pleaded from between clenched teeth.

Jeez, okay. He didn't have to be an impatient crabby pants about it. I reached out and petted the length of it with two fingers as if timidly greeting a live, rabid animal.

Sweat beaded on Mason's brow. He looked tortured, but he appeared to love every second of his suffering. "You are such a comedian. You know that's not what I meant by touch it. It's not a freaking dog."

"Um, no. I'd say this thing is more the size of a bull."

He gave a choked laugh. As much as he wanted me to get with the program, he was still having fun. I loved it. I'd never had fun while that other guy who-shall-not-be-named had been naked in front of me. I liked having fun with Mason.

"Now, why am I doing all the touching here?" Faking a pout, I sat back on my haunches and slapped my hands to my hips. "You haven't inspected one inch of me yet. Don't you like what you see?"

"I love *everything* I see." His eyes glazed with instability as he frantically clutched the sheets under him. I was worried I might've pushed him a little too far. A little dirty teasing was fine; driving a man to hormonal homicide was not.

His brow glistened as if he had a fever. "But if I touch you right now, that's it. I won't be able to stop. I wanted to make sure you have all your playtime in before I get started."

"Aww." I patted his belly, a bare three inches from the head of his oozing penis. "Thinking of me first. That's so sweet. Thank you."

"Yeah, I'm a frigging saint. Now will you *please*

touch my dick like you mean it before the damn thing explodes?"

"Oh, all right." I let out a resigned sigh as if giving in to his demands was such a bother. Then I leaned over and touched his dick—with my tongue—stroking it all the way from base to tip with a hot, wet stroke.

He shouted out my name and bucked us both a couple of inches off the bed.

"What did I do wrong this time?" I demanded, sitting up again to pierce him with a pointed look.

Panting, he stared up at me through a wild glaze. "N...nothing. That was...that was...perfect."

The dazed expression on his face made me pause. "Haven't you ever been licked there before?"

"No," he said in a strained voice.

"Really?" I arched an eyebrow. "What is wrong with the women of Waterford?"

He shook his head, still looking completely bowled over. "F...fellatio is more about my pleasure, and none of them really cared about my pleasure so...*oh*!...God."

His back bowed off the bed again as I took as much of him into my mouth as I could fit. Wrapping my fingers around the rest of the base, I sucked hard, being careful not to bite. Then I let my tongue roam, investigating every bump and vein. Next came a little deep throating.

"*Reese*!" His voice was high and strangled. "Oh, my God. Oh..." I think I actually *heard* his eyes roll into the back of his head. "...*shit*."

Yes, I give a damn fine B.J. if I do say so myself.

I knew he was right on the edge when he let go of the two handfuls of sheets he'd fisted his fingers around and sat upright. "I can't wait any longer. I need...I need to touch you. *Now*."

He pulled me off him, flipped me onto my back, and was on top of me so fast it knocked the wind out of me.

The kiss that followed was so hot, it melted my panties away. Literally. Well, okay, I think *he* ripped my panties away. But either way, after we were done giving each other mouth to mouth, I was completely naked, he had a condom on, and things had gotten real hot up in this loft apartment. My entire body throbbed with heat and moist, aching need.

Mason grasped my hip and manually draped my leg around his waist. I followed his lead and wrapped the other around him, hooking my feet together at the base of his back.

Sliding his palm up my thighs, he cupped my ass and lifted me enough to align our bodies. My core pulsed in anticipation, tightening my nipples into hard sensitive buds and tugging on the nerves in my thighs.

When he dipped in a finger to find me wet, we both moaned. Another digit followed. He stroked me until I arched and panted under him. His mouth did sinful things to my breasts. I never wanted him to stop.

After he pulled his fingers free, he replaced them with something much larger that nudged my entrance and made my vision gray. Oh, God. We were doing this. We were doing it right now. I held my body taut in eager excitement as his blunt tip pressed a little deeper.

The only other person I'd ever had sex with had been Jeremy, and he'd been so controlling and domineering, I wasn't absolutely positive what the normal procedure was. What if Mason wanted me to be more involved, or less involved, or...?

As if sensing my sudden insecurity, Mason

looked up, his face flushed. "Reese? Are you sure?"

That was it. His concern for me broke through all my fears about proper procedure. I needed this man now, in every way possible.

I nodded like a bobble-headed doll. "Yes. Yes. Please."

He set his forehead against mine and thrust forward, impaling me fully.

Oh.

God.

I sucked in a sharp, startled breath, not expecting so much, so soon. Oh, God. So very, very much. He hadn't hesitated once. My body couldn't adjust and I slapped his back in uncontrollable panic. "Stop! Wait, wait, wait."

He immediately fell still and pulled his shoulders back to look into my eyes. "What's wrong? Did I hurt you? Are you okay? I thought you said—"

He began to pull out, but I locked my legs tighter around him to stop any movement whatsoever.

I shushed him, needing silence so I could clear my head. "I'm fine. I'm fine." My mind was scrambled. I felt so stretched and full. He seemed everywhere. My thoughts were a scattered, dis-organized mess.

It was too freaking overwhelming.

"I just... I need a moment. I wasn't expecting it to be so...You're so big. Bigger than..." I looked into the worried, frantic face above me, and once again, that was all I needed. I grew famished. "Mmm."

My body warmed, adjusted, and accepted him. It actually relished the snug fit. In fact, it craved more and wanted to feel that delicious inner stretching again, wanted to feel him rubbing against the bundle of nerves inside me, and it wanted it right freaking *now.*

I arched up under him, burning for more. "Move, move, move," I panted.

Mason looked conflicted and a little panicked. "But you told just told me to stop."

I grabbed two handfuls of thick, wavy hair and clutched them hard. "Well, now I need you to *move.* Oh, God. Please, hurry. I feel so...I'm so...*Jesus,* what are you doing to me?"

Keeping a suspicious eye on me as his cheeks grew ruddy and his pupils dilated, he pulled out only to immediately rock back in. And oh my stars, the fit was just as snug and mind-blowing as his first plunge. I arched under him, moaning out my ecstasy in a low keen. "More."

Mason set a hand on the pillow by my face, watching me as he steadily pumped my body. "You confuse the hell out of me, Teresa Nolan, Reese Randall, or whoever the hell you are." His voice was raw and winded. "But I still can't get enough of you."

I was so happy he knew all my names and every part of me. There were no secrets between us. Just him and me, and this.

He plunged into me harder, shifting us just enough to slide deeper. Then he rearranged my legs, telling me it would make him feel bigger in me, and holy crap, he wasn't lying. Next he flexed his penis just so, hitting a spot that almost had me crossing my eyes. Damn, he sure knew what to do.

I thrashed my head from side to side, fighting the tightening in my loins as much as I embraced it.

"You feel so good, so good," I chanted from between chattering teeth. "So good."

Why were my teeth chattering? Why the hell was my entire body chattering? It seemed like the firmer my muscles pulled around him, the more my organs low in my abdomen swelled. And the more they expanded, the harder I shook.

"Christ," Mason bit out. His teeth clenched and neck tendons strained. "Don't say shit like that to me when I'm already on the edge. You feel good too, Reese. So...goddamn...good. But I don't want it to end yet."

I didn't either. Except the faster he moved, the better it felt. And the better it felt, the sooner it was going to end.

"Oh, screw it." I dug my fingers into his firm ass and moved with him, urging him to quicken the pace. "We can have long, drawn-out slow sex later."

He groaned again, though this was more like a whimper. "Promise?"

I nodded. "Yes. Yes. Right now, just light me up. *Please.*"

"On it." His hips slapped against mine. And...damn.

It was the first time I actually savored the carnal delight of this act. I cherished every wicked sensation vibrating through me. Hugging his hips tight between my thighs as he repeatedly entered and withdrew, I threw my head back and arched with him.

And yet, despite how hot and sweaty and primal it was, I felt a connection that ran so much deeper than the physical. The electrical current that had tethered us together the first moment I'd ever seen him across the college campus ignited inside me.

Mason's gaze was awed and amazed as he watched us come together. But he must've sensed the bond too, because he looked up and caught my eye. With a dazed kind of grin, he sank his fingers into my hair and held my face as if bracing himself for the big plunge off the summit.

"I love this," he said. "I love you. You are so beautiful."

I gripped him tight. "I love you, too."

And that was it. For a split second, he appeared overcome. Then he crushed our mouths together, buried himself deep, and sent me spiraling over the cliff. My entire system felt like a lightning rod, absorbing the shock of our union. Mason groaned and followed me into oblivion.

Until that moment, I hadn't realized I'd never had an honest-to-God orgasm before, because what happened to my body possessed every nerve inside me and shocked me from the inside out. The intensity kind of scared me. I cried out and clutched him hard, gouging out half moons into his back with my fingernails.

"Oh, God. Oh, God. Oh, God."

"Jesus, Reese." He arched and crushed us together as his cock pulsed.

I dug my heels into the base of his back until the earthquake, tornado, hurricane, and tsunami of sensations passed. And still, I felt rattled to the core. "Oh...my...God," I said one last time, my voice faint and exhausted.

Slumped heavily on top of me—which I loved—Mason chuckled against my cheek and kissed my jaw, then my throat, my collarbone. "Thank you," he said. "I've always wondered what it felt like to make love."

I turned my face to the side and saw his heart reflecting through the stained-glass windows of his gorgeous gray eyes. Realizing this was the first time I'd made love too, my lashes grew a little damp. Cupping his cheek where his five o'clock shadow prickled my palm, I murmured, "It *is* a million times better than that icky ol' straight sex with no feelings involved, isn't it?"

He teased my ear with his nose. "Fifty million times better."

Not one to be bested, I had to retort, "A trillion times."

"Infinity," he countered.

Wrapping my arms and legs around him, I burrowed my face into his neck. "Infinity times two."

With that, I pretty much just passed out underneath him, falling into a deep, peaceful stupor.

CHAPTER **TWENTY-SEVEN**

We woke some time later to my phone announcing an incoming text. Mason swung out an arm and grabbed it off the nightstand to pass to me.

It was from Eva. *His Jeep is in the driveway again. That gigolo better treat you right.*

This EX gigolo is treating me better than all right, I returned and gave the phone back to him to replace on the nightstand.

"What was that about?" he asked with his sleepy, sexy voice.

"Nothing." I curled into his warm side and ran my fingernails lightly over his chest. "I was just bragging a little to Eva."

My phone chimed again. I began to lean over him to retrieve it, but Mason caught my waist, halting me. "Don't you dare stop touching me like that. I'll get it."

Sighing contentedly, I caressed him a little lower. He groaned out his approval as he opened my text. "She said you're a lucky bitch."

I smiled, and a little something-something under my stroking fingers grew into a rather large something-something. "Why, yes. Yes I am."

He cursed and hooked an arm around my waist to tug me on top of him. This time around, I straddled his lap and did a little cardio exercise. Mason was even kind enough to show me how the backward cowgirl position worked. Bless his soul.

After round two, we took another nap. When we woke again, food became a little more important. I knew I didn't have much in my cabinets, but we went to investigate the kitchen anyway.

As I commanded him to stay seated at the table, I scurried around to collect all the breakfast friendly food I had.

From his seat, he took a drink of the OJ I'd gotten him and sighed, refreshed, as his gaze followed every move I made. "I finally know why a guy likes it so much when his girl wears nothing but his shirt around."

"Why?" I asked and wiggled in his shirt so the hem would ride higher up my thigh. "Easy access?"

"Well, that too." Eyes glittering with sensual awareness, Mason watched me open the fridge and pull out a couple of jars. "But I think it's like marking his territory. He knows just how much she's his when she's wearing his property."

I paused and lifted a non-impressed eyebrow. "Marking his territory?" God, he really was a guy, wasn't he? "So...I'm like a car tire you feel the need to pee on?"

His grin grew wolfish. "Peeing on you isn't quite what I had in mind."

I wrinkled my nose and stuck out my tongue.

He laughed and crooked his finger, beckoning me closer.

Unable to deny him, I drifted within his reach.

"So, here are your choices for breakfast." I set a jar of strawberry preserves on the table next to the loaf of bread and box of cereal I'd already gotten out.

He didn't look at the food. His gaze wandered to the bare skin on my thighs where his T-shirt ended. "I know exactly what I want for breakfast."

I snorted. "My God. Let a guy rock your world two times and he turns into a horny perv."

"Hey, I was a horny perv before." Snaking out his hands to grasp my hips, he swung me into his lap where I landed on his arousal pressing against his boxer briefs. "And you have no idea how hard it was for me to hide all the horny, perverted thoughts I had every time I was around you."

Licking my lips, I tilted my head back, letting my hair tumble down my back as I rocked against his erection. "Oh, trust me. I'm getting a pretty good idea just how *hard* it was."

He chuckled and kissed my throat. With a sigh, I sifted my hands through his hair and drifted languidly under the stroke of his expert mouth. He worked his way down until he met the collar of my shirt. With an irritated mutter, he gathered it up in his hands and ripped it over my head, tossing it aside.

"Oh, home girl," he chastised when he saw my bra. "This thing got to go." With three deft moves, he'd unclasped my bra and flung it across the room too. His gaze lit with approval. "Now that's more like it."

I laughed. "You are so—*Damn.*"

His mouth latched onto a nipple and I forgot what I was going to call him.

Mason Lowe was one incredible lover. He touched me with such reverence, his fingertips light and curious as they cruised up my spine while his mouth was bold and knowing, his tongue lavishing taut, puckered skin with deadly precision.

Without warning, he grasped my waist with both hands and lifted me off his lap to set me on the edge of the table. He stood up as he urged me to lie back. Then he leaned over me to give a little attention to my other breast.

Closing my eyes because this was so wild and crazy and amazing, I reached out and grasped the edge of the table for support.

Keeping my legs draped over the side, Mason fitted himself between my thighs and rubbed against me as he began to kiss his way back up to my throat.

"You taste so good," he rumbled against my flesh. "Feel so good. Smell so good."

I sighed. His touch kind of fried my awesome communication skills, so all I managed to reply was, "Y-you too."

Grinning, he lifted his face to press a tender kiss on the end of my nose. Then he gazed into my eyes and straight into me. "I love being with you, Reese." He looked down at my mostly naked body and let out a breath. "I love doing this with you. I love...I love you, period."

I swallowed, choked with emotion, and not at all used to hearing him say that. Wiping his dark hair across his brow and out of his eyes, I frowned softly. "You say that like it's the last chance you have to speak to me, like you're afraid I'm going to disappear any second."

His grin trembled. "Aren't you?"

"No." I shook my head. "I'm not going anywhere. This is real, Mason. I'm real, you're real, and this is really happening."

Leaning down, he hugged me and buried his face in my neck. "It feels like a dream, like I'm going to wake up any second and you'll be gone. I don't want to wake up from this."

"You won't. I promise." I wasn't sure what else I could say to reassure him, so I simply stroked his hair and let him rest on top of me. When I wound my legs around his waist and hooked my feet at the base of his spine, he hummed in approval.

Out of the blue, he said, "Hey, I thought you didn't eat fruit for breakfast." He lifted up off me just enough to snag my strawberry marmalade and eye me with arched, care-to-explain-this eyebrows.

"But that's jam," I argued. "Anything full of sugar doesn't count."

Mason unscrewed the lid. "Is that so?" He dipped out a pinkie full and popped the jelly-soaked digit into his mouth. Closing his eyes, he sighed deeply. "Yeah, that is pretty sweet. But I think it'd taste even sweeter...on you."

As his lashes opened slowly, the intent in his gaze made my body burn with all kinds of hormonal abnormalities, because it couldn't possibly be normal for a girl to get this turned on from a mere remark.

"You're not." Utterly aghast by what he was suggesting, my mouth fell open as he dipped his hand back into the jelly jar for more preservatives.

"This may get a little sticky." His grin looked wickedly pleased.

"Mason," I warned in a don't-you-dare voice, even though my body was heating in all the right places, and the muscles deep in my abdomen were contracting and preparing themselves for another earth-shattering orgasm.

He smeared one of my nipples and I gasped at the chill. But almost immediately, he leaned down and heated the area with a swipe of his tongue.

My back arched off the tabletop, and I had to clutch the edge with both hands.

"Incredible." He moaned as he licked the last bit of strawberry off me. "But I know where this would taste even better."

When he peeled off my panties, I nearly shot off the table. "Mason, oh, my God. You *can't.*"

Could he?

Holy shit, he could.

He caught my hip as soon as I sat up. "Shh," he murmured against my mouth just before he kissed me long and tenderly. His lips had the power to kill brain cells; it didn't even occur to me to resist after that.

I relaxed onto my back when he urged me down again. Then I opened my thighs when he nudged them apart.

He straightened nonchalantly and stared at me all spread open as his personal feast. He wasn't in any hurry to begin his meal, however. With a slow, sensual smile, he watched me while he picked up his glass of juice. I tensed, thinking he'd pour it on me and lick that off too. But he just took a long drink, his throat working as he swallowed.

His eyes never left mine as he finally lowered the cup, sighed, and licked a droplet of orange off his full bottom lip.

"Dear God." I panted, unable to look away.

His stare left my eyes to run over my completely exposed, waiting body. He examined me as if he were mentally mapping out everything he was going to do to me. I was already halfway gone into ecstasy land by the time he picked up the jar of jelly again. When he knelt between my legs and coated me with sugary strawberry wetness, I arched and squirmed, thrashing my head. Then I came hard against his mouth when he licked the glob of jam away.

He didn't stop there. Oh, no.

Scooping up another finger full, he started all over again, building me back up. This time, he took his mouth off me and fingers out of me just before I could come.

Replacing his tongue with something just as delicious, he pushed inside. My back bowed off the table as my thighs hugged him hard. Straightening to his full height, he hooked his arms under my knees and gazed down at me.

"Christ." He groaned, his eyes going unfocused. "You are so..."

"Beautiful?" I tossed out the breathless guess. "Amazing? Fun?" I couldn't come up with a fourth suggestion because I ended up crying out an orgasm instead.

"Yes," Mason hissed. His stomach muscles tensed as he thrust once more and shuddered inside me. "Yes."

~$~

Staring up at the ceiling in a dazed, sticky, satisfied mess, I wondered if one of Mason's clients had ever taught him how amazing strawberry jam could be.

I told myself it didn't matter where he'd learned such a neat trick. It felt so good; it shouldn't bother me. But it did. My heart felt charred and raw.

How many women had he given this exact treatment? How much money had he earned from it? How special did that really make it between us?

I hated how much this ate at me. What he'd been before he'd met me wasn't significant to what we were building right here and now. But I was so incredibly jealous of every other female who'd ever touched him or wanted to touch him.

Or looked at him.

He landed on the table beside me, pink smears on the corner of his mouth as he beamed with pride. I was grateful my aunt and uncle were not spendthrifts—they had to buy the best of everything—so we didn't cause the sturdy table to buckle under both our weights. It held us securely, and Mason looked so happy and content, I wanted to cry. Why did I have to have such unhappy thoughts when he was so pleased and satisfied?

"I've always wanted to do something like that," he said, sounding like a little boy who'd finally been allowed to drive the car.

Instant relief consumed me. Oh, thank God. He hadn't shared this intimacy with another woman.

I rolled toward him and threw my arms around his neck. He snuggled into me with an approving sound and hugged me back.

After kissing him lightly on the mouth, I said, "You know, we should do breakfast together more often."

His eyes sparkled. "You know, I totally agree."

~$~

It ended up, we did do breakfast together the next morning. Mason stayed all through Saturday. Yes, he let his mother know he wouldn't be home.

Since he'd been suspended from work and wasn't allowed to go near the Country Club for a week, he stuck around my apartment, and we remained inseparable for the rest of that lazy afternoon. Borrowing my calculus book, he did his math assignment while I worked on Virology. And let me tell you, naked homework sessions are a blast. I sat on one end of the couch and he sat on the other as we kicked our feet up and rested them on each other's stomachs...until this one time, my heel totally slipped just the teeny tiniest bit. It slid over his junk and kind of pressed against him harder that I probably should have. When I felt some swelling under my arch, well... my toes felt compelled to investigate further.

After that, we didn't get a whole lot of homework done. We did learn where the most sensitive places were on each other, however.

But as all honeymoons must come to an end, ours did too. Sunday morning, Mason woke me with a full body massage. After stroking every inch of my body until I was a pile of yummy, relaxed mush, he had his wicked way with me. And I have to admit, I really, really liked his wicked ways.

Kissing me as I drifted in a haze of semi-conscious post-coital bliss, he said, "I'll make you a deal. If you promise not to move from this spot and stay exactly as you are until I get back, I'll run out and find us some lattes."

I moaned in delight. "Sold."

He popped from the bed, looking way too energized for my taste. Once he tugged his clothes on—I know, boo hiss, clothes bad—he grinned and leaned down to kiss me goodbye.

I'm fairly certain he meant it to be a quick peck goodbye, but...I couldn't help myself. I sank my fingers into his hair—because I was actually allowed to touch it now, *squee!*—and opened my mouth under his, my teeth nipping at his bottom lip.

Groaning, Mason crawled back onto the bed and pinned me immobile under the covers so he could take over.

His eyes sparkled as he paused kissing me to grin. "So you want to tease, eh?"

It took us another twenty minutes of *teasing* each other before he finally rolled out of bed again.

"Don't move," he warned one last time before disappearing from my room. Footsteps, the jingle of keys, and the door closing marked his departure.

I sighed, feeling a little lost without him near.

It was sad, really. I'd had no idea a girl could become so addicted, so completely, and so quickly. With Jeremy—

Oh, why did I keep comparing? There was no comparison. I'd always been a little leery of Jeremy, deep down, as if my soul recognized he was no good. But either Mason had my soul completely fooled, or he was the man for me. I voted for option number two, hands down.

Feeling delicious and pleasantly sore in all the right places, I stretched languidly under the sheets just as a beep came from the nightstand.

I frowned because my cell phone didn't make that kind of boring tone. With a quick glance to the left, I discovered Mason had left his here. Worried it might be Dawn trying to reach him, I checked the ID.

When I saw the caller was *Landlady*, my blood ran cold. I should've felt guilty for opening her text and reading his private message. But, nah, I totally didn't.

I have Jeremy Walden's number dialed into my phone. Need you to come at ten tonight to keep me from pushing send.

With a gasp, I dropped Mason's phone.

That bitch!

I should've known she'd keep trying to use me as bait to blackmail him into sleeping with her. I mean, why didn't everyone suspect that of their evil, cougar landlady?

White-hot rage smoldered inside me. How dare she? How dare she hurt him like that?

I knew Mason. And every visit he spent in her

bedroom damaged him. It stripped away a part of him and transformed him into someone he despised.

Well, that shit stopped now. No one hurt my man and got away with it. Mason wasn't any woman's play toy. Not any longer.

He also wasn't the only one who could sacrifice himself to protect the people he loved.

So, that's pretty much when I completely lost my mind.

A plan formed in my head, and I just couldn't shake it away. It would be risky, putting my own safety on the line. It'd be slightly illegal, but heck, I'd always wanted to know what breaking the law felt like.

It might possibly blow up in my face too. But to free Mason of that woman forever, I had to try. And I didn't experience one iota of regret as I made up my mind.

Putting step one of Operation Save Mason into motion, I pushed *reply* and typed in "*I'll be there.*" After sending "Mason's" answer, I cleared both her text and my response from his phone completely.

~$~

By the time Mason returned with both his hands full of lattes, I had dressed and moved to the front room, disregarding his request to stay put. After that text, though, I hadn't been able to relax or remain naked a second longer.

He knew something was wrong the moment he saw me. His face filled with trepidation. "What happened?"

I didn't want to lie to him, but I couldn't tell him the truth, either, or he'd put a stop to my plans before I even started them.

I decided to go with the tactic he'd used on Dawn.

"One of your clients sent you a text message. I read it. Then deleted it."

See, total truth.

He stared at me a moment before coming toward me. "Good. I'm glad you deleted it." Sitting beside me, he placed the lattes on the coffee table before turning and taking both my hands. "But I don't like this look on your face, Reese. Talk to me."

I shook my head, not sure what to say. I was still too rattled from the message, too rattled from the plans I'd made. Too rattled by everything.

Licking my lips, I tried. "H-how often do you get a text like that?"

He winced and glanced down at our interlaced fingers. "It'll take a while for the word to get out that I'm done."

I nodded. "And how much longer after that will it take to convince all your clients that you're really serious this time?"

I don't know where these words came from, or why I used such a scathing tone to deliver them. I didn't want to pick a fight with Mason. I just wanted to gather him close and tell him I'd protect him always.

But the idea of texts pouring into his phone for days and weeks, maybe months, from women wanting sex bothered me. So the words kept spewing from my mouth.

"How long will they continue to slip you their business cards and tell you to call as soon as things between you and me get a little rough? I mean, how closely am I going to have to watch what I say? Because the first time I piss you off, you could just going running back to—"

"Stop," he demanded sharply and yanked me

into a hard hug. "I'm not going to cheat on you, Reese. I will never do that. I tried the other way. For *two* years. I didn't like it. I'm not going back. I just want you." A tremor rattled through him and echoed into me. "Don't break up with me already. It's only been one day. That's not enough, not *nearly* enough. Please don't give up on us yet."

"I won't." Bursting into tears, I sobbed, "I'm sorry. I don't know why I keep saying this stuff." Holy crap, why was I getting so emotional? It wasn't even close to my emotional time of the month. But I crawled into his lap and burrowed close. "I just want you too, Mason. I don't want to break up with you. I don't want to lose you at all."

"Shh." He gathered me close and kissed my hair, rocking me gently back and forth. "You're not going to lose me. It's okay."

He swayed with me, letting me cry out my tears. When I finished, he wiped the wetness off my cheeks and kissed my nose, ticking the diamond stud with his lips.

"I know it has to be damn near impossible for any woman to deal with a boyfriend who has a history like mine," he admitted, "especially being that it's a very recent history for me. And it isn't fair to ask you to. But I *need* you to. If anyone can get over what I was, you can. You are so strong. You are so amazing. You are... everything."

See, was it any wonder I was so obsessed with this guy?

I lifted my face from his neck and met his worried gaze. "I'll get over it," I assured him with utmost confidence.

I didn't care how hard it would be; I just knew I *would* get over his baggage. Because the alternative—losing him forever—would be unbearable.

He nodded and kissed me, but I didn't taste

passion. This kiss was desperate and seeking; he needed reassurance that I wasn't going to leave him. Kissing him back, I put my heart into it, and it seemed to pacify him.

We held each other on the couch, just like that, for the longest time. But for the rest of the day, I sensed a distance between us. I knew it was tension on my part—worry about the evening to come—and I suspected for him, he was worried he could lose me at the drop of a hat.

In an attempt to ease some awkwardness, I suggested we finish our *Harry Potter* movie marathon. We made it through three more videos before evening approached. That's when I stretched, faked a yawn, and kicked him out—politely, of course—telling him he really needed to go home at some point before Dawn labeled me Son Corrupter of the Year.

Seriously, though, I needed him gone so I could prepare for phase two of Operation Save Mason.

He looked like a kicked puppy as I walked him to the door, but he didn't beg his case to stay. Such a guy, he didn't want to appear whipped or anything, I guess. I put a little extra oomph into my goodbye kiss, trying to convince him how much I loved him.

But all the angst behind the glance he sent me before he jogged down the stairs and strode to his Jeep had me fisting a hand to my chest and wanting to call him back to confess everything. I watched from the opened door of my loft as he backed from the drive and disappeared down the street.

Then I blew out a breath, pulled on my big-girl panties, and got to work.

CHAPTER **TWENTY-EIGHT**

I dressed in all black. Remembering I'd left my car parked all weekend down the street from Mason's house, I walked to my destination and arrived without a minute to spare.

I figured the gate separating Mason's back yard from Mrs. Garrison's would be unlocked to allow him entrance for their ten o'clock rendezvous. And I was right. My heart pounded as I stole across her neatly trimmed lawn to her back door, which had also been left unlocked for him.

Scared half out of my mind, and yet excited that the time was here—I was really freaking doing this—I eased the back door shut behind me, hoping she hadn't heard me enter.

Music played from somewhere on the second story. I paused, listening to the muffled jazzy tune I could barely hear over my own harsh breathing. I couldn't believe I was seriously *inside* the devil's den. The air was warm and sticky and made me feel slightly suffocated in my dark-from-head-to-toe clothes.

Mind kicking into gear, I glanced around, not sure where to start my search.

Come on, Reese, think. If you were the computer of a slutty middle-age cougar who liked to blackmail her neighbor boy into having sex with her, where would you hide out all day?

My first guess would be the bedroom— obviously—but she was probably there right now, dolling herself up. For Mason.

I gagged at the thought.

He was so never going anywhere near that again.

Motivated by the thought, I stepped forward and glanced cautiously through the doorway of the back laundry room and into a dimly lit, state-of-the-art kitchen. I almost passed out when I saw a closed laptop sitting on her bar.

No freaking way. I couldn't possibly be that lucky.

Oh, well. I wasn't one to look a gift horse in the mouth.

I darted into the kitchen and seated my rump onto a barstool in front of her Dell. After cracking my knuckles and rolling my shoulders as if to pop my neck, I held my breath and reached for the lid.

No alarms sounded. No metal bars crashed down around me. No hidden trap in the floor opened up and dropped me into her dungeon below.

I was in the witch's computer. And the idiot witch hadn't even set a password. *Score.*

I stared sightlessly at her home screen a good minute, listening and practically waiting for footsteps, certain Mrs. Garrison would arrive now and murder me. But the first floor of the house remained silent.

Finally, blowing out a breath, I focused on step three of Operation Save Mason.

Clicking on the email icon, I rolled my eyes when I was sent straight to her inbox. Jesus, did the woman password protect *nothing*? You'd think she'd be a little more paranoid since she was so shady herself.

I shrugged again. Her loss. My gain.

Composing a new letter, I typed Jeremy's address, j_walden@ymail.net, into the *To* box.

In the subject line, I wrote: *Looking for Teresa Nolan?*

And in the body of the message I typed in my new name and mailing address. I was just entering the town and state when I heard high heels on the stairs.

My veins jolted with a surge of adrenaline.

But really. This was so awesome. I couldn't have scheduled her arrival any better than if I'd sent her an itinerary.

Enter one skanky landlady, stage left.

I was just finishing up the zip code when she strolled into the kitchen, carrying an empty wine glass and wearing a slinky green and black teddy.

Which Mason would *never* see her wearing.

She skidded to a halt when she spotted me, her stilettoes making her stumble. It was kind of comical, so I grinned as I waved at her in the most affable manner ever. "Hey. Cute nighty. *Victoria's Secret*, am I right?"

Then I laughed as I pointedly pushed the send button right in front of her.

"What the hell are you doing?" She stormed forward, jerking her laptop out of my hands and sliding it around to face her so she could see what I'd done.

"Oh, I just thought I'd come over to let you

know Mason wouldn't be able to make it tonight." With a shrug and guilty roll of my eyes, I confessed, "I kind of intercepted the text you sent him this morning." Wrinkling my nose, I sent her an apologetic cringe. "Sorry, but he never saw it."

"What..." Mrs. Garrison was too busy staring at her screen in confusion to listen to me. "What did you do on my computer?"

"I emailed Jeremy. Told him where I was and what name I was going under. I mean, wasn't that what you kept threating to do if Mason didn't keep *servicing* you?" This time I nailed a shocked expression like a pro. "My God, you weren't bullshitting him, were you?"

Mrs. Garrison clicked into her send history, and her mouth fell open as she read the message I'd just sent. "What...why..." She shook her head, at a total loss for words.

"Okay, I have to know," I said in a conversational manner as her face flamed red with confusion and anger. "Are those *genuine* Christian Louboutin shoes or knock-offs? Because I have *always* wanted to own a genuine Louboutin heel. And I would be pea green with envy if I knew you owned a pair. Are they very comfortable? Not that comfort really matters when your feet are wrapped in a pair of—"

"Are you *totally insane*? Why...why would you tell him where you are? You should be scared to death of this psycho."

"Oh, trust me, I am. But insane?" I snorted and waved an unconcerned hand. "What a subjective term. I mean, what one person might consider totally normal—like, I don't know...forcing her young, unwilling neighbor to have sex with her repeatedly—another person might think is totally repugnant. So, from *your* point of view, yeah, I probably look pretty much off my rocker right about now for sacrificing my own safety for the sake of saving the man I love from being blackmailed by a sick, vindictive, *old* spinster."

Mrs. Garrison's jaw tensed. "You're as annoying as you are crazy."

I pretended to think about it for a moment. "Meh. Maybe. My parents do keep trying to send me to a therapist. For the crazy part, not the annoying one. And I guess I can see where they're coming from. I mean, being pinned against a wall with a knife to my throat by someone I thought loved me did kind of mess with my head for a while. But, you know what, I'm kind of glad I did email him...oops."

I covered my mouth and giggled. "I mean, I'm glad *you* emailed him and told him where I was. I was seriously getting tired of always being afraid, of always glancing over my shoulder and expecting him to be hiding in every shadow." I let out a refreshed sigh. "I'm glad this is almost over, you know. And hey, if he kills me this time, *you'll* catch some of the blame for telling him where I was."

Vibrating with fury, Mrs. Garrison hissed at me. "Get out of my house."

I narrowed my eyes. "With pleasure." Tossing my hair, I slid off her bar stool. "Oh, but one more thing." I whipped out my hand and slapped her as hard as I could, actually wrenching her face to the side with the force of my blow. "Don't ever touch Mason again. Or I swear to God, I'll go even more psycho on your ass."

Mrs. Garrison straightened and wiped her face just below her nose with a trembling hand. When she came away with blood on her fingers, I gaped. Holy swinging palms, Batman; I'd drawn blood.

Cool.

"I hope Walden kills you slowly," she snarled, her hazel eyes glowing with hatred.

I grinned pleasantly. "If he does, I'll make sure to come back as a nasty poltergeist just to brutally haunt you." Twirling away, I strolled out of her house.

Mrs. Garrison had actually kind of disappointed me. She'd let me go without a fight. Humph. *Chicken.* I'd been all keyed up to kick some cougar ass, too.

Oh, well, such was life. *C'est la vie.* Maybe I could beat up the next woman who tried to hurt my man.

I drove home, feeling truly powerful for the first time in too long. As all those women had taken a piece of control away from Mason and made him feel cheap and used, Jeremy had taken away the same thing from me.

Fighting back, standing up for myself, taking control again felt nice. Felt good.

I felt like I totally needed to celebrate somehow.

As luck would have it, a familiar Jeep sat parked in my spot when I pulled into the Mercers' driveway. When I saw the sexy owner of said Jeep sitting on the top step in front of my apartment, waiting for me, I grinned.

Parking my car beside his, I killed the engine and leapt from the driver's seat, full of smiles.

"Mason," I squealed as I flew up all fifteen steps. "What're you doing here?" I crawled right into his lap and wrapped my arms around him. "Oh, my God. You have no idea how happy I am to see you."

Kissing him before he could answer, I took control of his mouth, much the same way I'd just taken control of Mrs. Garrison. I showed them both who was boss. Oh, yes, I did.

Mason didn't seem to mind as he kissed me back, thrusting with his tongue just as heartily as I was and entwining it with mine. Then, scooping me up by the butt, he cupped both cheeks and stood.

See, I told you he had some impressive muscles.

Not even breaking the kiss, he swung us toward my front door. "I couldn't stay away," he managed to explain breathlessly between kisses. "I couldn't leave things like they were. Jesus, where the *hell* have you been?"

"I'll explain later."

"Mmph." He seemed fine with that and kicked the door shut behind us as soon as we gained entrance.

We attacked each other. Right there against the door of my apartment.

I think I needed to release some of the adrenaline still thrumming through my system after my one and only stint of B & E as badly as he needed reassurance that I wasn't still freaked out over the text I'd read earlier.

"Wow," I said as soon as my tongue would allow me to speak intelligible words again. "I had no idea breaking the law could make a girl so crazy horny."

I wilted down the surface of the door until I was sitting on the welcome mat, pleasantly dazed by how amazing the evening had turned out.

Mason slumped down beside me. "Do I even want to know what you mean by that?"

I grinned. And told him everything.

His mouth fell open. "You did *what*? But, you... she...*how* could you send him your new identity? Are you *insane*?"

He sounded a little too much like his landlady,

so I scowled. Then I remembered I *had* sent that email, hadn't I?

"Oh, that reminds me. I'd better check my inbox of that new account I set up this morning."

I crawled to my purse I'd dropped beside the welcome mat and dug around inside until I found my cell phone. "I created it under the name Jeremy Walden. Need to check if I have any incoming messages." As I clicked my way into the inbox, I winked at Mason. "And what do you know, I do."

I turned the screen to show him the email from Patricia Garrison.

He gaped before sending me a stunned glance. "You faked her out."

I tossed my hair and preened. "Yep. Now...how would Jeremy respond to this letter?" Tapping my chin, I contemplated. "If you were a psycho stalker ex-boyfriend, what would you say?"

Mason scooted closer to be a part of the planning process. "Thanks?" he suggested.

"Perfect." I kissed his cheek and got a little distracted, needing to kiss his nose next, then his mouth. Before I totally lost my focus, I pulled back, bit my lip, and started typing.

Thanks. I owe you one.

"There." I pushed send and looked up. "That sounds like something he'd say. I'll delete the account later, just to make sure she doesn't reply."

Mason appeared overcome. "This was dangerous, Reese. I can't believe you risked so much just to free me from her."

"Hey." Cupping his face in my hands, I admitted, "I would risk it a thousand times over to help you any way I could."

He pressed his forehead against mine. "I still don't deserve you."

"But I'm here anyway," I teased, tipping my

face so that I could flutter my lashes against his cheek in a butterfly kiss. "Whatever will you do with me now?"

Tugging me closer, he settled my body against his and brushed the hair out of my face. "I guess I'll just have to cherish you with every breath I have."

CHAPTER **TWENTY-NINE**

Mason hadn't shown up on my doorstep with a lot of forethought. He totally forgot to bring a fresh pair of clothes, or his school things, otherwise we could've washed each other in the shower—kind of like how we'd squished into my dinky bathroom on both Saturday and Sunday to have way too much fun with the soap—and gone to classes together on Monday morning.

But, I had a feeling there'd only been one thing on his mind when he'd driven over the night before.

Such a guy.

He rolled out of bed and left me with a lingering kiss, telling me he'd sit with me at lunch. Then he was gone.

I rushed through my morning ablutions, hoping I'd get to see him before our first class. But no. I slunk into Brit Lit, depressed because I'd missed him. I didn't even realize Eva was absent from her typical seat next to me until halfway through the hour.

Yikes, I hope her breakup with Alec wasn't hitting her too hard. She had enough on her plate as it was. I also hoped she hadn't told her parents about the baby yet. I wanted to be with her, holding her hand when she did, and I hadn't exactly been available the entire weekend to do much hand holding.

God, I had to be the worst friend ever. I texted her during my free hour, but she didn't return my call.

I cringed, hoping it was only morning sickness keeping her from checking in and not anger over the fact I had totally blown her off for the past two days.

I thought of Mason all the way through calculus. We'd eventually gotten our math assignment done on Saturday, but I wasn't sure he'd been able to concentrate very well on his equations. I hoped his being with me didn't cause him to flunk.

Yes, I was beginning to worry about everything this morning. But something strange had me on edge. A feeling in the air, a freaky premonition that life was going too well. I wasn't sure what it was. I just seriously wanted it to go away so I could return to the euphoria I'd been dwelling in for the last forty-eight hours.

When I stepped out of class, I automatically glanced around for Mason. Sometimes, we passed each other coming and going here because he had class in this room directly after I did. Today, I really looked forward to brushing by him—wink, wink.

But a familiar face sitting on a bench not far from the doorway stopped me cold. A handful of students walked past, blocking my view, making me panic, because I was sure the vision would be gone when they passed. I told myself my paranoia was getting to me too much today. But after the students moved on, he still sat there, waiting.

For me.

My knees buckled and I had to clutch the wall to support myself. I froze, not sure what to do.

I could scream and run. I could approach him boldly. I could silently try to slip away, hiding behind clusters of people.

But I just stood there, staring at my psycho stalker ex-boyfriend as he leered back with one of his infamous gloating smirks.

"*Found you*," he mouthed the words so clearly I could actually read what he said.

I turned away from him, planning to stride off, even though I knew that wouldn't get me far. But then the worst thing possible happened.

Mason appeared, messenger bag slung over his shoulder as he approached his next class. He grinned when he saw me, a warm, private smile that held all the secrets of our weekend passion.

Oh, God. I loved him so much. I could not let Jeremy near him. Jeremy would *kill* him if he knew how important Mason was to me.

But nothing was going to stop either guy from approaching.

As Jeremy stood, I reacted before my brain could fully process what I was planning. I hurried to Mason. "Professor McGonagall," I gasped. "Thank God I ran into you."

Yes, I know I used a *Harry Potter* character for him, and a female one at that. But it wasn't as if I had a whole lot of a time to concoct a foolproof strategy. I was working straight from the hip here. And doing *just fine* if you ask me.

Besides, Jeremy had never once cared about my Harry Potter craze. He wouldn't know the difference. The clueless Muggle.

Rushing to unzip my bag, I said, "I know it was due last Friday, but I finished my paper and I would really appreciate it if you'd reconsider accepting it late."

As I yanked my graded Wife of Bath essay from my bag—which had received an A; boo *yah*!—I finally dared to look up into Mason's face.

Biting the inside of my lip, I prayed he would play along.

He blinked once, okay, twice. Then he said, "I told you no late assignments, Miss Randall."

God, I loved him. He fell right into line with my act perfectly. Then again, by the amused twinkle in his eyes, he probably thought this was some kind of kinky naughty schoolgirl foreplay.

"But I worked on it all weekend." The little hitch in my voice—because I was all keyed up about seeing Jeremy—sounded classic. Hmm. Maybe I should drop Virology completely and take up acting.

Mason lifted an unimpressed eyebrow. "All weekend, hmm?" The twist of his lips told me he knew otherwise. "On a paper you were supposed to be working on all *semester*?"

Jeez, did he have to play it quite this good?

I almost glowered at him. But I was still too freaked out about my psycho stalker ex hovering a mere ten feet away, listening to every word we said.

"Please," I rasped, the fear filtering through me until his expression finally sparked with concern. "Could you just give it a look?"

He nodded with a resigned sigh. "Okay, fine. But this is the last time I'll make allowances for you."

When he tried to take the paper from me, I jerked it back. "Wait. I...I need to sign my name."

My hands shook so hard that when I fumbled my way into my backpack, a tear actually dripped from my cheek.

Mason had mercy on me. "Here," he said, holding out his own pen, his brows wrinkling as if he was finally figuring out this was not a playful, bantering game.

"Thanks." I took it from him and lifted my knee to scribble *Jer is here* right below where my name was already typed onto the sheet.

I handed it to him and he barely glanced over what I'd written.

"I see." His eyes flashed to me. "You know, maybe we should go to my office and discuss this in more detail. I have an idea how you can make up some extra credit points."

"No." I shook my head. I needed to get him as far away from me—and therefore as far away from Jeremy—as possible before Jeremy realized who Mason really was. I took a step back. "No, I need to get to my next class."

Mason—damn him for caring so much—wasn't about to let me go anywhere by myself. "Reese." He grasped my arm. "Where?" he asked so quietly, only I could hear. He didn't even move his lips as he spoke.

Before I could answer—not that I was really going to tell him where Jeremy was—a familiar, super creepy arm slithered around my waist.

Jeremy's potent aftershave gagged me as he tightened his grip.

"There's my Reese's Pieces," he murmured in my ear, cuddling in close. "I've been looking everywhere for you, baby."

My entire body went rigid against his, and I could only imagine how white my face was as I gaped up at Mason.

I decided right then and there, I'd never seen him truly mad before. His jaw popped before he turned his attention to Jeremy and looked pointedly at the other man's arm wrapped around me.

Jeremy hitched his chin in greeting. "So, you're one of Reese's professors, huh? You look kind of young to be a teacher."

"That's because I'm not," Mason answered, his voice hard and tight. When he jerked his bag off his shoulder and tossed it to the floor by his feet, both Jeremy and I glanced down at it in confusion.

Neither one of us saw the fist that came streaking out of nowhere.

But seriously, Mason hitting Jeremy in the jaw was flat out amazing. He moved so fast, I had no warning until the slap of flesh and crunch of nose cartilage made me scream out a startled yelp. Jeremy's grip left me, and he toppled over backward, landing on his ass in the middle of the hallway.

"You hit him," I said in utter shock, blinking at Jeremy on the floor before I looked up at Mason with the same stunned gaze. "I can't believe you just hit him."

That hadn't been in my plans at all. But I liked this new turn of events. A lot.

"He tried to *kill* you," Mason argued with me as if he thought my shock was from disapproval. "Hell, yes, I hit him."

I gawked a moment longer before I shook my head. "But that was just so...*cool.*"

Mason's proud grin was instant. His eyes flashed with heat and he stepped toward me as if he wanted to do a little celebratory kissing.

But, of course, simply hitting the bad guys never kept them down.

One second, my wonderful, amazing, spider-killing, stalker-punching, ex-gigolo soul mate was shifting toward me, looking like he wanted to take me against the wall of the school's hallway. The next, he noticed something on the floor. His face contorted in horror, and he shoved me—yes, *shoved* me—aside before he dove on top of Jeremy.

I stumbled into the wall, taken aback. When I steadied myself enough to focus on the two guys rolling across the floor in a tangle of arms and legs, I was so shocked to watch them actually wrestling I didn't see what they were wrestling *for* until someone yelled, "*Gun!*"

Pandemonium reigned. Girls screamed. People scattered. And a stampede ensued. I was jostled back against the wall as a horde of students torpedoed past me. Crying out Mason's name in fear for his life, I fought the flow of fleeing traffic to reach him.

God, I was so stupid. I should've known Jeremy would be armed and dangerous. And since his knife hadn't done the trick the last time he'd gone after me, he'd pulled out the big guns this round—literally. Okay, honestly, it was kind of a small handgun he and Mason were fighting over. But I'm sure it still had the capacity to kill a person just as dead as a big gun could.

As soon as a path cleared for me to shove away from the wall, I scrambled toward the wrestling, grunting, swearing men on the floor. No one else had jumped in to assist Mason, so I decided I would, even though my heart was pounding in my chest.

But they were moving so much, constantly struggling to best the other, I had no idea how to help without getting in the way.

About to have a conniption fit, I cried out Mason's name.

Big mistake. My hysterical voice took his attention away from the psycho under him, and he glanced my way...just as the gun went off.

CHAPTER **THIRTY**

I paced the corridor of the hospital, ready to crawl out of my own skin. I hated waiting.

Why was this taking so long?

Did patching up bullet holes really take so freaking long? Or had the injury been worse than what people were telling me?

I rubbed the sides of my arms, so antsy and full of pent-up fear I wanted to scratch the wicked, terrifying sensation out of me with my bare claws.

"Miss Nolan, er, Randall, er..."

I whirled toward the approaching police officer. "Just Reese," I assured him with a tense smile. "Did you question Jeremy yet? Do you know how he found me?"

I'd asked this same question earlier when he'd taken my initial statement, but at that point, no one had talked to Jeremy yet.

The officer—Mikrut, I think his name was— nodded. "Mr. Walden confessed that he tracked you through the phone bills he found in your parents' house when he broke in recently. It took him a few days to get a computer techno friend to trace the extra line to you in Florida, and then it took him another couple of days to drive here. From the gas station receipts we found in his car, I believe he's been in Waterford for at least seventy-two hours."

I shivered. That meant he'd already been here when Mrs. Garrison had blackmailed Mason. And he'd been here when Mason and I had hooked up.

Shaking my head, I buried my face in my hands. "So, it didn't matter that I moved halfway across the country, that I changed my—"

A comforting hand landed on my shoulder. "You won't have to worry about him again. Not for a long time."

With a snort, I lifted my face and sent him a disbelieving sneer. "Yeah, until his daddy gets *this* trial dropped too."

Officer Mikrut shook his head. "Not after everything he did today."

I blew out a breath. "So that gives me what...?"

"Let's see. Two counts of attempted murder. Firing a weapon in a public school. Breaking and entering. Resisting arrest. I'd say...twenty to thirty years?" The cop shrugged.

I liked that guess. "Thank God."

He smiled. "Have the doctors come out with an update yet? I really need to question—"

"No." I shook my head savagely, not wanting to think about why it might be taking the doctor, or nurse, or anyone, so long to come back with an update. "Not yet."

"Don't worry so much," he told me with a soft smile. "I've seen people pull through with wounds much worse than this one. I'm sure everything will be fine."

"Thanks." I nodded, but I wasn't convinced.

Officer Mikrut drifted away to speak to a nurse. I hoped he got more information than I'd been getting. Feeling drained, I slumped onto the nearest bench in the quiet hospital hall just outside the stuffy waiting room and rested my head against the wall.

As I closed my eyes, someone sat next to me. "I got you a white chocolate mocha espresso."

Tears filled my lashes and my throat burned. I shook my head. "I don't think I could drink anything right now. But thank you."

I reached out blindly and instantly found a warm hand.

"Come here," Mason murmured and pulled me into his lap.

I curled into the fetal position and rested my cheek on his shoulder. As I soaked his shirt with tears, he kissed my hair.

"Eva's going to be okay. I know it."

I covered my mouth. "I still can't believe he shot her. He shot my *cousin*."

"I know. But she's related to you; she's tough. She'll pull through."

I clutched him hard. It was all still a lot to take in.

After Jeremy had put two rounds in the ceiling of Waterford County Community College, Mason had managed to elbow him in the face and wrestle the gun away moments before a swarm of law enforcement had shown up. Thanks to Eva.

Apparently, Jeremy had broken into my apartment this morning after I'd already left for class. Eva, running late, had intercepted him. He shot her—I know, I know, I still can't believe I said that either—and then left her bleeding body lying on the ground outside the Mercers' four-bay garage so he could find me at school.

According to Officer Mikrut, Eva had been lucid enough to pull her cell phone from her purse, dial 911, and warn them Jeremy would probably be at the college looking for me right before she lost consciousness. That's why they'd already been on campus when the first errant shot was fired outside my calculus class.

"Did you finally get hold of her parents?" Mason asked, kissing my hair.

"Yes. They're on their way now." Aunt Mads and Uncle Shaw had left for one of Uncle Shaw's work conferences the night before. "They had just gotten off the plane in Phoenix when I reached them."

"And what about Alec? If she's really carrying his baby, don't you think he'd want to know about this?"

I tensed, a little miffed he wasn't as sure Eva's baby was Alec's as Eva had claimed it was. But then, I knew he wasn't exactly an Eva fan.

"It *is* his baby," I hissed, "and, no. He *broke up* with her after finding out about it. I'm not calling that dick unless E. asks me to."

"Okay, okay," Mason assured me in a placating voice. "I'm sorry. I just—"

"It's fine." I curled closer to him and rested my head on his shoulder. I hoped E. didn't hate me for blurting out her secret to Mason, but I'd been freaking at the time, worried about her life and her child's life. He had assured me he'd keep quiet until she wanted the news made public. But I wasn't so sure there *would* be any news after today. Even if Eva survived, what were the chances of her baby making it too? "I just hope they're both okay."

"They will be. The cop said she was shot in the shoulder. That's nowhere near the fetus."

"But—"

"Shh." He stroked his hand down my spine.

I closed my eyes, soaking up his unquestioning

support. I didn't know how long we held each other like that, with me wrapped up on his lap and our faces tucked close together.

When I heard footsteps drawing close, I lifted my head to see a doctor approaching. "Oh, thank God."

But the man under me tensed. "Shit."

I glanced at him, alarmed. "What's wrong?"

Just as I spoke, the doctor glanced into the nearest waiting room. "Mercer family?"

"Here." I leapt off Mason's lap, forgetting his strange behavior, until he reached out and grabbed my fingers as if to draw me back to him.

The doctor turned toward us and faltered in her step when she saw him. "M-Mason?"

His fingers tightened around mine as the woman's gaze skipped questioningly from him to me and back to him again.

And suddenly, I understood.

I whirled to him and slugged him on the arm. "You have got to be kidding me. A doctor? A frigging *medical* doctor?"

He looked as if he were going to be beaten with a whip as he shied back, his face pallid and petrified. "I...I'm sorry."

The doctor jerked backward as if she was going to run off.

"Hey!" I sliced her a killer glare. "Aren't you going to tell us how Eva is?"

She paused and cleared her throat, coloring slightly. "Of course. Sorry..." She nervously pushed her platinum blond hair out of her face, making the sleeves of her white coat droop down enough to reveal the Michael Kors watch strapped around her wrist.

Damn, why did all of Mason's ex-clients have to have such good taste in fashion?

"Miss Mercer is stable," she said. "Her vitals are strong and she's awake and lucid."

"And the baby?" I blurted out.

Dr. Slut nodded. "Still has a heartbeat."

I slumped against Mason, and he gathered me close, kissing my forehead.

His ex-client glanced curiously between us before returning to business. "You can see her in a couple minutes. Once they have her in a private room, I'll have a nurse come back and take you to her."

"Thank you," Mason said, since it seemed obvious I wasn't going to speak to her again.

She nodded and gave us a tight smile. "At least now I know why my call was never returned." Gaze settling on me, she added, "Nice nose ring."

I turned to pin Mason with a scowl as she hurried off. "Why do all your ex-clients remark on my nose ring?" Even Dr. Janison had said something after class one day when I'd been walking by to leave her Brit Lit lecture.

Mason smiled faintly as he tapped my nose. "Because it reminds them how young they no longer are."

I frowned, bewildered. That made no sense. "Younger people do not have a monopoly on nose rings, you know. I've seen plenty of them on women —and men—of all ages."

"Ahh, but it looks hot on you." He paused to nod his head after the departing doctor. "It makes *them* look grasping and old."

Though his words pacified me a little, I still wanted to be pissed. I slugged him in the arm again. "And I thought you said all your clients were bored, rich housewives. Successful doctors, college professors, and landladies don't exactly fit into that category."

Mason flushed and glanced around as if I'd screamed the accusation. "I said *most* of them were," he muttered under his breath. "Not all."

Realizing this wasn't the place to make a scene, I fell moody and silent.

I thought about Mason's shady past and how many freaking horny women there were in Waterford panting after him and thinking they owned him. Then I thought about Eva and her baby, Jeremy and his prison sentence, Alec and his impending fatherhood. Actually, I don't think there was a thought that didn't swirl through my busy, muddled head.

Mason stayed quiet beside me, holding my hand and smoothing his thumb over my knuckles. He remained my one constant. Despite what had just happened, the assurance of his love steadied me, and by the time the nurse arrived to lead us back to Eva, I was doing okay, breathing easily and ready to see my cousin.

She was awake and sitting up in bed, cognizant and cracking jokes the minute we walked into the room.

After taking one look at the companion at my side, she set her hand over her heart. "Aww. A get-well-soon present already? ReeRee, you shouldn't have. Is he going to strip and do a little dance for us, or what?"

Mason's hand tightened in mine, but I only tugged him closer. "Sorry, E. But Mason is retired from all that."

"Is he?" Her blue eyes narrowed on him with suspicion. "Well, he better stay that way if he's going to keep hanging around you. I didn't get shot for you by one douche just so you could get your heart broken by another."

"It's too bad the first douche didn't shoot your

sunny personality right out of you," Mason mut-tered.

"Okay, okay." I held up my hands, playing ref-eree. "No more mudslinging. On any other day, I might be able to handle two people I love absolutely hating each other but...not today. All right? Truce?"

Mason winced and had the grace to look regretful. "Truce," he grumbled, glancing away.

Eva, on the other hand, lifted her eyebrows. "Did you just say the l-word...in reference to the *gigolo*?"

"She did." Mason sent her a challenging, hard look. "And for your information, I *will* be better for her than the last douche. I would rather die than hurt Reese."

Eva eyed him for a long, scrutinizing moment before she sighed and relaxed back against her pillow. "If you lie, I'll be putting a bullet hole in *you*, buddy. And trust me, they're not fun." She winced, suddenly bringing it to my attention how pale she was. "I swear to God, this pain reliever they gave me isn't working *at all*." She shouted the last two words toward the doorway as if she wanted everyone in the hospital to hear how miserable she was.

I panicked. "Do you want me to find a nurse? I'm sure they can give you some more—"

"No." E. set her hand protectively over her stomach. "The less drugs they pump into me, the better it will be for the baby." Then she sliced a wide-eyed look toward Mason and narrowed her gaze threateningly. "You didn't hear that."

He shrugged—the good man. "Hear what?"

The mention of her baby made me think of its asshole father. "I didn't call Alec. I didn't know what you wanted done there."

"Don't." She reached for my hand. "I don't

want him here." Her chilly fingers wrapped around mine. "I just want you...and I guess your gigolo boyfriend can stick around too, if he behaves."

I smiled and rolled my eyes. It was going to be useless to tell her to quit calling him that, wasn't it?

"I mean it, Reese. I know I can be a total bitch, and...and pretty full of myself."

Mason snorted; we both ignored him.

"And you should probably hate me for the way I came onto your boyfriend—even though I really did do that to show you he would be an unfaithful bastard. But you're still the best friend I ever had." Tears welled in her eyes. "Thank you for being here for me. I love you."

Wow, near-death experiences truly brought out the best in my cousin.

With that, I turned into watering pot number two. "I love you too, E. Always." We hugged and bawled all over each other. Mason stepped out of the room, pretending to use the bathroom.

When he returned, Eva and I had settled some, but we still kept dabbing tissues at our moist eyes and then laughing at each other.

Mason and I stayed with her until Aunt Mads and Uncle Shaw arrived. When Eva gave me a look, letting me know she was going to drop the baby bomb on them and wanted to do it by herself, I took Mason's arm and ushered him from the room.

As we walked out of the hospital, hand in hand, he was quiet. Contemplative. But seeing Eva and actually getting to talk to her gave me a certain relief, and I was ready to talk.

I bumped my shoulder into his. When he glanced over, I held up a hand in a universal what's-the-deal signal.

"I'm sorry," he said again, letting go of my hand to wrap his arm around my shoulder and pull me tight against him.

I set my fingers over his heart, already trying to soothe him. "About what?"

He glanced away. "I had no idea Dr. Masterson was the one taking care of Eva."

"Mason," I interrupted when he opened his mouth to say more. He looked so sick with regret that I leaned up and kissed his chin. "I need to confess something."

He paused and crinkled his brow with a confused frown. "Okay."

I pulled him to a bench by a small ornamental tree in front of the hospital and sat us both down. Taking each of his hands, I looked him in the eye. "When you tackled Jeremy today and that gun went off, my heart stopped. I swear, it literally stopped in my chest. I thought...I thought he'd shot *you*, and I was ready to die right along with you."

Pausing to wipe at my dry face, I blew out a deep breath and shook my head. "Then it went off again, and I was certain you were dead."

Mason didn't say anything; he just tightened his grip on my hands.

I sent him a watery smile. "You cannot believe how relieved I was to see you roll off of him and take control of his weapon. I couldn't believe you were actually alive, that I was so lucky. Even after I found out about Eva and I paced the halls of the hospital, wondering if she was going to make it or not, I still felt...lucky. I'm just so glad it wasn't you."

Eyes glistening with love, he breathed out a reassured sound and yanked me close for a hard embrace.

"Do you understand what I'm saying?" I asked against his neck. "It doesn't matter how many women paid you for sex. I won't leave you because of them. I don't think I could ever leave you for any reason."

He kissed me, tasting of relief and devotion. His lips told me he didn't think he could ever leave me either.

"But running into your old—and I mean, like, five years younger than God, old—clients is beginning to get annoying. We might have to move away from Waterford County, where no one knows how much you used to charge."

Mason lifted his eyebrows at my suggestion. "Where exactly did you have in mind?"

"Well." I bit my lip. "I've been missing Ellamore. A lot. They have a great medical program at their university, and I'm sure their engineering department rocks too. Besides, it didn't matter how far away I ran; Jeremy still found me. So I'm done running. I want to go home."

He winced. "But *Illinois*? What about Sarah and my mom?"

I only had to think about that for half a second. Snapping my fingers, I grinned. "I got it. We could bring them with us. My mom manages a hotel. She's always looking for good, dependable employees. She could get Dawn a job no problem."

Mason shook his head, his eyes sparkling with a reverent glint. "You have a solution for everything, don't you?"

When it came to keeping us together, I would definitely find a solution. I fluttered my lashes at him. "So what do you say? If we can get your mom on board, do you want to look into enrolling at Ellamore in the spring?"

His mouth cut me off. "Yes." His lips pressed against my neck next. "Yes. If it makes you happy and keeps us together, my answer will always be yes."

EPILOGUE

Four Months Later

Inhaling the tart odor of wet paint, I filled my roller with another batch of what the hardware store had called Nifty Turquoise and applied it to the wall, only to step back and admire my handi-work.

"Damn, I'm awesome."

Behind me, Sarah giggled from her wheelchair.

"Shh." Putting a finger over my lips, I whirled around to wink at her. "You didn't hear me say that."

She laughed again, her gray eyes twinkling with a mischief she had definitely inherited from her brother. "You're awesome."

"Okay, *that* you could hear." I waggled the roller in her direction, threatening to paint her, and her laughter turned into delighted screams.

Once she settled down, I propped one hand on my hip and studied the bare, half-painted room. "You know, when this dries, I think the color you picked out is going to be amazing."

Sarah clapped and chattered about her excitement, agreeing with me.

After moving out of Mrs. Garrison's rental house, Mason had found a place that was actually affordable and close to Sarah's new school.

Yes, I said *new* school.

In Ellamore, Illinois.

Can you believe that? I talked him and his entire family into moving back home with me. Now Dawn and Sarah had their own, snug, two-bedroom bungalow, and Mason and I were renting a place close to the university.

I'm not quite sure how he'd been able to convince his mom to pull up all her roots and move across the country to live near us, but she had agreed to the deal almost too readily.

I think she had been as eager to leave Waterford as Mason had been. Both of them had a past they'd wanted to escape. And they both seemed so much more laid back and relaxed now. Knowing his old landlady could never touch him again, Mason had bloomed in the past few weeks. And I loved every inch of the new man he'd become even more.

He was a spectacular, caring, faithful, totally hot boyfriend.

As if hearing my praising thoughts, he popped his head into Sarah's new room. "Holy...*Jeez*. That is one bright color." His eyes widened with horror.

"I know." I beamed as I displayed the wall like a pro Vanna White imitator. "Sarah loves it."

When he glanced at his sister, she clapped and cheered, so Mason simply cleared his throat, remained respectfully silent about his opinion, and picked up a roller to help me finish the walls.

See? Spectacular.

At some point, Dawn arrived and wheeled Sarah away, saying they were going to go grab some lunch, but Mason and I were so busy working we barely spared them a farewell.

We really were busy—until his mom and sister left, that is. Then things got a little...well, let's just say they got busy in an entirely different way.

We were still very much in the lovey-dovey, touchy-feely, kissy-cuddly stage, you see. And since Eva had arrived on our doorstep two weeks ago after her parents had disowned her, our love nest apartment had been disrupted by my troubled pregnant cousin, who took over our extra bedroom. We could no longer just do it anywhere.

It was utterly aggravating.

So, these days, we attacked each other the moment we were alone.

Mason had just laid me down on Sarah's bed—*hush*, don't you dare tell—and was frantically trying to unsnap the button on my jeans when my cell phone rang.

"Damn it." He rolled off me to lie on his back and cover his face with his arm. "If that's Eva, I'm going to kill her. I swear that cockblocking woman has it out for me, trying to keep me from ever having sex again. It's been *forever* since I was last inside you."

I rolled my eyes. "Oh, my God. It was three days ago."

"Exactly." He groaned as if he were in pain.

Checking the ID on my screen, I poked Mason in the ribs. "You were wrong. It's not E." Answering the call, I said, "Hey, Mom. No, I haven't changed my mind yet."

Both of my parents wanted me to go back to being Teresa Nolan again. But so much had happened in the past few months, I really didn't *feel* like Teresa Nolan anymore. I was Reese Randall now.

But I guess that wasn't why she had called this time.

"Reese." The serious note in her voice had me holding my breath.

I bolted upright, instantly alert. "What happened now?"

Mason rolled onto his side toward me. Before I could even turn his way for support, he took my hand, helping me brace for the worst.

"Jeremy..." my mother started.

My throat dropped into my stomach. "His trial was dropped again," I croaked, my skin chilling to icicles. "Wasn't it? He's free?"

"No," Mom said. "No, not at all. He's dead, honey. He got into a fight in jail and was stabbed to death. Two days ago. I think the newspaper called it a...a shanking or something like that?"

I covered my mouth with one hand and met Mason's eyes.

"*What's wrong*?" he mouthed.

I shook my head and turned away, still not sure how to react. I had certainly never wished this kind of harm to come to my psycho stalker ex. But I'd technically been finished with him since the beginning of my junior year. There were no lingering feelings of affection at all.

There was just...oh, God.

Relief.

Mom talked a few minutes longer, but I kind of shrugged her off, thanking her for calling and letting me know but saying I had to go.

When I hung up, I told Mason the news.

He was mostly quiet, studying me intently. "Are you okay?"

I nodded, looking more through him than at him. "Yeah, I..." Finally, I focused on his face. "I'm free."

His grin was slow and approving as he took my hands and squeezed my fingers. "We're both free."

"Free at last," I sang out, grinning, only to brighten. "Ooh, that reminds me..." I paused with an arch of my eyebrows and tilt of my head. "Actually, I have no idea how *that* reminded me, but it made me remember, for some strange reason. Isn't it odd how one thing can remind you of—"

"Reese!" Mason cut in, his exasperated voice and amused grin telling me how badly I was rambling.

"Right." I got back on track. "I wrote you a poem."

He wrinkled his brow into frown. "You wrote a poem? For me? Really?"

I bobbed my head enthusiastically. After digging into my pocket, I yanked free the multi-folded sheet of notebook paper I'd ripped out of one of my binders.

His throat worked as he swallowed. "Wow. That's...that's really sweet."

"Thanks." I tried to toss my hair over my shoulder before I realized I had it up in a ponytail. God, I loved being able to wear my hair up again.

Mason waved his hand. "Let's hear this thing." He sounded excited.

I nodded, clearing my throat and straightening the wrinkles in the page so I could read aloud what I'd written.

Way down in the boondocks of Waterford,
The girls liked to pay for their manly sword.
Goodbye, Mr. Mason Lowe.
Oh, what a gigolo.
Too bad he's retired to Ellamore.

Mason stared at mc, stunned speechless. Then

he shook his head and cracked a smile. "*Manly* sword?"

"What?" I shrugged. "I never claimed to be a *good* poet. You try to come up with something that rhymes with Waterford."

I'd been stretching it enough to make Ellamore go with Waterford.

"Hmm. Well, thanks *so much*. It's simply romantic. Brings a tear to my eye. Seriously."

I scowled, afraid my sarcasm was rubbing off onto him a little too well. Shoving at his arm, I pretended to pout. "Hey, you said you wanted a limerick. And limericks are *not* romantic. I looked it up. They're witty, humorous, nonsensical, and kind of dirty." I shook my rumpled scrap of paper in his face. "So this is what you got, buster."

"I never said I *wanted* a limerick written about me. I said there probably *would* be."

I snickered. "Well, now there is. Don't you just feel...immortal?"

He shook his head and pulled me into his arms. "You are so weird. But I don't think I could love you any more than I do right now. Thank you for my dirty poem. You're amazing, and I'm the luckiest guy on earth."

See, had that been so hard for him to say?

I flushed, pleased by his praise. "Well, you're welcome."

We kissed, and life was perfect.

"And I love you too," I felt inclined to add.

"You know," he murmured thoughtfully, pressing his forehead against mine as he toyed with the collar of my partially unbuttoned shirt. When he oh-so-accidently slipped the next button free, my sleeve slid off my shoulder. His fingers coasted over my bare skin. "The more *retired* and free I feel lately, the more I actually want to be tied down again. To you."

I frowned until the significance behind his words took root. Did he mean…?

He didn't mean…*marital* ties. Did he?

I sent him a suspicious glance, but he only winked.

~THE **END**~

ABOUT THE **AUTHOR**

Linda grew up on a dairy farm in the Midwest as the youngest of eight children. Now she lives in Kansas with her husband, daughter, and their nine cuckoo clocks. Her life's been blessed with lots of people to learn from and love. Writing's always been a major part her world, and she's so happy to finally share some of her stories with other romance lovers. Please visit her at her website

http://www.lindakage.com/

ACKNOWLEDGMENTS

To Sandra Martinie, big sister extraordinaire, who reads everything I write and gives her insightful advice. Yes, you may feel very, very sorry for her!

And to more amazing family members: Cindy Alexander, Nancy Crumpacker, Jamie Alexander, Katie Cap, Kayla Crumpacker, and Alaina Martinie. Thank you so much for helping me proofread.

Ivy Bateman, amazing author and cherished friend. Thank you for your wonderful counsel and manuscript guidance.

And that same acknowledgement goes to Lisa Filipe, blogger for Tasty Reads and owner of Tasty Book Tours. She took time away from raising her precious baby to beta read my work.

More praise goes to Carol Kilgore, crime fiction with a kiss author plus mentor for my first adventure into self-publishing.

To the amazing blogger, Courtney Wyant, whom I

will *never* forget, plus her Auntie Andrea for both of your mad beta reading skills. Thank you, thank you, thank you for your sunny and bright dispositions, which has always kept my morale high.

To my editor, Laura Josephsen, I totally love working with you. I can't say enough nice words to show you my appreciation.

Another round of thanks goes so Ashley Morrison of the blog, Book Labyrinth. She so graciously took the time to read and give a very precise, organized, and brilliant feedback to one of my earlier drafts.

For, Claire Ashgrove, awesome author and one of my first critique partners and writing friends. You are so much more than a mere proofreader. Thanks for your help in making this story flow.

To cover artist, Sarah Hansen, of Okay Creations. I'm not worthy! And I'm still in love with every cover you produce.

I'm very grateful to my husband and daughter, who ground me to reality as I go through all my writing ups and down. You guys are my everything.

And finally, thanks to the Good Lord for still putting up with me!

LATEST **RELEASE**

July 2013
from *Omnific Publishing*
FIGHTING FATE

CHAPTER ONE

Paige Zukowski dressed in the dark, her fingers fumbling over the buttons on her blouse. She tried a breathing technique to calm her rattled nerves. Inhale. Hold. One, two, three. Exhale. Hold. One, two, three. Inhale...

The buttons were mismatched. She frowned and started over, forgetting whether she was on inhale or exhale. Only when she was about to pass out because she was still holding her breath did she let a lungful of oxygen rush from her chest.

Oh, well. Breathing was overrated anyway. She gave up on the entire relaxation attempt and closed her eyes as she worked her way higher. Trace used to tease her relentlessly about fastening things from the bottom up.

"You just gotta do everything backwards, don't you, Pay Day? You're supposed to start at the top and go down. You miss less buttons that way, plus it keeps your gig line in order."

She'd raised an eyebrow at that one. "My what line?"

"It's a military term." He had shrugged with his usual nonchalance. "Something to do with making sure your buttons, belt buckle, and fly run a straight column down the front of your body."

Paige's derisive snicker had told him what she'd thought of that. "Are you joining the Army now? Since when do you know *military* terms?"

Lying way too comfortably on her bed with his legs stretched out and crossed at the ankles and his arms resting behind his head, he had merely sent her a cocky smile. "I know everything."

And he had. Her brother had been the brightest, most promising member of their family. He'd been going places. Even after his funeral, the college acceptance letters had poured in, inviting him to attend their university with a full ride.

He'd been anticipating the letter from Granton University the most. And it had come with a complete scholarship included.

Two weeks too late.

Her own nostalgic smile dying, Paige tried not to remember his infectious grin, though it was hard, particularly this morning. She left the top two buttons unfastened so she wouldn't feel as if she was choking through the entire day, and cold metal brushed the back of her hand as she manually tried to straighten her crooked gig line. With a sigh, she wrapped her fingers around the cool amulet draping her neck. A ruby embedded in a Celtic-looking cross. Trace had given it to her on her thirteenth birthday since ruby was her birthstone.

It was big, and clunky, and kind of gaudy, but in the three years he'd been gone, she'd yet to take it off. She squeezed the shape of the cross into her palm and whispered into the dim dorm room.

"For you, Bubba. I won't let you down."

A buzz echoed around her. Paige nearly jumped out of her skin, freaked for a split second that the ghost of her brother was responding...until she realized her cell phone was simply vibrating across the corner of her new desk, announcing an incoming call.

On the other side of the room, sheets rustled from the shadowed corner, giving her another heart attack. Still not used to sharing her space with anyone else, especially a complete stranger, Paige dashed a worried glace in the direction of her roommate's bed as she leaped toward her phone to silence it.

"Hello," she answered in a harried, hushed voice, trying not to wake Mariah, though honestly, Mariah hadn't seemed all that worried about not waking her when she'd come stumbling in at two this morning, cursing across the dark room until she'd turned on the light over her bed and jerked Paige from a restless sleep.

Huddled under her covers, Paige had feigned unconsciousness until Mariah had changed into a camisole and shorty shorts, then passed out face first on top of her covers, the reek of stale alcohol and cigarettes filming the air. Paige had waited five minutes before she'd tiptoed across the floor and killed the lights. It had taken her another hour to fall back to sleep in between counting every time Mariah tossed and turned, making the springs on her mattress screech and moan.

"Hello?" a quiet voice breathed back. "Why are we whispering?"

Paige sat on the edge of her bed, relieved to hear her best friend. "Because my roommate's still asleep."

She squinted through the dark, wondering if actually she should wake Mariah. Her new roomie probably wouldn't like being late on the first day of class. But if she was the type to habitually come in at two in the morning, then maybe she was smart enough not to schedule an early course.

Paige wiped at her tired, dry eyes, wondering what had possessed her to sign up for anything before nine herself.

Rookie freshman error, she decided.

"Ah. So...how's it going with the whole room-mate thing?" Kayla asked. "She okay or what?"

Stray beams of morning light filtered into the room, giving Paige a glimpse of her organized desk. She studied the four-by-six framed photo of Trace nestled next to the television.

"She's...fine." She'd really only talked to Mariah for a couple of minutes before some guy had knocked on their door and whisked her roommate away. But those few moments hadn't been pleasant. "We're still getting used to each other."

"Hmm. So, are there any available hotties there asking you out yet?"

Paige rolled her eyes. "Not hardly."

"What! No available hotties at all? What kind of college are you at?"

With a snicker, Paige corrected, "No one's asked me out."

"Oh." Kayla sighed. "Well, they will."

"Kayla, I didn't come here to date a bunch of—"

"Yeah, yeah, yeah. You're there because of Trace. And I'm telling you right now, that's the worst reason in the world to move so far away from home to attend a school you don't even like."

Paige's back straightened with indignation. "I never said I didn't like—"

"Well, you don't love it the way he did. Paige..." Kayla sighed again, this time sounding like a wise old parent tired of repeating the same lecture.

Paige gnashed her teeth. "Look, I can't talk about this right now." It was her first day of school. Besides, they'd been over it before. A lot. Nothing had changed her mind so far. Nothing would change it now.

So what if her best friend in the world thought Paige was crazy for trying to live a dead boy's life for him? It wasn't as if she had her own future to look forward to. After Trace's funeral, her world had collapsed. Her parents had turned away from her, too entrenched in their own misery to help her deal with hers. Her mother had descended so far into depression she'd looked right through Paige. And after her mom was gone, her father had drowned himself in booze. Paige had lost everything.

The only way she'd been able to dig her way out of the agony had been to focus on Trace's lost dreams, to decide she'd live them for him and become what he'd always wanted to be.

"I really need to get to class," she said, standing up and slipping into the sandals she'd set out last night to wear with her first-day outfit.

Kayla sighed. A third time. Really, it was too much. "Sweetie, you know I love you. I just want you to be happy. But—"

"Love you too," Paige broke in with fake enthusiasm. "Talk later." Disconnecting the line, she cringed, telling herself she'd call back and apologize after she actually survived her first day of school. Right now, she had other worries.

She had college to start, a first class to find, a dead boy's life to fulfill.

Busy, busy, busy.

A minute later, Paige pushed her way from her dormitory and halted in her tracks. The campus of Granton sprawled before her, teeming with activity. Thousands of students strolled the sidewalks while another thousand sat cross-legged in clusters on the grass as bicyclists darted between the foot traffic and an endless amount of cars filed into the parking lots. Half a dozen digital billboards sat perched in front of buildings, scrolling messages and advertisements across their screens. And a marching band practiced the *Party Rock Anthem* somewhere in the distance.

It was so hectic, so crowded. So intimidating. After living in a town of two thousand people her entire life and attending a school of barely three hundred, Paige huddled against the entrance of her dorm building, tempted to scurry back inside and hide under her blankets for the rest of the semester.

"Trace." She groaned under her breath, squeezing her fingers around his gaudy amulet. "Why'd you have to pick such a huge school to dream about?"

If her brother were here now, she'd be tempted to strangle him...right after she hugged him silly and reprimanded him to never die on her again.

"I can do this, I can do this, I can do this," she chanted as she forced her numb legs to move, trudging down a slight decline to the cafeteria. But when she entered Gibson Hall, the smell of bacon and sausages made her stomach churn, and not in a good way.

"I can't do this." At least not food. Not right now.

She turned around and walked right back out. Okay, so she'd just get to her first class and set up early. Unfolding her map of the campus, she hunted for her eight a.m. course.

As the first to arrive, she selected a seat in the front row, changing spots a few times until she had herself positioned near the exit yet close enough to the center to provide a decent view of the instructor's podium. She wanted to be the perfect, exemplary student.

When a trio of chatty guys entered the lecture hall, she'd already tugged a laptop from her bag and set it on top of the desk. After it booted, the screen lit with its wallpaper. Trace had picked out the M. C. Escher design as the background as soon as he'd bought the laptop, saving all the money he'd made mowing lawns between his junior and senior years of high school.

His computer had only been six months old when he'd died.

A year ago, Paige had decided she wouldn't let his hard-earned mowing money go to waste. She wouldn't let his dream of Granton die with him. She'd taken over his computer, and now here she sat, ready and willing to take over the rest of his life. In another four years, she planned to graduate with a Bachelors of Business Administration and find a job he would be proud of in the marketing world.

Logging into the processor, she pre-saved a word document and minimized the screen, prepared for an hour of copious note taking. Nothing was going to distract her from her studies. She had a goal to meet, her brother's dream to realize, and his future to begin.

"Good morning!" A loud voice ripped her attention from the two Escher hands drawing each other on her computer. "This is World Regional Geography. If you're in the wrong room, there's the door. If you have no respect for professorial authority, feel free to follow the other lost souls out the exit because I will not accept impudence."

Paige gulped and glanced surreptitiously behind her, surprised to see hundreds of other students had arrived while she'd been dazing off. They filled nearly every seat.

When no one stood from the sea of blurred bodies to leave, she slowly swiveled back around to face the professor.

Dr. Presni—as her class schedule labeled him—was a short, stout man with an irritable disposition, thick eyebrows, and a bad comb-over. Without introducing himself, he announced he would take roll call today, but after that, attendance was entirely up to the student.

"Marissa Abbott," he began, starting down his list.

"Here," the return call echoed from the back of the room.

The scratch of a check mark followed as Presni noted her presence. And so it began all the way through the alphabet. With her Z surname, Paige figured she had a while to wait before he called on her. She relaxed, tuning out, and studied the front of the room. A white board and stark, blank walls stared back. Yeesh, maybe she shouldn't have sat in the front row. She felt self-conscious. Singled out. She eyed the exit just to her left. It looked so welcoming.

"Rupert Waltrip...Alison Wutke..."

Paige refocused on the teacher's droning voice—really dry, droning voice. It was going to be hard to concentrate on his lectures with a voice like his, all arid and—

"Logan Xander."

Logan Xander?

Paige stopped breathing. Icicles crystalized on her brain, freezing her motionless.

That name.

Oh, God. That name.

Why would the professor say that name? Of all the names in the world, why—

"Here." A voice answered, claiming ownership of that horrendous name. He sat too close behind her and a tad to her right.

She couldn't help herself. Paige whipped around to look. She had to know.

There he sat.

Three rows back. Two seats over.

Logan Xander.

It had been three years since she'd last seen him. He fixed his dirty-blond hair shorter these days, shaved to a buzz cut. And his face had aged, the planes and angles sharper and more defined. Matured. But there was no way she'd ever forget what he looked like.

He must've caught her abrupt reaction to his name, because he glanced her way. Their gazes caught and held, and all the air in the room stalled, leaving her suffocated.

Dying.

A great, crushing tremble clutched her, wracking a painful shudder up her spine. Immediate tears throbbed behind her eyes. She blinked repeatedly, but her retinas remained scorching dry, giving her no relief from the horror she was beholding.

A bewildered frown wove through the center of Logan Xander's brow as he stared back, obviously not recognizing her.

She clenched her teeth and fisted her hands. She wanted to strike out, physically, verbally, any way possible, to make him remember the way she remembered. How dare he forget her when she would know his face—his name—for the rest of her life?

At the front of the room, the professor called, "Paige Zukowski?"

Finally, Xander reacted. His eyes flared wide and his face drained of color as he glanced at the professor, then back to her. His mouth dropped open, forming a great big, dreaded O.

Fear and rage and pain overwhelmed her.

A whimper sobbed from her throat. Humiliated for letting her distress echo into the room, she spun away, fumbling as she grabbed her things off her desk, not even closing the laptop as she swung out her arm and swiped it into her bag.

People were staring, gasps of surprise coming from her left and right, everywhere behind her. She didn't care. She had to escape.

Run!

A pen fell from her bag, but pausing to retrieve it seemed preposterous. It became collateral damage.

She tripped trying to stand too quickly, her legs tangling in the confining desk/chair combo. The professor lifted his head from his roll call and gaped at her over the top of his wire-rimmed glasses, his bushy brows and mustache twitching with confusion.

She didn't bother to explain herself. Couldn't speak if she'd wanted to.

Springing toward the door, she shoved it open and wheezed for air when she reached the hall. She didn't pause or slow down until she was outside and two blocks from the building containing Logan Vance Xander. All the while, she kept glancing over her shoulder, worried he might've followed.

He hadn't, thank God.

Of course he hadn't. Why would he? But, seriously. What was he doing here? How could he step foot onto the grounds of Trace's dream school?

How *dare* he?

It wasn't right, shouldn't be acceptable. He'd destroyed Paige three years ago, annihilated her entire family. He didn't deserve a second chance—a college degree—when Trace had nothing but a headstone and silly epitaph.

Tears streamed down her cheeks with a hot vengeance. She sprinted all the way back to her dorm room, her book bag repeatedly clouting her in the spine, spurring her onward. Grateful to find her roommate gone when she slammed inside, she huddled in her bed and wept hard, her body shuddering with the shock of discovering a murderer attended the same university as she.

And not just any murderer.

Her brother's murderer.

Made in the USA
Middletown, DE
28 January 2021